ANDREW M. GREELEY

❧ *Second* ❧
Spring

A Love Story

❧

**The Fifth Chronicle of
the O'Malley Family in the Twentieth Century**

A TOM DOHERTY ASSOCIATES BOOK
NEW YORK

SECOND SPRING: A LOVE STORY

A Forge Book
Published by Tom Doherty Associates, LLC
175 Fifth Avenue
New York, NY 10010

www.tor.com

Forge® is a registered trademark of Tom Doherty Associates, LLC.

ISBN 0-765-34238-3
EAN 978-0765-34238-6
Library of Congress Catalog Card Number: 2002032549

First Forge edition: April 2003
First mass market edition: May 2004

Printed in the United States of America

0 9 8 7 6 5 4 3 2 1

In memory of
Roger Brown,
St. Angela, 1942

DESCENDANTS OF

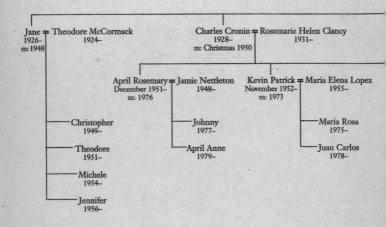

Jane = Theodore McCormack
1926–   1924–
m: 1948

Charles Cronin = Rosemarie Helen Clancy
1928–   1931–
m: Christmas 1950

April Rosemary = Jamie Nettleton
December 1951–   1948–
m: 1976

Kevin Patrick = Maria Elena Lopez
November 1952–   1955–
m: 1973

Christopher
1949–

Theodore
1951–

Michele
1954–

Jennifer
1956–

Johnny
1977–

April Anne
1979–

Maria Rosa
1975–

Juan Carlos
1978–

JOHN E. O'MALLEY

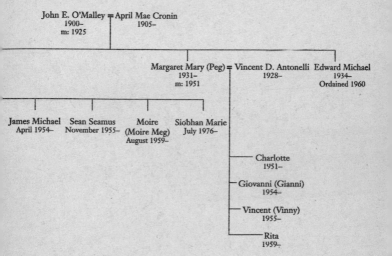

John E. O'Malley = April Mae Cronin
1900–   1905–
m: 1925

Margaret Mary (Peg) = Vincent D. Antonelli   Edward Michael
1931–   1928–   1934–
m: 1951   Ordained 1960

James Michael   Sean Seamus   Moire   Siobhan Marie
April 1954–   November 1955–   (Moire Meg)   July 1976–
                                 August 1959–

Charlotte
1951–

Giovanni (Gianni)
1954–

Vincent (Vinny)
1955–

Rita
1959–

❧ Chuck ❧
1978

"You might," the naked woman said to me, "make model airplanes."

"Ah," I said, as I caressed her firm, sweaty belly, an essential of afterplay as I had learned long ago.

"You always wanted to make them when you were a kid."

The full moon illumined the dome of St. Peter's in the distance and bathed us in its glow, as though it were doing us a favor. Over there the cardinals were doubtless spending a restless night in the uncomfortable beds in their stuffy rooms. None of them had a bedmate like Rosemarie with whom to play, worse luck for them and for the Church.

"You said . . . Don't stop, Chucky Ducky, I like that . . . You said that you were too poor to buy the kits."

"I did not!" I insisted, as I kissed her tenderly.

"You did." She sighed. "You don't have to stop that either."

My lips roamed her flesh, not demanding now, but reassuring, praising, celebrating.

"I did not!"

There had been a time, long years ago, when I would have tried a second romp of lovemaking in a situation like the present one.

"Or you could take up collecting sports cards. You told all of us that you couldn't afford that either."

"I never said that!"

"You did too!" She giggled as I tickled her.

"I guess I'm in my midlife identity crisis," I admitted.

"You can't be, Chucky Ducky darling." She snuggled close

to me. "You haven't got beyond your late adolescent identity crisis."

One of the valiant Rosemarie's favorite themes was that I was still a charming little boy, like the little redhead in the stories she wrote.

"Mind you," she whispered, "I like you as an adolescent boy."

"Oh?"

"Only an adolescent boy would be so nicely obsessed with every part of a woman's anatomy."

That would be a line in her next story. I wondered how the *New Yorker* would handle the spectacular lovemaking that preceded the line.

"A man could become impotent at the possibility that his bedtime amusements would become public knowledge."

"Ha! . . . I don't know about you, Chucky Ducky, but I'm going to sleep now."

She pillowed her head on my stomach.

"Chucky love," she sighed, now well across the border into the land of Nod, "you're wonderful. We really defied death this time, didn't we?"

That would be in the story too. I had become a character in a series of *New Yorker* stories—a little red-haired punk as an occasional satyr.

Rosemarie Helen Clancy O'Malley had found her midlife identity as a writer. Her poor husband had found his identity as a character in fiction. On that happy note I reprised in my imagination some of the more pleasurable moments of our romp and sank into peace and satisfied sleep.

❧ Rosemarie ❧

1978

I stirred my second cup of tea in the Hassler breakfast room, on the top of the hotel, and watched the Dome steam in the morning sun.

Instead of wondering about the outcome of the conclave, I worried about my poor husband.

In bed he was indeed the delightful adolescent who had learned a lot of tricks and a lot more of wisdom in pleasuring a woman. Our sex life wasn't always great, no one's is. But it was mostly good and often great, sometimes almost transcendent.

Our romp of the night before had left me in a state of pleasurable and self-satisfied complacency. It had started off routinely enough and then suddenly we both warmed to the task and it expanded to the edge of the transcendent, perhaps because the future of our Church was at stake in the conclave, a Church to which we were irrevocably committed despite its flaws.

I rejoiced in my condition as a woman animal, rational indeed to some extent, like a self-satisfied lioness lounging on her back in the sands of the Kalahari. Someone had rolled my nightgown into a ball and thrown it across the room. I refused to leave before we found it. Both of us blamed the other, but I was fibbing as Chuck knew very well.

Out of bed he was a mope, a sad sack, an old man long before his time.

He rarely touched his cameras. I had to insist that he bring the Nikon along for our trip to Lucerne and Vienna. He had not wanted to fly to Rome when we heard of the Pope's death. He had lost interest in recording great events and saw no reason to produce a portrait of the next Pope. I insisted again. He agreed, as he always does when I insist.

"You can quote me in a story," he said with a laugh, "that I had learned long ago that it was bootless to resist the orders of the monster regiment of women."

I had given up long ago any effort to convince him that he was not only quoting John Knox out of context but actually misquoting him.

He had stopped reading his beloved economic journals. He did not enjoy his children, not even the darling little Siobhan, currently being spoiled rotten by her Grandma April. He was not especially interested in his three grandchildren, two of them redheads like himself and Siobhan. Adoration from the next couple of generations did not much interest him. He is clever enough to cover that up, so the kids and grandkids adore him all the more.

He has stopped reading the papers since our unfortunate expedition to the White House to photograph Jimmy Carter. Nor did he vote for Gerry Ford. "It is not fair, my beloved, to say that he cannot walk and chew gum at the same time. However, you add the obligation to talk while he walks and chews gum and you befuddle him."

When President Ford assured everyone that the people of Poland were able to choose their own government, Chuck writhed. "Thomas Jefferson, where are you when we really need you!"

Yet when we went to the White House to do a portrait of Ford, we couldn't help but like the man. We spoke of Michigan and New Buffalo and Grand Beach and the Tabor Hill wines which we drank and which he served at state dinners. He was a genuinely nice man.

"You would like to spend time with him," I said on the plane back to Chicago. "Unlike Johnson or Nixon."

"And Jack Kennedy?"

I considered that.

"Sometimes those Boston guys, God be good to both of them, were like chalk scratching against the blackboard. They were fun, but you weren't altogether sure they were human. Gerry Ford you know is human."

Poor dear man.

Chuck tried to give up on exercise, but I wouldn't stand for that. However, he made little effort to beat me at tennis and gave up on his efforts to learn windsurfing. "Ridiculous for someone as old as I am," he protested.

That was the problem. On the coming September 17, my darling little redhead punk would turn fifty. The strands of white in his wire-brush red hair were increasing. He would not cover them as I promptly did when any gray appeared in my hair. Chuck was getting old, he thought. Life was slipping away and was pointless anyway.

He still made love with me, but I was almost always the aggressor. He was very good at the art of ravishing me, better than ever perhaps. It made him happy for a little while.

As I sipped my tea and worried about him, his lips touched the back of my neck, sending a shiver down my spine and causing my nipples to firm. No man should have that much power over a woman, right?

Wrong!

"You weren't the woman in my bed last night, were you?"

"Certainly not!"

"I didn't think so. Whoever she was, she had no modesty at all."

"Couldn't have been me. I'm Irish."

"Right."

"You were straightening up the room for the housekeeper?"

"I couldn't leave it a mess for the poor Giovanina."

"You made the bed?"

"Well . . ."

"Chucky, this is a high-class hotel. She'll remake the bed anyway."

"Yeah, well . . ."

My husband is, to put it mildly, fastidious. I'm a pretty good housekeeper—for someone whose origins are Irish. Chuck makes Missus, our Polish defender of order in the house, seem slovenly.

Also he keeps obsessively neat files, each one carefully labeled in his neat, precise printing. On the other hand he dresses like a slob—this morning in tattered jeans and a Notre Dame tee shirt which had seen better days thirty years ago. Out of place in the breakfast room of the Hassler? My poor Chucky looked like someone who came in every morning to walk the dog.

"*Per favore,* cornflakes?" he asked the pretty waitress with a pathos that would have been appropriate for an orphan in a Dickens novel.

"Certainly, *signor,*" she said with a big smile.

The little bitch thinks he's cute.

When she returned with the cereal and a big pitcher of cream, Chuck murmured, "*Mille grazie,* Paola."

Of course, he knew her name. For a couple of days the Hassler was his precinct. Like a good precinct captain, he had to know the names of everyone. Some traits are so ingrained that even a midlife identity crisis couldn't demolish them.

"You notice the major change in Catholic doctrine the last couple of days?" he asked.

I poured him a refill of his tea.

"How can they change doctrine when the Pope, poor dear man, is dead?"

"They did just the same. They wouldn't let women in slacks or shorts into the wake in San Pietro. Then they permitted slacks, then even shorts if they were not too short, then they gave up on that judgment call. Bare shoulders and spaghetti straps are still sinful, however. Nonetheless, I think there has been a real corruption of Catholic truth."

"It's because everyone is on vacation. Even the poor Pope was on vacation when he died."

"Did him a world of good, didn't it?"

"Chucky, that is a very old joke."

"I am a very old man . . . Paola, *ancora una volta?*"

"*Sì, signor.*" Paola rushed away.

"The little bitch thinks you're adorable."

"Women do. Cute little old guy."

It was not just the advent of his fiftieth birthday which bothered my Chuck. His real problem had been caused by John Kennedy and Pope John XXIII almost twenty years ago. Both men had believed that change in our country and our Church were possible and necessary. Jack Kennedy had invited Chuck to be part of his project when he sent us to Germany as ambassadors. Pope John had launched an Ecumenical Council that had created great hope among the parish clergy and the laity for change in the Church.

John Kennedy had died. Chuck served under Lyndon Johnson till it became clear that Kennedy's successor had decided to escalate the war in Vietnam. He turned down an appointment as UN representative and walked out of the Oval Office, to return in 1968 as one of the "Senior Advisers to the President" who had gathered together to tell Johnson that it was time to get out of the war.

(He had called former Secretary of State Dean Acheson "Dean" and that frosty man had called him "Charles.")

One of our children disappeared into the dropout underground during the war and another had his foot blown off by an American mine. Richard Nixon became President and Chuck, who had marched at Selma (because I had insisted), dropped out of politics.

Paul VI had appointed us to the commission which was supposed to find grounds for changing the birth control teaching. Then when we recommended a change and the reasons for it, he ignored us and caved in to the curial reactionaries. Chuck gave up his hope that the Church could really reform itself—though he continued to be a practicing Catholic and even a lector at Mass. Chucky navigating the syntax of St. Paul was a comic delight.

If Kennedy and the Pope had left things alone, my husband would be a distinguished photographer with a worldwide reputation and no sense that he had failed. You can only experience disillusion when someone sets you up with illusions. At our silver anniversary celebration a couple of years ago, he had smiled brightly and seemed to enjoy every moment of it. I cried all day because I knew that I had never deserved a husband like Chuck. He had prevented me from becoming an incurable drunk. Now he was in trouble and there was nothing I could do to help him.

The young radicals of the late sixties had fallen all over each other in "selling out." The blacks, or African-Americans as some of them insisted that they be called, had retreated into self-segregation. Disco music became popular as a retreat from rock and roll but not from drugs. Black musicians hated it. I love to dance. Chucky hates it, but he's learned to be presentable on the dance floor to please me (which is very generous). I dragged him off to a disco dance hall one night. We lasted maybe ten minutes. We were too old and I couldn't stand the smell—a mix, I thought, of sweat, urine, and pot. He wanted to go back to take pictures. I said that he might be beat up by some pothead.

Besides, disco wasn't radical and didn't represent anything except maybe the survival of the psychedelic drug culture (though without rock and roll), which was maybe what the sixties were all about anyway.

We liberals had rid the country of Nixon and defeated Ford by less than one percentage point, so inept was our candidate. There were no causes around. Why bother if all your hopes were to turn to dust?

"What did you think of our supper with Msgr. Adolfo last night?" I asked him when Paola had delivered the third helping of cornflakes, rolling her eyes at me.

I rolled my eyes back.

"Trastevere is a nice place," he said as he spilled a spoonful of cornflakes on his tee shirt. "Great old church, nifty restaurant. You can take me there anytime you want."

I paid the bills on these trips with my credit cards because my husband, as obsessive as he was about neatness, has never been able to cope with finances. He would have put us in a pensione somewhere instead of the most expensive hotel in Rome and would have worried for days if he knew how much our suite in the Hassler cost. Deep down in the murky subbasements of his character, he was still afraid that the Great Depression would return.

"And his opinions on what your friends over there are going to do?"

The cardinals were no friends of ours, but that's the way we Chicagoans talk.

"I wonder if it matters." Chuck sighed. He considered another dish of cornflakes and reluctantly decided against it.

"*Ancora, signor?*" Paola asked.

"*Basta.*" Chuck grinned at her.

"*Sì, signor.*" She grinned back. "More toast, *signora?*"

I shook my head and smiled, just to let her know I didn't think she was flirting with my cute little husband.

Msgr. Raimundo "Rae" Adolfo was like a character from a Fellini film, sleek and handsome with thick, jet-black hair, a neatly chiseled face, even white teeth, flashing black eyes, and just the faintest hint of cynicism in his quick smile. He did something for the Secretary of State who was kind of the Vatican prime minister. He had adopted us for some reason and insisted that Chuck must do a portrait of the new Pope.

"Well, that depends on who it is," Chuck had said as he was gulping down his pasta.

Adolfo shrugged, as he often did, a sign of a man who had seen everything and would be surprised by nothing.

"It will be very close," he sighed. "The whole project of the Vatican Council is at stake. My former boss, Cardinal Benelli, in his intervention just before the conclave said that collegiality is the most important issue, whether the Pope is willing to share power with the other bishops. You could see the tight jaws of his old enemies in the Curia."

"They really think they can repeal the Council?" I asked, deftly turning over my wineglass.

I'm quite good at that. I've had enough practice.

"Not explicitly. However, they can ignore it and return to governing the Church the way they did before 1960. They forced the long delay between the Pope's burial and the opening of the conclave so they would rally around a candidate. Pericle Felici, who opposes everything, has been on the phone every day. They will all vote for Siri of Genoa, who is very conservative and also authoritarian. They are saying that the last Pope was weak and we need a strong man now. Siri is very tough."

"And the good guys don't fight back?" Chucky said as he looked in dismay at his empty pasta dish. I shook my head as a sign that he'd had enough.

"For once," Adolfo sighed again, "they organize themselves. Leo Suenens does not go back to Brussels as he pretends but rather remains in northern Italy. He too knows how to use the phone, as does Benelli. They are ready, I think."

"Pope Paul ended the Council when he issued the birth control encyclical," Chuck insisted, his voice bitter.

Only two events made my poor husband bitter, the escalation of the Vietnam War in 1965 and the birth control encyclical in 1968.

Adolfo would not permit himself to discuss that subject.

"Yet much remains, Carlo. If Siri wins, you will realize just how much."

"He wouldn't put the Mass back in Latin, would he?"

"Slowly and gradually he would restrict the number of times it might be done in English. They're not opposed necessarily to a vernacular liturgy, only to the decline, as they see it, of papal power."

We were both silent for a moment. Above us a lovely full moon looked down benignly on the glittering mosaics of the Church of Santa Maria in Trastevere. In a city of such beauty, how could there still exist such ugly realities as corruption and power lust?

"Who's our guy?" Chuck asked.

Adolfo hesitated.

"You must understand," he said finally, "that there are very few Italian cardinals left who are capable of being Pope . . . Illness, ah, peculiarities, age. There is talk of Albino Luciani from Venice. He is a good man, a simple *padre di compagna,* a priest of the land, what you Americans would call a good parish priest. He walks the streets of Venice talking to people. He smiles and is witty and would never overturn a vote of his priests' council. However, it is said that he is not sophisticated. One also hears that he has very poor health."

"The best we can do?"

"I'm afraid so. Some of the Curia will support him, as will the Europeans and the Americans. You can never tell what will happen inside the conclave, however. One must pray."

"Indeed one must," I said.

Adolfo lifted the bottle of Frascati, noted my overturned glass, and offered some to Chuck. He declined with a lifted finger. Adolfo poured a small portion for himself. Two very abstemious Americans, he must have thought.

I don't look like a drunk you see, not at all. I haven't had a drink in almost twenty years and don't propose ever to have one again. I almost ruined my marriage and my life. Chuck saved me along with a couple of first-rate psychiatrists, in-

cluding a little witch with immense and kind gray eyes named
Maggie Ward. If you've been sexually abused by your father
and routinely beaten by your mother, drink is one way to escape.

"It is said that he has an open mind on that issue which is
so important to you . . ."

"And to all the Catholic married people in the world," I
interrupted.

The Monsignor smiled briefly, his teeth flashing in the can-
dlelight on the table.

"Of course . . . You remember when the so-called test-tube
baby was born in England? Everyone here condemned it naturally. Luciani began his very mild comment by congratulating
the couple on the birth of their child."

"How dare he!" I said ironically.

Adolfo smiled again. He enjoyed me. Most men do, though
I have a hard time admitting that to myself.

"This man Suenens has a lot of clout?" Chuck asked.

"That is one way of putting it, Carlo. He was one of the
great men of the Council. He was the Great Elector of the late
Pope Paul, who would have made him secretary of state if the
Curia had not threatened to resign. They would not have of
course . . ."

"Paul was never strong on courage against those guys, was
he?"

Msgr. Adolfo sighed very loudly.

"I'm afraid not . . . Later he ostracized Suenens because he
called for more collegiality between bishops and the Pope."

"I thought Pope Paul supported that."

"He did, but his feelings were hurt by Suenens's criticism."

I expected Chuck to argue that a Pope can't afford to have
such sensitive feelings. However, he said nothing.

"So we pray tomorrow for this Albino Luciani," I said, filling the silence.

"We pray fervently, Rosamaria. So much is at stake."

"You think he will win?"

He hesitated.

"How do you Americans say it? I don't want to jinx the
outcome?"

At my insistence we walked back to the Hassler. We needed

exercise. Chuck put his arm around my waist, just high enough so that his fingers were close to my breasts. A full moon sometimes does that to a man. I would be ravished before the night was over. To make sure of that outcome, I leaned against his arm.

A couple of Italian men made lascivious comments about me. I ignored them. Chuck didn't hear them.

"You remember what Father Ed said to us?" I said.

Ed was Chuck's brother, six years younger than he was, three years younger than Peg, who was my age and my life-long coconspirator. He had been the secretary of our crazy Cardinal O'Neill and, by his own admission, had barely kept his vocation and his sanity. Chuck gives me credit for per-suading him to resign from the job.

"Ed talks all the time," Chuck replied. "Always has since you signed on as his confidant."

Father Ed's name is Edward Michael. He likes to be called Michael or Ed. Chuck insists that he is Ed just as he insists that I am Rosemarie, though to everyone else in the family I am Rosie.

I like being called Rosemarie, it makes me feel elegant. And sexy.

"About the revolution not ending when the bishops went home."

"Oh yeah . . . Well, he said that the bishops thought that they'd had a nice little quiet revolution during the Council and they went home feeling quite euphoric about what they had done. However, the enthusiasm spread to the lower clergy and to the laity and within ten years they . . ."

"We . . ."

"All right, WE had swept away just about everything in the Church we didn't like or seemed silly—birth control, mastur-bation, divorce, married priests, women priests, priests and nuns leaving their vocations, Confession before Communion, Mass every single Sunday. Yet we remained Catholic, vocif-erously so . . . That the conversation?"

"Yes."

"And he said that the bishops really didn't understand this change or that no one could ever turn it around?"

"Not even a Pope?"

"Paul VI sure tried in 1968."

"And failed?"

"You win, Rosemarie, you always do."

"Chucky, you should not play with my boobs in public!"

"I don't think the Pope has made a rule against that!"

However, his fingers retreated a bit. Not too far, however. My hormones began to rage. No way he was going to fall asleep as soon as we returned to our suite.

"Do you think our children will worry about these problems?"

"No, I guess not."

"Yet they'll still cheer for the Pope whenever they're in Rome. And you know why?"

"Because they're Catholic," he admitted. "Always will be, can't ever be anything else."

"Right! We must remember to call your mother and see how Siobhan and Moire Meg are doing."

"Don't miss us at all."

We climbed up the Spanish Steps, though Chuck pretended to be too old to try such a venture. I insisted.

I kissed him passionately as we rode up in the elevator.

He undressed me as we talked to our daughters on the phone, two exuberant and loving young women, both of whom insisted that we should have a good time during our vacation.

"Chucky and Rosie," Rosary freshman Moire Meg instructed us, "you totally need to have a good time."

We did the rest of that night anyway. Our worries about the future of the Church drifted far away.

❧ Chuck ❧

1978

The gloriously dressed Italian cop warned me in a tone of voice reserved for grown men who were behaving like little children as I leaned out of the base of the obelisk to get an angle shot of a group of very little kids charging through a gaggle of earnest nuns. I didn't understand the words but I knew I'd better climb down. If he had not helped me the last few steps, I might have fallen on my face.

He shook his head in dismay. Crazy little American.

As I climbed down, shamefaced, I saw my wife frowning at me from a distance. The frown matched the cop's tone of voice—would you ever grow up?

Rosemarie knew the answer. Rarely did she interfere with my antics when I was pursuing my profession. After all, she was responsible for seducing me away from accounting. She caught my eye, grinned, and waved.

She was wearing a lemon-colored sundress with spaghetti straps—defying the Vatican's ban on such garb inside the Basilica itself.

"I might just for the hell of it try to walk in."

"No way they'd miss you," I said.

She sniffed in response, an archduchess dismissing an annoying peasant.

I waved back.

The sundress was not necessary. The day was warm but not unbearably hot like the Roman August is supposed to be. As I watched her a couple of Roman males half my age must have made some lewd comment. She withered them with a quick contemptuous glance. It would be worth my life to try to defend her from such crudities. My Rosemarie could take care of herself.

My father had warned me once that beautiful women of a certain sort become even more beautiful as they grow older. My wife, in her middle forties, was more appealing than ever, not untouched by age, but made richer by it. I remembered the amusements of the previous nights. You are a fool, Chuck, I told myself, for not making love to her on every possible occasion. Why must you be such a mope?

Maybe after lunch this afternoon . . .

The morning crowd in the Piazza San Pietro was nervous. It was too early for white smoke. The cardinals would not elect a Pope on the first or second ballot. Still they might. Who would it be? What would he be like? What would happen? It was like a crowd at the Bears season opener, expectant but prepared to be disillusioned.

Once I had the image of a Bears opener in my head it was easy to get the pictures I wanted. I scurried around the Piazza snapping shots with my Nikon of the kids waiting for the first smoke to appear out of the funny chimney above the Sistine Chapel. They were having a grand time. Some of them climbed on the obelisk, others sat on the bench around that pagan fertility symbol, yet others chased each other under the Bernini Colonnade. Teenagers flirted with one another, the boys acting like macho lovers, which seemed to be the required posture for all postpuberty Italian males.

There was nothing even remotely sacred about the atmosphere of the place. The giant Piazza was a vast playground through which anxious nuns, busy and self-important priests, and unsmiling German tourists walked. The kids ignored these trespassers in their park. Occasionally a cop would warn the kids to cool it a bit, just as he had warned me. The *ragazzi* paid little attention. It was their holiday after all.

The pageantry of the Vatican is elaborate and solemn but the crowds that swarm at the fringes of the show are not particularly religious.

The Romans are almost all Catholics. But most of them are not too serious about it, unlike northern Italians in places like Milan. So they don't worry about the politics of the Church.

There are too many memories of the days when the Pope was the absolute civil ruler of Rome. They cheer for the Pope because they're Romans, but then they go home and become anticlericals. As Edward said once, Romans and their priests never speak to one another on the streets.

"At least they don't spit on one another."

So as a matter of principle I always say *buon giorno* to a priest or a nun when they cross my path, like we'd do in Chicago. When in Rome do as Chicagoans do. They look at me like I'm crazy.

Several police buses were tucked away in a side street behind the colonnade. Cops, carabinieri if I remembered the uniforms correctly, were strolling around as if they didn't expect any action. The crowds no longer rioted after the election of a Pope as they had in the good old days. The cops didn't seem to mind when I took their pictures too.

Maybe my theme would be *Rome Prepares for the Election of a Pope*.

Solemn ceremonies, unsolemn people.

I joined my wife.

"What would I have done," Rosemarie demanded, "if that cop had arrested you for endangering your life?"

"Gone to the American consulate over on the Via Veneto and demanded my release."

"Who would have taken your pictures . . . Chucky, stop ogling my boobs!"

"Can't help it! My shots are not worth taking . . . Nothing religious about this scene at all."

"It frosts me," she said, changing the subject, "to think that those guys up there who are deciding the future of our Church are all elderly celibate males who have no children and don't find women attractive."

"Some of them do."

"They were taught in the seminary that they were not supposed to."

"Some of our evangelical friends are governed by married men who have children. They're not sympathetic to feminism. But they presumably do sleep with their wives."

"They don't enjoy it."

"Rosemarie!"

"I'm being a bitch, Chucky. Sorry . . . I get so angry at those guys up there telling me how often I can sleep with my husband."

"Do you pay any attention to them?"

"Not anymore." She took my hand. "A lot of people still do."

"It used to be," I said, "that the priests of Rome went into St. Pete's several times removed and chose their bishop. Then they brought him out on the balcony. If the crowd cheered, they crowned him. If the crowd booed, they went back and tried again."

"Women got to shout?"

"Who could have stopped them?"

"I like that."

"Probably made more noise than the men did. Women usually do."

"CHUCKY!"

She had not relinquished her grip on my hand.

Msgr. Adolfo materialized next to us, wearing a beige sport shirt and black slacks. He always appeared mysteriously.

"Nothing will happen this morning," he said briskly. "They'll be getting the feel of things. They were all whispering about Luciani going in. Now they'll see whether there are really enough votes for him. It'll be over this afternoon. He was the first bishop Pope John appointed, you know."

"What if he should die?" Rosemarie asked.

"That's an odd question," the Monsignor said cautiously.

"You yourself said that his health is poor. What if the same bunch of creeps had to vote again in the next couple of months?"

"They would have to think the unthinkable—a *straniero*, a foreigner. There are no more acceptable Italian cardinals . . . But, Carlo, I will be asked tomorrow. Will you make a portrait of the new Pope before you go home?"

I wondered who would ask him.

"I can't. I didn't bring my Hasselblad with me."

"CHUCKY! We can buy another camera."

"They're expensive."

"You can afford it. It's tax deductible."

"Really?"

I could never quite understand such matters, despite my degree in economics.

"Really!"

"What will we do with two of them?"

"You'll give one to your daughter ... Our oldest child, Monsignor, is following in her father's footsteps. She specializes in children."

Rosemarie removed her portrait gallery from her purse.

"This is April Rosemary, our oldest daughter."

"Looks like her mother," I said helpfully.

"This is her son, Johnny Nettleton. His grandfather served with Chuck in Germany after the war when Chuck got the Legion of Merit."

"Market mistake."

"And this is her niece Maria Rosa O'Malley and Maria Rosa's baby brother, Juan Carlos."

"Latins. Parents do jazz."

"Finally, this little redhead imp is April Rosemary's sister Siobhan Marie. Just like her father."

Adolfo smiled genially at our little act, as he had smiled at the dialogue about the new Hasselblad.

"Beautiful children. Many redheads in the family."

"Three—Maria Rosa, Johnny, and Siobhan. Four if you count my husband."

"You let one in and pretty soon the whole neighborhood goes."

Rosemarie did not tell him that our eldest had disappeared into the radical underground during her freshman year at Harvard. She had finally clawed her way back to us, fragile and uncertain. She was still not sure that she deserved to be forgiven, especially by her mother, whom she had idolized. Then she had suffered postpartum depression after Johnny's birth and was struggling out of it.

"We must call her this afternoon, Chuck, and tell her that she's getting a new camera."

"Secondhand."

"No, you keep the old one and she gets the new one I buy this afternoon."

Naturally, my wife would buy it, lest I swoon over the

cost—even after she had negotiated the dealer down to a reasonable price.

"What are our guys doing up there?" I asked the Monsignor.
The Piazza was filling up with people. Time for the kickoff.

"The American cardinals?" he asked in surprise. "They are
doing nothing at all. They wait till others tell them what to
do, then believe that the Holy Spirit is whispering in their
ears."

"That dumb?"

"Carlo, the joke in the Vatican is that the American cardinals are so dumb that even the other cardinals notice it."

"Especially our own man from Chicago."

"He is a terrible man. Papa Montini tried to replace him
earlier this summer, but in the end he lost his nerve."

"Just as he did on family planning," Rosemarie said.

She simply wouldn't let it go. Not that I blamed her.

"*Fumato!*" someone yelled.

"*È bianco! È bianco!*"

The smoke trickling out of the funny old chimney did indeed look white.

"Too early," Adolfo murmured.

The crowd went wild. Kickoff time. Everyone fantasized
that the Bears would run it back for a touchdown.

Then the white smoke stopped. A moment later, a thick
plume of unquestionably black smoke gushed into the sky
above the Sistine Chapel.

"*È nero! È nero!*" The crowd groaned—as if the blackness
of the smoke were not obvious to everyone.

The Bears had fumbled the kickoff.

❧ Rosemarie ❧
1978

Though it was not yet noon, Chuck and I wandered into a trattoria on the Borgo Pio for a dish of pasta before we went camera shopping. The sky had turned gray as if the black smoke from the Sistine Chapel had suffused the heavens. The little eatery was all brown wood and pasta smell. The waitress looked at us like we were crazy. Only mad dogs and Americans ate the noon meal an hour before noon instead of an hour after like civilized people did. There were three British journalists sitting at a nearby table already eating pasta. They weren't even Americans. Probably wanted to get their siestas started early.

As I did, though I couldn't consume wine to put myself to sleep like they did.

My lemon sundress occasioned some attention when we walked in, which it was designed to do. The Brits gulped almost audibly. Probably figured I was some aging Italian movie star. Hardly a Chicago Mick.

They were frantically concocting strategies in which their man, Cardinal Hume, would win as a compromise candidate. My husband muttered to me, "Compromise has passed from England to the second and third world. If they need a compromise they'll go for a Pole or a South American."

"Let them dream," I said.

The deflation of the enthusiasm in the Piazza after the smoke turned black had depressed my poor dear husband.

"No matter who's elected, he won't get rid of our madman."

These days Chucky tended to obsess about the small stuff.

What difference did it make to us or our family if our sociopath Cardinal remained in office?

Our family is kind of complicated. I'm Chuck's wife, thanks be to God. I'm also his kind of unofficial foster sister. We were, as the Irish would say, half raised together. He had never quite been a foster brother, but his sister Peg (nee Margaret Mary after whom our Moire Meg was named) was the sister I always wanted but never had, closer to me and I to her than any sister could possibly be.

It was in second grade when she found me sitting on a step in the old St. Ursula school weeping. She had stayed after school to help the nun clean the erasers.

"Why are you crying, Rose?" she asked me gently.

The nuns didn't accept such names as Rosemarie in those days.

"No one loves me," I sobbed. "My mommy doesn't. My daddy doesn't. S'ter docsn't. The other kids don't."

Peg sat down next to me and put her arm around my shoulder.

"I love you, Rose."

"You do not, Margaret."

"Yes I do. Call me Peg."

"Will you be my sister, Peg?"

She didn't miss a beat. Peg never missed a beat.

"I'd love to."

I was dragged home to the O'Malley house and introduced as Peg's new sister.

Later, Peg and I had our first periods on the same day.

You can imagine what most families would do under such circumstances.

Not the Crazy O'Malleys. I was solemnly and seriously welcomed as their new sister. Later I would learn that her mother and father had known my parents and already felt sorry for me.

Chuck was an obnoxious ten-year-old and did not seem too happy at the addition to his family. Yet his blue eyes were so kind. I figured that I'd judge him by his eyes. I still do. I fell in love with him on the spot and have never recovered. I'll never forget the day he kissed me at our cottage in Lake Geneva. I knew then that we would never escape each other.

I spent most of my free hours at the O'Malley flat, a half block south of our home at Thomas and Menard. My shrinks told me years later that my instinct to seek out a family which would welcome and love me had been the decisive turning point in my life. I wouldn't have said it that way in second grade, but somehow I knew it even then. I clung to them for dear life, like a drowning swimmer to a raft.

Later, after the war, when they moved to their new home in Oak Park, there was an extra guest bedroom which was always called Rosie's room. I slept there often. I never was brave enough to tell April O'Malley what my father did to me.

When my mother, incoherently drunk, tried to kill me with a poker from our fireplace, Peg saved my life. She pushed her away and then Mom fell down the stairs into the basement. Father Raven and Mr. O'Malley advised us how to explain it to the police. Chuck was away in Germany then, but eventually he figured it out.

He says that when we were young Peg was like a sleek mountain cougar and I like a prowling timber wolf. We were both flattered. Later he said, "When your cougars and timber wolves have young to protect, they're even more dangerous."

So I was the soprano voice to match Chucky's tenor at all the O'Malley family concerts. They were my only real family, yet I was never quite part of them. My fault, not theirs.

"Pardon me, sir," one of the Brits said to my husband, "may we ask if you are a journalist?"

"Nope." Chucky held up his Nikon. "I take pictures."

"You wouldn't happen to be Charles O'Malley, would you?"

"You look too young to have created so much impressive work . . ."

"Charles Cronin O'Malley," I said. "He was born at a very early age, you see."

Chuck loved an audience, especially of admirers. He needed to perform this drab August day for an audience. He would say the same of me, but that's not true. Well, not altogether true. The music shows we'd put on at Petersen's ice cream store on Chicago Avenue near Harlem were his ideas. Mostly.

They introduced themselves. I was presented as "my first wife, Rosemarie."

We were invited to join them. I accepted before Chuck had a chance to decline.

"You're here to cover the conclave, sir?" the youngest Brit asked.

"More or less," Chuck admitted. "They want me to do a portrait of the new Pope."

"You have any idea who that will be and when he'll be chosen?"

"Albino Luciani," Chuck replied confidently. "This afternoon. Patriarch of Venice. Wanders about the streets of that city talking to people. Parish priest type. Charming, smiles a lot. Nice little man. Not an intellectual but who needs an intellectual? First bishop Pope John appointed. A coalition of moderate curialists led by Benelli and Europeans whom Leo Suenens has organized tested this morning whether they had the votes. They'll call in their markers this afternoon. Don't expect white smoke, however. Like most everything else, the Vatican can't make the smoke work. Doesn't have good health. If he dies soon, they'll have to go with a Pole or a South American."

It was vintage Chucky. He had absorbed everything that Adolfo had said and regurgitated it back as his own. I stifled my laugher.

The Brits were impressed, as well they might be. We chatted for a while. They complimented him on his work in Ireland, a subject on which Chuck didn't generally trust English comments but he would accept praise from whomever it came.

The lunch was delightful. Chuck had two helpings of pasta and a glass of wine, which improved my chances of being ravaged when we were back at the Hassler.

To facilitate that for which my body was already tingling, I called the game on account of darkness. We had to buy a new Hasselblad for the papal portrait. Chuck collected their cards and promised to send them some autographed books, a promise which I would keep.

I paid the bill too, over the Brits' not completely sincere protests.

"That was quite a show, Charles Cronin O'Malley," I told

him, as we crossed over from the Borgo to the Conciliazione. "They're convinced that the great picture taker is also a skilled Vaticanologist."

"I had to give them something to write home about," he said airily. "Now that Luciani fellow had better win."

"I was afraid you would start to sing."

"Like the good old days at Petersen's . . . Good idea. I never thought of it."

We found a presentable camera shop across the Tiber on the Corso, just as the owner was putting up the shutters for his siesta. I made Chuck stand outside.

"Hasselblad, *signor*," I said.

He put the shutters aside. With appropriate gestures he showed me three models. I pointed at the most expensive one. He quoted a price which I guess was too much by half. I shook my head and acted like I was about to leave. We haggled for a while and finally settled on a price, which was probably ten percent too high, but for us worth it and more.

I gave the box to Chuck, who had been leaning disconsolately against a shuttered window. He pounced on it eagerly.

"New model," he said as he tried to pry open the box. "Better than mine."

"It can wait till we get back to the Hassler."

"Yes, ma'am."

"And April Rosemary gets this one. Nothing secondhand for our daughter."

"Certainly not!"

It was stuffy in our suite, so I slipped out of my sundress as I dialed April Rosemary.

Chuck picked up the dress and hung it neatly in a closet. Long ago I had tried to stop such behavior. I gave it up when I realized that it was not a reflection on my neatness but only a manifestation of his peculiar need for order.

"Dr. Nettleton's house," our daughter said softly.

"And his wife's too!"

"Hi, Mom! You and Dad still in Rome?"

"How's my grandson?"

"Johnny's such a sweet, quiet little boy," she sighed. "No trouble at all."

Still down, poor kid. If the kid was sweet and quiet, it was his mother's fault that she was depressed.

"And the baby's galoot of a father?" Chuck asked from the other phone.

"He's fine. He works so hard."

"Did he find himself a job?"

"Oh, yes, I should have told you when I picked up the phone. He's going on the staff at Loyola, so we'll buy a home in Oak Park I guess."

Great news, listlessly given.

"So you guys can walk over to Petersen's when your mother and I give our little shows."

"That will be fun."

"April Rosemary, your father's supposed to do a portrait of the new Pope . . ."

"If they ever get around to electing him," Chuck intervened.

"And he left his Hasselblad at home, despite what I told him. So we had to buy a new one today."

"I'm so sorry."

"You shouldn't be, dear, because Dad says he'll give you the new one when he gets home."

"That's wonderful, but they're too expensive."

Spoken like her father's daughter.

"I said give, not sell."

"Thank you very much, Dad."

"I'm sure you know whose idea it was," Chuck said.

"Thank you, Mom."

"Mope," I said when I hung up.

I kicked off my sandals. Chuck carried them to the closet.

"Were you ever that way?"

"Sure, after Jimmy was born; of course, I had four kids, not just one."

"How did I act?"

"You were sensitive and sympathetic and supportive, like you always were."

"Really?" he seemed surprised.

"It's all hormones. Women usually get over it."

He sat on the couch and opened the box with his camera—a little boy with a wonderful little toy for which he did not have to pay.

"She sounds pretty bad."

"I'm sure Jamie has her on medication."

"She'll be all right, won't she?"

He examined the lens with care like it was a newborn baby.

"Certainly," I said with more confidence than I felt.

"She's worried," I had said to Maggie Ward, "that she's an addicted personality like her mother."

"And her mother is worried about her own responsibility for her daughter's presumed addiction?"

"Well . . ."

"How many times do I have to tell you, Rosemarie, that you turned to drink because of the trauma of sexual abuse by your father. That doesn't mean you're an addicted personality. You don't overeat. You gave up smoking long ago. You gave up coffee because your husband likes tea . . ."

"I screw more than most women."

"Good for you! . . . Your daughter's problem is like that of the soldiers who used heroin in Vietnam. They gave it up when they came home. It wasn't easy but they did it. They weren't addicted personalities either."

"She's worried that she'll pass it on to her children."

"So were you. And don't you say you did, because you know that you didn't. April Rosemary will be fine once she gets over her postpartum blues."

All I had wanted was reassurance, but it doesn't last very long.

I stood behind him in my half-slip, my nipples rock hard.

"That camera must be fascinating."

Chuck looked up from his adorable new camera. He put it aside and drew me down next to him on the couch.

"Poor Rosemarie, her eldest daughter acts like a mope and so does her husband."

We clung to each other for a long time, our embrace a rebuke to all the things that can go wrong in life.

Then his fingers slipped under the elastic of my panties and my body was filled with warmth.

"Chucky Ducky, the more I know you and the more I love you"—I sighed—"the more mystery you become. Nice mystery though."

❧ *Chuck* ❧
1978

The big TV screen in the Vatican Press Office switched back and forth from a picture of the smokestack above the Sistine to the façade of St. Peter's. No action in either scene. A few of the press corps were snoozing in the chairs in front of the screen. Others were crowded into the workroom, sending off dispatches for Sunday morning papers without knowing whether the smoke would be black or white. I was glad I was a picture taker.

My wife was milling around outside, picking up local color. Maybe she was thinking about something for the *New Yorker*.

I was trying to commune with the deity, which is always a good thing to do.

I'm sorry, I told Him. Or Her. Or Whatever. I really am.

You have given me a great wife—beautiful, intelligent, funny, and a great lay, you should excuse the expression. I neglect her. This afternoon I was more interested in my new camera than in her. How much of a goof can a guy be? She's standing there ready for love and I'm fooling with the lens. Then, when I wake up to the possibilities, I don't do it very well. I don't deserve her. I never did. I'm bored and disillusioned and a couple of weeks short of my fiftieth birthday. My life is a lot more than half over and I haven't done a damn thing with it. I don't seem to comprehend that Rosemarie is enough and more than enough. How can a man be bored with a woman like her in bed with him every night. Msgr. Raven says that the spouse is like You. Well, if You're anything like my Rosemarie, You're a wonderful person. I should have nothing to complain about. So the Church and the country and the archdiocese are run by idiots and madmen. So what.

And I'm almost fifty and I haven't done any decent work in the last eight years. Maybe I should stop trying.

I have the distinct impression that no one was listening. I don't blame You.

People were running out of the Press Office. I looked up at the screen. Smoke pouring out of the chimney, apparently black. I don't have to rush out, I'm not a reporter, just a picture taker. Still, I'd better put in an appearance. Rosemarie will worry about me.

Sure enough it was black smoke, thick, determined black smoke. No doubt about it this time. They'd finally figured out how it worked. The crowd was already dissipating. The poor Brits that I had conned at lunch would know what a faker I was.

Well, I WAS a faker.

There was no problem finding Rosemarie. Her white sleeveless dress with the V neck and the tight skirt would stand out in any crowd. No wonder the nasty nun in the Press Office glared at her. Which may be why Rosemarie had worn it.

"*È grigio*," she said to me. "Gray smoke."

"Looks black to me."

"Vatican Radio says it's black. RAI says it's black. The cops are packing up. I think there are little spurts of white."

I studied the now fading plume.

"Black. Let's go have some supper."

"Wait a few more minutes. I have a hunch."

I never fight my wife's hunches.

It was getting cold. I glanced at my watch—7:15. The sun had disappeared behind the Sistine Chapel. It was turning cold. I must have dozed during my prayer in the Press Office. Catching up on the sleep I had missed last night and earlier in the afternoon. I enjoyed a fleeting image of Rosemarie at the height of joyous sexual abandon. Like I say, I told Whatever, a good lay.

I glanced again at my watch—7:19. I'd give her one more minute. Then we'd go over to the Grand Hotel for supper.

"*Attenzione!*" A public address system demanded. The door of the balcony of St. Peter's swung open. A cross bearer and two acolytes emerged. Then a man in red. What was his name? Funny one. Pericle Felici.

Well, they had yet to figure out the smoke thing. What if you had an ancient symbol and couldn't reproduce it when it had one of its rare moments?

Great way to run a Church which depended on its symbols!

Rosemarie grabbed my arm. She was into this stuff. Great pageantry. Oddly enough my heart was pounding too.

"Annuntio vobis gaudium magnum!"

Loud cheers. My Rosemarie was screaming.

"Habemus Papam!"

Okay. He was announcing great joy, we had a Pope. What the hell else would he be doing out there if he was not announcing the election of a Pope?

"Eminentissimum ac reverendissium dominum . . ."

Another burst of cheers cut him off.

"Dominum . . . Albinum Cardinalem Sanctae Romanae Ecclesiae . . . LUCIANI!"

I discovered that I was screaming too.

"Qui imposuit sibi nomen Johannem Paulum Primum!"

Ecstatic cheers.

Combining the names of the last two Popes, nifty political idea. Chicago pols would understand.

"Those Englishmen will certainly be impressed!" Rosemarie enthused. "Chucky the prophet."

"Chucky with a quick mind and a quicker tongue," I said, quoting one of my grammar school teachers.

Somehow I wasn't impressed anymore. How would this nice little country pastor cope with a worldwide Church of a billion or so people? How would he cope with the fat little psychopathic paranoid who was ruining our archdiocese?

Rosemarie
1978

I knew the smoke would be white, I just knew it.

Besides, Msgr. Adolfo said we'd have a Pope by day's end and we did.

The moon turned itself on for the celebration. The Italian Army band played happy music. The crowd which filled the Piazza was happy and relaxed, one more Italian Pope and a nice man at that.

Chuck snapped a few available-light shots before it was too dark.

"Let's go have supper," he said.

"Let's go back into the Stampa and watch his blessing on the big screen."

"I can't take his picture in there."

"No, but you can take pictures of the people inside. Besides, I want to see what he looks like."

My poor husband was down again. I was unbearably complacent because of our lovemaking after lunch. He was so sweet, so gentle, so tender. I thought I would lose my mind. He seemed content too.

He was happy when he made love to me, but such activity only occupied a limited amount of his time. Sex alone would not save my poor Chucky Ducky, but it might help. I certainly enjoyed it. How could a man who was such an accomplished lover think he was a failure in life?

We waited in the crowded auditorium of the Sala Stampa for the first appearance of the new Pope to give his first blessing *Urbi et Orbi*. He emerged somewhat hesitantly from the balcony door and smiled at the cheering throng. The whole world lighted up.

"Wow," Chucky murmured. "I know what my portrait will focus on."

"Awesome smile," I said. "Totally. Like Msgr. Mugsy or Msgr. Raven walking the streets of St. Ursula."

He was a little man with spectacles and salt-and-pepper hair. Nothing particularly impressive about him except his smile. Once you had seen the smile nothing else mattered.

"He'll win the world with that smile," I told my husband.

"He'll have to do more than smile to solve the problem in Chicago," he replied.

Chuck seemed to believe that he personally was responsible for the Archdiocese of Chicago. Or perhaps only for avenging the terrible harm it had done to his brother.

❧ *Rosemarie* ❧
1973–1976

Our new Archbishop, Thomas John O'Neill, had come in 1965. He brought with him a great reputation for supporting racial integration, one which he tried immediately to live down. He was a fat, ugly little man who could on occasion be very charming. However, priests did not like him much and neither, after a while, did the laypeople, save for the very wealthy and the very powerful, whom he cultivated assiduously, especially newspaper editors. "I could commit incest at solemn high Mass," he once boasted, "and it would never make the papers."

This boast immediately echoed around the city and won him no friends.

He tried to cultivate the Mayor and did not get to first base.

Peg's husband, Vince Antonelli, a great big gorgeous sometime linebacker at the Golden Dome, explained. "The Mayor and Mrs. Daley know frauds when they see one. That guy is a fraud. The Mayor has already had to cover up for a drunken driving ticket."

One of his early schemes was a fund-raising drive for the whole Archdiocese, Project Resurrection. It was not clear how or for what the money would be spent. However, its main purpose seemed to be to enhance his own image. The fund-raisers leaned hard and the parish clergy, some of them eager to please the new Archbishop, cooperated. Others did not.

Since we were big fish (though Chuck didn't believe that) one of the high-powered fund-raisers came to visit us, by appointment, though the appointment was made to fit his schedule. It was Monday night and the Bears were playing on *Monday Night Football*. My husband was aware that the Bears always lose on *Monday Night Football*, and most other times too. Yet he must torment himself by watching them.

He was not eager to meet the man, who began by saying that the Cardinal had sent him personally to talk to us.

"We know," Jack Gaynor said, "that you will want to support the Cardinal just as everyone in Chicago does."

The question was addressed to Chuck, who, as man of the house, was presumed to have both the money and the purse strings. I was the good, dutiful wife and mother. It was shortly after Chuck's return from Vietnam, the death of Bobby Kennedy, the birth control encyclical, and the Chicago convention riots. My husband was not in a particularly good mood.

Jack Gaynor, slicked-down hair, a tailor-made double-breasted suit that wasn't quite tailor-made, and shifty gray eyes, was apparently unaware of our participation in the birth control commission or of Chuck's picaresque adventures "in-country." The whole nation, I thought, knew about that.

Chuck didn't give me a chance to respond.

"Certainly we want to support the Cardinal. However, we'd like to know how the money will be spent. We're not the kind of people who are willing to buy a pig in a poke, even when the pig is wearing red buttons. Certainly it won't cost much to remodel the Cathedral, which is all we've heard about."

"The Cardinal has many expenses, Mr. O'Malley," Gaynor said easily. "Education, hospitals, seminary training, missionary work. He also wants to create a Catholic television network which will put him in instant communication with every parish in the Archdiocese."

"Why?"

I relaxed. There was no need of my intervention.

"Well, so he can coordinate instantly the work of all the priests. He can speak to them each morning about his plans for the Church in Chicago."

"Ah," Chuck mused. "Wouldn't the telephone do just as well?"

"CNET, as we're calling it, would enable the Cardinal to give direct instructions to every priest the first thing in the morning. It would use high channels on UHF."

"Would the laypeople participate?"

"Eventually we would hope to have attachments for every Catholic television set in the Archdiocese. The Cardinal has great faith in the importance of technology for facilitating the work of the Church."

"Aha! And there would be the technology for the priests and eventually the people to respond to him?"

"At the present time"—the fund-raiser was becoming uneasy—"we have no plans for that."

"So it's one-way, high-tech communication?"

Jack Gaynor was beginning to suspect that my pint-size, apparently harmless, husband was having him on.

"I suppose you could call it that."

"How will the Cardinal know that all the priests are listening to him every morning?"

"He feels confident that the priests will be eager to cooperate. We will have the best equipment that money can buy. There is no substitute for excellence in the work of the Church."

"And the software?"

"I beg pardon?"

"The programming which will appear on this network after the Cardinal's daily plan of battle?"

"We will purchase the best educational material that is available for use in the Catholic schools."

"But not create any of our own?"

"Not at the present, no. We will make our facilities available to secular companies which are willing to rent them."

"At less than the going rate, I presume?"

"I presume so . . . Can we put you down for a quarter-million-dollar pledge?"

Jack Gaynor pulled a pledge card out of his expensive briefcase.

"No," my husband said flatly, without even a courtesy glance in my direction.

Our flummoxed visitor asked, "How much then?"

"Nothing until we have a clear statement of how the money is to be spent other than a silly television network."

"You are not willing to support the Cardinal and his work?" Gaynor seemed shocked, even scandalized.

"At the present time we are not . . . Rosemarie, would you be so good as to show Mr. Gaynor to the door?"

This was our me-Holmes-you-Watson act.

"Certainly, Charles."

"By the way, Mr. Gaynor," I asked, "will any of this money be used to pay off the Cardinal's driving-under-the-influence tickets?"

The poor man didn't answer.

"Wasn't that a little too much, Rosemarie, my love?" he said in the tone of voice of a man who was very proud of his wife.

"Not after your show . . . The poor man was only trying to do his job."

"He's corrupt," Chuck argued.

"Even corrupt people have to earn a living."

"I'm calling John Raven," he said, punching in the Monsignor's number. I picked up another phone.

The Bears fumbled again. Fortunately, Chuck didn't notice.

"John, Chuck O'Malley here. I'm delighted to learn that the Cardinal plans to wake all you clerical loafers up in the morning with his own personal TV network."

"One of his guys visited you, huh?"

"A quarter million dollars for a megalomaniac TV network!"

"My husband has a way with words, Monsignor," I said gently.

"Well, at least I didn't ask him whether they would use some of the money to pay off his DUI tickets like a certain shameless Irishwoman I know did."

John Raven laughed in spite of himself.

"Rosie, you didn't?"

"Would I say something like that?"

"You certainly would . . . Look, Fatso had these same guys do a big fund-raiser on his last stop. Great success proved that he was a tough, effective executive. He didn't realize it wouldn't work in Chicago."

"We had an Ecumenical Council a few years ago, if I remember correctly. The Church was supposed to be updated. Then they send a crazy man to Chicago. What the hell is going on?"

"He knows how to play the Roman game. During his many visits over there he gives important curial people a thousand-dollar bill and asks them to say Mass for his mother."

"That's why they sent him to Chicago!"

"Part of the reason anyway. As they say at City Hall, he picked up his markers."

"Hell of a way to run a Church."

"You won't get any argument from me."

"What will happen to the fund-raising?"

"He'll get some money, especially from the rich conservatives who think a Cardinal can do no wrong. The pastors will drag their feet. The fund-raisers will announce that the drive is a big success, collect their fees and depart and we won't hear another word about it."

I frowned. I had never heard John so bitter.

"The birth control decision and a madcap Cardinal. Thank you very much, Pope Paul!"

"Did you notice what your friend said about the birth control encyclical?"

"No . . ."

"Neither did anyone else. He prepared a nonstatement before it was announced and then went off to Alaska."

"That's not a very conservative response," I said.

"Rosie, he's not a conservative. He has no principles. He's concerned only about power, his power. I don't think he believes in God."

"John!" I protested.

"I don't mean that he denies the existence of God. Only that God is irrelevant to what he says and does. He's embarrassed when anyone talks about religion."

"Oh," I said meekly.

"What are you guys going to do about him?" Chuck said, flipping off the TV after an interception.

"Hunker down in the trenches until he goes away."

"You won't be able to hide this from the laity, John," I said.

"We were not planning on hiding it from people like you, Rosie. Most Catholics will find out that he's strange eventually. The more devout won't even admit it to themselves. If anyone is going to get rid of him, it will have to be us and I don't think we're quite ready to do that yet."

We had a lot to worry about in those days. April Rosemary, unsure of herself and us, was going off to Harvard, kids were rioting in the streets, we were trying to elect Hubert Humphrey (and almost did), and Chuck was working on his exhibition *1968—Year of Violence*. There was no time to worry about a crazy Cardinal. I did ask Maggie Ward, whose brother-in-law was a priest who had been on the birth control commission with us, what Monsignor Packy Keenan thought of the Cardinal.

"He asks me how I would diagnose him, which is of course, Rosemarie, what you want to know. I am afraid that it is a rather straightforward case. He is what is generally called a psychopathic paranoid or sometimes a borderline personality."

"What does that mean?"

"It's a characterological syndrome about which we know very little, though such a man is very dangerous—Hitler and Stalin for example. The person does not have a conscience. No one else is a real person, save perhaps for a dominating woman. I am told there is one such woman in the Cardinal's life. She replaces the dominating mother who may have caused the problem in the first place. The syndrome is marked by a deep fear of total destruction. One develops a vast array of defenses to protect the self. The protections are increasingly bizarre. Finally, as he grows older the whole structure of the personality breaks down. The Cardinal is a desperately frightened man. I tell Msgr. Packy to stay away from him. He won't of course. Poor dear thinks he can save the church. You too, Rosemarie. I know that you and Chuck are reckless adventurers, witness his recent adventures in Vietnam. This one is not your cup of tea."

She didn't know about Chuck's taking on Lyndon Johnson earlier in the year. The Cardinal sounded a lot like Lyndon.

"You mean he's a mama's boy?"

"Precisely, Rosemarie. For all his bluster, the Cardinal is a weakling, utterly emasculated by his mother."

I told Chuck what she had said while we were working on the prints for his show—at the Metropolitan no less, but only because the Art Institute hesitated.

"It does sound like LBJ," he agreed, rubbing his eyes.

"However, that lovely little woman is right as always. He's not our cup of tea."

He became our cup of tea four years later. In the early autumn of 1972 our eldest son Kevin, a tall devilishly handsome Black Irishman whom I imagined riding with Phil Sheridan's cavalry in the Shenandoah Valley, had returned from Vietnam with a Distinguished Service Cross and without a foot. The venue for our solemn high welcome-home party was, as such must always be, at the house of Chuck's parents, John (as in John the Evangelist lest anyone think his patron saint was John the Baptist) and April Cronin O'Malley. The latter was never known as "Mom" but as "the good April." My husband's family earned their name the Crazy O'Malleys.

Kevin was thin and pale and walked with a cane. However, his slow sweet smile was unchanged. Maria Elena, his gorgeous future wife, drank him in with her vast Latin brown eyes. We all would rather have had him back in one piece, but we were glad to have him back, especially since the idiots at the Pentagon had insisted for several weeks that he had been killed in action.

I mourned permanently for our daughter April Rosemary, who had disappeared into the hippy underground. However, I had become good at covering up. As Maggie Ward had said, if I survived those days without returning to my drinking ways, I would never drink again. I hope she was right.

So we had the usual musicale with the jazz band of my three sons on their horns, Gianni Antonelli pounding the drums, Maria Elena doing her Latin jazz vocals, and the good April backing it all up on the piano. I did a few wordless vocal variations around my future daughter-in-law's songs.

Then Father Ed drew me aside and whispered, "I'd like to talk to you and Chuck for a few minutes."

My heart jumped. Something evil was coming in the night. Darkness was already closing on Chicago, a late afternoon in autumn when winter was beginning to growl. Outside, oblivious to our merriment, snowflakes were beginning to fall.

Edward Michael, to give him his full name, was the gentlest of all the O'Malleys. Slim, handsome, sexy, he was six years younger than my husband, intense, and unbearably idealistic. "There should be a big 'I' on his forehead to warn people," my husband argued. "He's a true believer looking for a cause."

"The pot calling the kettle black," I responded.

He was, I had often told my husband, Chucky "lite"—his brother without the great talent, the acerbic wit, and the touch of divine, usually, madness.

"No red hair either."

His slight form, his sandy hair, and his compassionate eyes cast him as the perennial "young priest" even though he was now nearly forty. He had marched at Selma and joined the war protests at the 1968 convention in Chicago, even though the Cardinal ordered him not to.

"Fatso thinks he should have a monopoly on public attention," John Raven had commented, with uncharacteristic nastiness.

In his early years in the priesthood, I had become his confidante. The poor kid thought he was inadequate as a priest and should leave the ministry before he did more harm to the poor laypeople. Chuck claims that I kept him in the priesthood.

"He doesn't want to leave," I reply. "He wants to be a priest."

"I feel sorry for women who marry priests," Chuck would say. "They make creepy husbands."

I did not necessarily disagree with the general statement. Nonetheless I would reply, "Father Ed would make some woman a fine husband."

"So long as she was prepared to make all his decisions for him."

We were both therefore uneasy when we drifted into Chuck's father's architectural studio at the back of the rambling house on East Avenue. As usual blueprints and file folders were scattered about the studio. Outside the snow was getting thicker.

"What craziness do you think it is this time?" Chuck whispered to me.

"The Cardinal has asked me to help him out," Ed began. He has the same pale blue eyes as my husband, but his are usually anguished while Chuck's are vibrant, usually with mischief.

"Well, Edward, he needs help," Chuck said carefully.

"What would you be doing?" I asked.

Fr. Ed, dressed in a clerical shirt and wearing a dark green sweater I'd given him for Christmas just after Chuck and I were married, leaned forward in the easy chair his dad used to talk to clients.

"I'd be his secretary and vice chancellor. I'd live with him in the mansion on North State. Advise him at every step of the way. He knows he has problems and needs help. He's my bishop. A priest can't turn down a request for help from his bishop."

He raised his hands as if appealing for our help. He was a good guy and I loved him, but when it comes to religion he gets a bit wimpy.

"What happened to the man you'd be replacing?" I continued.

"He's resigned." Fr. Ed waved his right hand in nervous dismissal.

"From the priesthood?"

"Yes."

"Was there a prior predecessor?"

Fr. Ed hesitated and lowered his eyes.

"He left too . . . So did his vicar for religious. Married a nun."

"Oh."

"I'm not going to quit the priesthood, Rosie, you know that."

"Isn't he a little bit, uh, crazy, Edward?"

"Not really, Chuck." He looked up again. "He's often misunderstood. He's not from Chicago, you know. It takes a long time to understand this city. He wants me to help him because he says I come from a family that really knows Chicago."

"Even if they live in Oak Park . . ."

"Will you guys support me? I'll take a lot of heat from my priest friends. They'll say I've sold out."

"Then they were never really friends, bro. We'll stand behind you."

"Count on us," I echoed my husband.

"Great!"

He gripped Chuck's hand, hugged me, and bounded out of the studio to rejoin the party.

"Well done, husband mine."

"Same to you . . . We're going to have to blot up the pieces eventually."

"One more victim."

He thought for a moment.

"I was wrong."

"I reject that possibility."

"I said the 'I' on Edward's forehead stands for idealist. Actually it stands for innocent . . ."

Chuck put his arm around my shoulders and led me back to the party. His fist was clenched. The poor dear man is not vengeful at all, save when one of his is endangered. Heaven help the Cardinal if he hurt Fr. Ed.

Chuck didn't mean it when he threatened to kill my father if he touched me again. He was just trying to scare him. He wept with me at the wake after the Outfit had blown him into tiny pieces. Then he told me the story about his parents' courtship at Twin Lakes and the gypsy woman's prophecy about me and how terribly sorry he felt for my own father.

Chuck's hate vanishes quickly. Still, Cardinal O'Neill had better be careful. Charles Cronin O'Malley is not the kind of man that you push around. Or his family.

I don't believe in gypsy prophecies, by the way.

April and Vangie pretended to be delighted at the appointment.

"I always thought that Michael would be a fine bishop," the good April said, donning her Pangloss glasses. "And the poor, dear Cardinal really needs someone to help him stop doing so many stupid things."

"I'm glad I'm not building churches anymore," Vangie said. "He's a very difficult man. Always comes out swinging until you stand up to him."

A couple days later, when I was struggling to figure out how the new Radio Shack computer with a word processor worked, John Raven called.

"Rosie," he said in that magical voice which had brought peace in my times of trouble, "is it true?"

"Yes, John. It's true. My foster kid brother will become secretary for that psychopathic paranoid who is ruining our Archdiocese."

"Why?"

"Because he believes that a priest should help his bishop when the bishop asks for help."

"Does he want to be a bishop himself?"

"Ed? Gimme a break!"

"Sorry, Rosie . . . The man is mad. He's destroyed all the power structures in the Archdiocese. He controls everything, which means that he controls nothing. We have terrible problems and nothing gets done. No one knows what happens to the money. He hires private detectives to shadow priests. One has been following me for weeks in search of my mistress . . ."

I couldn't help myself. I laughed.

John relaxed and laughed with me.

"All right, Rosie, all right. He destroys the people who work closely with him. The smart ones get out. One guy got himself a job in Rome because he realized that his chances of becoming a bishop would go up in smoke if he stayed around the Cardinal for long."

"If he's so bad, John, why don't the priests get together and do something about him?"

"Like take out a contract?"

"Like complain to the Pope."

"You can't dump a Cardinal, Rosie."

"You could go to the local media."

"They know some of it. They're afraid of the story."

"I can't believe that the Pope wouldn't listen to priests."

John sighed.

"The truth is that there is not enough courage in the clergy to really take him on. We gripe and complain and talk about nothing else. But we're afraid to fight."

"No balls?"

"I won't argue with that . . . You and Chuck keep an eye on Ed."

"We plan to."

"His parents?"

"They're concerned too, they just pretend not to be."

"Poor dear Cardinal needs someone to help him?"

"Almost verbatim."

I found Chuck in his obsessively neat darkroom working on the portrait of a beautiful woman of about my age whose husband wanted an erotic pose—the usual stuff, arms folded over her boobs, and very pretty boobs at that. She obviously wouldn't have minded if they weren't covered, but the poor dolt husband was afraid of her.

"Stop staring at her," I ordered him, as a print appeared in the magic of the chemical tray.

"I'm admiring the artist's skill."

What her husband didn't realize was that Chuck sees the erotic appeal in all women, no matter how old they are. Moreover, he has the weird ability to catch them at the moment when they reveal who and what they are. No sexual exploitation there. The woman in the chemical bath was sweet, like I say, and lovely and impish and very determined. Her husband had never seen that combination in her. The picture would scare the living daylights out of him. Serve him right.

Incidentally, Chuck sometimes sees them wrong. I am not the Irish warrior goddess his camera thinks I am. Well, not always.

"I bet the idiot never saw her that way," I said. "The picture will surprise him and scare him. She's a lot more than a pretty body."

Chuck thought about that.

"God gave us lovers, I think, because he thought it would be a good thing that there would be someone in our lives who could surprise us and scare us out of our daily monotony."

"Oh, Chucky." I began to weep as I always do when he turns mystical and says something profound.

"You can use that quote in your next story if you want."

I pounded his arm in mock protest.

Then I told him about my conversation with John Raven.

He stirred the chemical bath on the woman's bare shoulders.

"Why do priests put up with a guy like the Cardinal?" he asked.

Obviously a rhetorical question.

"Maybe if you take sex out of a man's life, he becomes passive aggressive. You suppress your hormones long enough, you don't have any masculine reaction."

I touched his hand, maneuvering it away from the bitch's shoulders.

"I don't think most Protestant clergy would behave differently. It must be that men of God are reluctant to take on someone who claims to be God's representative."

"Maybe we'll have to do something about it, husband mine . . . No one would accuse you of suppressing your hormonal instincts."

"What could we do about it?"

The idea appealed to him.

"We'll have to wait and see."

As winter reluctantly retreated temporarily and spring dubiously poked its tiny nose into our world, Chuck and I returned to our tennis and golf. He wasn't doing much of anything. When he wasn't working on a formal portrait, he devoted himself to unsystematic reading of Victorian novels, the people in which seemed to be more interesting than the people of late-twentieth-century real life.

"The men were such courteous gentlemen," he informed me with the tone of an academic expert, "even when they were cads, which most of them were."

He didn't lose interest in me, but in truth he didn't seem as interested as he used to be.

He and Moire Meg had long and complicated arguments about gender in the Victorian era, with my daughter arguing the apparently reactionary position that women ran things then too despite their economic dependency.

We saw little of Father Ed during the winter. He spent a few hours with us on Christmas Day. The rest of the time he was busy "helping the Cardinal."

Even the good April went so far as to comment, "I don't believe that job is really good for Edward's health."

He was able to preside over the wedding of Kevin and Maria Elena Lopez at St. Francis Church, but he had to miss the dinner because the Cardinal needed him. The bride and her family were much too polite to notice. Kevin was too much in love to care.

"What the hell is the matter with Uncle Ed?" Jimmy, a sophomore at St. John's up in Minnesota, asked me with his usual blunt clarity. "The Cardinal is more important than we are."

"Uncle Ed is an idealist," I replied, waving off the question.

"Oh, yeah." Jimmy nodded as if he understood. "Priests have to be idealists."

As I watched my three handsome, Black Irish sons on the altar at Mass, I felt very proud of them and very old. Too bad that the old Black Horse Troop in which Chuck's father had ridden with its silver uniform and red plumes did not exist anymore.

As for the groom's father, he wore his precinct captain mask. All the Mexican-Americans doted on him. He learned the names of all the uncles and aunts and would never forget them.

"Real Irish," one of the aunts said to me admiringly.

"You got that right," I said, rolling my eyes.

It was a great night—two musical families merging in a jazz mode with dazzling variations. Chuck and I actually sang a substantial part of our repertory to a mariachi background. They loved us.

"Mariachi music," my husband assured me, "is actually wedding music from the state of Jalisco."

"I needed to know that."

"And my brother is a stupid son of a bitch!"

"CHUCKY!"

Even the good April said to me, shaking her head in bemusement, "Father Edward Michael should have stayed longer."

I had the feeling that the whole family wanted me to do something about my youngest foster sibling.

Anyway, on a bright day in early May of 1974 we played golf at Butterfield Country Club, which Chuck preferred to Oak Park because, as he put it, "At Butterfield the drunks are all Catholic drunks."

He is a terrible golfer. He plays because his father likes to beat him. Also because his wife likes to beat him.

"Can't say I'm not a good sport," he would grumble.

We encountered that gorgeous little witch who reads my soul, Maggie Ward, and her husband Jerry Keenan in the dining room. Msgr. Packy Keenan, Jerry's brother, was with them. Packy was with us at St. Crispin's Day when we gave Paul VI a way out on the birth control encyclical which he decided he didn't want.

Maggie always pretends that she hasn't seen me in ages.

"Spring agrees with you, Rosemarie," she said. "You look wonderful!"

For a moment I fill up with affection for Maggie. Along with my husband she's saved my life. And still does.

"Thank you, Dr. Ward. Someday soon you'll have to teach me how to look even more beautiful when I'm a grandmother."

"You can tell she writes for the *New Yorker*," Chuck said.

"More likely old-fashioned Irish blarney," Maggie said.

"We have a little of that in our family too," Jerry Keenan admitted.

Shrinks are not supposed to interact with their clients, especially in country club dining rooms. The little witch breaks all the rules.

We talked about Richard Nixon for a while. Chuck assured all of us that Tricky Dicky would be out of office by the end of the summer.

"Not quite a Greek tragedy. He doesn't have the stature for that," Maggie mused. "But still a tragedy."

"Lyndon would have been all right," Chuck informed us, "if he hadn't gone to West Texas State and Nixon would have made it if he hadn't gone to Whittier College."

"Men destroyed by their own feelings of inferiority?" Maggie asked, fascinated as always by how smart my husband could be when he wanted to.

"The real issue before the house," Chuck went on, "is whether Leo Kelly and Jane Devlin will get together again, now that he's back in Chicago as provost at the University."

"It's been twenty years," Msgr. Packy said sadly.

I had suspected for a long time that Msgr. Packy had a very soft spot in his heart for Jane.

Jane and Leo were classmates of Chuck's. They dated in the forties and would surely have married if he hadn't been killed in action in Korea. By the time the Marines had admitted their mistake and he returned a prisoner of war without a couple of his fingers, Jane had already married Phil Clare, a lout who had been unfaithful to her on their honeymoon.

If Chucky Ducky had ever done that to me, I would have killed him.

When Jane finally had sense enough to sue for divorce, I

made Chuck call Leo, whose dippy-hippy wife had shed him years ago, leaving him with an adorable little girl child, and tell him that he should look for a job at the University of Chicago. Leo had laughed it off, but we knew he'd be back.

"Some one of these summers," Chuck told the Keenans, "he's going to show up at Lake Geneva with that diffident smile. I leave it to you, Dr. Ward, and the various other matriarchs involved to see that matters arrange themselves."

"You can count on me, Dr. O'Malley."

"Now, then," Chuck continued in his professorial mode, "the next order of business, Monsignor, is a detailed report on what is to be done about our paranoid sociopath Cardinal."

Packy Keenan, a big athletic man with a red face and snow-white hair like his brother and his father, laughed, but his heart wasn't in it.

"He's a strange one, Chuck. Some nights he consumes a gallon of ice cream and a bottle of bourbon and gets on the phone to bishops all over the country, complaining about us. Then he calls one of us and complains about the other bishops. That woman who he claims is a relative but really isn't hangs around all the time. No one knows what happens to the money. Then he goes off to places like the Royal Hawaiian or the Athens Hilton and holes up in a room. His staff sends him a mail pouch every day."

"Oh," I said.

"How's Ed doing, Chuck?"

My husband paused.

"You guys gotta get rid of him," he said.

"Ed?"

"No, Cardinal O'Neill. A bunch of you have to go to Rome and tell the Pope to fire him. Tell His Holiness that his behavior is bizarre, that there's a big scandal brewing, and that the priests and people hate him."

"That would be impossible, Chuck."

"That's what John Raven says too," I said.

Chuck continued to destroy his large T-bone steak.

"I'll come with you," my husband declared, turning to his mashed potatoes. I positively hate him when he devours food that way and doesn't put on any weight.

"Nervous energy," he tells me.

"They wouldn't listen. He's a Cardinal."

"Tell them that if they don't get rid of him, the media will eventually break the story."

"They won't risk offending the Catholics of Chicago."

"Eventually they will."

The next day I was in the darkroom shuffling, carefully so as not to disturb his order, through a file labeled "MENARD AVENUE."

Am I free to disrupt his sacred precincts? As I told him long ago, as long as I sleep in the same bed as he does, I can poke around whenever and wherever I want. The rules, however, are different when I'm working on a story. He may not look at it, even think about it, until I'm finished with my first revision.

Who makes these rules? I make them. I make all the rules.

Chuck shuffled into the darkroom.

"Looking at my Menard Avenue files?" he said plaintively, hinting that would I please put them back in proper order.

"Look at this one."

It was a shot, released by remote control, of the whole family at Twin Lakes.

"Sure were a lot of us . . . Dad and the good April are so young."

"Younger than we are now . . . Jane is exuberant about becoming a woman, you are pretending to look like a sullen French painter, those two she-tigers next to you are a frightening pair . . ."

"Conspiring about something, probably against me."

"And poor little Ed . . ."

Chuck took the picture from my hand and studied it closely. Then he looked at it with his magnifying glass.

"If I took the picture, that's the way he had to look in those days, kind of left out."

"Bullshit! You couldn't even see him when the shutter went off . . . How would you describe him?"

"Sad," Chuck replied, frowning. "Trying to catch up. Youngest child?"

"Moire Meg is our youngest and she's never tried to play catch-up. Depression child, maybe."

Chuck nodded.

"Maybe . . . He was always kind of quiet. I never felt he was competing with us. I guess he might have been."

"Competing with YOU!"

"That should have been easy, Rosemarie."

"Gimme a break!"

"Anyway, this is the past. We have to do something in the present. Or the immediate future."

"Get him out of that job."

Chuck nodded solemnly and removed the file from my hand. He paused to carefully check the pictures.

"It would be interesting," he said, deep in reflection, "if we could measure what those kids expected of life then and how it compares with the present."

"The amazing thing to me," I replied, "is not that the O'Malley family was willing to acquire another daughter without any fuss and bother, but that I had the nerve to push my way in."

"I would have vetoed the project," he said, extending his arm around my waist, "except that I thought there might be a chance to see you with your clothes off, not that I would have known what to do in such circumstances."

"Or do now."

Several days later Ed called and told us in an edgy voice that the Cardinal would like us to do a portrait he could send around to the rectories of the Archdiocese. I accepted before my husband could decline.

That's another rule we keep.

The man was fat and short and ugly, but genial in an ingratiating way. He wore a carefully tailored cassock with a short cape, red buttons, and red trim, no cummerbund or zucchetto, however.

"Well, Mr. O'Malley," he said, "you'll have a real challenge to make something out of me. I don't want any fancy stuff. Just a picture of me as I am, all of me!"

He brought us drinks, diet cola for me, red wine for Chuck. Father Ed hovered uneasily in the background. He was so thin and haggard that I had hardly recognized him.

Chuck likes to say that the camera always lies. It never takes a picture of someone as they are, but rather as the camera and the photographer want to see him.

"Once a person realizes that we are mountebanks and charlatans, the rest is easy."

His principle, uttered casually but adhered to implacably, is he wants us to see the subject as he is but in the best possible light. A two-year-old boy child might be an outstandingly ugly little brat, but we must see him in the light of his parents' love and with the possibility of life stretching out before him.

His task that afternoon was to find something good in an ugly paranoid psychopath who was a prince of the Holy Roman Church. I don't think he did a very good job of it. Chuck's lens saw Cardinal O'Neill as a sawed-off, overweight Mephistopheles with a genial Irish grin. However, the Cardinal praised the results and eagerly sent copies to all the rectories in the Archdiocese. I had seen this reaction frequently in the last couple of years. If O'Malley had done it, then it had to be good.

"He's not making them pay for it," Chuck sighed. "Unlike those TV antennae on every Catholic school in Cook and Lake Counties which no one ever uses."

Actually there was some stuff that they used in the schools, most of which could have been purchased or leased on videotape.

Afterward we went into supper in the dining room of the Cardinal's mansion. It was one of the strangest evenings in my life. He asked us what Jack Kennedy was like. Before we could answer, he told us stories about Kennedy's love affairs, some of which could not have been true. Then he talked about conversations he had with Eisenhower and Nixon and Ford.

"What about LBJ?" Chuck squeezed a question into the ongoing babble.

"We didn't get along too well," the Cardinal said, wolfing down a huge scoop of potatoes. "He was offended when I told him he should get us out of Vietnam."

"Back in 1965?" Chuck asked innocently.

"Let me see, yeah, it must have been then."

I had the uncanny feeling that he was about to recycle Chuck's life story back as his own. Father Ed said very little, stared glumly at his plate, and barely touched his food.

"Of course, I've been over there several times. In-country. The Holy Father wanted to ordain some bishops in the North that the Communists wouldn't know about. It was scary stuff at first, then you get used to it. One time it looked like I was sure to be caught, then a black Marine helicopter picked me up in the nick of time. Believe you me, I was glad to see those Marines."

"I can believe that," Chucky said pleasantly.

Chuck would know because a Black Huey had yanked him out of the South China Sea just before a North Vietnamese fishing boat had beat them to it.

"I've had to do a lot of things like that, especially when I was a young bishop. In and out of Russia and China to ordain bishops for the Underground. The Holy Father said to me, 'Eminence, we can no longer ask you to risk your life for us.' "

"That was very considerate of him." Chuck nodded in approval.

The bastard was enjoying the show.

"I could tell you stories that would blow your minds," the Cardinal rushed on, as a nun removed his plate, the last one on the table. "I shouldn't talk about most of them. The CIA wants me to keep my mouth shut. They warn me that someone on the other side may have put out a contract on me."

"I'm sure the local boys on the West Side would stop that," Chuck said with an absolutely straight face. "They're all good Catholics."

"They've promised me they would. I trust them to keep their word."

"Men of respect, Your Eminence."

This can't be happening, I thought. This is a dream. This crazy man cannot be a Cardinal Archbishop. The nun brought in the biggest dishes of chocolate ice cream I've ever seen in my life. I gently eased mine away. Father Ed ignored his. The Cardinal and my husband dug in.

"Now tell me what you think of this Congressman Boylan. I hear he's a bit of a pinko, alcoholic too."

Father Ed cringed.

"Timmy?" Chuck said. "Oh, I don't think so. When he came home from the war he tried to destroy the beer supply on the West Side in a place on Division Street called the Magic Tap because the proprietor has a pretty good magician. We'd sit there hours on end talking about Joyce and Proust, while he drank beer and I sipped on Coca-Cola. No Diet Coke in those days. He hasn't drunk anything since then. He's a real credit to our neighborhood and to the Church."

The Cardinal turned immediately to the question of Mayor Daley's health.

"I hear he's got only a couple of months to live."

The Mayor and the Cardinal were barely on speaking terms.

"He seemed healthy the last time we discussed the situation in Northern Ireland," Chuck said blandly. "He has some strong views on that as I'm sure you know."

The Cardinal consumed his ice cream before Chuck had finished his. Both of them had rings of chocolate around their mouths.

"Well," said the Cardinal, "I have to run. I have to sign twenty-five hundred *celebret* cards before morning. You'll have to excuse me. I'll be looking forward to your proofs, Chuck."

He bounded up the stairs. Father Ed, a ghostly presence, showed us to the door.

"What's a *celebret* card?" I asked.

"It says that the bearer of the card is a priest in good standing and asks that he be permitted to say Mass. We're supposed to carry one with us when we travel."

Father Ed spoke in a whisper.

"Does anyone use them anymore?"

"No."

Chuck and I were silent until we turned on to the Congress Expressway (as we Democrats still call it) and raced toward the safety of Oak Park.

"One flew over the cuckoo's nest," I said.

"Bedlam, Donnybrook Farm . . . And he's our Cardinal."

"It shouldn't have surprised us, Chuck. It's what Fathers Raven and Keenan have been telling us. He's round the bend."

"Monsignors . . . the Vatican can't know how bad it is."

"I wouldn't bet on that. We've got to get Father Ed out of there."

"Did you have fun?" Moire Meg asked when we were back at the house. She was poring over an algebra problem.

"Not exactly," I said.

She looked up, her green eyes flashing.

"Like the monkey island at Brookfield Zoo?"

"That's a fair analysis." My husband sank into an easy chair.

"Poor Uncle Ed."

Indeed poor Uncle Ed.

Summer at Grand Beach was delightful. It's hard to worry about anything during summer at the Lake. Yet being a mother, I worried, especially when I retreated to the tower which was my workroom. (I could pull up the ladder and be isolated from all the world.) I worried more about Moire Meg than I did about Father Ed. I remembered how crazy I was at that age (drinking at Lake Delavan).

"That one is not to worry about," my husband contended. "She has more common sense than we did at that age."

Too true. But that is not enough to stop a mother from worrying about her daughter, especially since she's lost one already. April Rosemary, I knew, was lost to us forever.

Father Ed didn't come to the Lake once that summer, not even to baptize my first granddaughter, Maria Rosa O'Malley, a red-haired Latina of almost intolerable beauty. He was scheduled to do the ceremony, but called at the last minute to say he couldn't make it.

Msgr. Raven, who was on vacation in Long Beach at a houseful of priests and was coming anyway, did the honors. He didn't say anything about Father Ed's absence. The little hellion screamed through the ceremony and went ballistic when John poured the water on her head.

Her two grandmothers passed the baby back and forth, each of us claiming with total dishonesty that this new grandchild looked like the other's family.

"The red hair," Lupe Lopez argued, "it is just like your husband's."

"Look at everything else and she looks just like you, Lupe, and your daughter."

In fact the howling little brat was patently an O'Malley.

No one said much about Father Ed's absence.

"I really believe that the poor boy needs a long rest," the good April observed.

"We have to get him out of there," her husband agreed.

They were simply too nice to figure out how to do that.

Chuck and I plowed along, he with his darkroom and I with my stories. Neither of us made much progress. It was as though our lives were on hold and still slipping through our fingers.

Then surprise and wonder returned.

On a day in September when Moire Meg and I had been shopping, we returned to the house to learn that April Rosemary had phoned to say that she was coming to visit us and with a young man and would not be sleeping in the same bedroom with him.

Our daughter had clawed her way out of the world of drugs and sex and rock and roll, recovered her health, and found herself a fiancé who was a medical school graduate and the son of Chuck's commanding officer in Germany after the war. They would be married shortly after our silver wedding anniversary and live in Chicago, indeed in Oak Park. She had not called us until she was sure that she was in full control of her life, the sort of thing that a daughter of mine might well do.

The Crazy O'Malley celebrations went on for a week. Father Ed did not come to any of them.

My daughter was still fragile and vulnerable, still feeling terribly guilty because she had let us down. We were so happy to have her back that our forgiveness was easy and automatic. However, she could not forgive herself.

"Give her time," Maggie Ward insisted. "She'll be all right . . . I presume you don't fight?"

"Certainly not!"

"Nor does she fight with the cute red-haired genius?"

"Poor Moire Meg walks on eggshells."

"And her father?"

"She never fought with him. Now she talks photography since she intends to follow in his footsteps."

"You'll know she's all right when she begins to fight with you. It's not healthy for mothers and daughters not to fight. Don't worry, it will come."

Naturally I worried. That's what mothers are for.

"Where's Uncle Ed?" she asked me one day as she helped Missus and me prepare dinner. Missus, our Polish housekeeper, humored us, though she considered us a nuisance in the kitchen.

We really didn't need a housekeeper anymore. However, it would have broken Missus's heart if we told her that.

"He's working on the monkey island at the zoo," Moire Meg informed us, dashing into the house in her Trinity High School uniform and hugging all three of us.

"Monkey island?"

"She means he's the Cardinal's secretary."

"A real loony bin," Moire Meg said. "You guys should get him out of there."

"We know that, dear," I said, realizing how much I sounded like the good April.

"Maybe we should all just go down and liberate him," April Rosemary suggested, then bit her lip at the word from her hippy past.

"We thought of that, darling, but Uncle Ed has to make his own decisions."

That was certainly true. Nonetheless, we could have taken him aside and told him what we thought. Only he was never around to be taken aside.

Still, we had our daughter and son back and the Vietnam mess was over. Chuck and I were approaching our silver anniversary with great joy. Our sex life was the best ever. We enjoyed each other. We didn't fight, mainly, he said, because he had learned to keep all the rules.

Well, he didn't keep all the rules. He often broke the one about pawing me only in the bedroom. I had, however, lost interest in enforcing that rule. I did enforce, however, the rule about his undressing me in the darkroom or in my office or in the exercise room downstairs. Usually.

My daughters insisted that I try on my wedding dress because they said I would still fit in it. They were wrong; we had to let it out in a few places.

"Only a little bit," Moire Meg told me. "You're some cool broad, Rosie."

I was embarrassed by this stuff. I had been such a little nitwit in 1950. I actually tried to talk Chuck out of the marriage after the rehearsal the night before because I insisted that I was spoiled goods.

Thank God he would have none of that.

Anything else in the years to come—all the rules he broke—had already earned forgiveness.

Not that you can earn forgiveness. It has to be done freely. I thanked God a lot.

Chuck fit into his wedding formal with perhaps a few more adjustments.

"See!" I crowed. "It's a good thing I forced you to exercise."

"I still look funny in it."

"Cute," I said. "Not funny. Really cute. You're skinny anyway."

"Slender," he said with a wicked grin.

"No, I'm slender because of lots of hard work. You're skinny naturally. It's all right. I like you that way."

So then, since we were in our bedroom, I began to undress him.

Then on the first Sunday in Advent, the day of the first blizzard of the year, Father Ed showed up at our door, wearing black trousers, a knit shirt, and a white summer windbreaker.

"I'm quitting." He shivered.

He must have lost at least thirty pounds.

We dragged him inside, pulled him to the fireplace, wrapped him in a blanket, and gave him a strong shot of bourbon.

"The man is evil incarnate. If I had stayed there any longer, I would have killed him."

He continued to shiver.

A psychotic interlude?

We called Jane's husband Ted McCormack and Msgr. Keenan.

"I'm leaving the priesthood, Packy," Father Ed told the Monsignor. "I've lost my faith."

"You have not lost your faith and you're not leaving the priesthood," someone said. "I told you once you couldn't leave without my permission. I haven't given my permission yet and I won't!"

I recognized that the voice was mine. Father Ed leaned his head in my lap and sobbed.

"Well, that's settled."

I looked up at the four men in the room. They were smiling at me. I had done their work for them.

"Okay," I went on. "The man is a nutcake, an escapee from the monkey island over at Brookfield, a psychopathic paranoid. The Vatican has to get rid of him. However, Ed, you're out of there now. And we'll worry about him. Like the good April has been saying all summer, you need a long rest."

"At the parish down in Tucson," Chuck suggested, "where you used to go in the winter."

"When you come back," Msgr. Packy said, "you can come live with us. We need another priest at the rectory."

"Okay." Father Ed sighed.

He sat up straight and touched my arm.

"Thanks, Rosie."

"Be my guest."

"I know a good doctor you can talk to down there," Ted added, "if you want to."

"Post-traumatic stress syndrome," Chucky said.

Somehow that made all of us laugh.

"I'll fly down there with you," he added. "I need to escape from all this anniversary lunacy for a day or two."

Monsignor Packy took him back to the St. Agedius Rectory. "Keep him in a priestly atmosphere," he said.

Ted lingered to talk with us.

"Why did he stay there so long?" he asked.

"He's a churchman," Chuck explained. "He was trained for years to believe in loyalty to his bishop."

"Infantile, isn't it?"

"To say the least."

"Rosie," Ted said to me, "I tell Jane all the time that her sister is an astonishing woman. If I said that of anyone else, she'd quite properly be jealous. But when you're the subject, she nods and agrees, as though it's a self-evident truth. Now I have more evidence. You saved that poor man. He'll have a hard time in the weeks and months ahead, but he'll be all right."

I sat on the couch, my head bent over my clasped hands. I was drained, empty, exhausted. After he'd shown Ted to the door, my husband sat next to me and extended his arm around my shoulder.

"Never try to tell me again, woman of the house, that you're not a Celtic warrior goddess."

I sobbed in his arms.

Moire Meg stumbled into the house, covered with snow.

"Totally shitty weather," she announced. ". . . What's wrong with Rosie, Chuck? You beating up on her again?"

My husband and I dissolved into laughter.

Father Ed came back for Christmas and our anniversary. Afterward he and our parents escaped from the blizzards to their house in Tucson. He seemed much better.

The anniversary was fine, even though I was a nervous wreck, just like I had been on our wedding day. Msgr. Raven preached at the Mass. I was too spaced-out to hear most of what he said. A lot of it was about me, too much probably. When he finished, everyone in the church—and we had filled St. Ursula—rose and cheered. Chuck rose, lifted me to my feet, and waved. Then he sat down. They continued to cheer. The kids ran up and hugged me. John must have made me sound like the strong one in the marriage. That wasn't true and it wasn't fair. I tried to be graceful, however, and waved back.

At Butterfield, Chuck began the ceremonies by saying, "You all know that the weather was about this bad when Rosemarie and I began our marital pilgrimage. I kind of remember that someone had said a few years before that it would be a cold day in hell when someone as classy as Rosemarie Helen Clancy would agree to go to bed with an insignificant little punk like me. He might well have added that it would be even colder when she stayed twenty-five years in the same bed. I was astonished then and I'm still astonished. I have reason to believe that if I continue to behave, I'll continue on probation in this relationship."

My turn. I forgot what I had planned to say.

"It's a year-to-year thing, Chuck. You have improved a little bit since 1950, so I think I'll keep you, on approval of course."

It wasn't very funny, but it brought the house down.

Then we began our usual duet of "Rosemarie." After twenty-five years everyone knew the lyrics all too well. We sang most of the rest of the day.

Then we drove down to the house on the lake where we

had consummated our marriage twenty-five years before.

"Well at least you're sober this time," I told him, as we entered the house.

"Just as hungry," he said.

We played around a lot, then sailed the skies with love.

I remembered to thank God before I fell asleep. And Christopher Kurtz, Chuck's friend whose body still lies in the frozen ground near the Chosin Reservoir in North Korea. He had been, I always believed, the good angel in our marriage.

As the bicentennial year began at the Biltmore in Phoenix, where it was warm and wonderful, I discovered that I was pregnant with what would become Siobhan Marie. Chucky and I wept with delight.

It was of course crazy. However, for all my "elderly" status we wanted another kid around the house. The Irish are sometimes that way.

It was the easiest of all my pregnancies and the easiest childbirth too.

"When do we have another?" my husband asked.

I threw the latest issue of the *New Yorker* at him.

Before we returned to Chicago we visited Dad and the good April in Tucson and took them and Father Ed to supper at El Charro. Father Ed seemed better, a touch of the light was back in his eyes. Msgr. Packy had arranged with the personnel board to reassign him to St. Agedius.

"I knew he'd be fine if he had a long vacation," the good April whispered contentedly, as we walked out into the soft Tucson air, "he'd be just fine. Poor boy works too hard. He should relax more like Chuck does."

She knew better than that. She usually knows better than that. There are, however, in her oracles many layers of meaning.

Chuck did not bring a camera with him to Arizona, the first time in our marriage he had traveled without one.

"I finally beat the mistress," I said, as we lolled by the side of the pool.

"Mistress?"

"The camera."

"Please put more sun cream on my back," he asked as he rolled over.

We were lying in the shade of a vast umbrella, a precaution that I insisted on because of Chuck's Irish skin.

"Why no camera?"

"I divorced it."

"Why?"

"She's become boring."

I decided not to push, as I usually would have. Nonetheless I worried.

We returned to Chicago, which was soaking wet from a late-January thaw. The melting snow sought out all the water-courses, natural and artificial, which drained our city on a swamp.

We announced our good news and the welcome-home party turned into pandemonium. No one protested.

"Just when I've outgrown dolls," Moire Meg observed, "I'll have a live one to play with."

As the celebration wound down, Jimmy, my second rider in Phil Sheridan's cavalry, joined us in my office—now the conference room for the family—saxophone still in hand.

"You guys got a minute?"

It was something important, scary. I didn't need a new crisis.

"As many minutes as my favorite second son needs."

He sat down on the red leather couch and rested his sax next to himself.

"I think I've made a career decision," he said uneasily.

"You're not planning to get a job just because you're graduating from college," my husband said. "That's against the rules, isn't it?"

"Not for a while yet . . . I want to be a priest."

God help us, that's all we need.

"A monk like those up in St. John's?"

"Nah. They're good guys, but it's too cold up there. Besides, I don't want to break up the jazz group."

"That's certainly an important consideration," his father said, probably half meaning it.

"What kind of priest?" I asked.

"An ordinary priest," he said, as though I had asked him a silly question. "Like Msgr. Raven or Msgr. Packy, you know."

"That shows a good taste in role models," Chucky continued. "Msgr. Raven made me marry your mother, which was an excellent choice even though I didn't have much to say about it."

"And like Father Ed?" I asked.

"Yeah, sure. I don't think I could ever be as serious as he is. The good thing about the priesthood is that there is room in it for all kinds of people. As Joyce said, Catholic means Here Comes Everybody."

"You know what Uncle Ed is going through now?" I asked.

"Oh, yeah." He picked up the sax and began to finger the keys. "The Cardinal is obviously a psychopathic paranoid, poor man. Jesus never said a perfect Church or a perfect priesthood. I'd never get mixed up with someone like him, though I admire Uncle Ed for trying."

"Don't you want to marry?" I pushed the point.

"That would be nice. Still, I want to be a priest. If they change the rules, I might marry. I don't know. I think it will be a long time before they change the rules. The guys who are running things want to hang on to their power."

"And," Chuck said, "if they let people like your mother anywhere near power, those guys would be dead."

"You better believe it."

He raised the sax to his lips, then put it aside.

"I want to be able to help young people like Msgr. Raven helped you."

A spear to the heart. There was a new breed aborning.

"You told your siblings already?" Chuck asked, while I was trying to control my tears.

"Yeah sure, all of them, except the little guy, and I can't tell him yet, though M.M. says it will be a she. They think it's totally good, especially that we will keep the jazz group together."

I burst into tears of pride and hugged him.

"I'm so proud of you, Jimmy."

"You might go easy on the bachelors in your parish," his father warned him. "Poor guys never have a chance once the clergy and the monster regiment take over."

"As Mom always says, you're misquoting poor John Knox. Still, I take your point."

"Did you think we'd disapprove?" I asked, wiping my eyes.

That really surprised him.

"Gosh, no! Why would you do that? . . . I better tell the guys."

He stood up, slung the sax over his shoulder, and left my office, playing "When the Saints Come Marching In!"

In the recesses of the house, the band joined in.

"We can't escape from the damn Catholic Church," Chucky complained. "It won't leave us alone."

"What will Fr. Ed say?"

"He'll be happy like everyone else. His grandparents will be delighted."

"Chuck, Msgr. Raven didn't make you marry me."

"Actually, he kind of did. He pointed out that you were the best deal I was likely to find. It helped that since I was ten or eleven I wanted to see you with your clothes off."

I blushed as I always did when he said something like that.

"You're being lewd!"

"Just lascivious. That means wanton. Little boys, as much as they pretend not to be, are always wanton when they think of little girls."

"The little girls don't know that."

"Yes they do," he insisted. "In fact I wanted to see you with your clothes off and kiss you everywhere."

"And you finally did?"

"Come to think of it, I did."

"And were you disappointed?"

"Not that I remember."

"You can sit here and talk dirty if you want, I'm going to join the celebration."

In April Chuck and I flew to Washington because some national Catholic group was honoring him. Chuck loves to be honored.

To our surprise the Apostolic Delegate was there. To everyone else's surprise too.

"Ah, Dr. O'Malley," he said to Chuck with a charming French accent, "your work is very interesting. I was particularly impressed with your portrait of the Cardinal of Chicago. He was good enough to send it to me."

"My brother-in-law was the Cardinal's secretary at that time," I said, with my nose tilted into the air.

"But of course. Father Edward Michael O'Malley . . . He is well now?"

"He's much better, Archbishop," Chuck said tentatively. "He's back in a parish near where we live."

"Oh, yes. St. Agedius parish. You of course go to St. Ursula because your father was the architect there. Perfectly understandable. I am told that he won a prize for it. He is well, I trust?"

"Very well."

"And madam your mother?"

"Indestructible."

"Excellent . . . I would like to meet your brother. However, protocol prevents me from inviting him. If you would be so good as to ask him to drop me a note requesting a meeting, I would then be delighted to invite him to lunch at the Delegation."

I showed him our family photo display.

"And this young woman, how does she call herself?"

"Moire Meg—Margaret Mary actually."

"She will soon have a little brother?"

"She claims it will be a little sister."

"Excellent. God bless all of you . . . And you will relay my message to Father O'Malley?"

"Yes," Chuck replied. "We certainly will."

What a marvelously Irish way of doing things.

"He came to meet us," I said to Chuck later in our hotel room. "And just to send that message to Father Ed. What do you make of it?"

"I think Rome is worried about your good friend on North State Parkway."

"And wants to collect documentation about him?"

"That man knows a lot, Rosemarie. He wasn't afraid to admit that he had checked us out carefully."

Two days later, I called Ed at St. Agedius.

"Your brother and I want to talk to you and Msgr. Packy. This evening."

"Anything up?"

"The Apostolic Delegate wants to see you."

"Maybe I don't want to see him."

"Your call, Ed," I said. "He seems to be on the side of the angels."

"I don't know that I believe in angels anymore."

"You and Packy will be home?"

"I guess so."

"We'll see you at seven-thirty."

"He doesn't seem much interested," I reported to my husband, who was sitting in my office, pretending to peek at the draft of my new story on the monitor.

"How can you trust a system that sends a madman to one of the most important dioceses in the world?"

"Your friend at the Delegation seemed like one of the good guys."

"I know, Rosemarie, I know. We can't blame Edward for being suspicious."

He was certainly suspicious that night.

"Okay, I go see him and tell him all the craziness in Chicago. He takes it all down and sends it off to Rome. First thing they do is send it to Cardinal O'Neill. He puts his spies on me. Nothing happens. They absolutely will not replace him. That sort of thing isn't done."

"Then, Edward," my husband said, "that's their problem. You've done your part."

"I've already done my part," he said stubbornly. "I'm still a Catholic and still a priest"—faint grin—"because my sister-in-law won't let me quit. Okay. I don't want to have to deal with the Vatican or the Delegate or anyone else who sent that bastard to us."

"They're probably assembling a dossier," Msgr. Packy said. "That's what they do when complaints exceed a certain level. Sometimes they do replace cardinals when the complaints are about financial matters. They dumped Cardinal Lecaro of Bologna recently on those grounds."

"He was a good guy," Father Ed said. "They never go after the bad guys."

"He was framed, Ed," Msgr. Packy said. "Later they admitted they were wrong and apologized."

"A lot of good that did."

"I tell you what, Packy,"—my good husband put on his Chicago politician look—"you write a letter to the Delegate and tell him that you and Father O'Malley would like to have an appointment with him. Like Rosemarie said, he knows who you are. Then the two of you could fly down there. I might come along to wait in the hotel."

"Bring John Raven too," I added.

"That all right with you, Ed?" his pastor asked.

"Sure," Ed said easily. "With a monsignor around, I won't lose my temper."

"I'll write a neutral kind of letter. I won't mention you guys. Just say we'd like to meet with him. Then the ball is in his court. Okay?"

"Fine," Ed agreed, though without much enthusiasm.

"I'll come too," I said.

"Depends on the baby," Chuck reminded me.

"Siobhan Marie won't mind one plane ride. She's really a very nice little girl."

Moire Meg had won me over to her expectation.

When the lunch at the Delegation was finally arranged, I was only two weeks from my due date. Chuck ordered me to stay home. For just that once I let him have his way.

"Maybe I should stay home," he said dubiously.

"Don't be ridiculous. You missed a couple of births before. April Rosemary and Moire Meg will be here and Peg is just down the street."

Rosemarie, I told myself, you're an idiot.

In truth I was scared, more than I had been at any time except for the first time. I realized what an enormous chance I had taken. The child seemed healthy enough, active, but not a nuisance. Everything seemed fine.

Chuck called me from the hotel in late afternoon.

"It apparently went well," he reported. "The Delegate was cordial and sympathetic, not defensive at all. They made the three points about Cardinal O'Neill we had agreed on, misuse of funds, bizarre behavior, and *odium populi,* which I gather means hatred among the people."

"Not that we matter."

"He's interested in a dossier from a number of priests, not many and not a representative body. Prudent and respected priests. He wants us to keep it secret. He'll pass it on to Rome with his recommendations. He made no promises, except to say that he knew that the appropriate people were very interested in the situation in Chicago. Packy says they've set up a kind of a commission in Rome to review the situation. There's no guarantee."

"Father Ed?"

"The Delegate was very gracious to him, praised him for his courage and integrity . . . How are you?"

"Fine."

"No problems."

"None."

"Sure?"

"Chucky! I've been through this five times. I know what it's all about."

I didn't mention the minor twitches of pain that usually indicated that the full labor process was maybe a week away.

"I'll fly home on the nine o'clock plane."

"That's not necessary, Chucky."

"Hell it's not."

He arrived home just as I was dressing to go over to Oak Park Hospital.

"In the nick of time," Moire Meg said.

"You won't be a couple of weeks late as you were when I was born," April Rosemary added.

"You have a long memory, young woman."

"I'm scared," I told them all. "What if . . ."

"She'll be fine," Chuck said confidently.

Somehow I knew he was right. I was still scared.

Siobhan Marie arrived two hours later, a tiny womanly Chucky with the bright red hair and the funny little face and the sweetest smile, though her big sister April Rosemary insisted that neonates that age haven't figured out how to smile yet.

"She's totally gorgeous, Rosie," my no longer youngest daughter informed me. "Are we ready for another redhead?"

"We already have three!"

"Three?" Chucky protested. "I can only count this one and Maria Rosa."

"What about yourself?"

"I'm not a baby!"

All three of us laughed at the new papa.

April Rosemary, practicing her new vocation as a child photographer, hovered round us constantly. She snapped away with her father's reckless disregard for the cost of film—the only extravagance in which my husband ever indulged.

I caught her crying once as she reloaded the camera after we had returned home.

"Something wrong, hon?"

"I wish I were Siobhan Marie and was just starting my life . . . I know that's silly, Mom. I'm just being silly."

She picked up her pliant little sister and sang the Connemara lullaby.

She arranged a "redhead shoot" with Maria Rosa, Chuck, Moire Meg, and Siobhan.

"What do you think, Daddy?" she said.

He was holding our daughter like he'd never had a babe in his arms before. Moire Meg was cooing over her. Maria Rosa was not sure she liked this stuff.

"I'm not going to second-guess you . . . Until the shoot is over!"

"You never second-guess me! . . . Maria Rosa, can I see that beautiful smile?"

"Smile at the baby, Rosa," Maria Elena begged.

The little girl looked, somewhat disdainfully I thought, at her tiny aunt and murmured something that might have been translated as "bybe." She decided to smile.

Two or three excellent shots caught the fire in this crowd of unruly Celts. Chuck praised them extravagantly. Moire Meg dominated the picture, perhaps because of the three women in it she was old enough to be a matriarch. She rolled her eyes at me.

"Scene stealer," I said.

"Little brat."

"Gorgeous young woman!"

"Mo-THER!"

I recovered quickly and was able to be sleek and presentable for April Rosemary's wedding, at which Father Ed did officiate, the family priest again. The poor child was so nervous. She clung to Jamie Nettleton's arm as though she would collapse if he let go. At the reception we secured my new daughter with Missus in one of the side rooms, where I nursed her when she claimed to be hungry. God had blessed me not only with a healthy baby but also one who believed that the night was for sleeping.

Her grandmother spent some of the party time with Siobhan Marie, beaming proudly.

"It's wrong of me to say it, Rose," she said, "but I do believe that this is the prettiest of all your babies and of all my grandchildren."

"Don't say that to Peg or Jane."

"I won't, but they'll know it's true."

When the music and the dancing began and the Boston guests joined in with loud if off-key gusto, April Rosemary seemed to relax and joined the celebration. I watched her anxiously.

"She'll be all right, Rosemarie," a woman said behind me. Maggie Ward, who else.

"She deserved a happier life than this one," I argued.

"Would she have found a better husband?"

I didn't answer. I don't like those crooked lines of God arguments because you can't prove them either way.

"You've seen the latest redhead?" I asked her.

"Show her to me."

Sneaky little witch that she is, I was sure she had but wanted me to display my new pride and joy.

I picked the infant out of her crib and placed her in Maggie's arms. Unfaithful child that she was, she nestled into the arms of this strange woman and fell promptly to sleep. Tiny tears slipped down Maggie's cheeks. Perhaps she was remembering her first daughter, who had mysteriously died before she knew Jerry Keenan.

"She wants to go home with me," Maggie said, handing my daughter back to me.

"A pregnancy at my age," I said, because I felt the need to apologize, "is not the sanest thing I've ever done. I guess we lucked out."

"You always luck out, Rosemarie," she said as if she were a priest imparting a blessing.

April Rosemary became more anxious as the time drew near for her to leave with Jamie. She covered it well enough, but a mother can tell, right?

I found her in the room where she was supposed to be changing to the blue suit in which she would travel. She sat on the couch, head buried in her hands. She looked so pretty in her lingerie. Lucky Jamie.

I embraced her. She collapsed in my arms.

"This is not going to work, Mom. It really isn't."

"I felt the same way twenty-five years ago, hon. It'll be just fine. Jamie is a strong, sensitive, loving man, just like your father."

"That's what Dad tells me." She giggled. "He says I'm lucky!"

"He's right, as always . . . At least when he agrees with me."

We both laughed.

"I'm not afraid of lovemaking with Jamie . . ."

"You're afraid of married life."

"Terribly . . . Will you help me out of this thing?"

"I was too."

"Really? I don't believe it! You've been a wonderful wife."

So quickly do they forget the traumas of childhood.

"You will too!"

We got her into her suit and fixed her makeup and sent her out to her happy husband.

There's not much you can say in such circumstances. I did what I could.

She had a bright smile on her face when she and Jamie climbed into the car and waved happily, at me especially I thought. Mothers always think that.

There was a little tear in my husband's eye as he waved.

Meanwhile, our priest friends were busy collecting their evidence.

"How can they ignore all the stuff you've collected?" I asked John Raven, after we officially welcomed Siobhan into the Church, a ceremony through which she slept contentedly.

"They're pretty good over there at denial. Their main fall-back position will be that the simple laity would be shocked if the Cardinal is replaced. In fact, I've learned that they tried a couple of times earlier to remove him."

"They DID?"

"They offered him a couple of jobs in Rome, impressive in

name but without much power. He slithered out of them. The Pope could have insisted but did not."

"That's a bad sign. We may have to go over there after we've sent the dossier."

"How do they know what the simple laity think?"

"It's a projection of their own fears."

"And an excuse for keeping power."

"You got it, Rosie."

Our problems with this Church to which we were irredeemably committed despite the Cardinal's faults were not over.

Sean O'Malley, the youngest and most charming of my three Irish cavalrymen, came home from college with a most untypical frown on his dark Irish face. He had not chosen St. John's, where he could have played basketball like his brothers, or Notre Dame, to which his grades and test scores entitled him. Instead he went to a small but highly praised Catholic liberal arts college in Illinois.

He cornered us in my office, deep in gloom.

"Dad, can you be gay without knowing it?"

I gasped, silently I hope.

"My friends who are gay say they've known it since they were kids."

"This priest out at school told me that I was gay and was afraid to admit it!"

I kept my big matriarchal mouth shut. Chuck was doing just fine.

"As far as I have observed, you find girls attractive?"

"You bet! But he said I was in denial."

"Is he a psychologist?"

"No, he teaches New Testament and works in pastoral ministry."

"Ah, and what led him to advance this pastoral diagnosis?"

"He made a pass at me and I shoved him away."

"A pass?"

"He tried to, uh, grope me."

"After the pass how did he react?"

"He tried again."

"And you?"

"Slugged him, uh." He smiled wryly. "I knocked him down."

"You reported this to the school authorities?"

"The president called me to his office before I could figure out what to do. He said I was excommunicated for hitting a priest and expelled me from the school."

"Without due process?"

"Huh?"

"I mean there was no formal hearing."

Seano shrugged.

"He said I had no rights because I had excommunicated myself."

"Indeed . . . Your mother will tell you that I was summarily executed in a similar way at Notre Dame back in the late Medieval Era."

"Oh, she's told us that often. She sounded real proud of you."

"That's the way your mother is . . . She likes troublemakers."

He laughed.

"We all know that, Dad!"

"Your exams are finished?"

"Just finished."

"So you have all your course credits?"

"Father Peter said that he was impounding my credits because I struck a priest and was now defaming him with false charges."

"Indeed . . . There have been no other incidents between this priest . . . What's his name?"

"Father Maximus . . . He makes passes at guys all the time. They fend him off usually. Some parents have pulled their sons out of the school. It's gone on for a long time."

"Where was the site of this interaction?"

"In the sacristy after Mass."

How many sacrileges was that? Three at least.

"As I remember, Sean, you have maintained a 4.0 average out there."

"Well, yes."

"I would propose—and I'm sure your mother agrees—that we take legal action to recover your credits. Do you object?"

"No way."

"No way we should do it?"

"No way you should not do it."

"Moreover, if Uncle Vince agrees, we will also sue them for sexual abuse and force them to clean up their act."

"Get rid of Father Maximus?"

Would Sean be reluctant to push matters that far?

He pondered the question.

" 'Scuse my language, Mom. Get rid of the bastard."

While Vince and Chucky were conniving with the state's attorney where the school was located, our team of dossier collectors went back to the Apostolic Delegation.

"I thought I knew everything about our mutual friend," Packy told me before they left. "I didn't know the half of it, not even a third of it."

I fretted all afternoon as I waited to hear from both Washington and from Chuck and Vince. I was in no mood to work on a story and I couldn't play with Siobhan Marie because the little brat wanted to sleep after she was fed.

Father Ed called first.

"They serve good food at that place," he began. "The men that work there are entitled to it."

That was the old Ed, beginning with an irrelevancy.

"And the Archbishop said?"

"He looked through everything very carefully. Then put the dossier on the desk—it's really a big pile of stuff—and shook his head in dismay. He said something like 'I have seen madness before but this material is not only beyond my experience but beyond my expectation. We knew some of it, naturally, but it was only, as you Americans say, the tip of the iceberg.' "

"Then what happened?"

"Packy asked him what he would do with the dossier. He seemed surprised at the question. 'Naturally I will send it on to the Congregation for the Making of Bishops.' And Packy—you know how pushy he can be—asked whether he would make a recommendation. Again the Archbishop was surprised. He said something like, 'But of course I will recommend that a coadjutor will be appointed at once.' "

"That's a relief."

My daughter woke up and whimpered, which meant she wanted a new diaper. Dainty little brat.

"Maybe. He warned us that his recommendation might not

be followed. He said we might be invited to Rome to consult with the Congregation."

"And you said?"

"I said I'd be glad to go . . . He was very nice to me. Praised my courage, which I don't deserve."

"You do too . . . Will the other priests go with you?"

"Sure . . . Do you think Chucky will go with us? Give us last-minute advice before we go into the Congregation?"

"It will be hard to keep him away."

"Hey, great," he said, as though he were surprised. "Be sure you tell him when he comes home."

"Count on it."

My daughter's whimpers were growing a little more insistent. I cleaned her and powdered her and wrapped her gently in a new diaper. She sighed happily. She was not yet ready to eat, so I put her back in her office cradle—one in the office and one in our bedroom. She went back to her peaceful sleep.

"Bless you child," I said, kissing her tiny forehead, "for having such a precise schedule. You inherited that from himself, I'm sure."

Several days later we took Siobhan Marie for her first ride in the country. I was driving my new Benz because I'm the best driver in the family. Peg sat next to me playing with my daughter. If she could have more children, she would certainly try to match me, as we had matched each other all our lives.

We had relegated our husbands to the backseat where they belonged. Chuck was spoiling for a fight with Father Peter, Vince eagerly awaiting a legal battle.

Like most of Chuck's friends, Vince is a big guy—a former linebacker with broad shoulders and thick arms. Peg had kept him in good condition like I had kept Chuck in good condition. He was wearing a blue three-piece suit and a white shirt with a bright red tie. A matching red handkerchief peeked out of his jacket. His cuff links were the colors of the Italian flag. Vince knew how to look like a Sicilian thug when he wanted to, and especially when he wanted to hint at an Outfit connection to scare someone. Peg, slender as ever, wore a demure light gray summer suit. She complained that she would have to stay in the car and tend to Siobhan while we went in to confront Father Peter.

We entered the outer office of the president of the college at eleven o'clock, the precise time of our appointment. They kept us waiting a half hour, standard clergy practice I had been warned.

Finally, a shrewish secretary reluctantly admitted us into the inner sanctum with a sneer of disapproval.

Nun, I thought.

If the priest who made the pass at Sean was Father Maximus, the president ought to have been Father Minimus. He was shorter than Chuck and weighed maybe three times as much. His oversize bald head glowed in the summer sun coming through the window into the Victorian presidential office. His tiny black eyes, set in a soft fleshy face, were mean. Kind of guy who a few years ago might have worked for the Inquisition. A sleazy-looking fellow of approximately the same build lurked behind him.

Neither of them introduced themselves. Nor did they ask us to sit down.

"I am," Vince announced from his six-foot-three height, "Vincente di Paolo Antonelli. I have the honor of representing Dr. and Mrs. Charles Cronin O'Malley and Master Sean Michael O'Malley."

I stifled a giggle. Vince's middle name was Paul. Where did the di Paolo come from? Heck, maybe it was his real name.

The shyster interrupted.

"There's no question of readmitting that young man to the college. He is excommunicated for striking a priest. The case is closed."

"Your name, Counselor."

"Frye, Andrew Frye."

"And you're Father Peter, the president of the college?"

"Yes," he sneered in a high-pitched voice. "We do not want that kind of young man in this college. He is excommunicated."

"The issue is not whether he will return to college here. The issue is whether we destroy your college before the day is over."

"He is excommunicated," Andrew Frye insisted. "If you

knew any canon law, you would know he is excommunicated.".

"We are not ignorant peasants, Father," Vince said softly.
"I consulted with two canon lawyers at the Chicago Archdiocese. They assure me that if a person is defending himself,
especially against sexual attack, there is no canonical penalty.
I'm sure you know that."

"The police have cleared Father Maximus," the president
jeered. "They wished to arrest the young man but we advised
against it."

"Just as they have cleared him six times previously," Vince
said, consulting a list. "This time without even talking to the
victim."

The state's attorney had told Vince that there had been
plenty of proof in the six previous cases to bring an indict-
ment, but that he had hesitated because of the intense Catholicism of the people in the country. "We'd never get a
conviction. Priests can't do anything wrong out here."

"The psychiatrists have cleared him too!"

"Again, Father Peter," Vince continued to be the man from
the Near West Side (where the Outfit used to be), "I would
remind you and the counselor that we are not ignorant peasants. Professional psychiatrists never clear anyone. They
merely estimate the risks. This college knew about Father
Maximus's propensities and nonetheless reassigned him to
work with young men. You're responsible for his behavior
and I mean legally responsible."

He still hadn't asked us to sit down. Chuck guided me to a
broken-down couch and then sat patiently next to me.

"Go ahead and sue us!" Andrew Frye shouted. "You'll
never win."

"That isn't the immediate issue," Vince replied calmly.
"Unless you give us a copy of Master O'Malley's academic
record . . . Let me see, his average is 4.0, is it not?"

"That makes no difference." Father Peter tightened his jaw,
which made him look even more ugly.

"And he was captain of the basketball team?"

"We do not want that kind of scum in our college."

I saw my husband's fists clench.

Keep your temper, Chuck! Please!

"And played the clarinet in your jazz band? And acted as head of the volunteer program here?"

"Those facts are all irrelevant!" Frye shouted again.

"Legally, perhaps, but hardly in terms of media reaction . . . Let me continue. Unless we receive a copy of his transcript now, we will call upon the state's attorney to ask that he issue a warrant for the arrest of Father Maximus. We will of course not hesitate to reveal our charges to the media. The local press may be reluctant to report the facts of the case. We will, however, make them known to the Chicago media. Your school will be dead."

"You wouldn't dare!" Father Peter yelled at us.

"Try me."

"Father Maximus has a serious spiritual problem. We are convinced, however, that he has pulled himself together. We must protect him from young men with homosexual tendencies."

"If it comes to that, Father Peter, we will subpoena you and you will be able to repeat that charge on the record and under oath."

"I'm not afraid of you."

"You should be, Father." Vince smiled easily. "You should be. As I say, it is within our power to destroy this college. We would be reluctant to do so because it is reputed to have a fine academic record. We will do so, however, if necessary."

"I will not give them to you."

"I will also go into the Circuit Court of Cook County this afternoon and seek relief in the form of compelling you to release this transcript to us. Counselor Frye will tell you that we will certainly get that injunction. Our request for it, given Dr. O'Malley's prominence in Chicago, will be front-page news. We are reluctant to do this, as I say, but you should not believe that we will not."

"Why Cook County?" Frye demanded.

Vince spread his hands soothingly.

"Master O'Malley is currently a resident in Cook County. Let me assure you that you will seek in vain for a change of venue."

"Can they do this, Andrew?" Father Peter asked, turning to the lawyer, as though it were his fault.

"I'd say give him the fucking credits."

"Please, Counselor, there is a lady present as well as a priest."

This time my husband had to suppress a snicker.

Father Peter drummed his fingers on the desk for a moment. Then he pressed an intercom button.

"Sister, will you make a copy of O'Malley's transcript and bring it in here?"

I knew she was a nun.

Chuck and I were enjoying the show. We knew that Seano was all right. We knew they'd take him with open arms at either Loyola or St. Procopius. We knew that we'd win in court. So we played the spectator sport of watching Vincente di Paolo skewer these creeps.

Uninvited, Vince sat in a chair opposite us.

"You hate priests, don't you, Mr. O'Malley?" Father Peter asked.

"Dr. O'Malley, Father. Economics. University of Chicago."

Chuck never claims the title. However, it seemed the thing to do just now.

"All right, Dr. O'Malley!"

"I have been not ungenerous to this school, have I, Father Peter?"

"I believe you have," he admitted grudgingly.

"You've handled these matters before by buying off the families and sending Father Maximus away for a few months. We are not the kind who can be bought off. Moreover, my brother is a priest and my second son is entering the seminary at Mundelein this autumn. We are here to protect the priesthood from sick pedophiles like Father Maximus and cowardly priests like you."

Father Peter turned purple, the exact color of my summer frock.

Before he could explode, the nun banged into the office and threw the transcript sheets on his desk like they were a copy of *Playboy* someone had found in the dorm. One of the sheets slipped off the desk.

"Take them!"

Vince picked the sheet off the floor, added it to the pile, and gave me the stack of papers.

"Does it seem complete, Rosemarie?"

I studied the transcript carefully. He really did have a 4.0 average. The last sheet listed his various extracurricular activities, among which he was to edit the school newspaper in the fall and was the senior class president.

"Everything in order, Rosemarie?"

I was always Rosie to everyone else, except John Raven and Chuck. However, for the moment, Peg's husband was willing to waive that rule.

"It's a record of which a parent would be very proud. If he didn't go to Mass every day out here, Father Maximus would never have had a chance to grope him—in the sacristy after Mass."

"Well that's it for today." Vince gathered up his briefcase. "Oh, one more thing. I went into the Circuit Court of Cook County yesterday to file a motion in the name of Sean O'Malley for civil action against the school, you, Father Maximus, and your religious order. We have kept the suit a secret, but here are the papers and a demand for your records on Father Maximus. It's the kind of petition which could easily be changed to a class action suit. We don't want to ruin the school, though we will if necessary. We're asking for monetary damages and for a letter signed by you, the provincial council, the present provincial, and the president of the order over in Rome, in which you will promise that Father Maximus never again is assigned to work with boys and young men. Incidentally, we have notified your provincial in Chicago of the suit."

He handed the suit and the papers to Frye.

"You are hereby notified of our suit. I'm sure, Mr. Frye, that you will counsel settlement. You've bought people off before. Now you will have to buy us off and at a much higher price. Otherwise, I promise you on my mother's grave, we will destroy the college."

Vince's mother is still alive and a dear, sweet woman. His oath was part of the Outfit image he had created.

I looked at my husband. His lips quivered.

"We will fight it every inch of the way," Father Peter promised.

"Do that and it will make my day," Vince renewed his

promise. "We will make a lot more money and the result will be the same."

We rose from our seats and walked to the door.

I was the first one out because my brave warriors honored and respected womenkind.

I pushed back into the office and pointed my finger at Father Peter.

"It's people like you and Father Maximus that turn the priesthood into shit."

"I was wondering what you were going to say for the last word," Chucky said, as we walked out of S'ter's office. "While in general I disapprove of scatology in a woman, there are exceptions. This was one of them." He embraced me. "You're wonderful."

"Naturally."

Vince told us that the religious orders and the dioceses were following the advice of their litigators to play hardball with victims and families "because they are the enemy."

"The parents rarely have enough money to pay the bills for legal action. We were the wrong people to try to stonewall."

"Bye, S'ter," I said, as we walked out of the president's suite.

We high-fived one another as we left the administration building.

"Will they settle?"

"Sure they will. Eventually. Even that sleazebag lawyer of theirs will tell them that they will never win in Cook County. Lucky for us that the provincial office is in Chicago. That's why the provincial is at the top of the list of defendants."

"Poor man." I sighed.

"He had to have made the decision to reassign Father Maximus to the college after the previous complaints . . . The Church has yet to learn the risks it takes when it reassigns a pedophile priest. Once the word gets around to tort lawyers that there is money to be made in this kind of litigation, the Church and its insurance companies will lose a lot of money."

"The lawyers will take such cases on contingency?" Chuck asked.

"Sure, why not? The Church has brought it on itself."

In the car my baby was playing with Peg.

"I fed her from the bottle and changed her diaper, but she said she didn't want to go back to sleep till her mommy returned, didn't you, Siobhan Marie?"

I seized my child and held her close. She cooed contentedly. If April Rosemary were to be believed, the kid couldn't at this age differentiate her mother from any other nice person.

Still, my kid certainly knew who I was. Aunt Peg would never woo her away from me. As she grew up she would know that Aunt Peg was a very nice woman, but not Mommy.

Right?

Anyway, she went right to sleep. Peg drove us home.

Seano was delighted with the outcome.

"I can play basketball at Loyola," he said, clutching his transcripts. "It will be great to be living at home again. I missed Chicago. I'll get my MBA there too."

"It's a shame that terrible man ruined your senior year in college," I said.

"I was getting a little bored," he replied. "Chicago is a great place. Besides, there's lots of cute girls at Loyola . . . Will we really drag those priests into court?"

"If they don't settle the suit pretty soon, we sure will."

"I'd like to testify at a trial against them." So much for my worries.

The summer was filled with bicentennial hype which offended both me and my husband. I kind of wanted to go to New York for the tall ships parade, but Chuck said it would be easier to watch it on television. Besides, I didn't want to take our new child on a plane ride till she was a little older.

He spent the summer reading Victorian novels and poetry and arguing with Moire Meg about them—when he wasn't spoiling our new little brat rotten. He hardly touched his camera.

We didn't participate in the election campaigns. Both of us were tired of politics. We were able to contain our enthusiasm for Jimmy Carter when he was nominated, especially when he referred in his acceptance speech to "Eyetalians."

"Just the kind of man you need to get out the Catholic ethnic vote."

We both were furious when he chose Walter Mondale for vice president. Fritz was a nice man, but his wife was opposed on the record to Catholic schools. Patently the candidate either didn't care about getting the Catholic vote or didn't know anything about Catholics. He ran an incredibly inept campaign and blew a twenty-two-point lead during the run up to the election. He just barely squeaked by with less than a one percent margin—against the man who had pardoned Tricky Dicky.

Jimmy had begun his four years at Mundelein, which he seemed to enjoy. "It's nothing like it used to be," John Raven told us. "They have cars. They drive into the city. They read newspapers and watch television. They have vacations the same time as other colleges do. It looks the same on the outside, but it's a different place, thank God."

Seano was happy at Loyola. He had moved into an apartment near the school and was playing basketball. Moire Meg would be a senior at Trinity next year, right down the street, so "I can stay home and take care of poor Siobhan Marie."

April Rosemary, home from her honeymoon and living in an apartment downtown till Jamie finished his residency, was not getting good grades at the Art Institute but said she was learning a lot. She wanted desperately to be pregnant.

Seano's college was stonewalling. One of the Cardinal's lawyers called Vince and first pleaded with him to drop the suit, then threatened him.

"You're wasting your time," Vince said he told him. "The longer they mess around, the more money we'll demand for a settlement."

"You'll be doing grave harm to the Church, Vincent."

"Not as much as you're doing."

Our priest revolutionaries were summoned to Washington the week after the election. The Delegate suggested that they fly to Rome to meet at the Congregation for the Making of Bishops. They wanted Chuck to come with them. I was in no mood for Rome. Besides, I didn't want to drag our poor little daughter across the Atlantic Ocean.

❧ Chuck ❧
1976

I consumed two dishes of chocolate gelato in a sidewalk café on the Conciliazione while I was waiting for the rebels, as Rosemarie and I called my brother and our two priest friends. We had supper the previous night with our friend Rae Adolfo from the birth control commission days. He knew we were in Rome and wanted to talk to us. He was still a smooth, handsome character out of a Fellini film. Apparently his assignment was to tell us what to say to the Cardinal the priests were going to meet the next day. I suspected he was working for Cardinal Benelli, who was Pope Paul's chief of staff and allegedly the chairman of the special commission they had set up about Chicago. We chatted and gossiped and admired the Church of Santa Maria in Trastevere. Whatever he was supposed to tell us about the meeting was deeply implicit in the conversation.

"The Pope is not well." He sighed. "Not well at all. Another year or two, who knows?"

"And then?"

"It will be very difficult. The new Pope will be pulled in both directions, those who support the Council and those who oppose it."

"Don't they know that the laity and the clergy have already made up their minds?" Edward asked.

"They believe that they can still control what happens. They are wrong, *certo,* but they have no idea of what's happening. They live in their own little world."

"Ah."

"You have nothing to fear tomorrow. The Cardinal President of the Congregation for the Making of Bishops is of course on your side. He has relatives in a place near Chicago called River Forest . . . You know it?"

"Somewhat," I said.

River Forest was a wonderful place. However, not a few of the Outfit folks live there. Was this Cardinal "connected"?

"They tell him even worse stories. He merely wants to review the documents with you to be able to say that he has done so."

"Fair enough," Packy said. "What are our chances?"

"Everyone knows there must be a change in Chicago. Even the Pope. However, he remembers when enemies forced him out of his position on Papa Pacelli's staff and sent him into exile."

"Milano is exile?" Packy said.

"It is if your life has been in Rome."

"So our chances," I said, "are about what they were at the time of the birth control commission. All the work has been done. The Pope will have all the material he needs. He will stew over it for a while and do nothing."

Adolfo sighed heavily.

"Not quite the same, Carlo. In those days all the people who were whispering in his ear were against us. Now they are all on our side. You must not be impatient. It will take time. You remember what Pope John said of the man he knew would be his successor. He called him *il mio Amleto*."

"My Hamlet," John Raven translated unnecessarily.

I pounded the table—I really did.

"Listen to me, Rae, and listen closely. And tell what I said to your friend Benelli. Either they get that psychopath out of Chicago now or there will be a major scandal. The Chicago media have a hint of the situation, and more than a hint. There's material for the federal government to look into if they are of such mind. You can keep this sort of thing secret just so long in the United States."

There was silence around the table. Adolfo looked at the three priests.

"You agree?"

"The media are afraid of a negative reaction from the

Catholic laity," Packy said, "but less so than they used to be. Chuck is right."

"There's always the possibility," Edward, who had been silent through most of the meal, added, "that someone who worked for him would go to the police."

"Would you do that, Father?" Adolfo asked. "I do not say that it would be wrong if you did . . ."

"I don't think I could do it, Monsignor. Perhaps I am too much of a priest."

I pounded the table again.

"He knows that I think he should."

Rae nodded solemnly.

"Then I might say to those who will make the case that it is altogether possible that a layman or even a priest from the Cardinal's staff might reveal the problem to the civil authorities."

No one denied it.

"Very well. It is true that we have no sense over here of how government and church relate to one another in the United States. I am not sure that those who will make the case or the Pope himself will understand."

"In the big cities, where most of the Catholics live," I explained, "the civil authorities, who are generally Catholic themselves, have felt that they should let the Church take care of its own problems. They too are afraid of offending the Catholic laity whose votes they need for reelection. That's changing as sexual abuse becomes a national issue, especially if the abuser is a clergyman."

Adolfo raised his hands in a gesture of helplessness.

"If it has become an issue in America, soon it will be here too."

"In the Vatican?"

"I meant in Italy . . . I'm sure that it happens here too, though not very often. Not all of us who work over there are saints."

I let it go at that.

We were staying at the Columbus Hotel on the Conciliazione, which used to be the headquarters of the Knights of Malta. Nice enough place and right down the street from the Congregation for the Making of Bishops. The rooms were all right. I'm sure they had been remodeled once or twice since the eighteenth century. It was not the kind of Rome into which my beloved wife would have booked me. Nor would she approve of my sharing it with Edward in her absence. I had perhaps enhanced it somewhat in the description I had given her when I called the night before.

"Do you have the room to yourself?" she demanded.

Nothing was too good for Chucky Ducky.

"Uh, no . . ."

"Father Ed?"

Silence.

"Well, you won't pick up any little Italian bitch."

"Roman . . . They're the most beautiful women in Italy. Maybe in the world."

"Hmf . . ."

After our dinner with Adolfo I called her from the lobby of the hotel. Edward didn't ask why. Maybe he respected my privacy or maybe he was too tired to wonder.

"I want to know how my youngest daughter is surviving her father's absence."

"She hasn't even noticed."

"Has her mother noticed?"

"Maybe a little bit . . . What happened at dinner?"

I summarized the evening.

"Same old stuff, huh?"

"Probably. You protect psychopathic cardinals for the good of the Church, just like you protect pedophile priests for the good of the Church."

"Chucky, you sound angry."

"I'm more lonely than anything else."

Husband asks for tender sympathy.

"You've only been away two nights!"

Husband does not get tender sympathy.

"I miss you."

Husband makes renewed plea for sympathy.

Silence while wife reevaluates.

"I miss you too, Chucky Ducky."

Husband gets sympathy, feels much better.

"Fine world traveler I am."

"Well-married husband you are . . . I can hardly wait till you come back."

"Me too."

Mission accomplished.

I slept the sleep of the just man.

So the next morning I waited at the café and ate the gelato— Italian ice cream, the best in the world—and thought about my wife.

After our quarter century together, she still overwhelmed me, more indeed than she ever had. I melted whenever I saw her. Even after a couple of hours' separation. She hadn't changed much. She was still contentious, strong-minded, bossy, opinionated, funny, demanding, patient, tender, sweet, and loving.

That sounds vaguely like a text somewhere in the Book of Wisdom, though I don't think she knits fine fabrics like the woman in that passage. Fair enough.

She is also incredibly fragile despite all her talk, more vulnerable in her own way than poor little Siobhan Marie, the adjectives being required in any discussion of our sixth (and presumably our last) child—who may be little but is certainly not poor.

She has not escaped and never will from her harrowing childhood and young adulthood. She is always on the edge of falling apart. She never has and never will, but those experiences remain always with her. She cannot forget her last binge, which almost led to her expulsion from the family. Yet she blames me (usually half fun and full earnest as the good April says) for not making the threat years before. She's not at all sure that her binges had no effect on April Rosemary or the younger children, no matter how often Maggie Ward tells her not to worry about it. I tread on eggshells with her, lest I open the old wounds. Such caution became habitual years ago and requires little effort. Yet I worry that in our constant banter I might say the wrong thing.

She worries constantly, kind of like a second track on a two-track tape which provides background for her consciousness. She worries about the kids, each one in their own special category of worry, about my parents, who are growing older, about my sisters Peg and Jane and their families, about Edward, about the Church, about the country, about the whole world.

Mothers, she tells me, exist to worry. Fair enough, but, as we say in my economics trade, she is a couple of standard deviations above the mean on the maternal worry index.

She worries especially about me.

I really don't deserve such loving worry, though, being a man, I consume it like a sponge.

She has shaped my life. She knew from the beginning that God destined me to be a roving adventurer and that my camera was both the weapon and the pretext for that wandering. She rushed off to Little Rock when the locals worked me over— and correctly blamed President Ike. She clawed the overweight bums who tried to savage me in Marquette Park. She fought off the violence-crazed cops at the Conrad Hilton. Only her prayers could have sent the Black Huey to snatch me out of the South China Sea as the North Vietnamese fishing boat was about to pick me up. Don't you dare mess with my Chucky.

Chucky Ducky, that is.

Now she worries, mostly in silence, because I seem to have lost interest in the camera. What, she must be thinking, if I seduced him into this vocation and then he leaves? Edward must not leave the priesthood, no never. What if Chucky discards the camera?

I won't really ever leave it. It's not as much fun as it used to be. Too much has happened. I haven't done any major work since *1968—Year of Violence*. Okay, my portraits are pretty good and they'll make a nice book one of these days, much to the delight of my subjects.

Will I include the Cardinal against whom I'm conspiring at this minute?

I don't think so.

The romance is gone, however. It's not the camera. My eye is if anything better than it used to be. It's me. I'm getting old.

Or something.

I'm in a phase, as my sister Peg tells me. I'll grow out of it.

Maybe she's right. She usually is, as she would be the first to tell me.

In the meantime, my Rosemarie has found her own career as a writer. She is very, very good. She's no longer Charles Cronin O'Malley's wife. I'm Helen Clancy's husband, perhaps even the prototype of the little redhead punk who appears all too frequently in the stories. She supported me in my career when it started. Should I not support her in hers as it starts?

Except she doesn't need my support. She wrote her first several stories without my knowing about it.

So there's no way to pay her back. She would be offended to know that I was thinking that way.

I'm getting old, that's the problem. I'm burning out before my time.

I miss my wife.

The whole country is in a bad mood, maybe that's what's bugging me. All the radical kids are rushing for cover, grabbing for the good life while they can. The conservatives are crowing, though I don't know why. Everyone is blaming the Vietnam vets, who happen to be a handy scapegoat. The turncoat liberals are repudiating their heritage. The Catholic radicals are repeating the clichés of last year. They arrive everywhere too little and too late. The blacks have retreated from the old integration ideal and replaced it with separatism.

The economy is in bad shape and will get worse. I don't read the economic journals anymore because they seemed archaic as well as arcane. Everyone knows that the problems began with Lyndon's decision to fight the war on the cuff. You don't raise taxes, you keep the regular economy going, and you cause inflation. Then Tricky Dicky tries price controls and takes us out of the Bretton Woods Agreement. That doesn't work and inflation continues. The Arabs cut off the oil spigot and we try a new form of price control—"allocation." That means that everyone waits in line. Time is money.

Anyone who has had an introductory course in economics knows that the only way to deal with a shortage is to let the law of supply and demand set the prices. Is this hard on the poor and on others? Then provide them with some form of tax rebate. The same course also teaches that if you want to curtail the use of a product, you put a tax on it. That's the way they do it in Europe. In this country we launch moral crusades in favor of "conservation." Put a dollar a gallon tax on gas? That would take money away from the Saudis and put it in American research projects. It would also be hard on the poor? Again give them rebates. However, the politics of the country don't permit such rational behavior. Most of the members of Congress are economically illiterate.

So we have inflation and unemployment and no economic growth. We have leaders who can't lead either because they don't know what to do or do know what to do but lack the courage.

All of this in the midst of the Vietnam hangover.

No wonder I don't read the economics literature anymore.

And I'm almost fifty, which is probably the real reason I've lost all my energy.

When Dad was my age in 1948, he was riding the exciting postwar economic wave, making more money than he thought he ever would, and building some of the best postwar subdivisions and churches. He was my age and he was young. I'm his age and I'm old.

I want my wife.

My three unindicted coconspirators appeared down the street. From a distance they seemed content.

I signaled the waiter.

"Signor, ancora quattro, per favore!"

He rolled his eyes but brought the ice cream in time for their arrival. They didn't seem at all surprised but promptly dug into it.

"It went well enough," John Raven, the oldest, summed up the meeting. "He's a nice man, very sympathetic. Says it's all terrible. Should never have happened. Promised us that something would be done in a few months . . ."

"Do you believe him?"

"I think his sense of urgency," Packy observed, "is not very great. One senses that he thinks it's a shame and something should be done about it. However, the Church has been around a long time. It's seen worse and it has survived. Rome is timeless . . ."

"And we are not," Edward said sadly.

"The Pope is the problem?"

"Sure," Packy agreed. "He doesn't want to hurt Cardinal O'Neill's feelings. He's not quite persuaded that the situation in Chicago is as terrible as we say. He knows there's a problem, but he operates on the Roman premise that if you wait long enough, every problem goes away. Though Cardinal Sergio told us that we could expect something in a couple of months, the Pope will agonize over it, vacillate, hesitate, agree and then disagree, and it will more likely take a couple of years. The atmosphere here sees little difference between months and years."

"Hell of a way to run a Church, huh, Chuck?" John Raven said.

"I was just reflecting on how the way we've been running the country since 1965 is a hell of a way to run a country."

"Cheer up, Chuck," my brother said brightly, "things are not all that bad."

I did tell Rosemarie that comment when I reported to her after our debriefing with Rae Adolfo, who thought the session with Cardinal Sergio had gone very well.

"Well," she said, "Father Ed has always been less melancholy than you. He's more like Jane. You're more like Peg."

"Huh? We had to struggle to keep that guy sane and in the priesthood and now he ends up bright-eyed and bushy-tailed and I'm the melancholy one."

"You and Peg," she said, with a woman's passion for the precise repetition of what she had said.

Oh.

"Well, I'll see you tomorrow afternoon, if the plane isn't late."

"I'll meet you and bring the kid."

"You don't have to do that."

"Yes, I do, Chucky Ducky."

❧ *Chuck* ❧

1976

So we won back the White House in November, not that it was worth all that much or that the man who won it would know what to do with it. We also suffered a great sorrow in Chicago (where we were of course still registered voters because of our two flats on the Chicago side of Austin Boulevard). Despite the implicit conviction of most of us that he would never die, Mayor Daley went to heaven in December of that year, a reward which he deserved, if for no other reason than his put-down of that pompous phony Walter Cronkite during the 1968 Democratic Convention in Chicago.

Late in the afternoon, Vince called.

"The Mayor died this afternoon," he said, "in the doctor's office in that old building at 900 North Michigan. He was pronounced dead at Northwestern Hospital. Some of his family were trapped in the rickety elevator at 900 North. It should be on the news in a few moments. I'll stay in touch."

The Chicago journalists, whatever East Coast ideology they might have brought with them, were sufficiently acclimated to the city to play the news straight. "A city mourns" was their theme. The people they interviewed on the streets were clearly stricken, many of them in tears.

The national programs returned to the convention and the Martin Luther King campaign in Chicago and repeated their old clichés. They still didn't get it. They never would. That pompous phony Walter Cronkite admitted grudgingly that he had always been a popular mayor but added that his legacy had been tainted by the convention disorders.

As though the Mayor was in the street throwing feces at the rioters.

I could never figure out why there was so much East Coast hatred for the Mayor. He was Irish, he was Catholic, he talked funny in public (but not in private), and, most of all, I think, he was in Chicago, a city which, if you lived in New York, it was all right to hate.

Prejudice against women or blacks or Hispanics (and more recently gays) was wrong. Prejudice against Chicago was all right, indeed it was high virtue. None seem to have noticed that he had won two elections after 1968 by overwhelming margins—the last one with a 70 percent majority, including a 70 percent black majority. I guess the reason you didn't have to pay any attention to that was that you could assume that Chicagoans by definition were victims of false consciousness.

"We should say some prayers for him," Moire Meg reminded us.

We gathered around the little shrine in our small room in the back of the house and said the rosary. What else could we do?

The baby slept peacefully.

Vince called later with details.

"Tomorrow before he's brought to the church to lie in state, there will be a small private wake at the funeral parlor. The family would like you both to come. I'll stop by later with a sticker for your car, so the cops will let you pass. They also will have tickets for you for the funeral."

"Vince doesn't still work for the Mayor?" Rosemarie asked.

"Vince, as you well know, is in a very successful private practice."

"Then what was their relationship?"

"He had lots of clout."

"Why?"

"Because the Mayor liked him, which we will both agree shows his good taste, because he knew when to show up and when not to, because his instincts are good, because the Mayor trusted him completely."

"Did the family call Vince today or did he call them?"

"Vince was around. Maybe he went to the hospital when he heard the Mayor was being brought over there. Maybe he waited in the background. Maybe the family saw him and called him in. Maybe. Whatever happened, you can count on it, your brother-in-law's behavior was impeccable."

"I almost said, Chucky, that he's come a long way. But the truth is that, like you, he's always been what he is."

"Except when he came home from Vietnam and you had to straighten him out."

"I get a lot more credit than I deserve."

This was absurd. However, my wife could not admit even to herself how many marriages survived because of her intervention. Including maybe our own.

The funeral home was right across the street from Nativity Church, just down Lowe Avenue from the Daley family bungalow. The Mayor used to say when he walked down to the church for daily Mass that it would be easy at his wake to get his body to the church.

"They'll just have to carry it across the street."

The prewake to which we were invited was early in the afternoon before the crowds would gather later for the lying-in-state in the church.

Rosemarie was driving my Chevy because, as she said, her Benz would be out of place in Bridgeport. She has little confidence in my abilities at the wheel. Vince had told us to turn west on Thirty-seventh Street and park a quarter block down from the funeral home. That part of the street was mostly clear of cars. A cop waved us on. Rosemarie rolled down the window—letting in a frigid blast of winter air—favored the cop with her best smile and showed him our pass. His expression changed from one of stern warning to one of infinite courtesy.

"Park right here, ma'am. Nice to see you."

I doubt that he knew who she was, much less that she wrote stories for the *New Yorker*, stories featuring a hopeless but cute little redhead. He knew she was a friend of the family and beautiful, either one of which characteristics was sufficient.

We shivered as we walked the short distance to the funeral home. It was the coldest day of the year so far, though worse was clearly yet to come. Somehow in our city the first cold days seem far worse than the routine ones that came later. Rosemarie clung to my arm, huddling against me for protection against the wind and the cold and death. Under her cloth coat—my wife does not believe in expensive furs—she was wearing her black dress from the time of our visit with Pope Paul. She would be especially striking, which was the general idea.

Inside the funeral parlor the atmosphere was of the typical Irish wake with one major exception. The Daley men wept intermittently. I didn't use to be able to do that myself, though in a marital union with my wife, one learned to cry if only in self-defense.

Vince and Peg were already there. Vince was if not quite in charge—no one really was—seemed to be directing some of the flow of mourners. There were maybe thirty people milling around.

"Smashing," my sister whispered to her constant partner in crime.

"And the same to you," Rosemarie replied.

When the two of them were together, even in this unusual setting, I always felt that they were conspiring. Against me.

Vince introduced us to Mrs. Daley, whom we'd met a couple of times before.

"Oh, yes, Chuck. I remember you. Dick loved your pictures. He said you were a genius. Your sister is Vincent's wife, isn't she?"

"She got all the beauty in the family, I'm afraid, ma'am."

"You have all the sympathy of which we're capable, Mrs. Daley," said my better half, remembering that it was a wake.

"Thank you much, dear. Pray for us. We're all alone now."

Then she made the connection.

"You're the one who writes those funny stories, aren't you? We all love them, especially those of us who are married to Irishmen."

Ground open up and swallow Chucky, please.

Then tears rose in her eyes.

"I miss him so much."

A priest swept in and began to intone in a chantlike voice a decade of the rosary.

Rosemarie made a face, not at the prayer but at the clerical singsong.

"Why can't they pray in their natural voices?" she whispered to me.

"After years of boring people from the pulpit, they don't have natural voices."

After the prayer, we approached the casket to pay our respects. The man inside didn't look like the "mare" at all. Which of us does look like ourself when life leaves the body behind?

My wife was weeping, not sobbing (that would show no class) just lamenting to herself the loss of a man she hardly knew but who was one of us.

We shook hands with the children and their spouses, handsome people whose hearts were broken.

We then did what the Irish do at wakes, we went to the back of the funeral home and sat on the card chairs which had been lined up like the pews in a small church.

"What are we doing here?" I asked my wife as she dabbed at her eyes.

"Your sister is married to that nice Italian boy Vincent and the Mayor thought you were a genius."

"I'm NOT a genius," I said impatiently.

"Yes, dear," she said, patting my arm patiently.

Vince and Peg joined us, his eyes always on the door, waiting for the entrance of someone who was his responsibility.

"What happens now?" I asked.

"They'll elect Mike Bilandic mayor. Then in ten, twelve years, young Rich will take over."

"Does he have the moves?"

"All his father had and more."

Another priest came in and we had to pray again. Rosemarie made a face as she knelt on the floor.

"They should have kneelers," she complained.

After the priest left, shaking hands with almost everyone in the room, Vince gave us our tickets for the Mass.

"Get here early. The hangers-on will be trying to sneak in. They're real pests."

"Why are we here, Vince?" I asked. "We were not this important to the Mayor."

"Because you're Peg's brother," Rosemarie cut off the answer, "and because the Mayor thought you were a genius."

"And because Mrs. Daley liked my wife's funny stories about Irishmen."

Outside the steeds of night raced across the sky and cold winds swept across the Lake. Crowds were already lining up for the beginning of the wake inside the church. I realized that this was an important historical turning point for my city. The neighborhoods, which the Cronkites of the country despised, would turn out in massive numbers for one of their own.

Rosemarie, her hand shivering, tried to start my Chevy. It didn't want to start. After several tries, she jabbed the keys at me.

"Charles Cronin O'Malley, get this car started."

I turned the ignition once and the Chevy leaped into action.

"It's all in knowing how," I said modestly.

"How do you turn on the heat?"

I pushed the levers at the top.

We eased out of the parking place and picked our way past cops and toward Halsted Street.

"Heaters in these American cars are no good . . . Chucky, I'm freezing."

I snuggled close to her. She didn't, under the circumstances, seem to mind.

"Such wonderful, low-key people," she mused, as we warmed up. "They couldn't be pompous and self-important even if they wanted."

"Folks from the neighborhood."

"Right! The media will never be able to understand that."

Nor did the editor of the *New York Times*, who turned space in the op-ed page over to one of the Mayor's most vicious critics.

I still couldn't figure out why I was at the private wake.

"We shouldn't have been there."

"Speak for yourself . . . If you want, I'll drop you off at Thirty-sixth and Halsted and you can wait in line with the rest of the city."

"I'd have to walk home?"

"You bet."

"I guess I won't."

"You're just angry because Sis Daley agrees with me that you're a genius."

I dropped the issue.

"You were striking in your papal dress."

"You're just saying that because you want to sleep with me tonight."

"What's the point in being married on a cold night like this unless you snuggle up with your spouse?"

She rested her hand on my knee for a moment, banishing all the cold in the car.

"You'll want to do more than snuggle up."

So I did.

And so we did later on, exorcising death with a commitment to life and love.

Local TV at ten was filled with pictures of massive lines of people slowly edging into the old church.

"The national news had some of these pictures at five-thirty," Moire Meg informed us. "They were like totally awed."

That long lines of people on Thirty-seventh Street and on Lowe waited to get into Nativity the next day despite the terrible cold and a windchill which hovered near zero astonished the national media.

The next day as Rosemarie, in the same cloth coat and a different black dress, worked our way through the police lines for our reserved seat—which now I was willing to accept— we encountered a national CBS reporter and cameraman.

"Dr. O'Malley," she asked. "You are Dr. O'Malley, aren't you?"

"Sometimes Ambassador O'Malley, sometimes Chuck."

"Are you surprised at the big crowds of people who have passed through this church and are here waiting for the Mass to begin?"

"We call it the Eucharist these days . . . And, no, I'm not surprised at all."

"Why, sir?"

"Well, he was one of us and we loved him, unlike phony Chicagoans like Studs Terkel and Mike Royko."

"A zinger," my wife said. "You didn't mention your good friend Walter."

"They would never have used it. This they might."

"I don't think they will."

For once in the last ten years of our marriage, Rosemarie was wrong. They did use it.

"Like you were totally good," Moire Meg assured us breathlessly. "And, Rosie, you looked totally beautiful."

"Not embarrassed by your father?"

"Oh, no! You smiled like you were kind of proud of him."

"Imagine that."

So it had been when we were in Bonn. The media stories were all about the Ambassador's wife and children.

Inside the church I settled into the torpor I desperately seek when I know that I'll have to sit through a long and wandering homily which all the Irishwomen in church would insist was wonderful. Well, not my wife. She was actively anticlerical. I was only passively so. I would turn them off. She would squirm and mutter to herself.

Someday a group of people would assemble in a church for my obsequies. I hoped Edward would avoid the clichés.

What could be said about me?

I had been a decent son and husband, not spectacular but on the whole more good than bad. I had remained faithful to my wife. I had tried hard at the good father role and at least none of my kids hated me. I had tried to serve my country a couple of times and eventually given up in despair. I had taken an unconscionably large number of pictures, a few of them were presentable.

He was born, he grew up, he loved, he lived, he died. Not much to remember. A few good deeds, not many bad deeds. A life that was not completely wasted.

He could have done so much more.

I know. My reveries turned to prayer.

What more can I do between now and my own funeral Mass?

I was sad when we trudged back to Oak Park after the ceremony finally came to an end.

Sad for the Mayor, sad for all who must die.

Sad for myself.

Sad sack.

❧ Chuck ❧
1977

"None of us on the Hill trust this guy," Timmy Boylan informed us.

Timmy's body and mind had been shattered in the Hurtgen Forest, three days after he had arrived in the First Division as a replacement in September of 1944. A big, handsome Black Irishman with thick black hair that covered half of his forehead, he recovered his bodily health in an Army hospital and returned to the neighborhood, where he promptly set about destroying the existing beer supply on the West Side. Though he was two years older than I, we became friends of a sort because we both read books.

"Charles C.," he'd say with a roguish laugh and a crooked grin, "we're misfits. We read books because we like to read."

I'd sit in the Magic Tap with him for hours on end, sipping Coke while he downed brew in great gulps, arguing about Proust.

"These are our times lost, Charles C. Only since we're both misfits, we'll never be able to recall them."

I'd hold up my camera. He'd laugh.

I tried to persuade him to see Dr. Berman, the shrink with whom I had shared a darkroom in my days in Bamberg, defending the United States from the Red Army. To my astonishment, he did. Then he stopped drinking and began to date, even half court, a lovely, freckle-faced Irish kid named Jenny Carlson from St. Lucy's. He enrolled in "The Pier," as the first branch of what would become the University of Illinois at Chicago Circle was called because classes were held in the cavernous halls of Navy Pier. Brilliant kid that he was, he aced his classwork and seemed destined to earn his visa to suburbia in record time.

Then he disappeared again, without saying a word to poor Jenny or Dr. Berman or to Charles C. O'Malley. Rosemarie and I hunted him down in Ireland, where he was seeking the simple life as a hotel manager out in the Irish-speaking reaches of the County Galway, a stone-sober hotel manager. Eventually, Jenny, by then a nurse, dragged him back to the neighborhood where he belonged. They had a couple of kids, he became in rapid order an assistant state's attorney, a judge, and a member of the House of Representatives of the United States of America.

He still had the roguish laugh, the crooked grin, and strange notion that he and I were kindred spirits, indeed that we understood each other. We were both frauds, he seemed to hint, and we knew it but no one else did. Rosemarie and Jenny (from whose face the look of absolute worship never disappeared) and the two of us were eating supper in the Monocle, a restaurant in the Capitol Hill district of our nation's capital.

"That's what Pat Moynihan said at lunch today," I replied.

"In the Senate Dining Room, I hope, Charles C.," he said, his black eyes twinkling. "Rosemarie H. deserves at least that."

"She deserves the White House Mess," Jenny announced.

She and I were sipping from a half bottle of wine. Our mates had turned over their glasses.

"Actually, the State Dining Room," I countered.

We all laughed again.

"What's the matter with Jimmy Carter that you guys don't trust him?"

"He treats the Congress of the United States," he said, rubbing his fingers through his thick silver hair, "like we are the Georgia State Legislature. He sends his poor white trash staff up to us with his marching orders. Then when we get set to march, the white trash change their minds. Drives poor Tip O'Neill crazy."

"Tip" was the legendary Boston Irish Speaker of the House who had guided the Congress through the impeachment years.

I had not particularly liked Jimmy Carter. Maybe it was Irish Catholic prejudice against his Southern Baptist piety. He had admitted during the campaign that he had looked at women with lust in his heart.

"What's the point of God's creating women," my good wife had protested, "if not to stir up desire in men? How does that pious dope thinks the species continues itself?"

That's the kind of thing Rosemarie says when she's offended.

"It's like he's running a government in exile over a true American who has to work in a foreign country that is not responsive to his wishes. Because he walked to the inauguration and carries his own bags and doesn't have a chief of staff, he figures he represents the America of Andrew Jackson which is the whole of America."

"Because he's a peanut farmer and a Southern Baptist," Jenny joined, "he thinks the rest of us are."

I was not surprised. I had kind of expected that Carter would be ineffectual.

"He's supposed to be very bright," I suggested.

"Nuclear engineer and that stuff," Tim chortled and waved his arms. "That's a pretty narrow field and it doesn't teach you anything about how to work with a Congress for many of whom presidents just come and go and they go on."

"He's not a liberal?" Rosemarie asked. "I thought he was."

"He says all the right things . . . Another steak, Charles C.?"

"I'd say yes and my wife would veto me and I don't have enough votes to override."

"Chucky!"

"In response to your question, Rosemarie H., he makes all the right liberal sounds and, God knows, he believes them because they're part of his personal religion, but he has no idea how to get legislation on them through Congress. Worse than that, he never will."

"Ronald Reagan waits in the wings," I said.

"God forbid, Charles C."

"Isn't Hamilton Jordan acting as chief of staff?" Rosemarie asked.

"He pronounces his name as Jerden. Tip calls him Hambletonian Jerkin, which is a pretty good name. He doesn't have a clue. Even some of the Southerners in Congress call him 'poor white trash.'"

"And the President and his personal family?" my good wife asked.

"They use the same words," Jenny Boylan said. "Timmy and I think it's cruel. See what you think tomorrow afternoon."

The remnants of the meal were cleared away. The waitress offered dessert. The other three declined. I ordered chocolate ice cream in line with my principle that it is at least venially sinful to refuse dessert. My wife, good woman that she is, sighed audibly.

"So, Charles C., what about this UN job that presidents seem to want you to take?"

"Huh?"

"The rumor is all over the Hill that Jimmy Carter will offer it to you tomorrow afternoon."

"Huh?" Rosemarie said.

"News to me." I put down my teacup.

"The story is that you were the best ambassador in the Kennedy years, that LBJ offered it to you because you were perfect for the job, and that you turned it down flat because you were opposed to the Vietnam War."

"I don't know who ranks the ambassadors," my wife answered for me as she often does, "and LBJ never really offered it to him. He just bullshitted around like he did all the time."

"Rosemarie," I pleaded weakly, "such a terrible expression to describe the behavior of the President of the United States."

"Accurate," she replied crisply.

"Well, Charles C., if he offers it to you, will you take it?"

"No," I said firmly. "No way."

"Why not?"

"I would not want to serve in an administration which has a big majority in Congress and doesn't know what to do with it."

Rosemarie did not intervene in the conversation. Generally her silence means agreement.

"You were a great con in Bonn, Charles C. You charmed everyone. The ideal non-diplomat diplomat."

"If you check the article in the *New York Times* newspaper about that interlude, you'll find that I was a success because of my witty and beautiful wife and dazzling family."

"That's not altogether true," aforementioned wife commented.

"You are one of the great cons in the history of the West Side of Chicago," Timmy persisted. "Did you not con me into believing that this lovely woman was pining for me and thus trick me into giving up my Connemara paradise—mind you, Rosemarie H."—he put his hand on Jenny's—"you are part of the con."

"I don't think, Timmy, that I want to try to con the whole world about an administration that doesn't know what it's doing or how it's doing."

"Secretary of State we might consider," my wife announced, without any prior consultation.

"I fear," Timmy grinned his best crooked grin, "that Cyrus Vance has that job all sewed up."

"Genetic entitlement," I said.

In the years since, I have been grateful to Mr. Vance. I would have taken that job if offered. Then, I would have had to cope with the mess of the Iranian occupation of the American Embassy and President Carter's inability to do anything about it.

The next afternoon we traipsed across Lafayette Park from the Hay-Adams *en famille*. Moire Meg carried Siobhan, whom she referred to as her "big sister" because her mother, she argued, had to help with the shoot.

The Carters were amiable people. I don't quite know what poor white trash means, except that you don't own a big cotton plantation. I would describe them as just plain folks from down home with a strong strain of authentic Baptist piety. They were about as different from my clan as anyone in America could have been. Yet we all found it hard not to like them.

"Not everyone has to be from the West Side," Moire Meg whispered to me.

"As your grandmother April would have said, it's not their fault."

Siobhan's little sister giggled, as she always did when the wisdom of the good April was cited.

The President and his wife made a big fuss over our youngest to which she replied characteristically with coos and grins.

They also invoked God's blessings on her.

Our two daughters were seated in the Cabinet Room with lemonade and cookies while my good wife and I prepared for the shoot.

Jimmy Carter was not an easy subject. I try to capture my people at their very best while at the same time being honest about them. In my portrait of this President I wanted to show him as the intelligent, sincere, and devout man he was and leave it to others to wonder whether there was anything about him that suggested he should be President.

All I could get at first was a man who was tense, laboring under an enormous strain, perhaps suspecting that the job might be too much for him.

"How many presidents have you photographed, Charles?"

"One way or another," my wife answered for me again, "five. Eisenhower, Kennedy, Johnson, Nixon, and Ford."

"Did any of them seem relaxed in their job?" he asked.

"Not at all, Mr. President," I answered. "They all were trying to learn a job that no one can ever really learn."

"I know what you mean," he said with a faint smile that I managed to capture.

"I think the problem with America," he said, "is that we're in the slough of despond. The war, the protests, the scandals have sapped our spiritual energy. We need to renew those energies. We need to rediscover the faith that we've lost."

That was the same message that he delivered later when he came down from the mountain (Camp David) to urge rejuvenation on America. The media quickly dismissed his Gospel message. The problem was not spiritual but the incompetence of the presidency.

"I've been saying pretty much the same thing," I said as I signaled Rosemarie for a slight shift in the lighting. "The country is in an acute hangover."

He laughed and I caught part of it. That was the shot we'd use in the end.

"How long do such hangovers last, I wonder?"

"A couple more years maybe."

Rosemarie frowned. Obviously it would take longer.

Some presidents are unlucky. Jimmy Carter didn't get many breaks. On the other hand, presidents have to make some of their own luck.

He and Mrs. Carter were delighted with the final portrait we sent them.

"Can I have a private word with you, Charles, before you leave?" the President asked.

"Certainly," I said.

Rosemarie, who was folding one of our lights, glared at me.

"You have given much of your life to government service of one sort or another, Charles," he said as we sat at the massive oak table in the Roosevelt Room. "I hesitate to ask you for another commitment. Yet the government needs men like you. I realize that President Johnson offered you this job before and you declined. I wonder if I could persuade you to represent us in New York at the United Nations."

"He didn't quite offer it, Mr. President. He hinted at it, which was his way."

For one terrible moment I was tempted to quote Rosemarie that he had bullshitted around about it.

"So I understand." President Carter smiled.

"These are different times, Mr. President. I went to Bonn fifteen years ago. The world has changed and I've changed. I have new family obligations and responsibilities, this new daughter who has tried to charm you, a bunch of grandchildren. I'm afraid at this time I can't really take on that task, as much as I would like to."

That was a lame excuse. I could hardly have said to President Carter that I had a lot more confidence in Jack Kennedy than I had in him, even if that confidence might have been somewhat mistaken. I could not say I felt more comfortable with an Irish Catholic than a Southern Baptist. I could not say that I would take Secretary of State if it were offered. I could not say that I was certain his administration would foul up.

A spasm of disappointment flickered across his face—sadness and not anger. I wondered how many other men had turned him down for other jobs.

"I understand, Charles," he said. "You really did not give your best reason for not wanting the job. You're an artist with a wonderful talent. You should not let government service interfere with that. I almost hoped you would say no. I would have felt guilty interfering with your art."

"I'm not really an artist, Mr. President."

"I'm sure your wife would disagree with you." He smiled broadly. "She'd be right too."

In the Cabinet Room our youngest was doing her best to stand up with considerable help from her mother and sister. Soon she would be walking. Soon I would be the father of a contentious two-year-old, contentious and charming.

I had a few recollections as we left the Oval Office and trudged through Lafayette again, the first buds of the cherry blossoms peeking out as they tried to make up their minds whether this was a good idea or not—our first time in the Oval Office when Jack Kennedy (with Pat Moynihan in the room) offered me the Embassy in Bonn, an offer which my wife quickly accepted before I could decline, reporting to Jack later about Germany, turning down Lyndon's request that I withdraw my resignation, and warning him about the dangers of escalation in Vietnam, our meeting with him when the "Senior Advisers to the President" told Lyndon that the time had come to get out of Vietnam.

Those were exciting moments in my life. I had turned my back on more such exciting moments.

"What did he say?" Rosemarie asked.

I told her.

"What a wonderful man!" she said, her voice catching.

"He was right, Chucky," Moire Meg, sister in her arms, said. "Why would you want to work for the government anyway? All those media nerds chasing you around all the time."

So I tried to explain to her what I'd been thinking as we crossed the park.

"You mean President Kennedy thought you could change the world?"

"That's what he said, kid, and I think he meant it."

"He did," my wife said, "most of the time."

"That was a long time ago, wasn't it, Ma?"

"So long ago, hon, that you weren't even with us."

"Those must have been exciting times, Rosie."

She understood. She knew that she did not live in exciting times. Yet she understood how it was to live in such times and perhaps to regret that she didn't live in them.

"They were exciting, hon. Maybe we were only kidding ourselves."

"I kind of think," Moire Meg said hesitantly, "that doesn't really matter."

"Young woman," I told her, "you're wiser than the two of us put together."

We all laughed happily. Not to be outdone, Siobhan Marie joined in.

Rosemarie and I went to a concert at the Kennedy Center that night. Moire Meg insisted that she had homework to do. The next morning we took the shuttle up to New York. I was to attend the Publisher's Lunch at the *New York Times*. My uninvited wife came along.

Perhaps lunching with the Pope and his staff in the Vatican is a more solemn high event than the Publisher's Lunch, but it may not be. Everyone is neatly dressed, simultaneously relaxed and intense, urbane and deadly serious. My Ph.D. examiners were less threatening than the examination board we were facing, for all their graciousness.

Well, I wasn't threatened at all. It was another stage for the Chucky act, a truth which Rosemarie noted before we walked down from the Waldorf.

As in, "Chucky, please try to behave yourself. None of this West Side leprechaun game."

"Who, me?"

I knew some of the men already from my time in Bonn and my brief adventures in Saigon.

First question: Ambassador, you've been out of public service since 1965. Have you ever thought of returning to it?

Answer: No, I am not planning to move permanently to an apartment at the Waldorf.

Question: You mean the one the UN Ambassador lives in?

Answer: It's a nice place to visit.

Question: Do you lack confidence in the Carter administration's human rights foreign policy?

Answer: I'd like to see what human rights mean in Northern Ireland.

(Respondent's wife shuts her eyes because she knows what's happening.)

Question: Do you think that the United States in fact has a foreign policy?

Answer: Sure it does. Woodrow Wilson enunciated it—

Make the world safe for Democracy. That's what we thought we were doing in Vietnam.

Question: We failed there, did we not?

Answer: Tell me about it. No formal policy, no matter how exquisitely moral, dictates its own limitations.

Question: So you think that a human rights foreign policy is fine so long as it is aware of its own limitations?

Answer: That the world is gray and murky and problematic is hard for our American Calvinist culture to comprehend.

I continued to eat their admittedly excellent food while I talked. The dessert was some wimpy fruit compote. I thought of asking for a second helping, but resisted the temptation so as not to embarrass my wife.

Question: You think we are Calvinist here?

Answer: Certainly, especially your editorial writers!

Question: You have a doctorate in economics, don't you?

Answer: I think so.

Question: What do you think is the most important economic problem in America?

Answer: Other than too much poverty and discrimination against women, I'd say it's all been caused by President Johnson's decision to conduct a major war without increasing taxes. There's been an inflationary bias in the economy ever since.

Question: And the cure for that is?

Answer: Tight money for a couple of years. That takes courage and at present there's not enough of that around. Also we should stop talking about conservation and impose heavy taxes on gasoline. Anyone who knows anything about economics knows that.

Question: You are apparently not ready to return to public service now. What about the future?

Answer: What did the man say, never say never because never is a hell of a long time.

Question: I'd like to pin you down . . .

Answer: Impossible!

Question: Could you tell us precisely why you turned down President Carter's invitation to become America's UN representative?

Answer: I'm not prepared to admit that there was such an offer.

Question: If there were, would you accept it?

Answer: I'm a photographer, not a diplomat.

Question: Mrs. O'Malley, are you really Helen Clancy the writer?

New respondent brightens considerably at the prospect of taking over show.

Answer: What would ever make you think that?

Question: The spouse in the story seems to bear a remarkable resemblance to Ambassador O'Malley.

Answer: Really! They both have red hair, but I can't imagine why anyone would think the Ambassador is a little red-haired punk.

Question: One who is very sweet and wins all the arguments, however.

Answer: The Ambassador never wins the arguments, do you, Ambassador?

Answer: Not that I can remember.

Apparently I had passed the test. The conversation became genial and was dominated, as one might expect, by my wife. I told them about my new exhibition, which would be called *People* and would feature all my portraits. The publisher actually asked if I would do a portrait of him. Rosemarie agreed for me and jotted down a date. We'd have to return to New York.

"If I were a drinking man," I said as we walked back to the Waldorf, "I'd need a stiff drink after that."

We leaned our backs against a chill wind, which had arrived from somewhere.

"You did well, Chucky. You charmed them and flummoxed them. The crack about Calvinists will set them thinking for a long time."

"Fortunately, you were able to ride to my rescue when that woman asked you whether you were Helen Clancy."

"I wondered when they were going to get around to that."

We struggled through rush-hour traffic to get out to La Guardia for our late-afternoon flight to O'Hare. Siobhan Marie did not like all the shifting around that had occurred and was irritable most of the way home. However, she did not disgrace us by screaming.

"Was I this good in planes when I was her age, Chucky?"

"Don't ask!"

When we finally pulled up to our home in the dark, we were all exhausted. Too much, too much. I belong on the West Side of Chicago, nowhere else.

We were hardly in the door when Peg called to tell us that April Rosemary had a miscarriage.

My wife and my middle daughter both wept.

"I better go over there," Rosemarie said through her tears.

"I'll put what's-her-name to bed," Moire Meg said.

"Should I come?"

"No, Chucky, she doesn't need to see any man except her husband and him for not very long."

"It's hard for her," I said, trying to sound wise.

"It's hard for every woman who has one, especially hard for her. She probably had just begun to think she was pregnant and to make plans."

"There'll be other chances."

"Please God."

I was weary but I knew I wouldn't be able to sleep. I went down to the darkroom and began to work on the White House shoot. The shot of Jimmy Carter as he began to laugh looked like the best, as I thought it would. Indeed, it was the only good result of the afternoon's work. It captured the President in his essential if somewhat tense goodness, a man who could indeed worry about lusting in his heart after a woman, who could laugh but not without a sense of guilt. Would the right-wing critics complain that I was too kind to him?

Probably.

Would the young left-wing critics complain that I was too kind to him?

Probably.

I had stopped worrying about both groups, though their nastiness always astonished me.

Carter had some remarkable accomplishments during his administration—the treaty to return the Canal to Panama and the Camp David agreement between Egypt and Israel. I didn't think he should have refused to sell wheat to Russia because of their invasion of Afghanistan or pull out of the Moscow Olympics—and thus offend both the farmers and the sports fans in this country while having little impact on the Soviets. Finally, however, he was done in by inflation and Iran and his own well-meaning incompetence.

Someone knocked at the darkroom door.

"Pasta."

Moire Meg.

"Just a minute."

I secured everything that needed to be secured and opened the inner door. Then I closed that and went out to the exercise room.

"Bolognese," she said, pointing to a dish on the table where I ate when I was working. "And iced tea."

"The sister?"

"Glad to be home in her own little trundle bed and sound asleep . . . Pa, what's a trundle bed?"

"Kind of a bed with wheels that can be stored under a higher bed."

"You know everything, don't you, Chuck?"

"A lot of useless facts . . . Good pasta. Thank you."

"You're welcome . . . The trip to the East doesn't seem to have done you a world of good."

"I belong on the prairie soil of Illinois, kid, the West Side of Chicago. I'm out of place everywhere else."

"You did all right in Germany."

"That's because I was doing it for Jack Kennedy. Different time."

She nodded solemnly.

"The thing is that I know I could do well enough in the world of the White House and the New York Times, only I don't want to."

"I'm glad . . . Gotta get to my homework . . . Bring the dish upstairs or Ma will be mad."

"Can't let that happen."

Later, when I was closing up shop, Rosemarie appeared. I showed her the first crude print.

"Only good one I got."

She hugged me.

"Like I always said, Chucky, you're a genius."

"Yeah, well it's lucky this one turned out."

"Food?"

"The redhead brought me a bowl of pasta."

"So all's right with the world."

"She also warned me that I should bring the dirty plate upstairs or Ma would be mad."

"Would I get mad over a thing like that?"

"How's our oldest daughter?"

"Typical. Very brave. Very upbeat. Happy she knows she can get pregnant. Next time it will be all right. Nature's way of ending a pregnancy that wasn't going to work. Inside she's terrified."

"Jamie know?"

"I'm sure he does, poor dear man."

Winter had come, so spring could not be far behind. The Brit poet who had written that did not have to live in middle western America.

❧ *Chuck* ❧
1978

My picture of the "Smiling Pope" was on the front pages of all the Italian papers. Indeed, the smile was probably on the front page of every paper in the Christian world. We had lucked out. Some idiot priest who was a sociologist had been appearing at press conferences around Rome with a job description for the new Pope—"A hopeful holy man who smiles." If that were truly a description of the man we needed, then it was surely a prediction of the man we got. There were some complaints already—mostly from the French—that he was too simple, not very intelligent, not really bright enough for the job.

We went to his first General Audience in the Audience Hall that Paul VI had built, a big modernist monstrosity that kept the Pope a long distance from anyone who was not a bishop or who lacked clout. Since we still had clout in those days we were up close. Somehow they had provided an awkward English translation of the Pope's remarks on the paper the Vatican likes to use, which I suspect is recycled toilet paper. The talk was a tour de force, a simple little homily about God in which he advanced the radical notion that we must picture God as our strong father, but even more as our loving mother, a notion which Catholic feminists and Catholic antifeminists never seemed to learn about. I suspect that the Vatican establishment was horrified and did its best to cover it up.

I followed along in English. Rosemarie listened in Italian. His mixture of diffidence and laughter absorbed the crowded hall. Oh, yes, we had lucked out with this man from northern Italy.

"The funnies are add-ons to the text," Rosemarie whispered to me. "The man is really good."

Her perfume was, as always, dazzling. She could lean over to me, her breasts almost touching me, whenever she wanted to.

Paul VI had died without acting on Cardinal O'Neill. He had characteristically vacillated. Finally, earlier in the summer, Benelli had persuaded him to accept the report of his commission and appoint a coadjutor with right to succession in Chicago—in effect an administrator who would have complete control. Cardinal Sergio had been dispatched to Chicago to impose the change. The new Archbishop already had his papers.

Then the Pope called Sergio at Fiumicino Airport and added the condition that the change was acceptable only if Cardinal O'Neill agreed. There was a noisy shouting match between Sergio and O'Neill at the Cardinal's villa on the seminary grounds. But the Curial Cardinal went home with only the promise from Cardinal O'Neill to fight every inch of the way.

Then Paul VI died, leaving the problem for his successor.

News of the fight at the villa leaked around the city, but didn't make the media. Most priests didn't believe it. The laypeople we knew hoped it was true. Edward, now thoroughly recovered and deeply committed to his work with the young people on the Near North Side, was unperturbed.

"I never thought it would work."

I did, however.

Somehow the story of our trip to Rome to request the Cardinal's replacement did not become known for a long time. Most of the priests who had contributed to the dossier did not suffer for it. One man who had, many thought, a legitimate claim to be a bishop was blocked for the rest of his life.

Adolfo met us outside the Audience Hall, two blond and handsome Swiss Guards in tow. They saluted smartly. No one salutes better than the Swiss Guards. When they salute you, you begin to believe that you deserve it. Dangerous temptation.

"You noticed the apparent deviations from his text?" the Monsignor asked.

"We sure did!" my wife exclaimed.

"Impressive spontaneous wit, was it not?"

"If it was spontaneous," I said. "If it wasn't spontaneous, it was even more impressive."

"You are quite right, Carlo." Adolfo chuckled. "I saw his final draft. He had penciled in every comment and joke. He's a polished catechist."

"Even if he is not the intellectual the French seem to want?"

"Often the French do not understand."

The Monsignor and I laughed at our little anti-French joke.

"You have all your camera equipment, Carlo? Shouldn't you have more?"

"Real photographers do, Monsignor," my wife informed him. "You must understand that Chucky is not a real photographer. He takes pictures."

"Ah," he said, winking at me.

"When do you go up to the papal apartments?" I asked.

"Our appointment is in a half hour. Might I suggest that we arrive early. That will give you time to, ah, arrange your equipment."

I have no complaints against my professional colleagues who travel with enough stuff to establish a studio. I would rather do my portraits in the studio I have established at our house. But I don't bring a lot of stuff along with me on a shoot. Maybe I'm just too lazy. Or maybe I think it gets in my way. As Rosemarie says to me, "Chucky, you're a snapshot artist. Always have been, always will be."

I think that's a compliment.

"The Pope's health is good?" Rosemarie asked.

"Not at all, Rosie. It is quite bad. There is already fear."

"I assume he has the best doctors in Rome?"

"Ah, no, *cara*. The Vatican doctors are the ones with the most influence in the Curia. Excellent Catholic laymen, if you understand me."

"I don't think I like that," I said.

He shrugged as would a character in a Fellini film.

We were shown into the papal office, the Oval Office of the Catholic Church, all polished wood and thick damask drapes—

a place that would have done nicely as the office of a late-nineteenth-century funeral home. I shuffled around lining up my lights and taking light readings at various spots. Bright Roman sunlight filtered into the room. Maybe I should shoot Pope John Paul with available light. Rosemarie followed after me, adjusting the lights and the shade so that it was the way she thought it should be.

I had learned long before that it was pointless to argue with her about such matters. She was almost always right, not only in high theory but in actual practice. Adolfo watched our act with an amused little smile.

The Swiss Guards had vanished. However, I suspected they were lurking outside the big oak door, just in case the crazy little American with the beautiful wife might prove to be dangerous. Obviously, he was not a man to be trusted.

Then the door opened and Pope John Paul entered, his smile brighter than any illumination my flashes might produce. He was a medium-sized man (which means he was as tall as I am and that if my wife were wearing high heels she would have towered over him), spare of frame and girth, with brown eyes whose sparkle radiated through thick glasses. He stretched out his arms to us in a gesture of vibrant warmth. He was indeed a simple priest of the land of whom no one in his parish could ever be afraid.

Adolfo translated for us, though the ineffable Rosemarie needed little translation.

"What a beautiful book!" the Pope exclaimed, holding up my book *Kids*. "What beautiful *bambini*! Some of them are yours?"

We stood at his desk as he leafed through the book and we identified which of the kids were ours. Well, Rosemarie, dazzling in her black dress and veil, did the identification. I relapsed into my familiar role of the punk kid from the West Side who was out of place in the presence of royalty.

All I could think of was how much I loved her and how beautiful she was and how I would make love to her back at the Hassler—terrible dirty thoughts on the fifth floor of the Vatican Palace.

It had started with that whiff of perfume, Chanel I think, in the Audience Hall. My desire hadn't changed through the years, I told myself; it was if anything more intense. Now it was also erratic.

"And these are the children now!" The good Rosemarie informed the Vicar of Christ, as she pulled her foldout gallery from her purse. "This is April Rosemary, our oldest. She's studying photography, something her father never bothered with. This is Kevin, our oldest son, he's studying for a doctorate in musicology; the O'Malleys are a very musical family. And Jimmy is studying to be a priest, like his uncle . . ."

"He was Cardinal O'Neill's secretary for some time, was he not?"

"Yes," my good wife said smoothly, "he works with young adults now . . . And Sean graduated from college. Moire Meg graduates from high school."

"And a grandchild?"

My wife turned an attractive shade of crimson.

"We have some of them too. But this is our youngest, Siobhan Marie—Joan Marie in Irish—She's two and she's just like her father, a little Irish imp!"

"Red hair too!"

"Two of our grandchildren have red hair, so there's four of them in the family! All imps! Here's a picture our eldest took of them all!"

This was part of the priestly role of which I had never been aware. The priest was expected to marvel at pictures of children, whether they appeared marvelous or not. This man was clearly a pro at it.

"Three generations! How beautiful!"

So he knew who we were and probably that I had been involved in attempts to remove Cardinal O'Neill. Not only a hopeful holy man who smiled, but a smooth operator too. Very interesting. Maybe there was hope for the Church after all.

"Perhaps we might do the portrait now," Rosemarie said, not at all hesitant to give instructions even to the Pope.

"Yes, it would be good," agreed the Pope with a smile.

How wise of God to have created woman for man to reverence, adore, desire, and make love with. How convenient for humans to pair off one with another so the loved and desired person was always more or less available. First of all I would unzip her black dress. . . .

*   *   *

Then professional responsibility took command. Temporarily.

It would be an easy shoot and yet a very difficult one. Our new Pope was telegenic. It would be easy to get a shot of his smile and his twinkling eyes. Yet I had to capture something else. What was it—determination? Willpower? Or merely the shrewdness of a priest of the countryside?

I suspected that he was a man who could make the tough decisions as they came along and have a good night's sleep afterward. Or at least no worse than any other night. No more Hamlet.

We talked as I fired away. Finally, I came up with the right question.

"What is the toughest part of being Pope?" I asked.

His smile was unwavering, but there was steel in his answer.

"Protecting laypeople from the mistakes we poor priests make."

I continued shooting, but I knew that I had captured just the right expression. Before September it would be on the front page of every newspaper in America.

When we had finished and I was packing up the equipment—God forbid that the Grand Duchess Rosemarie should dirty her hands with such work—he gave my good wife several handfuls of rosaries, medals, and holy cards and imparted his blessing on us and all of our families.

"May they always be a consolation to you and you a consolation to them!"

The second part sounded difficult.

When we left his office I felt like I had made a weeklong retreat, exhausted, exhilarated, happy!

"You are impressed, no?" Adolfo asked, as we took the elevator to the ground floor.

"Enormously," I admitted.

"You noted that he alluded to the Chicago dossier?"

"Very indirectly."

"He is an Italian, after all." The Monsignor laughed. "He has read the whole dossier and is deeply troubled by what he read. He does not like the thought of hurting Cardinal O'Neill, but he realizes that it is necessary to do so. He will do it before the month is over. Also he plans to invoke another commission on birth control."

"One more?" Rosemarie, whose eyes were glowing with admiration for the man who had blessed each of her children so warmly, sighed.

"Their task will be to find a way to go beyond Humanae Vitae without contradicting it."

"That won't be easy."

"On the contrary, *cara*, that will be very easy."

"God grant him a long life to do all those good things." Rosemarie sighed, an Irishwoman's prayer that, even though things are supposed to go wrong, this time would be an exception.

I had returned to my lascivious, indeed tumescent, thoughts about my wife. We were packed for the trip tomorrow, at my insistence. There would be nothing much to do all afternoon. I would undress her very slowly, admire her nakedness, revel in every curve of her lovely body, and then make her mine, just as she would make me hers.

Her breasts had obsessed me since the first day they had made their tentative appearance. I had fantasized about them for years. The fantasies never stopped after we were married. Though they were not as firm as they once had been, they still made me delirious with desire. How clever of God to arrange such delights.

"You will send us several prints?" Monsignor Adolfo asked, as we walked out into the Belvedere Courtyard, to the accompaniment of the usual salutes of the Swiss Guard.

"A half dozen or so," I replied. "I know which one I'm going to use, however."

"He's all instinct, Monsignor," Rosemarie explained. "He's read the books and studied the masters, but he knows what he wants to do. A little undisciplined, perhaps, but natural brilliance."

We said "*ciao*" to one another and promised that we'd meet again. None of us knew how soon that would be.

"Charles C. O'Malley," she protested as we walked out of the gate and into Italy, "it is unspeakably obscene to have dirty thoughts about me in the papal apartments. You embarrassed me terribly."

She didn't seem upset, however.

"I did no such thing," I insisted.

"Chucky Ducky, I've slept with you so long I can smell your lust."

"I was thinking how wise God was to have created woman for man to reverence, adore, desire, and make love with. How convenient for humans to pair off one with another so the loved and desired person was always more or less available. I thought that was a perfectly presentable thought to have in the papal apartments, especially when my wife was so beautiful and charming that even the Pope was impressed."

She paused to consider that.

"That's very beautiful, Chucky Ducky," she said, a catch in her voice. "Seductive of course, but still quite lovely."

"Thank you."

She stopped, opened her purse, and drew out her "Helen Clancy" notebook in which she made notes for her stories.

"How did that go again?"

I repeated my words.

She nodded, jotted them down, and then closed the notebook briskly and returned it to her purse.

"You're not going to quote the little redhead punk as saying that in one of your stories?"

"I might just," she said aloofly.

"You'll accuse the poor little guy of lusting after you in the papal apartments?"

"I might just . . . After all, Chucky Ducky, when I know a man is thinking that way about me, my body begins to act up too."

"Really?" I extended an arm around her waist.

"Gimme a break!"

"I had another gift in mind."

She pretended to try to squirm out of my partial embrace, but without much sincerity.

"You think you can do anything you want to me, anytime you want."

"I know I can."

"That's because you're so perceptive and so sweet." She sighed and collapsed against my arm.

It is not good, I reflected, for a man to have that kind of

power over his woman. Well, I had worked at it a long time.

So we made love in the afternoon in the heat of a Roman August and felt very good about everything, especially about the future of the Church we both loved. Also we were pleased with God's arrangement for men and women.

Back home in Chicago we reported to our families and friends about the new Pope: yes, what you saw was the real thing. This time we lucked out. We distributed prints of the shot I knew would be the best. Rosemarie adjured everyone to pray for his continued good health.

"He's a wonderful man," she said, "but he's under terrible strain."

The plans for my fiftieth birthday on September 17 continued apace. I was, needless to say, barred from any participation in the plans. The monster regiment of women had taken charge, especially my sister and my wife and my two older daughters and my mother. I imagined all too easily the good April saying of some madcap scheme, "I think that's cute and I know poor Chucky would love it."

She knew full well that I wouldn't love it. What she meant was that I ought to love it, whatever it was.

I was relegated to playing with Siobhan Marie, who assumed as a matter of right that, since I wasn't part of the serious planning, I had plenty of free time to play with her. She was, as should not have surprised me, a very bossy playmate.

"What do you think of this?" Rosemarie handed me a letter.

The handwriting was obscure, deliberately so I decided as I deciphered it. It was on cheap, lined paper of the sort we used for tests in grammar school.

O'Malley,

I am writing to you to inform you that I shall come to Chicago in November to learn your tricks with the camera. I propose to devote my life to honest photography, especially photography which tells the truth about patriarchal discrimination against women, the young, nonwhites, and gays and lesbians. I believe you have a serious moral obligation to share your secrets with me so I can present an alternative to your racist, sexist, ageist, homophobic vision of the human species. In studying with you I will engage in honest dialogue about the meaning of photography as art. I will not become a wage slave or an assistant to you as that would reveal false consciousness. However, I expect to be paid a wage commensurate with my talent and experience.

Ms. Diana Robbins.

"Oh," I said, handing the letter back to my good wife. "It's a joke, it's like someone on *Saturday Night Live*."

"No, it's not. She's real. I asked April Rosemary whether there were still young people like that. She said there were. Her exact words were, 'Not all of us grew up.' "

"How's she doing?"

"Coming out of it. Has begun to enjoy her kid. She'll be all right."

"What should we do with that?" I gestured at the letter.

"I'll write Ms. Robbins a nice note, which will infuriate her more than a nasty note, and explain that you don't work with students, unless they're doctoral candidates in economics and that your skills with a camera are innate and instinctive and that you don't even understand yourself what you're doing. I'll tell her that she'd learn a lot more by studying your work itself than by hanging around with you."

"I don't know, Rosemarie," I said. "Maybe we could help the poor kid."

"You really are the original bleeding heart liberal, Chucky. She's a spoiled rich brat who's working out her conflict with her mother. She'd drive you crazy. April Rosemary said it sounded like something she might have written when she was working out her conflicts and that no way should we let her anywhere near you."

"I guess so," I said.

"I know so."

That settled that.

"Another thing," my wife continued, taking a deep breath under her maroon University of Chicago sweatshirt, an action which always had an effect on my libido.

"Bad news?"

"Probably."

"Oh?"

"Sean has a girlfriend."

"SEAN!"

"That's right."

"Serious?"

"I think so."

"He's much too young."

"No younger than you were when you forced me to marry you."

"That was different."

She grinned.

"You sound like it's your seventieth birthday next week instead of your fiftieth."

"Things were different then."

"I doubt it."

"You don't like her?" I demanded.

"She's a sweet little thing, pretty in a waiflike way. Orthodox Jewish."

"Jewish!"

Our children married Catholics, right?

Well they didn't have to. Good liberals that we are, we had always told them that we must not discriminate against other religions. We must respect all religions and all people.

Yeah, but still that didn't mean . . . did it?

"Don't be a curmudgeon, Chucky. He loves the poor little kid. There's no way we can talk him out of it. We have to be supportive and hope that they're both happy."

"You sound like they're planning marriage."

"He is. I'm not sure about her."

"What does Moire Meg say?"

Moire Meg was the next sibling after Sean and they were very close.

"She thinks it's silly. She goes 'April Rosemary had to flake out, Kevin had to go to Vietnam, Jimmy had to become a priest, now Seano has to fall in love with an Orthodox Jew. They're all testing us to see how we'll react.' "

I ignored her lapse into teenage language. At least she didn't say, "she goes, like."

"Did you ask her how she'll test us?"

"She said that would be juvenile."

"What's this young woman's name?"

"Esther Stern."

"Her family is Orthodox too?"

"No, that's why this letter"—she gestured at the note from Diana Robbins that lay on her desk—"reminded me of her. Her family is completely secular. They called themselves Starr, Edward and Eloise Starr. Esther was named Eileen. She didn't go to Jewish school, never had a bas mitzvah, indeed had nothing to do with Judaism till she went to Loyola to study biochemistry before going to medical school. She loves computing too. She met our son in a programming class. She chose Loyola because she wanted to be near her family. She's an only child. Now she won't talk to them because they've betrayed their heritage. They have a Christmas tree every year, for heaven's sake. Now she's discovering her Jewish identity . . . Or so Seano tells me with great respect in his ideas for the poor child's honesty and integrity . . . Oh, yes, she wants to migrate to Israel and live in an Orthodox kibbutz."

"Wow!"

"She is sweet, Chuck. She so much wanted me to like her."

"Her family is not opposed to their romance?"

"I gather from Seano that they are not exactly enthused because they think Catholics are religious fanatics. On the other hand they hope that Seano will win her away from her hyperorthodoxy."

"Will he?"

"I don't think so. He has too much respect for her religious identity to even try."

"Why didn't he tell me about it?"

"He's afraid you won't understand."

"Me!"

"He's wrong of course." She reached over and touched my hand. "Since that incident at the college out in the boondocks, he's a very confused young man who thinks everything is clear in his head . . . I'm telling you because he wants to bring her to the family birthday party."

"What family?"

"Don't be a dolt, Charles Cronin O'Malley. The party that

the family is having for you at your parents' house. That's the small party."

"Small party!"

"An intimate gathering of the family and a few friends—the Boylans, the Murrays, the Mayor, people like that."

"How many people?"

"That's not clear yet. We're still working on it. The other party—"

"What other party!"

"The public party at the Drake."

"I won't be there."

"Yes you will, Charles Cronin O'Malley. Don't worry about it. We'll tell you what to do."

"I'm sure you will . . . What does all this have to do with what's-her-name?"

"Esther."

"Yeah, Esther."

"Well, Sean goes like she's practically a member of the family. So he wants to invite her to both parties. So we said yes, though Moire Meg says it's silly. She doesn't even know you."

"So you're warning me that I should not be surprised when this waiflike creature appears, clinging to my youngest son's arm?"

"How did you know she's a clinger?"

"Figures."

"You will be nice to her, won't you?"

"I may be turning senile, but I'm not turning uncivil . . . The poor child will feel terribly out of place, won't she?"

"Yes, Chuck, she will. I didn't even suggest that to Seano. He thinks everything will work out just fine."

I felt like I was turning not seventy but eighty.

Could this child, raised in a completely secular environment, really turn to Orthodox Judaism? Or was she swept up in a late-adolescent identity crisis, like the one my wife argued I had never worked through?

What the hell did I know?

However, she had never been to an O'Malley family party. The music, the singing, the dancing, the storytelling would scare away a lot of Irish people I know. Not for nothing are we still called "the Crazy O'Malleys."

Well, there was nothing I could do about it except leave it all to heaven, who perhaps knew what would be best.

I was dispatched for a "complete physical checkup by a specialist." This activity was depicted to me as an exercise in high virtue, almost like a plenary indulgence, as though the checkup would prevent future illness while all it would in fact do would be to give me more things to worry about.

The internist at Northwestern Hospital who had been assigned to my case was a dyspeptic fellow who probably had not smiled since his first bowel movement. He was also profoundly skeptical when I told him that I had never smoked, I drank only an occasional glass of wine, exercised regularly, and normally eschewed sex as an exercise in temperance.

I actually said that, since one of my demons had taken over.

He hesitated, pen poised over his sheet of questions.

"Really, Dr. O'Malley?"

I had insisted that I wanted to be called "Doctor" because I had a degree in economics from The University. He looked at me like I had stolen something precious from him.

"I am an artist, Dr. Hoffman. I find that sexual activity weakens the creativity that drives my work."

As I recount my interaction with him, I am ashamed of myself. I was taking out my displeasure with the monster regiment by hazing this pathetically sincere man.

I was in that kind of mood. Running away from aging.

"Could you be a little bit more specific about your frequency of sexual relations?"

"With my wife or my mistress?"

I was confident that at some point he would realize that I was pulling his leg and smile.

Like, no way.

"Well, both."

"I don't have a mistress right now. So it would only be with my wife. We don't do it very often, only four or five times a week. We did it more frequently when we were younger."

He wrote down my answer thoughtfully.

"Your relationship with your wife is satisfactory?"

"It sure is. As long as I do what she tells me to do, we get along fine."

He wrote that down too.

Actually that wasn't the truth. Most of the time I did what Rosemarie wanted me to do because I trusted her judgment and her love. When I disagreed—like once a year—I always won the brief argument.

I then went through one of those stress tests in which you run on a board with an uphill grade while they monitor the behavior of your heart. Then you lie down on a table and they monitor the course of the radioactive stuff they have injected into your bloodstream.

"The photography doesn't have very good composition, Dr. Hoffman," I observed.

"Perhaps God would have designed the heart better if he had taken that matter into account, Dr. O'Malley."

I began to wonder then who was pulling whose leg.

The final verdict about Dr. Charles Cronin O'Malley at fifty and counting was delivered in a tone which I chose to interpret as disappointment.

"Your health is quite good, Dr. O'Malley, for a man of your age."

I felt like I was eighty.

"I am concerned only about your weight."

"I'm not overweight!" I protested.

"Most men your age are overweight, Dr. O'Malley, even obese. You're a tad underweight. That might reduce your resistance to serious infection."

"Not for lack of trying," I said. "Maybe I should eat more ice cream, though I can't stand the stuff."

"It might be good for you."

"Well, I'll see what I can do."

"Life expectancy?" I asked at the end.

"Both your parents are still alive?"

"Yes. Dad has just turned eighty. Mom is seventy-six."

"Thirty more years, plus or minus five."

That was not unreasonable. I would die eventually, but not, in the ordinary course of events, soon. The issue was what I would do with thirty years plus or minus five. That was my problem.

"Better check my pension investments."

"That would be a good idea," he said soberly.

When I finally escaped my "complete physical," I called my good wife.

"How did it go?" she demanded anxiously.

"There's good news and bad news."

"What's the bad news?"

"The bad news is that I am in good health for a man of my age."

Sigh of relief.

"And the good news?"

"Doctor says I must have sex more often!"

"Chucky!"

"I told him we did it only four or five times a week and he said that wasn't enough for someone as healthy as I am."

"Chucky!"

"He also said I should eat more ice cream because I was too skinny!"

"He did NOT!"

"Well, he said I was underweight and I told him how I hated ice cream and he said that I should force myself to eat more of it. So we'll have to go to Petersen's tonight before we work on increasing my sexual outlets per week."

"You're impossible!"

"You always say that."

"I'm so glad you're all right."

Now the poor woman was crying.

"Except for not having enough sex."

Now she was laughing and crying at the same time.

"I love you, Rosemarie."

The laughing and crying increased. I started to cry too.

"And I love you too."

I then went to the University Club for lunch with Max Berman, my old friend from darkroom days in Bamberg when we used to have Talmudic arguments about human guilt while we produced our respective photo prints.

Max had not changed much through the years, a little less hair, a little more haggard, but the same sadness in his eyes and same melancholy in his voice, even when he was being very funny. He was everyone's favorite rabbi, even if he was a psychiatrist.

"So, Chuck, you had your 'complete physical' today? So what did the good Dr. Ernest Hoffman have to say? Doubtless he was very earnest?"

"He said I would live a while longer."

"Ah, and how much longer?"

"Thirty years plus or minus five."

"It is a mistake to teach doctors statistics, no?"

"Maybe I shouldn't have told him that I wanted him to call me Dr. O'Malley."

He chuckled softly and rubbed his hands together.

"You must tell me the whole story."

Over my lobster bisque, I recounted in full detail my experience with the earnest Dr. Ernest. Max gave up on his clear consommé and contented himself with laughter. While no story that I have ever told in all my life has lost anything in the telling, it didn't seem to me to be quite as funny as Max thought it was.

"It was not wise to send you to a doctor who was German and not even German Jewish," he said, dabbing at his lips with his napkin.

"Huh?"

"He did not realize of course that the Irish way with death is to laugh at it, indeed to laugh obscenely. You were laughing at death, of course, to cover up your fears of mortality—which medical examinations always create—but because it is Irish to stare death in the face and laugh at her."

"Yeah?"

"But of course"—he waved his hand—"is not that the way of Irish wakes? Is that not why in the wakes in Ireland before your Church stepped in and ruined them, people made love in the fields around the house where the wake was happening? Your culture even in America says 'Fuck you, death.' No?"

"Maybe."

"Did you not tell him those outrageous stories about your sexual life to assert the Irish way of things? Why else would you have done that?"

"You guys know too much."

"A physician who was Irish or one who knows them all too

well, as I do, would have continued with the joke, knowing that it was but a harmless form of denial."

"Yeah?"

"Yes, Chuck, definitely."

I thought about it.

"I guess so," I admitted. "It sure was fun."

"Naturally . . . So now we come to the core of our little problem: what are you going to do with those thirty more years?"

"Plus or minus five."

"Naturally."

The previous winter I called Max and told him that I ought to see him occasionally to discuss my problem.

"What problem?"

"Fiftieth birthday."

"Naturally. We must have lunch."

We alternated between the Standard Club and the University Club.

"Shouldn't I be on a couch or something?" I asked at the first session.

"Naturally not. We are not trying to take your personality apart, Chuck. It would probably be impossible and in any case a mistake. No, no. We merely want to help you to discover a new direction or perhaps only a renewed direction for your life. It will be a very benign experience for you."

What the hell did I know?

"So," Max asked, "was that comment you made earnestly to Dr. Ernest about a mistress perhaps a form of wish fulfillment? Do you perhaps want a mistress?"

"I have one, Max. She also acts as my wife."

"So . . . you are never tempted?"

"I couldn't possibly be unfaithful to Rosemarie. It would break her heart. Besides, no mistress could possibly be as good a lover as she is."

"You really believe that?"

I thought about it.

"Yeah, I really believe it. We probably don't make love as often as we used to, but that's because I'm tired at night, probably from worrying about what to with the rest of my life.

However, our lovemaking is a lot more, uh, imaginative than it used to be."

I described for him in expurgated form our tryst that began in the papal apartments.

"I agree that the interlude sounds imaginative. You have become skilled at, as they say, turning her on?"

"It's mostly knowing the signs that she's ready."

"Ah . . . and she can turn you on?"

"All she has to do is open a button or a zipper and I become a ravager—or something like that."

We dug into our Wiener schnitzel. Outside the Lake was calm and turquoise under a pale blue sky. My imagination was playing with the idea of opening a button when I returned home.

"Sure, I encounter women that I'd like to take to bed. Who doesn't? But I don't and I won't. Rosemarie is too much for me as it is."

"So then you have an ideal sex life?"

"No one, Max, as you well know, has an ideal sex life. I think we're getting better at it as we both become more reckless."

I had not thought of it that way before. So now I would have to be more reckless. Maybe today. If there were signs that I could. Or, even better, signs that I should.

"Just the same," I continued after a moment's thought, "I worry about it."

"Aha!"

"What if as I grow older, the glow goes away? What if as her career progresses mine languishes? What if she grows tired of me? What if she's entering her time of full sexual maturity and I'm exiting mine? What if she wants more love than I'm capable of giving?"

"You are faithful but you fear that she is not?"

"I'm sure she is."

"But may not always be if you do not measure up to the demands of her own emotional growth?"

I had not thought about these things, yet they must have been hiding just beneath the surface of consciousness or I would not be talking about them so easily. "She's three years younger than I am," I said foolishly.

"You will have your usual chocolate ice cream?" Max said.

"It's not as good as thinking about my wife," I said. "However, for the moment, it will do."

I ordered two dishes of chocolate with hot fudge sauce.

"Naturally you have told her about our conversations."

"She knows that I have lunch with you every week. I assume that she guesses what we're talking about."

"You haven't told her, however."

"No."

"Why not?"

"She does not tell me about her conversations with your winsome little colleague Maggie Ward."

Maggie was one of the more delightful subjects for my errant fantasies.

"Ah, yes, the ingenious Dr. Ward. I would think it would be hard for a man to be her patient . . ."

"Or very rewarding."

We started in on our ice cream. His cappuccino and my iced tea were brought to the table.

"You feel competitive with your wife's career."

It was a flat statement.

"If I feel anything, it is the wish that mine was only just starting as hers is."

"You realize that the same theme runs through our conversations. Your problem is not sex, not your wife, not your health, but the conviction that your career as a photographer is over."

"And that it never was very much to begin with," I added.

"Chuck"—he sighed—"you must realize that is nonsense."

"That is very directive and judgmental, Dr. Berman."

"Naturally."

I pondered and pushed away the remnants of the chocolate ice cream, very unusual behavior for me. We always encountered this problem as our conversations wound down.

"Look, Max, I admit that by any sensible calculation I have had an extraordinarily successful career. I could rest on my laurels for the rest of my life. Maybe I'd like to do that. Maybe it would be a good thing."

"Only you don't feel like you're a success. And your Church and your country have disillusioned you. You'd put away your camera tomorrow if you could find something more challenging, only you can't and know you probably won't."

"Something like that."

Max sighed loudly. He's from Brooklyn, yet there were times in our conversations he sounded Viennese. Deliberately.

"Ya! You Catholics believe in the Holy Spirit, don't you?"

"We have to."

"Isn't there a line, in St. John I believe, about the Divine Wind blowing where He will?"

"Or She."

"Yet you are unwilling as you approach the critical day of September seventeenth to wait for the Spirit."

It was my turn to sigh loudly.

"You win!"

By which I had meant that he had won the argument. In principle I had to wait for the Holy Spirit.

On the ride down the elevator I told him about Esther Stern nee Eileen Starr.

"She is naturally rebelling against her mother, her father to some extent, but her mother especially. If your parents are secularized Jews, then Orthodoxy is a wonderfully effective form of revolt . . . You have no idea, Chuck, how utterly without religion are the truly secularized Jews. They don't keep Passover or the High Holidays."

"Her parents have a Christmas tree."

"Naturally. However, it has no religious meaning for them. Rather it is a sign of their rejection of what they took to be the yoke of Jewish law. Perhaps there was strict orthodoxy among some of her grandparents or great-grandparents."

"Is this a passing phase in her life?"

"Most young rebels return eventually to the culture in which they were raised, perhaps with some modifications, especially if there was warmth in the family life. Presumably she can find some religious meaning in a moderate form of Judaism which would not be such a harsh rebuke of her parents . . . Yet I wonder why she would seek out a goyish young man with whom to fall in love."

"Irish goy, the worst kind."

"Naturally."

We walked out into the oak-paneled lobby of the University Club.

"Perhaps," Max continued, "she is considering at some subconscious level two options—either to become Orthodox or to become Irish."

"There'll be no pressure on her to do the latter."

"Ha! When she is swept up in that family culture of yours, she will realize that if she wishes to marry your son, there is no other option, no matter what her formal affiliation might be."

"I hadn't thought about it."

"It is surely a more tolerant culture."

Max turned toward Michigan Avenue and the garage where his BMW was parked—a strange car for a man who was obsessed about German guilt for the Holocaust. His head bowed, his shoulders sloped, his thin hair disheveled by the light lake breeze, he looked like the traditional rebbe pondering the intricacies of a dictum in the Oral Torah.

I walked over to the L station at Randolph and Wabash for the ride back to Oak Park.

Are You anywhere around, Holy Spirit, Divine Wind, Paraclete, whatever? I am ready to receive Your message. I waited in a corner of the L platform just in case. There was, naturally (as Max Berman would have said) no message.

In the absence of the Holy Spirit I might as well go home and make love with my wife.

Why not?

She was in her office, windows open so the soft September breezes slipped through it. She was wearing white tennis shorts and a black Fenwick tee shirt and her reading glasses—which replaced her contact lenses when she was tired.

"Clean bill of health in body and soul," she said, not looking up from the list she was studying intently.

"Here're the test results." I diffidently offered her the two sheets of paper.

She grabbed them and read them carefully, like a mother considering a second-grade report card.

"Well, it looks like you will survive a little longer." She tossed aside the test results and returned to her list. "I'm arranging the table seating for the dinner at the Drake."

"I can think of a lot more pleasant things to do on a warm September afternoon," I said, kneeling beside her and not restraining the impulse of my fingers to slip under her tee shirt and touch her flat stomach muscles.

"Chucky! I'm working!"

Nonetheless her eyes grew round and soft as reason warred with Eros.

"That can wait."

Her back arched in anticipation.

"Not here, not right now!"

"Yes here, yes right now. It's Missus's day off, the baby is sleeping, and Moire Meg won't be home from school for a half hour."

"Regardless." She sighed as I tickled her ribs. "Should I expect this every afternoon when you come home from your session with Dr. Berman?"

"That's not a bad idea."

"You have only one thought on your mind while all the rest of us have to worry that we won't get this party right."

"The only one who could ruin the party is me, and you know I won't do that."

"I promised you an orgy after the parties are over."

"I don't want an orgy now, just a little tender affection."

"You talked about me with Dr. Berman?"

"Sure."

"What did you tell him?"

"What do you tell Maggie Ward about me?"

"That's different . . . The internist gave you a new lease on life, so you want to celebrate by loving me."

I managed to push up the tee shirt from my alma mater and lower a bra strap.

"Dr. Berman asked if I had ever wanted a mistress."

"And you said?"

"That with a wife like you I didn't need one."

"Bullshit, Chucky Ducky, but it was sweet of you to say it."

I licked her breast lavishly, then concentrated on its nipple, drawing on it like a nursing child.

She groaned.

"It's not fair, Chucky Ducky. It's not fair."

"Yes it is."

"Well, I suppose it is. I was tired of that damn list any-way . . . Oh I love you so much!"

When we were finished and lay exhausted in each other's arms on the couch in the office, she said, "You are improving at this sort of thing, Chucky Ducky. If this is what your midlife crisis does to you, it can continue as far as I'm concerned—What's that noise? Did I wake the baby up?"

"You did scream pretty loudly."

She pulled on her clothes and dashed away. I dressed more leisurely, sat at her desk, and resolved the problems about seating arrangements, just to show that I could.

She reappeared, a sleepy two-year-old redhead in her arms.

"Someone wicked entered her dreams and screamed at her. It's all right, Siobhan! See, Daddy's home."

The clever little brat grinned and extended her arms to me.

"How's Daddy's little sweetheart?" I asked her with an atro-cious lack of originality.

She cooed.

"Chookie!"

"You've been fooling with my list," my wife thundered.

"Just solving your problems."

She frowned and studied the list.

"Well, I guess you have."

"See!"

"See, Roosie!"

On the whole a good afternoon for Chucky Ducky.

I insisted after supper that we go over to Petersen's for malts, since my earnest doctor said I ought to put on weight. Our two daughters accompanied us.

"Just so you won't misbehave!" Moire Meg informed us.

❧ Rosemarie ❧
1978

Chuck behaved remarkably well during the celebrations of his birthday. I knew he would because so many of us had invested so much time and energy in our efforts to make the golden birthday a festive event. If at times his heart wasn't in it and he was worrying about what to do when he grew up, only a wife could tell. This wife saw only faint traces of angst. He did an excellent imitation of a man enjoying every second of the weekend, so excellent that maybe he really did enjoy it.

I'm afraid Esther Stern did not enjoy the noise, the jazz quartet—my three sons and young Gianni Antonelli with backup from the good April on the piano and myself and my daughter-in-law Maria Elena doing the vocals. Gianni was no longer "poor little Gianni." He was now bigger than his father and destined for the Golden Dome and Memorial Stadium.

"A little noisy, huh, Esther?" I said.

"It is all very interesting," she said cautiously. "We are generally not so loud in our celebrations."

"The Jewish weddings I've been to," I said, "are much louder. They're wonderful, dancing and singing and carrying the bride around on a chair. Our weddings are tame by comparison."

I did not add the full truth—Irish weddings are tame and too much of the drink is taken.

"I have never been to a Jewish wedding," she admitted.

"Try one. It makes this melee look quiet."

"Mrs. O'Malley," she asked softly, "you do not drink?"

"I'm a drunk, Esther," I replied candidly, perhaps too

candidly. "I haven't had a drink in, oh, twenty years."

Her reaction astonished me.

She embraced me and wept quietly.

"Please don't say that, Mrs. O'Malley," she said through her tears. "You are a good and wonderful woman. You are not a drunk."

I calmed her down and she slipped away from me. I remembered what Max Berman had told Chuck. Perhaps at some level she was choosing whether to be strict Orthodox or Irish Catholic. There had to be alternatives which were not so stark.

I didn't want another daughter. I had enough of them as it was.

"What was that all about?" Moire Meg appeared from nowhere.

"What?"

"Why was that fragile little doll crying?"

"She asked me why I didn't drink."

"None of her business . . . I suppose you gave her your standard answer?"

I admitted that I had.

"Not cool, Rosie. Not cool at all."

"I guess not."

"I wonder what her mother's like."

So saying, my all too perceptive middle daughter drifted away.

The good April embraced me for the third time.

"I think poor Chuck is enjoying himself," she said, as though she needed reassurance.

"Your son is too much the gentleman even to hint that he wasn't."

I had never thought of Chuck as a gentleman. Shame on me.

April Mae Cronin O'Malley had been my surrogate mother for most of my life. If God gave me the challenge of playing that role for someone else, I'd better do a good job at it.

"It would appear, thoughtful wife"—Chuck embraced me—"that we're expected to sing."

So we went through our act, doing all the old Chuck/Rosie duets and ending, of course, with that old clunker "Rosemarie," which we hammed up outrageously, though my husband's kiss at the end was altogether too passionate.

Well, it really wasn't but you have to say something like that.

Out of the corner of my eye I saw poor little Eileen/Esther, leaning against my Seano's strong arm, smiling happily.

She doesn't have to become Catholic, I said to God. After all she's a relative of Yours. She can become one of us and still be Jewish.

Then it came time for the speeches. Or speech—by a vote of four to one, the monster regiment of women voted that the only speaker would be Chuck. I deputed myself to be the mistress of ceremonies.

"The steering committee for this joyous event," I began, "voted four to one against limiting the speeches to one. I was the one who voted for the limitation so, since I'm the boss, there'll be only one speech."

Applause.

"The Birthday King will give that speech."

Boos.

"I am the mistress of ceremonies. My remarks will be brief."

Applause.

"They will last only a half an hour."

Boos, cat calls, imprecations.

"Actually, I will sing my intro."

(She sings "I've Got You Under My Skin.")

"In conclusion, I want to insist that I am one of the most fortunate women in the world. Gentle Souls, the Birthday King."

Tumultuous applause.

(My husband waits patiently for the silence.)

"As you all know, I had no choice about marrying Rosemarie. My mother and my sister Peg made up their minds to that before I reached the age of reason—at which I may have arrived by the time of my fifteenth birthday. I must say that they made a very good choice. I would have never dared to pursue such a lovely, intelligent, and witty young woman on my own. They pushed me into it and I'm glad they did.

"Usually."

More laughter and applause.

"So much of what I am today must be attributed to the

various women in my family from the good April all the way down to my daughter Siobhan Marie."

Loud cheers.

He lifted the little brat into the air.

Applause for her. She waved like the reigning monarch she was.

The whole performance was vintage Chucky. We used to joke that he had a fast mind and a faster tongue. In fact, he was rarely at a loss for words, even, when the occasion required them, elegant and graceful words. I never saw him write anything out beforehand (as I had written and then memorized my introduction). I suspect that he prepared very carefully and then pretended to spontaneity. Yet it was possible that he was one of the great ad libbers in all the world.

"I must thank all of these valiant women for my sartorial splendor tonight. I am a symphony in color-coordinated gray as befits a man whose systematic graying we are gathered here to celebrate. I warn you that this is the last time that you will see me in this outfit that I won't look like a slob. Something happens to a nice gray suit when I wear it for the second time. It adjusts itself, I suspect, to my own slobbery and thus defeats the efforts of the women in my life to make me look chic. However, I want to go on record as thanking them for their concern, as ineffective as it may be.

"My remarks tonight will be confined to my immediate family who are responsible for this gala if somewhat noisy event and indeed responsible for me.

"First of all, I must thank the good April Mae Cronin and her steadfast consort Vangie O'Malley for keeping the flapper era alive and flourishing not only when I was growing up but even unto this day. The Jazz Age is alive and well at least in this corner of Oak Park.

"I must also thank them not merely for bringing me into the world but even more for their courage in bringing me home from Oak Park Hospital. They must have had strong doubts about the wizened little redhead with the pinched face and the loud mouth, doubts which certainly have not diminished through the years. Chuck from day one spelled trouble, a contentious dissident, a white sheep in a family of black sheep, a soberside in a family which then and now and not without reason, are called the Crazy O'Malleys. My youngest son's date, the good Eileen, has been looking on in astonishment at this show. I have to say to you, kid, if you are looking for sanity in this clan, I'm the only one in whom you will find it."

General and deserved laughter. Chuck was the craziest of all of us, by far. Esther flushed happily and smiled broadly.

Count on Chuck to use her Irish name.

"Moreover, I must thank the women siblings who have bracketed me—Jane, who decided early on that I was a troublesome but funny runt who should be a source of constant impatient amusement, and Peg, who loved me so much that she was determined that I would amount to something. I don't know whether I have or not—the verdict isn't in yet—but it was not, Margaret Mary, for the lack of your effort and that of your constant ally about whom more later.

"Edward taught me what idealism really means and loyal and faithful service to a Church about which we all are ambivalent but which we cannot forsake. He dragged me kicking and screaming into the St. Crispin's Day of our generation at Selma, Alabama, and has more by example than by word kept the tiny flame of idealism somewhere in the subbasement of my soul from flickering out.

"I have learned more from my children than they have taught me, from April Rosemary courage and maturity beyond her years, from Kevin an unshakable sense of personal identity, from Jimmy an idealism which matches that of his uncle, from Sean the importance of laughter, from Moire Meg, for a long time our baby, wisdom and grace not only beyond her years but beyond the years of her mother and father put together, and finally from our new youngest, the redoubtable Siobhan Marie, the joy of having a child around the house. Since there is little reason to think that I deserve such an array of talent, beauty, and goodness around me, full credit must be given to their mother, who will claim it anyway.

"Academic authors like myself have the custom of saying that all the good things in their books are the result of the efforts of a long list of colleagues and the mistakes must be attributed to the author. I would ask you to accept the same judgment about me as I ease with some reluctance into my second half century—credit for that which may be admirable must belong to others and blame for that which is perhaps a little less admirable must be attributed to the skinny and wailing little red-haired organism that the flapper and her husband brought home from Oak Park Hospital.

"I return finally to the mistress of ceremonies as she suggestively styles herself. Rosemarie, my love, you have dragged me, often kicking and screaming, into a happy and productive life, one filled with joy that has spoiled me rotten. I serve notice that I expect exactly the same high-quality TLC in the next half century."

Then he began to sing "Night and Day."

Tears streaming down my face, I joined him in the chorus.

There was much hugging and kissing from the crowd.

I had been sure he'd do well. Yet I feared that he might become philosophical about life and death, youth and aging, success and failure, and all that stuff which was making him miserable these days.

Typical of my husband, he had made such a powerful case for joy that he actually experienced a good deal of it, despite himself.

Later in the shower as we gently caressed one another, I realized what a frail-seeming little punk he was—skin and bones and sex organs. I began to cry again.

"What's the matter?" he asked softly.

"You were very gallant tonight."

"Gallantry doesn't draw me into the shower with you, only hormonal drives."

"Silly! I meant you salvaged the party for the rest of us."

"I'm staring into the fog," he replied, kissing my breast, "waiting for the Divine Wind to disperse it. Until that happens we celebrate."

"What Divine Wind?"

"That's what Max Berman calls the Holy Spirit. Blows wherever She wants. Whenever She wants. Can't force Her hand."

"John three," I said. "Don't stop kissing me."

"I wasn't planning to . . . What's John three?"

"John's Gospel, third chapter. Where Nicodemus comes to

see Jesus and Jesus talks about the Spirit who blows where He wills."

"Really? I never heard that."

"It used to be in the Gospels at Sunday Mass every year, now it's there every third year. You don't listen to the Gospels!"

"Too busy fantasizing about women!"

"Shame on you . . . Chuck, we can't keep this shower up forever."

"Why not?"

"Because I can't think straight anymore."

"I like you that way."

By the time we turned to the matter at hand I was a blubbering idiot. I like myself that way.

As far as orgies go, it was very sweet.

"You notice Esther at the party?" I asked him as we clung to each other afterward, too spent to move into bed.

"That's her name. I blanked on it and called her Eileen."

"Sure you blanked on it!"

"She didn't seem to mind . . . She spent a lot of time talking to Moire Meg. What was the point of that, Rosemarie?"

"Moire Meg was sizing her up."

"That's pretty ruthless."

"Our penultimate child, Chucky Ducky, can be very ruthless when the welfare of someone she loves is at stake. That goes along with the wisdom and grace you attributed to her tonight."

"It did seem that they liked one another."

I didn't want to wake up the next morning.

"I'm going to sleep all day. I was battered and abused last night."

"You have a party this evening," he insisted, the very triumphant male the day after he had pleasured the woman beyond her rational control.

"I won't go to it." I buried my head in a pillow, secretly proud of myself.

"The promised orgy is only half over. Remember we have a suite reserved for ourselves at the Drake. Your idea."

His laugh was obnoxious. He had conquered me completely. Male warrior with the captured matron.

"Stop it, Chucky, I have to shower and get ready for all the nonsense."

"We can take one together."

"I know what that will lead to. The answer is no."

Somehow we were huddling again.

"Well," I said as I struggled out of bed, "I guess I won't forget last night for a while."

"Tonight will be even more unforgettable."

As the hot waters of the shower ordered my skin to wake up so I could get to work I understood that the night would indeed be even more memorable.

We should have a birthday party every month.

And we had asserted the triumph of life and love over death.

It was Peg's turn to do the introduction in the Grand Ballroom of the Drake. The Mayor was there and the Governor and the president of The University and a very elderly Msgr. Mugsy who asked the blessing before the meal.

Peg, trim and slender as always, brought her violin to the podium.

"My foster sister and sister-in-law sang her introduction. I'm going to play mine on my fiddle as my brother has always called it. The first part of the introduction is a capricious rondo by that fellow Mozart, which captures the vividness of my brother's personality, a vividness which has always guaranteed that there will never be a dull moment in our family. The second is a tune from our youth which looks brightly to the future."

The Mozart piece was pure Chucky—silly, wacky bravado. Like last night in bed.

The second piece was "Begin the Beguine," which in Peg's rendition was a shining story of hope surging to a hard-fought victory over melancholy.

"I thank you, Margaret Mary," Chuck began, "for the highly optimistic suggestion that I could dance the Beguine or anything else. When I hear you play it, however, I think I might like to try."

He was on another roll.

"I am wearing my economist's hat tonight," he continued. "I want to make an announcement of considerable importance.

Anyone who wants to leave the room and call the media should feel free to do so.

"The announcement is that I am now convinced that the Great Depression is over."

Applause from the audience.

"I realize that I am the last economist with a degree from The University to accept this phenomenon. However, I take my decision to mean that you can bank on it, you should excuse the expression, the prosperity of the postwar years is real.

"Every once in a while the media, having nothing better to do with their time, announce that some economic blip is a warning that Depression might be lurking if not just around the corner at least down the block. I will say to folks like the Mayor's good friend Walter Cronkite, folks, you weren't there! When unemployment rises to twenty-five percent, then you can start talking about Depression! Till then, go away and do something useful with your lives.

"I was a Depression baby. My parents were not. They faced up to economic horror with the confident, if totally unjustified, expectation, that someday their ship would come in. Clear-thinking realist that I was and am, I saw through this mythology. Their ship would never come in.

"Only when I returned from my hapless military service in Bamberg, I discovered that the vessel had indeed plowed at very high speed into port. Again, with the clarity of insight which has marked my whole half century of life, I insisted that it would soon weigh anchor and depart. It never did. I am now prepared to admit that I was wrong.

"Don't expect any further such admissions in the remaining years of my life!

"More seriously, I want to spend a few minutes tracing the impact on all our lives of the flotilla of ships which were crowding our ports in the late nineteen forties. Those years are, I think it safe to say, the axial era of this century, a time when everyone's hopes expanded exponentially—with the tragic exception of some of the nonwhite peoples in our society. We now take prosperity for granted, with, as I now ruefully admit, good reason.

"I didn't want to give up the Great Depression and still

don't. My good wife Rosemarie—who now follows me around with a notebook jotting down quotes to put on the lips of an utterly fictional character she has created out of her vivid imagination—does not trust me to make hotel reservations when we travel for fear I will put us in a cheap fleabag to save money. So she has reserved to herself, much the way the Pope used to reserve forgiveness for certain sins to himself, the making of such decisions. Driven by good sense and good taste, she always puts us in an acceptable place. Similarly, I leave to her, mostly in the name of making a virtue out of necessity, all financial decisions about the furnishing and decoration of our home, which is apparently an ongoing project.

"I say to you today, good wife, that you can continue to exercise power in these areas of our common life. I do promise, however, that I will no longer feel guilty about the comfort and convenience you choose.

"Well, not too guilty!

"My children roll their eyes when I talk about the Great Depression. They view it as a myth not unlike the biblical flood and of about the same era. They also refuse to believe that there was ever a time when TV did not exist or when the Mayor's good friend Walter Cronkite did not pompously pontificate on it.

"Some of them firmly believe that the Civil War was carried on television!

"What can I tell you!

"Each generation has its experiences which it believes are unique. My own children lived through the Vietnam era which was critical for them. The point tonight is not that my experiences are better or worse than that of earlier and later generations, only that they are different.

"Moreover, and this is the center of it all, I have thought for most of my life that my formative experiences were in the Great Depression and the war of my childhood. Now I have come to realize that far more important in my life were the surprises of the postwar world, surprises beyond the expectation of any of my generation. It's not merely that the reality of my life has been beyond my wildest dreams when I was a kid. Rather they are in a world which I knew then could not possibly exist. In the Kingdom of God's love there are always surprises. The ships did come in and they did stay, there was a revolution of expanding expectations. We Irish Catholics had demanded MORE for years and, Mr. Mayor, more was finally there and we took it. In the midst of the surprises, Chucky O'Malley took his camera in hand and ventured forth into the world to record all the surprises. I hope someday that someone will accord me a variation of praise that Walter de la Mare offered to G. K. Chesterton: he lived in an age of miracles and dared to take pictures of them.

"I can't believe all the surprises really happened. I can't believe that this beautiful, talented, and challenging woman is my wife, that this swarm of handsome and gifted young people are my children and grandchildren, I can't believe that Edward and Jane are my siblings and that Peg, in conspiracy with my wife, is still trying desperately to make something out of me. I can't believe that I have flapper era parents. I can't believe that so many people want to look at what the good April has always called 'Little Chucky's cute pictures.' Miracles, miracles everywhere. I don't deserve any of them, but I'll enthusiastically embrace all of them. And in gratitude to God I will try to continue to take cute little pictures of them."

Oh my! Peg and I both rushed to the podium. She struck up "Begin the Beguine" and Chuck and I joined her in a duet. Then the jazz group, which had been hiding its instruments, joined in.

Happy pandemonium.

The Crazy O'Malleys indeed. My darling Chucky was the craziest of them all.

The orgy that night was pretty crazy too. And pretty wonderful.

❧ Chuck ❧
1978

After the birthday parties, I settled down to work on my exhibition *People: One Hundred Portraits by Charles C. O'Malley*. My heart was not in the work. None of my shots seemed good enough to exhibit. None of my problems had been solved. I was still flailing around. I had gone through a good act at the time of my birthday, so good that it had almost persuaded me. Nothing, however, had changed.

"The Divine Wind blew by the parties," I said to Max Berman, "but She didn't drop in."

"In the Kingdom of God's love there are always surprises. Strong words, Chuck. You are saying you don't believe them."

"I guess I think the surprises are over for me."

"Ah, that makes God fairly selective, doesn't it?"

"I said all those crazy things at the party because in my head I believe them and my family wants me to believe. In my heart, or wherever the emotions are . . ."

"The unconscious, perhaps."

"Whatever . . . I'm not sure about them at all."

"Or about God?"

"Why should God bother about me?"

"Why should Rosemarie bother about you?"

"Fair point," I admitted grudgingly.

"Do you want some medication?" he asked abruptly.

"WHAT!"

"Perhaps some mild antidepressants . . ."

"Are you recommending them?"

"Naturally not."

"You think I am depressed?"

"You report that you fall asleep easily at night and then wake and cannot go back to sleep?"

"Not all the time."

"But often?"

"Yeah, I guess so."

"That is a sign of mild depression."

"Charles Cronin O'Malley depressed. Who would believe it?" I asked sadly.

"Very few people because you are such a superb actor."

Now I was really scared.

"For the moment I'd rather not rely on medication."

"I quite agree."

I never like the food at the Standard Club much. That day it tasted like lined yellow paper.

The always troubling Moire Meg reported to us at supper that night that we ought not to worry about Sean and Esther sleeping together.

"Not that I think you two are worrying about it," she added. "Esther's brand of Judaism says that a woman waits till her wedding night to give herself clean and pure to the husband."

"You sound skeptical, hon," my wife said.

"Not about chastity, but about the idea that it's a virtue only for the woman . . . She also says that she believes a man and a woman should have as many children as possible to hasten the coming of the Messiah."

"Oh, my," Rosemarie said.

"Yeah, well, we used to believe that too, didn't we? It doesn't consider the decline of infant mortality rates . . . She shocks her parents and her Jewish friends with that idea."

"Or the poor thing's health. A half dozen or a dozen pregnancies would kill her."

"Half dozen didn't kill you," she said with her patented wicked grin.

"I'm different."

"You sure are!"

"You think, Moire Meg," I asked, "that they'll marry?"

"I wouldn't bet on it. My poor brother has made up his mind. I don't think she has."

"What should we do?"

Our middle daughter frowned.

"When was I named the Ann Landers of the family? Just because Chucky says I'm a wisewoman, doesn't mean I am. Anyway, wisewomen were witches and they burned them at the stake."

"You didn't answer your father's question, hon."

"You both know the answer. You shouldn't do anything. If poor Seano wants to talk about it, you listen to him but don't argue. He'd want you to argue because that would confirm his determination. Boys are like that."

"Not girls?"

"Chisel it on stone, Chucky. This girl kid would never marry anyone unless you and Rosie were enthusiastic about him. I'll write it out in contract form and sign it for you."

"That would be sweet, hon, but it's not necessary."

"Rosie, you sound more like the good April every day. But it is too necessary, at least for me."

Well, that settled that.

On the last Thursday in September, we attended the wedding of Leo Kelly and Jane Devlin at the parish church. Msgr. Packy presided. The marvel was not that these two classmates of mine should marry. In 1948 it seemed like a sure bet, a much safer wager than one on a lifelong relationship between me and my present wife (and only wife). It took Leo and Jane thirty years to overcome the problems of war, death, suffering, confusion, and anger.

"A shame that they had to wait so long," Rosemarie commented after Mass. "They looked beautiful, didn't they?"

"Like two people who could hardly wait to get to bed."

"Chucky!"

"Well it's true."

"I'm sure they've been together for a couple of weeks, since whatever happened this summer at the Lake. I don't think they would have taken the risk of marriage unless they were dizzy over one another."

"It's different when it's official," I replied, as though I had reason to know, which of course I didn't. "You know that no one will take the woman away from you again, so you're free to enjoy her without any worry."

"CHUCKY!"

"And vice versa."

"Well, Leo did look very pleased with himself."

"He should. She'll be great in bed."

"How like a man to look at it that way," she sniffed.

"Only honest. Everyone in the church at a wedding knows that before the day is over the bride and groom will be fucking. We cover it up because we're embarrassed."

While I believed in the truth of what I was saying and while my imagination permitted itself brief images of the lovely Jane spread-eagled in the advanced stages of pleasure, I was playing the usual banter game in which Rosemarie and I indulged.

"Well," she sniffed in reply, "that's what they should be doing unless the groom has had too much champagne."

A vicious and unfair slash of the knife.

"Touché," I admitted.

The groom was now the provost of The University and the bride a high-quality travel agent. Both worlds were represented at the wedding, to say nothing of the neighborhood. My wife and I kind of belong to both the neighborhood and The University, but actually to neither.

"I thought Msgr. Packy was wonderful," Rosemarie said, as we waited in the reception line at Butterfield.

"Good loser."

"He loved her," Rosemarie agreed, "but he would never have left the priesthood for her."

"You're right. Still it's hard."

"Life is hard, Chucky Ducky."

In my foolish brain I wondered whether I would be better off with a brand-new wife to occupy my attention till my midlife crisis—or whatever—had disappeared. Then I realized that a brand-new wife would never put up with me as patiently as Rosemarie did. Or love me so much.

We hugged the bride and groom. They thanked us for bringing them together again, giving us more credit than a couple of phone calls merited.

They both looked proud of themselves, as they should have.

"Don't let her get away this time, Leo."

They both blushed.

"No danger of that, Chuck. I think for us 'better late than never' should possibly be just 'better late.' "

"Well," my wife said with some satisfaction as we found our table, "all's well that ends well."

That night in bed, she added another comment.

"We don't see many brides and grooms whose passion is as intense and focused as theirs, do we, Chucky?"

"Uhm . . ."

"The kids, even our own, are hungry for sexual release but they don't understand, can't understand the terrible binding power of love the way those two do. That's the way of it when the lovers are older. Sometimes anyway. Forest fire stuff. Only gets stronger."

"Uhm . . ."

"You agree?"

"Uhm-hum . . . I had another thought too. I said to myself that if you had a new wife like Leo does you might be able to break out of your midlife crisis or whatever the hell it is. She'd take your mind off it."

"You'd drive a new wife out of her mind."

"I thought that too. Then I realized that no new wife would love me as much as you do."

There was a pause while she digested this comment.

"That's very sweet, Chucky."

She turned on the light, grabbed for her reading glasses and the notebook which was always on the nightstand, and scribbled in it. Then she glanced over what she had written, nodded in approval, put the book back on the nightstand, and turned off the light.

"More dialogue for the punk."

"Maybe. I'll ruin him if he's too sweet all the time."

"I try to do my part."

Forest fire stuff. How do you sustain that when you're over fifty?

The following Friday about 4 A.M. the phone rang.

"I know it's early morning there, Carlo. This is Rae Adolfo. I thought you ought to know, the Pope is dead. I just offered Mass for him on Vatican Radio. He died in his sleep early in the morning."

I struggled in the darkness for understanding.

"The Pope died in August," I sputtered.

"The new Pope, Carlo, John Paul. He is dead."

"Really?"

This was all a tasteless dream.

"I'm afraid so."

"What happened?"

"The nun who brought him his coffee in the morning found him dead in bed. Some kind of stroke apparently."

"They will be saying he was killed."

"They're saying it already."

"We'll be right over."

I sat on the edge of the bed and tried to wrench myself out of a deep sleep. Had I really talked to Adolfo? Was our smiling Pope really dead? I shook my head in an effort to clear it. It couldn't be true. It was only a nightmare.

Rosemarie stirred on the bed.

"Who was on the phone, Chucky?"

"You heard it?"

"Certainly I heard it . . . One of your girlfriends?"

"Rae Adolfo. He says the Pope is dead."

"He died in August, Chuck."

"That's what I said. He meant the new Pope—John Paul."

"Oh my God, Chuck! Our smiling Pope!"

She threw her arms around me and sobbed.

"We have to go over for the wake," she said, an Irishwoman's immemorial cry.

Of course we had to go to the wake.

We flew out of O'Hare to Rome on Alitalia later in the day, first-class because Rosemarie made the reservations. Siobhan Marie was not happy about being translated to Gram's house again.

"Why do you have to go away?"

"Remember that nice man whose picture Daddy took when we were in Rome?'

"The Pop?"

"The Pope. He died, Siobhan Marie, and we have to go over there to pray for him."

"I'll pray for him too."

"Next time," she said to me, "we have to take that one with us."

I was too tired to argue. I dreaded the jet lag and the dreariness of Rome.

As soon as the plane took off, my wife kissed me good night.

"See you in Rome, Chucky."

She kicked off her shoes, pushed the recliner back, fluffed up a pillow, covered herself with a blanket and promptly went to sleep.

You can't beat willpower.

I tossed and turned, fretted and stewed, and woke up every time we hit a bump. I gave up and ate the spicy supper for which I knew I would later pay. A couple of lifetimes later the plane picked its way through clouds and rain and landed at Fiumicino.

Rosemarie opened her eyes.

"Are we there yet, Daddy? . . . Where's the bathroom?"

She had to wait until we got inside the terminal. Despite her long nap, she was not in a pleasant mood.

"Tell me again, Chucky, why are we here?"

"We have to go to a wake."

"I hate wakes."

"So do I."

"Why did you make me come?"

I would have lost my temper if I had not seen the corner of her lip turn up in a grin.

"We both knew we had to come."

"Why do the good ones always die, Chuck?"

"Darned if I know."

We found our elderly limo driver and directed him to take us to San Pietro.

"They killed him!" he shouted. "He was a good man, a saint. He would have remade the Church. They could not permit that. So they poisoned him. Everyone knows it is true, but no one will punish them."

"Who are they?" I asked.

"The priests *pro certo*. Who else? It is all about money. They don't want to lose their money."

It was true enough that many of the Italian clergy, impoverished and with heavy demands from their families, grasped for money in a way that would offend Americans. It was also true that the finances of the Vatican were rumored to be highly irregular, like those of Cardinal O'Neill in Chicago. Yet I could not see the priests of the countryside conspiring against one of their own. That some powers in the Curia might be happy to be rid of this unpredictable new Pope, I didn't doubt. However, they were not the kind of men who would kill a Pope.

Were they?

The rain fell in heavy sheets, the traffic from Fiumicino to the city was bumper to bumper. My stomach was already preparing for a violent protest.

Finally, after noon, Roman time, we arrived at St. Peter's. The rain continued. A dark and unruly crowd milled around outside the Basilica. Apparently the authorities had blocked entrance to the wake. We were blocked by black-clad carabinieri at the head of the street. I realized that the Press Office was only a few yards away.

"Rosemarie," I said, "I'm going to duck into the Sala Stampa to be sick. Wait for me here."

"Poor Chucky." She touched my hand. "I'll come with you."

"I'd sooner be alone," I said with a martyr's air.

"Don't vomit all over S'ter."

"What a wonderful idea!"

I strode into the Press Office like I belonged there. That's one of the secrets of Rome and the Vatican. If you're wearing a trench coat and act like you belong, no one will stop you. Alas, I could not find S'ter.

It took some time for my stomach to be sure that it had rid itself of my dinner. Unsteady on my feet, I stumbled out of the men's room and right into Msgr. Adolfo, whose harried face and rumpled clothes indicated that his usual polished veneer had fallen apart.

"Carlo! You are here so soon! You look terrible! Where is Rosemarie?"

"The Alitalia supper was too much for my digestive process," I said. "Rosemarie is outside in our limo. What's happening?"

He shrugged expressively.

"Everything has gone wrong, Carlo. The Pope is dead. We have lied about it, patently lied. Cardinal Villot, the *camarlingo*, forbade an autopsy. You may not, he said, subject the sacred body of the Pope to such indignities. The Italian media are saying that there is a conspiracy. So now, after the embalming, we are doing a secret autopsy in San Pietro itself. Only we deny it. Again everyone knows we are lying . . . Is your car in front? Come, we will get it and go around to the courtyard so that you may enter the wake as soon as they are finished with their ghoulish work."

"Thank you for coming, Rosemarie," he said gallantly to my wife. "One needs to see someone with great sense at a time like this."

"In all probability," he went on, "Papa Luciani died of a pulmonary embolism, perhaps in the bathroom. He had one before up in Venice. He has had circulatory problems for a long time. He takes, excuse me, he took a medicine called raffin for his circulation. It is very dangerous medicine which can also serve as a rat poison. It must be taken regularly and under a physician's care. He took it irregularly and there was no physician to supervise him."

"Why not?" I said, still not certain about whether I might need to run somewhere to be sick once again.

"For many years to come, Carlo, there will be conspiracy theories about which faction in the Curia wanted to kill him. You know enough about the Vatican to realize that for all its deviousness the present Curia is incapable of organizing an effective conspiracy. Our poor smiling Pope died of medical incompetence, an explanation which fits the Vatican perfectly. Unfortunately, it is easier in this place to believe in conspiracy than in incompetence."

"I thought the health office was right down the corridor from his apartment. Why weren't they supervising his health?"

"Papa Luciani's physicians up in Venezia would not send down his medical records until the Vatican asked for them. The Pope's doctors here would not ask for the records because that would be beneath their dignity. So they fought back and forth while the poor man died . . . I do not know. His health was not good. He might have died anyway. Yet if there were doctors who were watching him, he might have survived. We will never know."

"That's terrible," my wife exclaimed.

Our car had slowly eased its way to the entrance of the

Belvedere Courtyard. Two dripping Swiss Guards crossed their pikes to stop us. Then they recognized Msgr. Adolfo, snapped to attention, saluted us, of course, and permitted us into the courtyard.

The driver murmured an expression of awe.

"We stay here for a few moments, I think. I will tell you what seems to have happened. Last week, it is said, he felt pains in his chest. He forbade his secretaries to mention the pains to anyone. When they found him dead, late in the evening perhaps, they became fearful that they would be blamed. So they put him to bed, or perhaps back to bed. Sister Vincenza left the morning cup of coffee at the door. When she came back later it was still there. She knocked at the door. He did not answer; she pushed it slightly ajar and peeked in. Then she screamed. They called Cardinal Villot, the *camarlingo*, and of course he came immediately. They also summoned the doctors, who came reluctantly as you might imagine. They pronounced the Pope dead. He told the Sala Stampa to announce the death and say that the Pope had been reading the *Imitation of Christ* when he died. Everyone knew that was false. The lies have continued ever since, all for the good of the Church, you understand."

"Of course," Rosemarie agreed.

Every time I travel with her I must for some reason rediscover that she is immune to most of the infirmities involved in traveling seven miles high in an aluminum tube. She is unaffected by jet lag, motion sickness, dehydration, claustrophobia, or any of the other ailments from which we mere mortals suffer. She was now wide awake and eager to hear the whole story. I merely wanted to find a bed—anywhere but preferably in our suite at the Hassler—and sleep. Rosemarie, however, firmly believed that you ought to stay awake until the local time said you should be in bed.

Perhaps I could fake collapse. Come to think of it, that might be easy.

"What was he working on?" she demanded.

From the seat in front of us, Rae Adolfo's quick brown eyes examined both our faces.

"There is no reason not to tell you. The Chicago papers. He

had made up his mind to replace Cardinal O'Neill on Monday—and he wanted to review them one last time."

All three of us were silent. There was no point in trying to understand God's plans.

"You are not the only one who knows this story, are you, Msgr. Adolfo?"

"No, many of us know it. We will not tell the story now. It would not do any good. The conspiracy theories are too popular. Someday perhaps . . . Ah, I see that we may now enter the Aula of San Pietro."

We trudged through many corridors of the Vatican complex, elaborate soulless marble rooms in which the Divine Wind would not be welcome. Dumb place to run a Church which was supposed to specialize in good news and big surprises.

Then we passed through a covered passage and entered St. Peter's, a great big baroque monstrosity that had cost us Germany. Why did we need a place like this?

Up in the front, almost tiny beneath the vast gilt baldachino and in front of the massive marble altar, lay a simple catafalque on which rested the small body of our smiling Pope. The sickening smell of embalming chemicals and the hospital room lingered about him. Without his smile and his quick gestures, it was impossible to recognize him. Like most everything else in the Vatican the undertakers were not very good.

A few figures stood around the dead Pope—priests and a couple of laymen in formal clothes, papal nobility doubtless. Rosemarie was the only woman in the place, and herself in black slacks and a black blouse. Oblivious to all the others, she fell on her knees and prayed. I don't think they even noticed her, or the red-haired retainer who knelt next to her. Nor did they pay any attention to Adolfo, who apparently had enough clout that he could wander around Vatican City unnoticed.

"Take a picture, Chucky," she reminded me. "You're a photographer, remember?"

"Picture taker."

I removed my Nikon from my raincoat pocket.

"Available light?" Rosemarie asked.

"Certo," I said.

"There's not much of it."

"There's enough. He's not going to move, poor dear man."

"You might."

"No way. I have steady hands."

"I've noticed."

It was neither the time nor the place for a faintly erotic comment.

Adolfo watched silently as I finished a roll. Grisly pictures.

"Very steady hands," he said.

"This is all right?" I said, as I slipped the camera back into my pocket before the silent dignitaries noticed.

"They won't let the people who are about to come in take pictures but they will anyway. It is important to have a good record."

"We can distribute it?" Rosemarie asked.

"I would not have permitted Carlo to take the pictures unless I intended that. The world should know what death did to the smiling Pope of September."

"Death and bad embalming," I muttered.

"The September Pope is with God, Chuck," my wife reminded me.

Back in the car, Rosemarie, her lips tight and her face pale, said to me, "It's not like an Irish wake, Chucky."

"No it is not, *cara*. The Irish, being a hopeful people, laugh at death. We Italians, being a pessimistic people, rage at it. There have been terrible outcries in the Aula before. There will also be others before the day is over and during the funeral."

"Can I ask you a question, Rae?" I said, trying to make sure the right words came out of my dry mouth, which still tasted of vomit.

"Certainly, Carlo."

"What do you know?"

"Scusi?"

"You have tremendous clout around this place. You wander in right after the autopsy with two *stranieri*, one a beautiful woman. The creeps standing around the Pope's body don't notice you or us. How come? You either know someone or something that makes them afraid of you, so that you're invisible to them."

"Maybe it is the magic potion as in H. G. Wells, no?"

"Maybe."

"I'm afraid it is a trade secret, Carlo. However, it suits many people to permit me my invisibility. They feel that I play an important role, though they're not always sure what it is. So?"

"So," I said, feeling that I understood.

There were people in Mayor Daley's City Hall, only a few, who enjoyed the same invisibility. My brother-in-law Vince Antonelli had been one of them, even when he no longer formally worked for the Mayor. When the Mayor died, he withdrew from the game.

"You will have that role, no matter who the next Pope is?"

He laughed lightly.

"*Certo*. Everyone needs an invisible man or two. I make few demands. I keep important people well informed."

"Already," Rosemarie said, "some important cardinals have asked you what really happened?"

"Perhaps."

"And you have told them enough to satisfy them but not everything?"

"Perhaps."

"Why bother with us?"

"Because, *cara*, your husband is one of the most important people in the Catholic world, even if he doesn't realize it, no?"

"Yes," she agreed.

I was still too sick to wonder what that meant.

The car slipped out of the gate which separated Vatican City from the Republic of Italy. The salute of the Swiss Guard as we exited guaranteed us a wave through the traffic from the Italian cops.

Why did we need Swiss Guards? Why did we need Vatican City?

Did the Founder approve of all this stuff that accrued through the centuries? I rather doubted it. No one, however, had asked him.

I heard Rae and my wife agree that he would join us for supper at eight-thirty in the dining room of the Hassler. I knew that I would never eat again, especially not Italian food, so I didn't care.

I would not have found our suite without Rosemarie's hand on my arm. I was a wreck, a battered old man who probably needed Librium or something of the sort. Now I needed only sleep.

"You go right to bed, Chucky, and get a good sleep. I'll see that these pictures are developed and send them out to somebody. Reuters maybe so they'll go worldwide."

"We'll be like that someday, Rosemarie, like our September Pope."

"And we'll be with God too, darling. Now go to bed and sleep just as long as you want."

I managed to take off my clothes and collapse. The beds in the Hassler were very comfortable indeed.

One question tugged at the far edge of my consciousness. Why did our invisible Monsignor want those pictures to go 'round the world?

Several centuries later I awakened to the sound of rain and wind beating against the window and the sight of my wife in black lingerie applying her makeup. Normally that would be a sight which would ignite at least mild sexual desire. Now there were no such movements of the flesh. Indeed, I felt that such movements would probably never return.

"Are you awake, Chuck?" she asked as she inspected her face in the mirror.

"No," I said firmly.

"Here's the picture I sold to Reuters. It's on its way around the world. They're calling it *A Smile Extinguished*."

"Gross," I murmured.

"I don't think so . . . Here, look at it."

So I looked at it.

"Not bad for available light."

"It catches all the tragedy of this death."

"Uhm . . ."

"I called home. Dad and the good April have moved into our house to take care of Moire Meg and Missus as well as your youngest."

"Can't run the risk of Moire Meg convening her own party."

"And the next Pope will be a Hindu . . . Your youngest told me she was praying for the poor dear Pop and for us too and Gram and Gramps were taking good care of her. Which means they're spoiling her rotten."

I rolled over and buried my head in a pillow.

"April Rosemary called. She wants me to come home."

"Ugh," I muttered in disapproval.

"She hasn't been taking her medication. She and Jamie had a big argument. She told him that she was addicted once and doesn't want to become addicted again. He said that she was stupid. She said that she would work her way out of her depression without any medication. He said that was most unlikely. Now he insists that she swallow the pills while he's watching. She says she wants to leave him."

"How long?"

"How long hasn't she been taking the pills? Almost from the beginning. Her OB doctor, a woman, by the way, is furious too."

I burrowed deeper into my pillow.

"You're going home?"

"Certainly not," she said, surprised that I would ask such a foolish question. "I told her that it was time to grow up. Tough language, but she needed to hear that from me more than she needed my presence."

I did not want to cope with family, Church, world, life, God, or even my wife in black lingerie.

"Go 'way," I said.

"Chucky, darling, you've had enough sleep. Time now for your shower. Msgr. Adolfo will be here in a half hour for dinner."

"I don't want any dinner," I insisted.

"That's what you say now. In a few minutes you'll be so hungry you'll want me to call room service for a hamburger."

Two hamburgers . . .

"Do you think your friend Peg's husband is one of Mayor Daley's invisible men?"

"*Certo*," she said, chuckling. "Pretty big guy to be invisible, isn't he?"

I struggled out of bed and stumbled toward the bathroom. I closed the door and turned on the shower. Then I opened the door.

"Rosemarie, you look absolutely gorgeous in black lace!"

She glanced at me, her face covered with an appealing flush.

"Ah, you are coming alive, Chuck my love."

"Not for years, maybe not ever."

"The real *boffi* in the Curia," Adolfo said over our aperitifs—Cinzano for him, Cokes for us—"are trying to tell the world that the Pope died because the papacy was too big a job for him. Therefore, the next Pope should be a man of the Curia who understands what must be done."

"Who do they have in mind?" I asked.

"Cardinal Siri of Genoa, who else? He's been there a long time, made archbishop back in 1954. Bright young man in those days. He's never been in the Curia. They say he'll be a strong leader and we will need a strong leader in the hard times that lie ahead. They also say he's been passed over three times and he's entitled to it."

"Isn't the obvious response that if he's been passed over three times people have thought before that he was not the man for the job?"

"That is irrelevant, Carlo, to the logic of the Curia."

"Does he have a chance?"

"For the moment everyone is talking only about him. When the *stranieri* Cardinals arrive they'll remind everyone that he opposed the reforms of the Vatican Council on every possible occasion. That's why the Curia wants him."

"Who is the opposition now?" I said, just as I sneezed.

"My old boss, Benelli. He's a dynamo of energy. He made things happen when he was Paul VI's chief of staff. He is a man of the Council, though I would not say that he is a democrat. He gets things done. Many people hate him, but many respect him too. He was one of the leaders of the coalition which elected Papa Luciani. He knows the Curia and would probably shake it up more than any of the other *papabili*. I think he has probably made too many enemies to win."

"So what will happen?" my good wife asked. She had been watching me sternly since I sneezed.

Rae Adolfo shrugged.

"Stalemate. There are no other Italians available for one reason or another. We may at the end have a Pope who is not Italian."

"That would be an improvement, wouldn't it?"

"Perhaps. There are few *stranieri* who would be better than the Italians. The College of Cardinals does not have, how do you Americans say it, a very deep bench."

I sneezed again. Rosemarie's brow furrowed. She knew all about my colds.

Cold or not, I was wolfing down my *bistecca fiorentina* like I might not eat for another couple of days. I was a well man; a few sniffles would not interfere with my taking pictures at this conclave.

"Can we afford another funeral and conclave?" I asked brightly. No, I was not getting sick. No way.

"It is interesting that you should ask," Adolfo replied. "No one mentions that problem, but the simple answer is that we cannot. Both are expensive. We will have to borrow money from the Italian banks to pay for it. That is not a good idea. They already have too much influence. We will have no choice."

"The resources here are that thin?" Rosemarie said.

"Everyone believes, *cara*, that the Church is very rich—all the treasures, the Vatican Palace, the museums, San Pietro. To whom could we sell them?"

"You might sell the air rights over St. Peter's for condo builders."

"Believe me, if we offered the sale, there would be a long line of buyers."

I started to fade. What was I doing here in this creepy city? Why was I learning more about this creepy Church than I wanted to know? Why wasn't I back in Chicago struggling with my portrait exhibition? It was Rosemarie's fault for dragging me out of the peace and contentment of Cook County.

The papal funeral would be on Wednesday. Everyone hoped that the bitter rain which had lasted now for four days would end by then. The meteorologists said it would not.

"It fits the mood of the Church," Adolfo said sadly as he wished us good-bye.

I sneezed again in the elevator, several times.

"Why is it, Charles Cronin O'Malley, that every time I get you all to myself in a luxurious hotel suite in a romantic city, you come down with a cold?"

This was a reprise of my complaints about her ill-timed periods.

"I'm not coming down with a cold," I insisted. My voice trailed off in a cough.

"I shouldn't have let you stand outside in that terrible rain today. You know what rain and chills do to you."

All sensible people know these days that colds are caused by viruses and that one can stand out in a cold rain without a cap all the day long and not "catch" a cold. The viruses, being more sensible organisms than we humans, stay warm and comfortable inside the cabins of airplanes.

However, despite overwhelming scientific evidence to the contrary, all mothers are convinced that wet chills will be the death of you. Moreover, they are also convinced that various old wives' remedies like honey or a toddy of hot lemonade, whiskey, and honey will reduce the two weeks of a cold to something less than fourteen days. Evidence to the contrary does not shake these convictions. Having served as an apprentice under the good April, my wife was convinced that she could heal my cold quickly, if only I did what she told me to do.

I also, incidentally, had to drink a lot of water and fruit juice.

My only choice was to accept her tender loving care which soothed and comforted, even if it failed to heal. She would place cool compresses on my forehead if I had a fever and warm ones if I did not. It was like having a mother all over again, especially since she had learned it all from my mother.

The hot toddy of honey, lemonade, and whiskey would not cure anything. However, it would reduce me to a state where I was hardly aware that I was sick.

In our suite she found some fruit juice in the minibar and required that I drink it as well as consume a bottle of Pellegrino water. This was the beginning of her treatment. It was all very consoling and maternal. Since the virus exorcised every trace of desire from my body, there was no chance of taking advantage of her tenderness for other purposes.

She felt my forehead and declared that it was not fevered and promptly put me to bed.

"Drink all that orange juice, Chucky," she ordered me.

"Yes, ma'am . . . It's too red to be orange juice."

"Sicilian oranges."

"Oh."

"And take these two aspirin. They'll beat the fever."

"I thought I didn't have a fever."

"Take them anyway."

"Yes, ma'am."

Rosemarie, be it noted, never has a cold. It is not fair.

The next morning we had a medical consultation—my wife, the hotel manager, and an Italian doctor—round, short, bald, dressed in a neatly tailored three-piece suit and very smooth. I participated in the discussion only by coughing violently.

The first decision was that I would live. The second was that I need not go to the clinic. The doctor prescribed medicine which would dry my sinuses and control my cough. He adjured me to drink much water and fruit juice and sleep much.

Then, having exhausted the limited capabilities of medical science, Rosemarie turned to surefire remedies. Room service was ordered to bring a tumbler of bourbon, hot lemonade, and honey. A pretty young waitress appeared, pushing a massive table with these requirements neatly arranged on it. She was as solemn as a nurse in surgery.

Rosemarie explained in Italian that her poor husband had become the victim of a cold by standing outside in the rain and the wind. The young woman nodded sympathetically. Men were that way. She watched with considerable interest as the mysterious American cure was concocted.

"It is wonderful, *signorina*," I explained to her. "It is so powerful that you don't know you're sick anymore and you don't bother your wife with your complaints."

"Chucky!"

The kid grinned.

The harsh truth is that the toddy tastes awful. Moreover, no one in his right mind consumes a glass of unadulterated bourbon in a single swallow. Yet that was a requirement of the treatment, so I took a deep breath and drained the magic potion.

I did feel a little better, though I'm sure for the wrong reason. My wife tipped the young woman generously, too generously the lingering Depression kid thought, and dismissed her. Then she placed the required hot compress on my head and departed for the *farmacia*. I went to sleep.

I knew for sure and she probably knew that none of this medical attention would have the slightest impact on the curing of my cold. However, a wife and a mother had to do something. It would have been enough to give me the cough suppressant and antihistamine. However, such behavior would reveal a culpable lack of concern for the poor, sick boy child.

Sometime later, Rosemarie returned from the *farmacia* and made me drink some foul-tasting medicine which was probably an Italian version of NyQuil. I went back to sleep.

Later she called home, reported to the good April that I had "one of his usual colds," and then talked to Missus and to the baby. She required me to say hello to the latter.

"Hi, Siobhan. Are they treating you right?"

Her response was gibberish.

"Tell them to be good to you or I'll come right home."

More gibberish.

Rosemarie removed the phone from my hand.

Apparently our youngest missed us but not to the point of desperation.

Then I caught snatches of a conversation with April Rosemary.

"I'm glad you feel much better, dear. That's what the medication is supposed to do for you. You'll be fine . . . Don't worry about poor Johnny Nettleton. He's a good little baby. He knows you love him. He'll be fine."

Not easy being a mother or a grandmother, especially with a sick husband-child on your hands.

Sometime later I was awakened for lunch.

"Not hungry," I protested.

"Feed a cold, starve a fever," she said, as though she were the Pope speaking ex cathedra. "You have to get proper nourishment. Drink your orange juice. You need lots of vitamin C."

"Yes, ma'am."

"RTE has been showing pictures of the cardinals coming out of their meetings in the Vatican. Not a very encouraging bunch of guys. Also some arriving at the airport. Including Cardinal O'Neill, fat, ugly little man. Why should we women in the Church take seriously leadership that is all old, fat, little celibate males who don't have any women or children?"

"No reason I can think of . . . There was a time when some

of them did have women and children. That was probably worse."

"Also they say that Cardinal Lorscheider of Brazil is sick and won't attend. He is one of the good guys, isn't he?"

"That's too bad. The good guys will need all the help they can get."

"Also they're doing the poor little Pope's funeral Wednesday morning. Outside. Rain or shine."

"They're doubtless hoping for rain to keep the crowd down and thus prove he wasn't loved."

I was beginning to think like a Roman. There was always a "they" who were up to something nefarious.

"Are you planning on going?" she asked tentatively.

"I have to. Pump me up with medicine, wrap me in a coat and a hat and a scarf. I'll be fine."

"I'll have to run out and buy you a warm coat and a scarf."

"And gloves!"

"Chucky! You're making fun of me."

"Would I do that!"

"You do it all the time."

"You look awful pretty in that robe—kind of diaphanous, isn't it?"

"Chucky! This is no time for romance."

"I'll probably be incapable of that ever again. Still, it's always a good idea to invest a little in the future. Kind of nice thighs."

"Will you shut up!"

"It must be the bourbon in me talking . . . Hey I have a great idea for your next story . . ."

"Well?" She glared at me.

"The punk gets sick in a hotel room, Vienna maybe. He's a miserable patient, but the narrator cures him with her magical potions."

"It won't work. Everyone knows that a hot toddy never cures anything. A wife would make one only as a bit of magic or superstition."

"Oh . . ."

"But that could be the story! He gets better. Thanks her for the magic cure, which couldn't have cured him at all! Not bad. I'll have to think about it."

She reached for her ever-present notebook, providing me with a chance to grasp one of those nice thighs.

"You're terrible," she said. However, she did not pull away.

"I know."

Alas, viruses and romance are incompatible.

The next morning found me way up near the front of the Piazza (courtesy of a pass produced by Rae Adolfo), dressed for arctic cold, watching the dreary obsequies for Pope John Paul. The rain had paused, but thick black clouds scudded over the Piazza and in the distance flashes of lightning carved up the sky. There was none of the usual flair and drama which marks Vatican ceremonies. It was as though the Catholic Church wanted to rid itself of this troublesome little Pope as quickly as it could, end what had been a bad job.

I couldn't quite put my finger on what was wrong. The Sistine Choir was as good as ever, the performance of the clergy as punctilious as always. Maybe the grim-faced cardinals were worrying about the debt they were building up.

Or maybe it was my own virus-induced depression.

I encountered in my search for good camera perspectives the local *Time* man.

"They're certainly in a hurry to get rid of him, aren't they, Chuck?"

"You noticed that too?"

"There are now rumors that there was rat poison in his blood system."

"I hear he was taking raffin for circulatory problems. That is rat poison."

"Is that for attribution?"

"What does a picture taker know?"

"Right. A high-placed Vatican observer?"

"Why not?"

"Have you noticed the crowd?"

"Yeah," I said, "remarkably silent and sullen for a crowd here."

"Almost as if they would storm the altar and kill the cardinals if they could find a reason."

"They loved him, even if the cardinals think they are well rid of them."

"What do you hear about the conclave?" he asked.

"Probably a deadlock and then a foreigner."

"Really?"

"What do I know?"

I turned my camera on faces in the crowd. Perhaps the valiant Rosemarie would persuade Reuters to distribute some shots of angry Catholics.

"Chucky, where have you been?" that lovely woman demanded when I collapsed on the hard chair next to her.

"Taking pictures. That's what I do for a living."

"A lot of very sullen people here. They believe the Curia killed him."

"That's what my pictures say. Do you think . . ."

"That I can get prints and give them to Reuters? Sure. That's a good idea. Now let's get out of here. We've paid our final tribute to the man. Those rain clouds are closing in again and you look shaky on your feet."

Lightning crackled, it seemed, just above the Dome. Many of the onlookers scurried for cover. Some of the Cardinals opened umbrellas.

Rosemarie assumed the role of a blocking back and led me to our limo, parked just outside the Sala Stampa. The car escaped much of the crowd but not all of it. Our ride back to the Piazza Trinita dei Monti was slow and bumpy.

"If I can't have you, I want another hot toddy. I'm cold and wet and depressed and sad and sick."

"You're a real mess, my love. But you can't cope with me just now. My old wives' tale says only one toddy per cold. We'll give you cough medicine and that will put you to sleep just fine."

"Yes, ma'am."

Before I lapsed into drug-induced unconsciousness I saw that RAI was reporting the arrival in Rome of Alois Cardinal Lorscheider of Fortazaela in Brazil. The good guys had a strong ally and the Curia was caught in another lie, not that it would bother them in the least. I couldn't follow the Italian of the newscast very well. However, Cardinal Siri was mentioned often.

The phone rang. I ignored it. I was suffering from a cold. I had no obligation to pick up a ringing telephone. Then I thought of children and grandchildren in America and reached for it.

"O'Malley," I mumbled.

"Daddy?"

April Rosemary.

"I think so."

"Mom said you had a terrible cold."

"I would doubtless be dead already if she hadn't given me one of her legendary hot toddies."

"Oh, Daddy, those things taste good but they're not a cure for anything. Colds are caused by viruses."

"In a couple of years, kid, you'll be telling young Johnny Nettleton and his successors that they must button up when they go outside lest they catch a cold."

She giggled.

"You're being funny like you always are when you're sick."

"Leave them laughing says I."

"You were at the funeral this morning?"

"A drab, dreary affair. The Vatican wanted to get rid of the poor man with as little splendor as possible."

"The crowd looked awfully angry."

"At this very moment *Madame la vôtre mère* is trying to peddle some of my pictures of the crowd to a news service. They make the same point. The local folk firmly believe that he was poisoned."

"Was he, Daddy?"

"Kid, they gave the job to a man with poor health and then didn't insist someone take care of him. Same result."

"Oh . . . Tell Mom I called. She's been worried about me. Like a little idiot I wasn't taking my medicine. I just wanted to tell her that I'm feeling much better now. Jamie is such a dear."

"I'll report that discovery."

She giggled again.

"You're terrible, Daddy."

"At least on that you and your mother agree . . . Keep taking the medicine."

"Yes, Daddy. I will."

As I slipped back into my dream world, I wondered what I was doing weary and sick in a hotel room in a foreign country.

Why was I fixated on the outcome of an election for the leadership of an institution which was permeated by dishonesty and corruption? I was an old man. This was crazy.

I went back to sleep.

I found myself running through the endless marble corridors of the Vatican. A papal corpse was chasing me, waving a rusty crosier. I turned a corner, pushed opened a door, and found myself in a room filled with cardinals in their pretty red clothes. Burn him! someone shouted. Their crosiers turned into lances and they began to chase me. I ran out of the room, ducked around a corner, grabbed my camera, and leaped out to take a picture of the charging cardinals. They had changed into the 1945 Chicago Cardinal football team. Ed Murray was leading them. I dropped my camera and ran again. Suddenly the Sistine Choir appeared out of nowhere and intoned *"Tu es Petrus."* I wasn't Peter, I was Charles Cronin O'Malley. I ran right through them. The cardinals, still in 1945 NFL garb, were right behind me. Somehow I escaped into the Piazza. Raimundo and Rosemarie, the latter in a diaphanous red robe, told me that they were chasing me because they wanted to make me Pope. I was a compromise candidate.

This is a drug-induced dream, I told myself. This is a silly dream. I should wake up and get out of here.

So I did wake up. With a sigh of relief, I rolled over and went back to sleep. Marshal Goldberg, the great Cardinal back of that era whom I had met at a party, greeted me and dragged me to the papal throne inside of San Pietro. The rest of the cardinals, now back in ecclesiastical crimson, tied me to the throne. I will not be Pope, I insisted. Rosemarie, help me.

She charged up to the throne stark naked and cut the ropes. The cardinals fell back in horror at the sight of an unclothed woman. I followed her as we both ran down the steps and out of the Aula, knocking several TV cameramen down.

Then I was running again through the streets of Rome. This time Rosemarie was chasing me. She had become a science-fiction monster with several heads and a dozen or so hands, in each one of which there was a long and shining sword. I dashed into an old palazzo, perhaps the Farnese, down a long hallway, into a side room, and then into a closet inside the room. I slammed the door and collapsed on the floor, exhausted and gasping for breath.

The door burst open and Rosemarie dashed in. She began to carve me up.

"Rosemarie! Don't!"

I sat up in bed, shivering with terror. Rosemarie stood at the door in a chic new raincoat. She was carrying several shopping parcels.

"Chucky!"

I pulled the bedcovers over me and fell back onto the bed. I continued to shiver.

"A dream?" she said, depositing her parcels on an ornate chair.

"Nightmare," I mumbled.

"The doctors say that you are prone to them when you have a cold. Your whole organism reacts in anger at the viruses. You're especially likely to have strong reactions . . . Chucky, you're shaking like a leaf . . . Do you have a chill?"

I had terrified the poor woman.

"I want another hot toddy."

She sat on the bed and cuddled me. I stopped shivering.

"Nice new raincoat."

"It was on sale."

Naturally it was on sale. No Irishwoman ever buys anything that's not on sale. She didn't have to tell me this because it was her money she was spending. Yet the genetic programming requires the explanation.

"They wanted to make me Pope."

"No!"

"You wanted to make me Pope! You were chasing me with twelve swords, one for each of the tribes of Israel."

I wasn't sure that there were twelve. The tribes of Israel were a gloss.

"How could I have twelve swords?"

Her perfume was soothing, reassuring.

"You had twelve arms."

"A Rosemarie monster! . . . Do you really want a hot toddy?"

"No. I just want to go home."

"You'll have the cold at home too."

"I hate this stinking city and the stinking Vatican and the stinking papacy. I want out!"

"You don't hate the Church?"

"Course not. The Curia only thinks that it is the Church."

"It's your call, Chucky. I'm ready to go home if you are . . ."

"One good reason why we should stay?"

"It would be nice to have the next Pope in your new exhibition."

Typically my wife had thought of the important fact.

"I guess so . . . Well don't change the reservations."

She hugged me fiercely. This was perhaps what married love was all about.

"I'm sorry, Chucky. I didn't mean to wake you up."

"If you hadn't, they would have forced me to be Pope."

"I'm glad I came in the nick of time."

The dream was still terrifyingly real.

"Your eldest called to say that she had been a little idiot and was taking her medicine again. She sounded fine. She also alleged that her husband was a dear."

Rosemarie sank into a chair, a woman exhausted in the pursuit of good works.

"She'll be all right . . . It doesn't seem possible that this meek little child was a rebel in the Underground only a few years ago."

"Bad times."

"They were indeed . . . The photo editor at the Reuters bureau loved your pictures. Said the one from yesterday appeared all over the world with the credit line that I had insisted on of course. Bought these two today. Those kids look like real bomb throwers, don't they?"

I glanced at the prints she had sold. I had caught all the anger of the crowd at the funeral. The days were over when mobs would storm St. Peter's. Yet the idiots over on Vatican Hill ought to wake up to the truth that people knew about their fun and games and were not amused.

Nothing like giving the Divine Wind something to aim at.

"Are you up to having a bite to eat?"

I consulted my stomach. It wondered when I was going to ask.

"Only a bite."

"I'll call room service."

"I'd rather take a shower and try their coffee shop or whatever they call it."

"Good." She popped up from the bed. "You're feeling better already."

"If you didn't take such good care of me, I'd have to feel better."

"I like being a mother."

Which was what it was all about.

Outside the rain continued to beat against the window.

Perfect weather for burying a Pope.

Again I wonder if those terrible men who were in such a hurry to get rid of the poor Pope's body for the good of the Church might not have been ready to get rid of him for the good of the Church.

✌ Rosemarie ✌
1978

"I don't know why, Rosie," Dr. Kennedy, the internist at Oak Park Hospital, had said to me. "Maybe it is connected to the extraordinary sensitivity that makes him a great artist. However, Chuck's organism reacts very badly to virus assaults. He recovers of course, but they are traumatic experiences for him."

"He doesn't think he's a great artist . . . I mean he won't cut off his ear like that Van Gogh did, will he?"

"I think not. Yet even an ordinary cold will deplete his energies and leave him severely depressed."

"Is there any threat to his life in these events?"

"I don't think so. His health is excellent, as the tests at Northwestern indicated. A serious incident of viral pneumonia might present some problems but nothing we couldn't deal with."

I wouldn't be a wife and a mother if that were enough to stifle my worries.

I called Dr. Kennedy from Rome while Chucky was in the shower and described his symptoms.

"No difficulty breathing, no dark sputum, no tightness in his chest?"

"None of those."

"It sounds like a simple upper respiratory infection. Keep treating the symptoms. Remember lots of water and orange juice."

"He says that Sicilian orange juice doesn't count because it's so red."

He laughed.

"That's what Chuck would say . . . You might warn him about the depression which is inevitable with virus attacks, especially for him."

"I will."

I would not, however, quote the doctor. There was no point in my husband knowing that I was worried. Life would be very difficult without him.

Then I called April Rosemary. Jamie Nettleton answered.

"Hi, Rosie," he said, "there's a glow back in your eldest's eyes. She's doing fine . . . She says her dad is sick?"

"Her father's organism reacts badly to viruses. He has truly awful dreams."

"What's going on over there?"

"Awful stuff."

"Sounds that way . . . Here's April Rosemary."

My daughter was contrite for having caused so much trouble.

"It wasn't you, kid. It was your damn hormones. No one is responsible for their hormones. Don't worry about Dad. He's doing fine."

"He was so funny on the phone . . . Give him my love."

"And ours to Johnny."

Johnny's grandfather, Colonel John Nettleton, and his wife, Polly, had been Chuck's commanding officers during his time in Germany back in the nineteen forties. Apparently my husband had even then been too much.

He emerged from the shower, wrapped up in a terry-cloth robe, and collapsed on our bed.

"Woman," he said in his fake Irish brogue, and sighed. "I'm not long for this world. I need me tea and me praties."

"I can call room service and order tea and praties."

"And yourself taking me metaphors literally." He closed his eyes and smiled beatifically. "A dish of chocolate-chip gelato would do nicely, however, wouldn't it now?"

He was in one of his silly phases, which I adore and it's a good thing I do or I'd kill him.

"Ah, no, won't we go downstairs to have something more substantial, just as soon as I catch me breath."

"You should remember what Dr. Kennedy said to you."

He frowned.

"Which thing he said to me?"

"About depression during and after viral attacks?"

"Depression? Me depressed?"

"Yes, you depressed."

"I can be depressed if I want to."

"You can't help being depressed. It's physiological. You just have to remember not to take it seriously."

"How can I not take it seriously?"

"By listening to me."

"Oh, THAT!"

For the next couple of days we divided our day into three parts, morning photographs—or, as he would insist, picture taking—afternoon nap, evening early dinner before I put Chuck to bed. Each morning he would announce cheerfully that he had beaten the cold and each evening he would be almost incoherent at bedtime.

In truth, however, even in full health Chuck could be incoherent when he was in one of his moods.

"Conclave," he muttered one night as he was going to sleep.

"Hmm . . ."

"No," he said, "conclaves."

"That's right—there will be two of them this year."

"Great idea."

In all honesty, I would have liked some serious loving. That's what a woman has a husband for, among other things. Well, as a lot of women say, it's not the only thing in a marriage. Certainly not, but I'm not sure most of us would be able to put up with our husbands if there weren't some high-quality lovemaking on occasion. Taking care of the husband when he's sick is really what intimacy is all about.

Normally with Chucky this was hardly a problem. I haven't had any other lovers, so I can make no comparisons. However, from listening to my friends talk, I suspect that a lot of men are clumsy and insensitive, perhaps because their wives really don't want to instruct them. I lucked out with Chucky Ducky in more ways than one. Somehow, he *knew* me from almost the beginning. Maybe it's part of the artistic sensitivity which Dr. Kennedy talked about.

I could wait. Chucky Ducky wasn't about to go away.

He didn't know everything about me. No man ever knows everything about his woman (and vice versa, though I think we do better because we spend so much time with children). Sometimes I send him mixed signals, which is my fault. Still, he does pretty well. He works hard at it too.

It turned out the next morning that he was planning a book about the two conclaves, one that would portray both the splendor and the ugliness of the Vatican. That meant we would hang out in front of the Vatican each morning to take telephoto shots of the various cardinals, usually with the most unflattering expressions on their faces.

It was a profoundly subversive scheme. We both loved it.

"You're supposed to be a writer, woman, aren't you?"

"Some people think so."

"Then why don't you start taking notes?"

"For what?"

"For the text and commentary in this book—something like, how did you put it again, 'Why should women take seriously rules about sex from celibate men who have never had children, wear funny dresses, and don't particularly like women.' "

"Brilliant idea!"

I pulled out my notebook and began to write.

Everyone looks stupid, venal, and arrogant on some occasions. Church leaders (Catholic or not) probably look that way more often than the rest of us, since they figure they have a monopoly on God. However, cardinals about to elect the religious leader of a billion people, plus or minus as Chucky says, seem to look that way most of the time. So most of the shots we sent around the world that week and stockpiled for our book were not particularly flattering. Nor were those that we took in the Sala Stampa, particularly of my old friend S'ter. He who holds the camera, I realized, gets even.

Some of the men, like Franz Koenig, who came to talk to us in the Sala or at press conferences, were brilliant, gifted, honest men. We'd put them in the book, just to show that there were good guys too. The surprising thing was that the distance between the good guys and everyone else was so great, perhaps everyone else was insecure because they were not very bright.

"Your photographs," Adolfo said with a hint of a smile at supper over the weekend back at Sabatini's in Trastevere, "are attracting some notice around the world."

"Good," said Chuck as he destroyed a dish of pasta. "That's the general idea."

"What are they saying?"

"There is some suggestion that you are trying to make the cardinals look like fools."

"Who, me? Would I do that?"

"Men like Suenens and Lorscheider laugh and say they are merely realistic pictures of men hard at work on difficult decisions."

"*Certo*," I said. "What else would Chucky be doing?"

"Subverting the Church."

"How could they say that if they saw my picture of Papa Luciani?"

Adolfo laughed.

"And the next pope, you will photograph him?"

"If he'll let me," Chuck said meekly.

"And what will he look like?"

"There's a difference, Rae, between a formal portrait and a news shot. In formal portraits I try to present men as they are but in the best possible way. I don't lie, but I give them every possible break."

"Even Siri?"

"He has the same rights as everyone else."

"*Bene*. That will be useful should any questions arise."

"Will it be Siri?" I ask anxiously.

"There are two camps"—he toyed with his wineglass—"inside the Siri camp. There are those who realize their own weakness and hope to use a strong first-ballot showing to enhance their negotiating power. And there are others who believe their own propaganda and will fight to the bitter end, just as they or their predecessors did the last three times. They see it as their last chance to undo the Vatican Council—which of course is impossible."

"What would I think of Siri?"

"You would like him, Carlo. He is a nice man, though he doesn't speak English or any other foreign language. He has been in Genoa for thirty-four years. Very fatherly, very pleas-

ant, a little outspoken, powerful preacher, not very sophisticated, gentle with people."

"Theology?" I asked.

"The very best of the years before the War."

"Would they elect a pope who didn't know English or
French or German?"

"Or Spanish," I added.

"Hardly. You will notice that certain papers will report this
problem starting tomorrow. You see, the Siri people have a
little less than thirty votes . . . The coalition of the Benelli men
in the Curia and the northern Europeans have perhaps forty-
five. The rest of them, including your North Americans, have
no idea what's happening. They know neither the issues nor
the personalities. They want to be able to go home and say
that they have voted for the new pope before the final ballot.
They will think that the Holy Spirit has inspired them, when
in fact they will be responding to such questions as whether
a man can speak their language."

"You don't believe that the Divine Wind blows through the
Sistine Chapel?" Chucky said.

"We have had popes who raped women coming to St. Peter's on pilgrimage, we have had popes who were thieves,
popes who had mistresses and produced children while they
were pope, even popes who murdered their enemies, usually
by poison. Must we credit that to the Holy Spirit?"

Some of Adolfo's smooth exterior had slipped aside. How
could he stand to work in this place?

"There have been no truly bad popes," he continued, "since
1700. However, though none of them were bad men, they were
often not very good at their job. All your Divine Wind does
is guarantee that the Church survives us poor priests who are
responsible for it."

"Can we quote you?" I reached for my notebook.

"*Certo* . . . Not by name, *prego*."

"Experienced Vatican watcher?"

"*Bene*."

Two days later we did portraits of Cardinal Suenens, Cardinal Lorscheider, and Cardinal Benelli for Chuck's exhibition. I remembered that he had brought proofs of many of his
pictures along. We gave them to Adolfo as evidence that it

would be a serious show. They were impressed and agreed to the shoot. We found Suenens at the Belgian College. He is a handsome, charming man, former rector of the University of Louvain, and active in the resistance during the War. In a properly run Church, he should be pope and we wouldn't have this silly conclave.

We had to wait a long time for Lorscheider at the Brazilian College. He swept in with a warm smile and a gracious apology. He told us how much he admired Chuck's pictures. He was a tall German, blond and handsome. His family had lived for generations in Brazil. I decided that his smile qualified him to be a successor to the smiling September Pope.

Benelli was waiting impatiently for us in Adolfo's office somewhere in the bowels of the Vatican.

It looked like we would face one of his famous temper tantrums, then he saw me. His face relaxed into a broad grin. He bowed and kissed my hand.

He was short, bald, intense, quick of movement, with dancing eyes and a mobile face whose expressions changed constantly.

"I'm sorry," he said with an expressive shrug, "that my Brazilian colleague kept you waiting."

All right, I thought. If I had a vote, this guy might just get it, though sometimes he looks like a Sicilian thug.

Now as I look back on the pictures in the *People* exhibition, I think that they were three remarkable men and that Chucky's Divine Wind had done a pretty good job finding some decent leaders for the Church.

"You will photograph Siri?" he asked, as Adolfo was showing us out.

"Non, Eminenza," Rae said with a sweep of his hands.

All of us laughed.

I thought that maybe we would make love that night. Poor Chuck was wiped out from the portrait shoots, too tired even to wonder about the results.

The next morning the bad news was that some of the American cardinals were praising Siri's "long pastoral experience." Another name had surfaced, Giovanni Colombo, the seventy-six-year-old Archbishop of Milan. Some reporters said that he was a year younger than Pope John when he was elected Pope.

Others said that the election of a man twelve years older than Papa Luciani would be an insult to the Church. Cardinal Suenens was quoted as praising Colombo as a man who had been very open to change at the Second Vatican Council.

We had given up on our shoots in the Vatican. Chuck continued to be very tired.

Adolfo called in midafternoon when my poor husband was napping.

"I cannot believe that your American cardinals are so dumb."

"The system doesn't produce many bright ones," I replied, as if I knew anything about the system. "Do you know this man Colombo?"

"*Certo*. They are trying to find an Italian compromise candidate. He is their last hope. Siri is gaining still. Benelli tells me that he will not be pope, but neither will Siri. I think he knows something."

I turned on RAI to witness an interview of an American cardinal who said that while John Paul was a great man, he lacked the administrative skill and experience to be a pope. The Church needed in these troubled times a strong man, an able administrator, and a firm anti-Communist. Someone who was not Italian should not be elected, he insisted, because such a person would not understand Rome. Rome after all was the center of the Church, in a certain sense, the Church itself.

"Idiot!" I screamed at the screen.

"Mark his name down," Chucky mumbled. "We'll get a picture of him and put the quote in our book."

"Go back to sleep, Chucky," I snapped.

"Yes, ma'am."

I was losing it. The constant elation and disappointment of this very peculiar political campaign had captured and infuriated me. These dumb American cardinals who were ready to believe every lie the Curia would tell! I was playing nursemaid to a sick little boy, negotiating over rights to our pictures, damn, his pictures, getting film developed and printed, making notes for my commentary, and taking care of a family from a long distance.

Siobhan Marie was acting up, her patience stretched out beyond all reason. She wanted her daddy!

Daddy, was it? She could have him in his present useless condition.

"She's just tired, Rosie," Moire Meg assured me. "She does miss you guys. When you coming home?"

"Tuesday, Wednesday at the latest. What's new with Seano?"

"I am tired of hearing what a wonderful person Esther is. He's got it real bad. Soapy. I think he'll want to discuss his love with you and Chuck as soon as you return."

"I can hardly wait," I sighed.

"I miss you, Rosie."

"And Dad?"

"Oh, yeah, him too."

I pondered the end of the conversation. Was Moire Meg trying to make up for her slip of the tongue which hinted that the baby missed her father more than her mother? And what kind of a neurotic idiot was I to be worrying about such things?

We had to get out of this insanity. Soon. Maybe a portrait of a new pope wasn't all that important.

On Friday the thirteenth (the day before the conclave was to begin) Siri's luck ran out. An Italian newspaper ran a devastating interview with him which it had promised to withhold until the conclave began. The paper argued that he had said the same thing on several radio interviews. It was rumored that Cardinal Benelli was behind the leak, which his staff vigorously denied.

Cardinal Siri lost his temper apparently several times in the interview. He said he was the most maligned man in the world, that he was neither a liberal nor a conservative, but a supporter of the Gospel. He made fun of Pope John Paul and ridiculed the notion of collegiality. He warned against the evils of Communism, which were even more dangerous to the Church than recent foolish reforms.

"Communism" was a big issue in Rome because of the kidnapping and murder of the ofttimes Italian Prime Minister Aldo Moro by the "Red Army"—a bunch of crazy professors and graduate students whom, as Chucky remarked, the real Communist party would line up against the wall and shoot if they ever took over.

I translated the RAI story for Chuck, who was beginning to show some signs of life, though his cough was still terrible.

"I figure," he said, "that Benelli probably had someone else lean on the paper. No need to involve himself. Anyway, to lay down a barrage like that which would land only when he was safe inside was a sneaky trick. They had to print it. Imagine what it would be like if he emerged as the next pope with a story like that in the headlines."

"This is a rotten, sick place, Chucky."

"Yeah. Jesus would have been better advised to turn the Church over to angels—or some other creatures who don't cheat and lie and catch colds at the wrong time. Maybe to the timber wolves."

"You didn't choose to get sick, Chuck."

"That's true . . . Are they still playing the Communism card?"

"For all it's worth. It's in every paper. Someone arguing that the most important criterion for the next pope is that he will be strong in the face of Communist attacks on the Church."

"Have there been any such attacks while I've been out of it?"

"No."

"I guess facts don't matter now."

"How you feeling?"

"Somewhere between better and terrible."

"Remember that the depression now is physiological."

"I'm too depressed to feel depressed . . . What's the weather like?"

"Lovely Indian summer weather."

"Let's go for a walk."

So we went for a walk, hand in hand. I felt young again. We found a nice little *gelateria* off the Via Veneto and ordered two double scoops of chocolate ice cream.

My husband was recovering.

"Just like dropping into Petersen's back in the old days."

"Ice cream isn't as good, Rosemarie."

"Nothing is as good as Petersen's."

Chuck could only finish one scoop.

"Eyes bigger than my stomach," he sighed.

"You're getting better, Chuck . . . Can't waste good gelato. I'll finish it off for you."

He had several fits of coughing on the way back to the hotel. I gave him cough medicine and put him to bed. No romance for Rosemarie again tonight.

Saturday morning, the day the cardinals would go into conclave for the second time in seven weeks, he was more chipper.

"It all starts this afternoon, doesn't it, Rosemarie?"

"Starts or ends. Your Divine Wind will have a hard time getting in."

"Sure will. We'd better go over there. I want to get a shot of that American who said that it couldn't be someone who was not Italian. If they elect a *straniero*, we'll print his picture with the quote."

"You are one very angry West Side Mick, Charles Cronin O'Malley."

"Maybe it's just the cold."

It was a glorious day, warm, gentle, benign like a loving mother—which I had been once a long time ago. We wandered up and down the Conciliazione and pretended that we were tourists. We gaped at every nasty little nun and porcine pompous prelate we encountered. Chuck's Nikon banged away.

Dear God, these men and women have given up home and family to serve You. Could You not have organized a better, happier way for them to do it?

We ate a late lunch in the Columbus Hotel. Chuck destroyed the pasta plate and asked for another. His coughing fits were infrequent. He was coming alive again. Poor dear man. He'd be all right eventually. The midlife crisis, really a crisis of mortality, could no more keep him down than would this terrible cold.

Or so I hoped and prayed.

We then walked over to the entrance from the Piazza to the Sistine Chapel. The press were already seizing positions from which to hurl questions at the cardinals as they entered for the conclave. The usual crowd was filtering into the Piazza. They had forgotten the September Pope. There was new pageantry to consume and soon a new pope to cheer.

No one is as dead as a dead priest, Msgr. Packy had once said.

Especially, I reflected, if the dead priest had been a pope.

"You must be feeling better, Chuck." Msgr. Adolfo appeared behind us, as he often did, like someone from another world.

"I'm not long for this world," my husband protested. "I'm dying with me boots on. Someone has to take pictures of the cardinals."

"Anyone special?"

"That American idiot who endorsed Siri the other day."

"A stern crusader against atheistic Communism? Is there any content in that?"

"Nope," said Chuck. "It's a mantra. Makes them feel good."

"What's going to happen?"

"Siri won't be pope. Neither, I fear, will my former boss."

"Colombo?"

"I doubt it . . . Probably a compromise foreigner."

"Like?"

"Koenig of Vienna. Wojtyla."

"Who's he?" Chuck demanded.

"Cracow. Very gifted man, poet, playwright, actor, intellectual, wit. Man of the Council and from Poland. There'd be no question about anti-Communism. Probably too young, only fifty-eight. I don't think they want a man who might be pope for a quarter century."

"What's he like?"

"Strong, perhaps too strong. Has spent most his life under enemy occupation. That means a perspective very different from Western Europe or America. One advantage that he might have is your Cardinal Krol, not exactly a dazzling light, is also Polish. He might bring the American cardinals along as a group, which could tip the scales."

"A Polack Pope!"

"Chucky!"

"No problem here with that word, *cara*, the Italian adjective for Polish is *Polacco*."

"And in *Hamlet*," said my husband, triumphant in his phony little triumph, "does not the Polish king announce that he is the Royal Polack?"

"You're terrible!"

My feisty little lover was returning to me at last. I had missed him.

"The Divine Wind still locked out?" he asked Adolfo.

"*Certo.* Yet when they come out they will be confident the Spirit swept them along to His chosen decision."

"Hers," I said.

Adolfo drifted away.

"Will he ever be a cardinal, do you think, Chucky?"

"Too important."

"What do you mean?"

"Cardinals are a dime a dozen. Invisible men who get things done smoothly are few and far between. There aren't many lawyers in Chicago as slick as Vince."

The journalists crowded around us were speculating on the outcome of this very peculiar election. A gaggle of Brits was arguing for their man George Basil Hume. Their logic seemed to imply that because Hume was eminently qualified he would certainly be elected.

"Not a chance," Chuck said to me. "Do we have any pictures of him?"

"Some good shots. He's one of the few that doesn't look like a degenerate creep."

A wild cheer went up from the crowd. The crimson tide had appeared at the portico of St. Peter's and was winding its way in somewhat disorderly fashion toward the entrance to the Vatican Palace.

"He's that little man"—Adolfo was suddenly behind us—"with the rimless glasses and the pious little acolyte smile. Don't worry about missing it, the expression never goes away."

Chucky blazed away with his telephoto.

"I am ashamed," I said, "that he is the best my country can do."

"As my Irish friends would say, he's not the worst of them."

I handed Nikon magazines to Chuck as I often had. We didn't want to miss a shot. I wondered again what instinct it was that gave him the uncanny ability to see a perfect shot coming a moment before it was there. I'd never understand. Neither would he. My Chuck just saw the shot as it was forming.

Genius?

I never doubt it, though he never believed it.

Then the procession was over and the sun setting behind St. Peter's. We were almost a month into autumn and light was vanishing quickly from the European sky.

We walked around the corner and into the Borgo Pio for an early-evening dish of pasta. My husband was silent, melancholy, not typical moods for him.

"What thinking, husband mine?"

"Just that it's a long way from Galilee."

"It sure is."

We walked back to the Piazza, ambled over to the obelisk and looked up at the Vatican Palace. There were a lot of lights up there, some of them bedroom lights of men who had been crowded into offices and storerooms until they could elect a pope. Others corridor lights. As we watched some of the lights flicked off. Arm in arm we stood there, and wondered and prayed silently.

There were a couple of hundred people in the immensity of the Piazza, mostly tourists, cameras in hand. We had a couple of cameras slung over our shoulders but we didn't feel like tourists. We were Vaticanologists. A couple dozen cops were scattered around, mostly lounging and relaxing. The Dome of St. Peter's loomed radiantly in the background. Over our left shoulders a full moon shone down. The Sistine Chapel stood vaguely in the shadows.

Full moon over conclave, maybe we could get the jazz group to put together a piece when we went home. I'd do the vocals. April on the piano.

"Wouldn't you like to know what's going on up there?" I asked.

"We're probably better off not knowing."

Chuck was already half-asleep when we reached our suite at the Hassler. I told him that I didn't think we needed the NyQuil because his cough seemed to be cured. He agreed and promptly climbed into bed.

I had set aside a moderately sexy nightgown, which now seemed a waste of time. Nevertheless, I put it on and slipped into bed next to him. He was sleeping peacefully. I turned off the lights.

❧ *Chuck* ❧
1978

We arrived at the Vatican about eleven-thirty, after attending Mass at the Trinita dei Monti at the top of the Spanish Steps. I confess that much of my attendance at the Eucharist was distracted by a sense of lost opportunity last night. I had neglected my wife badly. There was something seriously wrong with me.

The Piazza and the top of the Conciliazione were already crowded with people dressed in their Sunday best—parents and children and many family dogs who amused themselves by pretending to fight with one another. They came, I suspected, because the weather was splendid and the Piazza was the place to be. They really didn't expect white smoke the first morning. But they didn't want to miss it either.

We crossed over the street which ran behind the left colonnade, where we found a good view of the chimney on the top of the chapel. Just as we worked our way into the colonnade, white smoke appeared from the chimney. The throng went wild. "*È bianco, è bianco!*"

I reflected that the smoke signal and the excitement it generated seemed to fit perfectly into Italian culture.

Then the smoke turned black. A vast sigh arose from the crowd.

"They still can't get it right," I said to Rosemarie, touching her arm.

I had resolved to keep her at the fringes of arousal all the day long. She didn't seem to mind.

Then it turned gray. For a long half minute it was clearly

white. The crowd cheered, but with a sense of reservation. Then it was definitively black. The crowd groaned its displeasure and quickly broke up. A couple of people near us, who had Radio Vaticana on their handheld sets, turned it off in disgust.

"Basta!" one elegant Roman woman exploded.

We wandered over to the Sala Stampa, where a Canadian reporter was telling everyone that Siri had won fifty votes in the first ballot and that by afternoon he would have half the votes. After that he couldn't be stopped.

"Do you believe that, Chuck?" Rosemarie asked.

I looked over the scratch sheet I had prepared.

"I don't see how he could have got more than thirty-five, forty at the most. Then, if the history books are right, his plurality will begin to decline."

"How did the word leak out, I wonder."

"Our friend Rae Adolfo, if he were here, would say that such matters can be arranged. I can't imagine that there are not communication links both ways. If almost everything around here is corrupt, why not the restrictions on the conclave?"

"What good does it do?"

"Someone might send a message inside that the people out here were delighted because they want Siri."

"That seems truly weird."

"Rosemarie, my love, where are we?"

"Right . . . Nothing here is weird."

We sat there for a while, holding hands and listening to the director of the Sala Stampa explain why there was a confusion about the smoke signals.

"Chuck O'Malley, Chicago," I said, raising my hand. "There doesn't seem to be any historical record of this happening before at earlier conclaves. Has modern technology made it more difficult to produce the right color smoke?"

"Chucky!" my wife whispered.

The man, an insecure and nervous priest who was trying desperately to protect his job, erupted into a long lecture in feverish Italian.

"What did he say?"

"That the Vatican has the very best of modern technology."

"Like the television studio it doesn't have."

Someone else asked him about the report of fifty votes for Siri.

He erupted again. There could be no reports from inside the conclave. All reports were false.

Our driver, whose respect had been won by Rosemarie's generosity, promised that he would be back by five.

"White tonight, no?" he asked. "Just like last time."

"Maybe," I said.

We lugged our equipment back up to the suite and collapsed into bed. My wife was, as always, right. We did need a nap, pure, you should excuse the expression, nap.

We slept so deeply that we would have missed the smoke if our driver hadn't rung us at a quarter to five. We were both logy and irritable and snapped at one another as we dressed.

"Why didn't you wake me up?" herself demanded. "I can't do everything in this family."

"You're the mommy," I replied. "It's your job to wake me up."

"Bullshit."

That is language she never uses. We went down to the car silently.

"Thank you for calling, Martino. We were both very tired."

"*Sì, signora*, tiring times for great artists, no?"

I almost said that I was not a great artist, but I thought better of it.

We arrived at the Piazza at 5:40. The crowd stood around listlessly. Nothing had happened. The sky was quickly darkening. A searchlight focused on the rickety old chimney. It will be hard to tell in the dark. What did they do in the days before searchlights!

The system is that they burn the ballots which will normally send up white smoke unless wet stuff is added to the fire to make it black.

By six tension had increased. The last time this had been the decisive ballot. Was something going wrong inside?

Much later we would learn that the two "scrutinies" (four ballots) had tested the relative strength of the Siri and Benelli forces and that neither had been strong enough. Siri had begun with fifteen more votes than he had at the previous conclave.

The curial propaganda had given him an impressive boost. The leaders of the European coalition were worried. Toward the end of the day, he was losing votes to Colombo. Many of the American cardinals would go to bed that night convinced that the Holy Spirit was directing them to vote for an infirm seventy-six-year-old man.

An orange moon rose over the Tiber and stood for a few minutes at the bottom of the Conciliazione, a perfect setting for white smoke.

At 6:05, the smoke went up again. It sure looked like it was white. We turned on our portable radio. "*È nero*," the announcer of Radio Vaticana said firmly.

The smoke continued to pour out, alternately white, black, and gray. The crowd groaned and dispersed.

"Drat," my wife said. "I wanted to go home tomorrow or Tuesday."

"Let's have a real dinner," I replied. "That nice little place over by the Gregorian University."

We found a table despite the crowd because the owner recognized my wife. Naturally.

The restaurant was filled with American Jesuits from the Gregorian and American journalists. We hid in our little corner and listened.

"It'll be Colombo first thing in the morning," one young Jesuit with a Boston accent informed the reporters who were hanging on every word. "They beat back Siri today but don't have enough votes for Benelli. He's angered too many people. Colombo will be the last Italian Pope, another elderly transitional papacy."

He was wrong, as it turned out. But much later, many of us found ourselves wishing that he'd been right.

We went back to the Hassler and made leisurely and peaceful love, restoring the union which had existed before my sickness.

How could a man with such a wonderful wife worry about his future? He should just go home and work on the *People* exhibition and our book on the conclaves.

The next morning the routine of white, black, and gray began early at 11:15, just as we arrived. However, someone had the bright idea of linking Vatican Radio with the powerful public address system which dominated the Piazza.

"*È nero!*" the voice said, almost casually.

Later we would learn that a line had been set up between the door of the conclave and Vatican Radio. Someone just outside would pick up a signal from someone just inside about the color of the smoke—one if by land, two if by sea or something like that. It was an interesting way to deal with a conclave that was appearing on worldwide television.

Still later we heard of the dramatic events inside. Before the ballot sheets could be collected, Giovanni Colombo rose to announce that he would not accept if elected for reasons of health and age. The cardinals were thunderstruck. He had scuttled their nice little compromise. Then Franz Koenig, Archbishop of Vienna, broke all the rules of the conclave and proposed that they proceed to the second ballot AND elect Karol Wojtyla, the Archbishop of Cracow. Koenig praised his education, his intelligence, his sensitivity, his leadership in the reconciliation between the Church in Germany and the Church in Poland. He said no one could doubt his anti-Communism, but it was a sophisticated anti-Communism, that of a man who understood both the weakness and the appeal of Marxist philosophy.

The other cardinals were thunderstruck. No one doubted Wojtyla's intelligence or abilities. Very few realized how young he was. Most knew that he had been an important figure in the Vatican Council. All knew that Koenig, one of the great men of the Council, would not recommend someone who did not stand for the same ideas of ecumenism and collegiality.

They cast their second ballots under the influence of a passionate appeal which broke all the rules of the conclave. Wojtyla fell short of the two-thirds by only one or two votes. In the afternoon they would elect him and the conclave would end.

The voice of Koenig was the voice, they firmly believed, of the Holy Spirit.

In the ensuing years, Franz Koenig might have had second thoughts. When it was time for him to retire as Archbishop of Vienna, the Pope appointed a Benedictine abbot who had impressed him at a Mariological conference, without bothering to consult Koenig. When that man retired from the Archdiocese and from the College of Cardinals under pressure of pedophile charges, John Paul named as his successor a young aristocratic Dominican who, for all his personal charm, was a reactionary.

His Holiness's idea of loyalty and the one in which we were raised in Chicago were very different.

Franz Koenig had locked the Church in for the rest of the century and beyond by that illegal intervention. He is, I am told, not a man to have second thoughts.

We were back in front of St. Peter's at five-thirty. The crowd was smaller—it was a workday—but enthusiastic, as if it knew that tonight we would have a pope again. The sky was clear, the weather was soft and warm again, and once more the orange moon hung over the Tiber as if it were waiting with bated breath for the announcement.

At 6:08 the smoke went up, unmistakably and permanently white.

"*È bianco!*" said Radio Vaticana.

The atmosphere changed at once to hilarity. We were all talking to one another happily. The main subject of conversation was whether the new pope would be a *straniero*, a foreigner. Some of our newfound friends were horrified at this possibility. Others thought it was high time.

A well-dressed and cultivated gentleman who spoke excellent English said to us, "I have a store of the best sparkling wine in Rome. If we rid ourselves of the Italian papacy, I will go home and break open that store and with my family drink to the future of the Church in Italy."

"What do you think, Chucky? No hedging your bets now."

"I don't think Colombo quite made it. That leaves only a foreigner. I'm betting on a Polish pope."

She considered me with glowing blue eyes that make my heart melt and my loins tighten.

"No bet."

The powerful lights went on behind the doors of the loggia of the Basilica. We continued to wait. They certainly knew how to drag out the suspense.

Then the door swung. The cross bearer and the acolytes emerged, then Cardinal Felici appeared:

"*Annuntio vobis gaudium magnum!*"

The required ecstatic cheers.

"*Habemus Papam!*"

Oh great, we weren't expecting that.

"*Carolum Sanctae Romanae Ecclesiae Cardinalem...*"

Charles? Who was that?

"Wojtyla!"

"Pope Chucky," Rosemarie giggled.

The cheer was modest at best. They weren't sure who this man with the funny name was. They knew he wasn't an Italian.

"*Qui imposuit sibi nomen Johannem Paulum!*"

Felici did not sound very happy.

"*È papa nero? È papa nero?*" a man next to me asked anxiously.

"*Non,*" my good wife replied, "*È papa Polacco!*"

"*Magari!*" he exclaimed, clutching his head.

"*Polacco?*" a number of others shouted.

"*Revera,*" Rosemarie said, "*È papa Polacco!*"

"The first non-Italian pope since 1522!" I said to herself. "And we are there!"

"Quick, who was the last non-Italian pope?"

"I've been sick all week."

"Adrian VI, Cardinal Breakspeare!"

"A Brit!

"That's right, a Brit."

All right, you've elected a Polish pope. What do you do as an encore for that?

The crowd did not disperse. They were hurt, angry. They wanted to see what this new man was like.

Not good losers.

We elbowed our way over to the Sala Stampa.

"The tradition is that he just gives the blessing and goes back into the Sistine. His first talk is to the cardinals at the closing Mass tomorrow."

My spousal tour guide had spent the week of my illness brushing up on the local folklore.

"He'd better say something to these folks now. They're not happy."

"Pope Chucky," she giggled again. "Your nightmare came true even if it was another Chuck."

An Italian military band struck up happy music at the edge of the colonnade. The moon was orange again, the sky was still clear. A new era had begun in the Catholic Church.

About 7:20 he appeared on the screen, a big man, not tall (though taller than I am by a couple of inches) but broad-shouldered and solid.

"May Jesus Christ be praised," he said in Italian.

"Now and forever," the crowd replied, somewhat surprised at the Italian.

Rosemarie whispered a translation to me, through her tears.

"Dearest brothers and sisters, we are still all grieved after the death of the most beloved Pope John Paul I. And now the most reverend cardinals have called a new bishop to Rome. They have called him from a distant country, distant but always so close for the communion in Christian faith and tradition. I was afraid to receive this nomination, but I did in the spirit of obedience to Our Lord and in the total confidence in His mother, the most holy Madonna.

"Even if I cannot explain myself in your . . ." he paused and chuckled, ". . . our Italian language, if I make a mistake you will correct me."

Laughter from the throng. He had won them over.

"Also I present myself to you all to confess our common faith, our hope and our confidence in the mother of Christ and of the Church and also to start with the help of God and with the help of men."

An enormous ovation leaped from the Piazza San Pietro. After all they really had another Italian pope.

One of the functionaries standing around him had tried to silence him, whispering "*basta*," which the mikes picked up.

The new Pope had ignored him.

Adolfo had said that the Archbishop of Cracow had been an actor before he went to the seminary. He certainly had magical stage presence. He had been close to tears when he spoke of being afraid of the nomination. He had clung to the railing of the balcony to control his emotions. The Romans loved him.

For the moment.

"An enormously impressive man," my wife said to me as we rode back to the hotel.

"Incredible," I agreed.

Both Rosemarie and I were elated and exhausted. I was also fading fast, my cold striking one last mean blow.

"I'm fading, Rosemarie my darling."

"I can see that, Chuck. By tomorrow you'll be fine."

So it was right to bed for Chucky Ducky and his wife and right to sleep. Time for us to go home.

On Tuesday morning, we were waiting with most of our equipment, at the entrance of the Sistine to catch the cardinals as they emerged from the conclave. We were reading the English-language translation of the discourse he had delivered to the cardinals at the Mass ending the conclave. He had touched every base, Vatican Council, collegiality, the synod of bishops. The opponents of the Council had been routed, now it would seem definitively. The Siri people were in full retreat. The Cardinal himself would in all probability never get his fifth chance.

"So, what do you think?"

"He was wonderful," Rosemarie enthused, the stars from last night still in her eyes. "And you, Chucky?"

"The big question, it seems to me, is whether the man can really make the leap from Cracow to Rome, from being the brilliant leader of a garrison Church to being the one who presides in charity over a worldwide pluralistic Church."

I know I said those things because my wife jotted them down in her notebook.

"Are you perhaps demanding too much?" Adolfo asked. "Can any of us leave behind our origins?"

"I probably couldn't leave behind my neighborhood," I admitted.

"He will do his best," Adolfo smiled. "You wish to do the portrait?"

"*Certo*," Rosemarie answered for both of us.

"Come to the Sala Stampa tomorrow at ten-thirty. I will be engaged at the time. They will, however, take you to the papal apartments. The Pope does not need a translator. Now here come the cardinals. Don't miss your shots."

The cardinals streamed into the courtyard in various stages of formal dress, Siri in full robes with a Roman hat, Benelli with a black cassock and crimson sash and skullcap. They seemed tired and distracted, no claims of a great spiritual experience this time.

Someone asked a sullen Cardinal Siri whether the outcome was a surprise.

"I am not able to say. Perhaps it was a surprise."

"What do you think of the discourse of the new Pope?"

"I do not remember anything."

Benelli was willing to say more, though he seemed nervous and agitated.

"The right man at the right time."

"A revolution?"

"There aren't revolutions in the Church, always continuity."

"Did you expect a foreign pope?"

The fiesty little man lost his patience completely.

"In the Church there are no foreigners, no boundaries, no divisions. There are no foreigners in the church."

Then he flashed his famous smile and disappeared into his car.

It was not much better up at the North American College on a hill overlooking the Vatican. Cardinal O'Neill took over before Cardinal Krol could crow about the victory for Poland.

"The Pope and I are very good friends. I recently spent ten days living with him in his home in Cracow. I had lunch with him the day before we went into the conclave. His election is a great victory for Chicago."

Even the other cardinals could not help look askance at this shameless nonsense.

Someone asked Cardinal Krol whether the Pope had been married as a young man and begun to study for the priesthood after his wife died.

The Cardinal blew up.

"That is a complete lie. It is a dirty Communist propaganda trick."

"I thought marriage was a sacrament, Cardinal?"

Krol was too angry to respond.

Several other cardinals told pious stories of how they had felt the Holy Spirit in the flowing of the votes.

The vehemence of Krol's reply made suspicions all the stronger.

The Pope himself answered the question later, quite calmly. "No, I never entered through that door."

"Strange metaphor," I said.

"Maybe not, Chucky. He's a poet after all. As well as all those other things." ·

A rumor persisted for some time that the young Karol Wojtyla had indeed been in love in the drama group of which he was a part. However, they had not married and were never intimate. She had died during the war. This rumor probably wasn't true either. None of the later biographers would pick up on it.

Cardinal Krol had embarrassed the Church and insulted the married laity by his vehement denial of a possible marriage. Other popes had been married men, even perhaps into the nineteenth century and taken major orders only after they lost their wives. It would not be the last time Cardinal Krol put his foot in his mouth.

We went back to the hotel and began to pack. There was a TWA flight to Chicago on Wednesday at three. We should be able to make it after the photo shoot.

The next morning we presented ourselves at the Sala Stampa at ten with our camera and lights. We both could hardly wait to get it over with and get away from the Vatican and Rome and Italy and back to our home and family.

No one seemed to be in charge, so we went to S'ter's cubbyhole.

"We're supposed to do a portrait of the Pope today at ten-thirty," I said tentatively.

"It is not permitted," she snapped. "It is absolutely forbidden."

"Why?" I asked.

"The Pope will not meet with degenerates."

"I see," I said, my fists clutched in rage. "What makes my wife and me degenerates?"

"You support mutual masturbation!"

"We served on the birth control commission for Pope Paul—"

"Pope Paul is dead!" she said triumphantly.

"May we speak with Monsignor?"

"Monsignor is gone." She seemed equally happy. "He is no longer the president of the Sala Stampa!"

Rosemarie grabbed my sleeve.

"Come on, Chuck, let's get out of here. We don't need his picture or anyone else's."

I followed her out of the Sala Stampa.

"Do we have a shot of her?"

"We do," she said, scribbling rapidly in her notebook. "And I'm writing down the dialogue . . . Chucky, as I keep telling you, you're one of the great Catholic laymen in the world. They need you more than you need them."

"We could find Rae . . ."

"We could go back to the hotel and pack."

Never argue with your wife when you know she's right.

Well, she was wrong about my importance. However, no Catholic ought to be told by the Church that he—and by implication his wife—are degenerates because they served to the best of their ability on a papal commission. This was not going to be a good papacy.

In our suite Rosemarie threw garments into her large collection of luggage with reckless fury.

I took her in my arms.

"Rosemarie, cool it!"

"They're evil, Chuck."

"Let's say they have a different style than we do."

She remained rigid in my arms.

"I did say cool it," I continued.

"Look who's giving orders in the family." She giggled and then relaxed.

The phone rang.

"Chuck O'Malley," I said.

"Adolfo here. I call to apologize."

"You didn't do it . . . Don't try to say it was all a mistake."

"No, it was not a mistake. It was done deliberately. The new president of the Sala Stampa is a layman from Opus Dei. They have their own agenda. The Pope did not know of it."

"He appointed the man."

"Yes, he did . . . Chuck, if you come to the gate of the courtyard at three, I will be there with the Swiss Guards and they will let you in. The Pope will see us at three-thirty."

"Adolfo?" Rosemarie whispered.

I nodded.

"We don't have to take that shit from anyone, Rae."

"Sister?"

"She said we were degenerates. Suppose I call some of our friends in the media and tell them . . . Catholic photographer thrown out of Vatican Press Office on charges of degeneracy?"

"You won't do that, Carlo. You would have done it already, a point I have made. I personally would not blame you if you did."

"Does the Pope know?"

"Yes he does."

"Will he apologize to us?"

"By deed at least."

Rosemarie had grabbed the other phone.

She nodded decisively.

"Okay," I said grudgingly, "we'll be there."

The Swiss Guards knew us well enough to salute us even before Adolfo appeared. The poor man was very apologetic.

"I should have come with you. Sister would not have dared to stop me."

"Not only did she stop us," I replied, "she insulted us."

"Sister is not the Pope," he said simply.

"Chucky is in a very bad mood, Monsignor. The last effects of his terrible cold."

"There will be mistakes made," he sighed. "A different kind of mistake than used to be made. We will be able to correct most of them."

"I understand that," I said in a tentative concession to graciousness.

"It could have been so much worse," he said mysteriously.

Upstairs we were introduced into the papal antechamber. A young, lean secretary with a round Slavic face glared at us, apparently to make sure that my wife's clothes would meet the papal standards of modesty.

He turned to Adolfo, who pointed at his watch. The punk obviously felt that no one should be admitted to the papal office without being made to wait. If they tried to delay us, I would simply walk out, no matter what my good wife thought.

See how tough I am!

Adolfo stared him down. The invisible man could be quite visible when he wanted to be. Patently he had lost none of his clout.

The young man stood up and walked grudgingly to the door of the papal office, opened it a slit, and slipped in. He seemed to be afraid that we might rush in after him.

He returned in a moment, opened the door wide, and bowed respectfully.

Rosemarie, who had picked up some standard household expressions from Missus, said something to him as she went in, first of course.

He flushed and smiled, a rather nice young man.

The Pope was waiting just inside the door.

The wife greeted him in Polish as she bowed to kiss his ring.

He replied and she answered.

They both laughed.

The Pope might be a charmer. Today he had met his match.

He took my hand and squeezed it.

"We have two Charleses in the room, do we not, Dr. O'Malley? Do they call you 'Charley'?"

"Chuck usually, *sanita*," I said as I kissed his ring. "Sometimes even Chucky."

"Chucky, I like that . . . Monsignor, thank you very much for bringing Dr. and Mrs. O'Malley to my office. Please stay and correct my English."

He was not as tall as he had looked the other day, maybe only two or three inches above me, which is not a heck of a lot. He was, however, solid with broad shoulders and a husky body. I could believe that he loved to ski, an activity which I thought to be folly. His face, like the rest of him, was square and solid and also handsome in an Eastern European way. His eyes were frosty blue and his smile slow and friendly.

He brought us over to his desk, on which were opened copies of *Kids* and *After the War*, my first book of pictures about Germany in the late nineteen forties.

The latter was open at the picture of Trudi, my sometime German mistress. The title was *Hitler Youth*.

"This one lives now? She wants so much to live in the picture . . ."

"Yes, Your Holiness, she lives in Stuttgart. Her husband is an official in a manufacturing company. Her son flies for Lufthansa and her daughter is in university."

There was no point in telling him that her son was my son.

"Chuck saved her and her mother and sister when the Russians wanted them," Rosemarie said.

The Pope had an interesting facial mechanism. He would purse his lips, roll his frosty blue eyes, and nod. It was an expression which could mean absolutely anything. The first time he made it, I think he approved of my saving Trudi and her family.

"And this one, the one waiting at the train for her husband to return from Russia? Did he ever return?"

"Yes, Holy Father," my wife answered for me. "He was the rector of the University of Bamberg for many years and his wife a Frau Professor. He is a senator now for the CDU."

The Pope laughed at the complexity of German titles.

"They came over to America for Chuck's fiftieth birthday last month."

This time the papal expression seemed to mean that it was impossible that I should be that old.

"Happy birthday," he said.

"And she was there when he got off the train?" the Pope asked me.

"It's not that kind of story, I'm afraid, Holy Father. She was at the Residenz, the American headquarters that afternoon, acting as a translator for the then Herr Oberbürgermeister of Cologne."

"So you were there to greet him for her?"

That was a good guess, a damn good guess.

"She had a feeling that he would come on one of the few days she was not waiting for the train from Leipzig. That day she asked me to represent her."

The hopes and the sorrows, the loneliness and the folly of my time in Germany all raced pell-mell through my imagination. It had been so long ago and I was so young.

"You were how old then, Chuck?"

"Eighteen, nineteen."

This time his enigmatic expression seemed to mean that I

was far too young to have had the adventures which the pictures implied.

He then turned to *Kids* and flipped through the pages.

"These three are yours, Mrs. O'Malley?"

"Rosemarie, Holy Father . . . Yes, those are my three Irish cavalrymen. The middle one is studying to be a priest."

"In Chicago?"

"Certainly."

He nodded.

"And this young woman"—he picked out Moire Meg—"must have red hair like her father."

"That's when she graduated from grammar school. She's in university now. She is just like her father, except much prettier."

"Four children?"

"Six, Holy Father. And two grandchildren with another coming. This is our youngest." She pulled Siobhan Marie out of her purse. "She too has red hair as you see and is an imp like her father."

He smiled at Siobhan Marie, like everyone must when they see the little kid's goofy, magical smile.

"And Chuck, what do you try to do in your portraits?" He was looking at Jack Kennedy and John Paul I.

"I try to catch who they are when that which is best in them is present, not so much to flatter as to challenge them."

The face again.

"So you will perhaps challenge me."

"I'll try."

I glanced over at Adolfo. He was smiling happily. The young secretary was beaming. We—that is to say, my wife—were doing a fine job. I was too excited by the conversation to remember how angry I had been an hour earlier.

"So, Rosemarie"—he gestured at the books and pictures—"do you think your husband is a genius?"

"I knew that, Holy Father, when I was ten years old and he was the obnoxious brother of my best friend."

There was no way to stop the woman when she was on a roll.

The frosty blue eyes sparkled.

"I'm not a genius, Holy Father," I protested.

"God has blessed you, Dr. O'Malley . . . Chuck . . . with enormous talent. You have done very well with it. I know you will continue your work. I will ask God to bless you and your work and your family . . . Now we must see how you can challenge me."

"I think we can still use available light," I said to my assistant, as she bustled around the papal office, setting up equipment.

She took a reading with a light meter.

"Probably you can for another half hour or so. Let's do it both ways to be sure."

"Yes, ma'am."

It was not difficult to find the right shot. Despite his many layers of complexity, the Pope was an easy man to photograph. What you saw was what you got—mostly. I tried to get a brilliant and gifted man who had grown up under oppression and was ready to fight for his beliefs, an intellectual garrison commander with gentleness and charm.

I managed a number of wonderful shots. I knew it would be hard to choose among them.

Rosemarie nodded approvingly.

"I think that will do it," I said finally.

"So quick?" He rolled his eyes and pursed his lips again.

"You're an easy model, Holy Father."

"Ah."

"Now we must have a picture of the three of us," he said. "Father Stefan, do you know how to operate Dr. O'Malley's camera?"

"Yes, Holy Father. It is a Hasselblad."

I put a new roll into it and gave it to the priest.

"Shoot the whole roll."

He did. There was nothing wrong with his eye.

The Pope blessed us and gave us medals to commemorate his election to pass out to our children and grandchildren.

"And one for the sister who was the best friend."

He made us promise to send him a copy of the picture and the book of portraits, blessed us, and said good-bye.

Outside in the antechamber, Rosemarie said something in Polish to the secretary. He nodded in agreement or approval or something.

"You two are very dangerous," Adolfo said, as we rode down in the elevator. "He realized immediately that you were not the degenerates that the people in the Sala Stampa said you were. That was very good. He will not forget you. You must stay in touch with me if there are ever any problems."

Yet the posters were up on us. We sent copies of the print of the Pope to both Adolfo and the Pope. Adolfo sent a nice letter. We heard nothing from the Pope. The same thing happened to the catalogue of our Art Institute exhibition.

When the Pope came to Chicago we were not on anyone's list to be invited to anything. The Lady Jane—Jane Byrne, the new Mayor of Chicago—was not on the list either because she and Cardinal O'Neill had become bitter enemies. She in turn managed to keep Sis Daley, the Mayor's widow, off the list though the local Polish clergy arranged for her to meet the Pope at the Polish parish he visited in the Bridgeport neighborhood. At the Eucharist in Grant Park it had been arranged that the Pope would give Communion to a hundred people, not including the Lady Jane. So the Mayor elbowed her way to the head of the line so she could be the first to communicate. At the end, there were two people and one host. The Pope shrugged and broke the host in half.

We didn't feel left out. We still had the huge enlargement of Father Stefan's picture, which we displayed prominently in our family room.

"He's been a bit of a disappointment," friends say to me.

I reply, "You can never really leave your neighborhood behind."

I don't receive invitations to lecture at Catholic colleges much anymore, which is fine because I've given up on lectures. The archdiocese pretty much leaves us alone, despite our charitable gifts. When Notre Dame awarded me its Laetare medal, Ted Hesburgh wondered why there had been a call from the Nuncio asking why the award had been made.

"I told him exactly why: you are a very important Catholic layman and a distinguished alumnus. What's the problem?"

"My wife and I are degenerates," I said.

I didn't point out that I had been thrown out of Notre Dame on a trumped-up charge of drinking on campus—Chucky O'Malley who doesn't drink! I didn't because the good wife was there watching me to make sure that I didn't start a fight.

"What makes them say that?"

"The birth control commission report."

Ted shook his head in dismay.

In my remarks I vigorously advocated honesty and fairness in the Church. It was received enthusiastically by everyone. Some of our friends who were there—Vince and Peg, Ed Murray and Cordelia—savored the irony with us.

The institutional Church left us alone and we left it alone. We are to the core of our beings parish Catholics, which is where we belong.

Anyway, Rosemarie and I were drained by the excitement of the visit with the new Pope on that Wednesday in October of 1978. We held hands in the back of the car, speechless and baffled.

"He's a great man," I said finally.

"And a very good man."

"It was kind of a spiritual experience meeting him."

"I know, Chucky, that I'll never forget it."

"I don't think he'll change any more things, like women in the Church, though he was perfectly charming to you."

"He never mentioned my stories."

"Perhaps he didn't know about them."

"That would be the problem, wouldn't it? Charm is no substitute for respect."

"I saw him as an intelligent and gifted garrison commander for a Church under assault."

"We're not under assault."

"Not in our neighborhood, Rosemarie."

"He grew up in a neighborhood under assault, didn't he?"

"That's the whole point."

"I still think he's a wonderful man."

We asked the driver to stop for a few moments by the Trinita dei Monte Church and slipped inside to pray for the Pope and the Church.

"That's the end of the year of the three Popes for us," I said, as we walked out of the church. "We have a lot of work to do at home."

"Including our book on the conclaves."

"I'd almost forgotten it."

"We have to do it, Chucky."

"Yes, we do. Only I don't want to think about it now."

We changed our reservations to the next day, ate a good supper at a trattoria down the street, made gentle love, and fell into peaceful sleep.

The plane was delayed in its departure and delayed even more in landing at O'Hare. It was eight-thirty before we finally cleared customs. We agreed that there would be no one waiting for us.

We had misjudged our family. Moire Meg, Seano, and Siobhan were at the door of the arrivals hall.

"Chookie, Rooshie!" our youngest shouted and rushed at us, clutching one of each of our legs in an elegant compromise. "Momeg say don't go 'way again."

Who would dare to argue with Momeg?

I picked her up and gave her to my wife. She hugged and kissed Rooshie and then was passed back to Chookie.

"I brought the lug along," Moire Meg said, "because I knew I couldn't cope with Rosie's luggage."

Rome was now far away. The ambiguous story was over. We were home, home to stay, I hoped, for a long time.

❧ Rosemarie ❧

1978

"The story can wait," I insisted. "We have to get the framing done first."

"It can't wait," my husband responded with quiet firmness. "I'll do the frames, you work on your story."

It was an order. I hear them rarely. Each time resistance and anger well up inside of me. How dare he! I give the orders, right?

"You're right, Chucky. You work on your pictures and I work on my story."

We had developed the protocol for such exchanges years ago. I work on the premise that when Chuck challenges me he's always right. After the exchange is over and I calm down I know he's right. In this case I should not neglect the revision of my story. Its final acceptance and the publication of the collection of my stories is important to my career.

It's a powerful sexual turn-on too.

"You are sexually aroused when you bend your will to your husband's?" Maggie Ward challenges me, the little soul-reading witch.

"Would that be wrong?"

"What makes you ask that question?"

"It's like when he told me to stop drinking, those were terrifying days and unbearably sweet."

I figured I would get points for that comment. I would have said in the past that he made me stop drinking. We'd spend the rest of the session arguing that he had done no such thing.

"Ah."

"I feel vulnerable and protected."

"And hence sexually aroused?"

"Safe," I say.

"Someone has drawn outer limits to your self-destructiveness and you wish to merge with him?"

"I guess so . . . and celebrate with him."

"Celebrate what?"

"Survival."

"A delicate dance, Rosemarie."

Often I would go home and flirt with Chucky after such a session. In our bedroom he makes me take off my nightgown and lie on the bed. Then with a single finger he traces delicate abstract designs all over me. His movements are slow and leisurely. My reactions are the same way at first. Then I become a tornado of twisting, turning, womanly hunger. He smiles and continues his unhurried amusements.

."Chucky Ducky, I am not a sex object to be played with."

He just laughs.

"Please!" I scream, as the warmth in my body becomes intolerable. "Let's finish it."

He laughs again, kisses me, and continues his work.

He thus demonstrates his complete control over me. And at the same time he reveals how much my need for happiness controls him.

I don't need that witch Maggie Ward to explain everything to me.

I cry out often. He continues to laugh. I fear that I will die of pleasure. Then finally, in an explosion of joy, we come together and ride to the stars.

"Well," I say. "I hope you're satisfied."

He laughs yet again. He knows what has happened. We cuddle in each other's arms and sleep long and peacefully.

Only that is not what happens on that rainy late-October night in 1978 when we have returned from the conclave and he works on the exhibition and I work on the story. We are too exhausted at the end of the day from jet lag and hard work. I'm even more to blame than he is because I am edgy from my struggles with the text.

We share our work at the beginning and the end of the day. Rather, he shows me his final scheme for cropping when we

start to work in the morning and the final result in late afternoon. There is so little change in the picture that most would
hardly notice it—as they will not notice the difference of the
hung portrait from the one in the catalogue (which is already
set in type). However, the final touch satisfies his need for
neatness before he presses two prints into the matte, one to be
carefully, indeed perfectly wrapped, and sent off to the Art
Institute by messenger, the other to be shown to me and then
locked in one of his cabinets against the day during the exhibition when someone has violated a photograph, a new anticipation in his preparations.

Indeed, he is much more uneasy about this exhibition than
any of the others. In the past he hasn't cared much about the
shows. He's done his work, he's taken the pictures, printed
them, matted them, and that's that. To hell with what anyone
thinks or says. Now he worries constantly about the reaction
both of the crowd and the critics. It's been too long since the
last one. He's also not sure that he has done anything worth-
while, a fear that never bothered him before.

Damn midlife crisis!

"Charles Cronin O'Malley! To hell with the critics!"

He grins at me.

"You're right, Rosemarie. They didn't like Mozart either."

He doesn't mean it. He continues to worry.

Sometimes in the day while we're both working in different
parts of our home, the baby drifts into my office with a load
of toys. She's breaking the rules that Mom (or in her case
Rooshie) is not to be bothered when she's at work in her
office. However, I have granted a temporary indult because
we abandoned her for so long during the conclaves. She plays
very quietly, interrupting her fantasy games only to periodically hug and kiss me.

"I love you, Rooshie!"

"I love you too, Shovie."

I wear my usual work uniform of jeans and either tee shirt
or sweatshirt. I have enough varieties of this garb to last at
least a month without repeating myself. However, since it developed that Moire Meg and I could wear the same clothes
and she began to "borrow" mine, I've had to stride into her
room, unbearably messy, and borrow mine back, usually with

threats of severe punishment if she kept it up. She'd laugh at me, as she usually does, which is no way to treat a mother, is it?

Late in the afternoon, the aforementioned Moire Meg ambles in, book pack over her shoulder, and pecks my cheek.

"How many sentences did we get through today, Rosie?"

"That's my Vienna tee shirt."

"I'll give it back."

The small one abandons me to rush to embrace her adored big sister. Little brat.

"Momeg! Momeg!"

The two daughters desert me and I continue to stare at the computer screen. Somehow revision is a lot harder this time.

Then Chuck arrives to show me, with the pride of a kid showing a drawing to his mother, the day's work—four or five pictures on a good day. I respond by admiring his work. His eye is as good as ever. Alas, he's not so sure.

Then I show him my work?

No way! I don't permit him to read a single word of a story before it's ready to be sent to an editor. He doesn't even look at the computer screen lest I screech at him that he's breaking the rules.

Is this asymmetry silly, even wrong?

Yes, it is. However, it's the way we work.

Two people afraid that their efforts are not worth anything.

Our love life is temporarily suspended because of darkness. Or rain. Or something.

Then one afternoon in early November—only ten days left before final delivery of our work—Seano shows up and asks if he can talk to us for a few minutes.

Certainly he can. I close the door to fend off his sisters. He's wearing chinos and a blue blazer and a blue dress shirt, open at the neck—business-school student and part-time worker at the Board of Trade. The shortest of my three sons (towering over his father by three inches), he is also the most handsome. His flawlessly carved face is touched by the late-afternoon shadow which could so easily become a beard if it were part of his current persona.

My heart is in my throat because I have a pretty good idea of what's coming. I hope that my husband is tuned in. Seano sits at the edge of one of my maroon leather easy chairs.

"I'm planning to marry Esther," he says, trying to sound relaxed and casual, "in June, right after I graduate."

"Is she planning the same thing?" I ask without thinking.

That stops him.

"I haven't asked her yet. I imagine I'll have to do some persuading. I'm sure I'll win her over."

What a dumb male thing to say. I almost responded, "Wanna bet?" I didn't. Maybe I should have.

"We respect you too much, Sean," Chuck says smoothly, "to try to change your mind. We'll stand by you."

Nice going.

"I know that," Sean says uneasily. "I'll always be a Catholic. I couldn't possibly be anything else. Esther respects that just as I respect her Jewish faith."

"You realize that it won't be easy," I chime in. "It would be all right if one of you was not a strong believer in your heritage."

"I think our love is powerful enough to support us through those problems."

My heart ached for this child of my womb who was repeating the easy clichés of one besotted by what he thought was undying passion.

"The children?"

"We'll raise them in both heritages and let them choose when they're old enough to make up their own minds."

A recipe for constant family infighting.

"Esther agrees to this?" Chuck asked.

"We haven't talked about it, but I'm sure she will. I thought we could discuss those things after we're engaged."

"Those things" were minor problems, hardly worth worrying about.

"When do you think that will be?"

"I plan to give her a ring at Christmastime."

"Not at Christmas, Seano," Chuck said gently.

"Why not?" my son seemed surprised.

"That's a Christian feast. As I remember her family celebrates Christmas much to her chagrin. Try New Year's."

"Oh, yeah, Dad . . . Good idea."

How naïve can a late-adolescent male be? Even when he's my own son, pretty damn naïve!

"I'm sure you understand," Chuck went on, saying all the things I should have been saying, "that Esther is in the midst of a particularly painful crisis with her own family, indeed a religious crisis. She is angry at them for denying what she takes to be her religious heritage. They are angry at her for buying into what they think is outmoded superstition. I won't speculate about the reasons for this conflict, but it is a wrenching experience for her."

"She's made up her mind that she's Jewish," Seano replied. "She won't change on that."

"I'm sure she has. However, you must realize that she's not Jewish in the sense that you're Catholic."

"What do you mean, Dad?" Sean was puzzled.

"You've been raised Catholic, you've been Catholic all your life, you've never been out of the Catholic environment, even when it was a degraded environment at that college you went to. Esther has only recently become a Jew."

"Her mother is Jewish. In Jewish law that's what makes Esther Jewish."

I wondered how much his experience at that rinky-dink college contributed to his sudden, late-adolescent passion.

Irrelevant question.

"As you would be Catholic if you had been baptized and then raised in a completely secular environment."

"I suppose that's true," he admitted, not seeing the point, the poor jerk.

"So you have to cut her some slack until she feels relaxed in her newfound faith."

"I don't plan to be married till summer," he said, somewhat defensively.

Summer was so far away.

Well, maybe it will all work out.

"That's your decision, Sean." I finally found my tongue. "We'll support whatever you decide. Your father and I are really suggesting that you should be very sensitive to Esther's current emotional state."

"We'd be about the same age you were when you were married," he said, not hearing a word of mine.

"That was different," Chuck replied, the usual idiot cliché.

"How was it different?" Sean bristled.

"You're a lot more mature than I was at your age."

Brilliant, husband mine!

Sean laughed and, sensing that the conversation was over, stood up.

"I wonder," he said as though it were an afterthought, which it surely wasn't, "whether we could have her over for supper on Sunday. Just us—and Moire Meg of course. She finds our whole family intimidating."

"Intimidating?" I snapped.

"Well, what she said was overwhelming."

"That I can understand. We are after all the Crazy O'Malleys."

"We'd be happy to have her for dinner on Sunday," Chuck said easily. "Why not?"

"Certainly," I added, again too little and too late.

"Gosh, thanks a lot," our son said fervently, and slipped out of my office.

"Well done, Chucky."

"Only because I more easily become phony."

"What's going to happen?"

"I think, as is usually the case in these matters, it will depend on Eileen . . ."

"Esther."

"Yes . . . Esther. It is usually the case that women bring these matters to closure. Either to force a marriage decision or to end the courtship, the former being the more frequent. At some point Esther will either go along with our son's wishes or brush him off. In which case we may need a blotter."

"Women see things more clearly."

"I recall hearing that said." He grinned at me. "I would not dream of debating it."

Moire Meg appeared at the door of my office in her tantrum modality.

"Rosie, your son is an asshole."

She was still wearing my Vienna tee shirt. For the first time that day I noticed the radiance of Indian summer outside the window and the front lawn bathed in gold-and-crimson leaves.

"I don't disagree," I said.

"That poor kid doesn't want to come here for supper on Sunday. She's scared stiff of us."

"Frightened of the Crazy O'Malleys?" the young woman's father asked.

She threw herself on the same chair that her brother had just vacated.

"Sure! I can't figure out why her parents let her go to Loyola. She was certain to encounter some Orthodox Jews at the Hillel Center or whatever they call it up there. She was also certain to stumble into the Irish Catholic Chicago subculture. She isn't prepared for either. My idiot brother is too tumescent to understand that."

"She has to choose between the two of them?" I said.

"Or retreating to the safety of Jewish secularism."

"We're a threat then to her newfound Jewishness?"

"Oh, yeah, Rosie, sure. I can't imagine that she could have lived in this city all her life and not know about our kind, except a few clichés. She finds us all very attractive. She told me so. Especially your husband, who is such a nice man, right? That's why she won't want to come here for supper. Asshole takes it for granted that she's dying to know the family better and doesn't even ask her whether she wants to show up here on Sunday."

"How do you know that?" I wondered.

"I asked him. He looked at me blankly and goes like, 'I know she'd love the invitation.' "

"And you said?"

"I told him he was an asshole. He seemed surprised . . . Rosie, there's something missing in his education, like how to relate to a woman."

"We do our best," I said defensively.

"Yeah, well, you two don't argue with her much. She'll come ready to play Talmudic games with us. Jewish people love to argue, like Chucky's friend Dr. Berman. She'll pick up a load of arguments at Hillel before she shows up here. Let me do the arguing. I'm her age and she thinks I'm a friend. Which I am. I'm the one to take her on."

She stood up, her displeasure vented on her defenseless parents.

"One question, moonbeam," her father asked.

"Yeah?" She smiled happily as she always did when he called her moonbeam.

"How did an eighteen-year-old like you acquire such wisdom?"

"Actually, nineteen, Chucky . . . And I learned all I know by growing up in this house."

She cackled like a Halloween witch.

"Hey," she said, glancing through the matted prints Chucky had brought up to the office, "this is a totally bitchin' picture of you, Rosie. Out of sight! Great work, Chucky! Best yet!"

"It's not me," I said firmly.

"Oh, yeah, it is, Rosie, totally."

"That's what I think too," my husband said.

"We won't discuss it now."

"Yeah, well, I'm not involving myself in this family argument," she announced, and flounced out of the office.

"I have made up my mind," I told my husband. "This does not hang in the exhibition."

I had told him that several times before. He usually said that, of course, was up to me. I knew however that he was scheming and conniving in search of ways to avoid my wishes.

"If you say so," he agreed. "It's your call."

It was a portrait he had made of me at Grand Beach the previous summer. It was not obscene or even erotic. I was simply not me. I was wearing an old maroon University of Chicago sleep tee shirt which fell modestly to my bare knees. I had not worn it for years. It was a student's tee shirt I should have thrown away. I forgot about it and, when Chuck rediscovered it somewhere in the disorder of the house, he got the brilliant idea of photographing me in it. It had been a loosely fitting nightie when I first wore it. Now it had shrunk after many washings, as such shirts do. It covered me but it left no doubt about the distribution of the various parts of my anatomy.

Moreover, I had a crazy look in my eyes and an even crazier grin starting on my face. I was also wielding a hairbrush with which I might have brushed my tangled hair or hit the photographer.

In fact, I had thrown it at him.

"I might just as well be stark naked," I protested.

"That wouldn't do at all," he argued. "This is much more erotic, but innocently so."

"It isn't erotic at all. It's just plain dumb."

I shifted back and forth between two arguments—the first was that it was indecent and the second that it wasn't me at all. What these arguments lacked in consistency, I made up by my own fury.

"Well," he said that afternoon when our middle daughter had withdrawn from the fray, "I'd like to remind you that a lot of our subjects say the same thing about their portraits, only to be overruled by their family's insistence that it was too."

"I don't care!" I growled.

"I won't hang it if you object," he said again. "I propose, however"—and his eyes narrowed—Chucky plotting—"that we ask the opinions of others."

"What others? That silly little teenage witch?"

"What a terrible thing to say about your daughter . . . No, I mean the high council of matriarchs."

"What?"

"Convene a board of judgment made up of all the womenfolk—the good April, Peg, Jane, April Rosemary, Delia Murray if you want, even Moire Meg so there'll be one vote on my side."

It was a dangerous and insidious proposal which I could not reject without looking bad, something which would never do in an argument with my husband.

"Then, if you want, take it to your next tête-a-tête with your friend Maggie Ward and listen to her judgment. If the vote in both venues is against me, then I will yield the field of battle."

"They'll all say that it is a stupid picture."

"If such womanly wisdom emerges, I'll accept the decision."

He was building a trap for me, ingenious little bastard that he was.

"Suppose they agree with you and I still don't want this idiotic picture hung?"

"It's your picture," he said, moving his hands as though he were smoothing something out.

"Well . . ."

"Up to you."

"You're a clever little bastard."

"I believe I've been called that before."

"You forced sex on me after you took that picture."

"Funny, I don't quite remember it that way."

"And how do you remember it?" I snapped, knowing full well that I would lose this argument.

"You threw the brush at me and then physically attacked me. I merely defended myself and one thing led to another . . . You seemed to enjoy one thing and another."

"That's irrelevant," I shouted. "This is not me."

Deep down in the lowest subbasement of my soul, I was scared that it might indeed be me. Then where would I be?

Nonetheless, I was confident that the High Council of Matriarchs, as my insidious little husband had called them, would support me. A woman had a right to her modesty, did she not?

I called April and told her that I was having a problem with a portrait of me that her son wanted to hang at the Art Institute and I wanted everyone in the family and Delia too, who was practically family, to look at it.

"Poor little Chucky is so clever with his camera."

This had been her standard reaction to her son since he was ten years old.

So the next morning we all appeared at the elder O'Malleys' home on East Avenue. April Rosemary had brought along little Johnny Nettleton, who seemed delighted at all the attention the various mothers showered on him. His mother was radiant again. The medication was doing its work.

Peg and her mother distributed coffee and tea and cookies. I accepted the tea and declined the cookies.

"Well, dear"—the good April called the meeting to order—"you have some kind of problem with a picture of you that Chuck wants to hang at the exhibition."

That was an uncharacteristically direct opening from herself. She was dying of curiosity. So were they all.

"He took this shot at the Lake last summer. I think it is silly and stupid and humiliating and is not me at all."

I unwrapped the picture with little attention to Chuck's careful work on its packaging and laid it on the kitchen table for all of them to see.

There was a gasp of astonishment and then dead silence.

"Poor dear Chucky is so clever with his cute little camera."

"April, you've been saying that since he was ten years old."

"Well, dear, it's been true since he was ten years old."

"It really is you, you know." Peg, my best friend in all the world, had gone over to the other side.

"It's the best thing Daddy's ever done," April Rosemary joined the consensus. "He reveals your beauty in a way that neither objectifies you or fetishizes you. You are a lovely and challenging woman in the middle years of life who isn't afraid of the photographer or anyone who looks at the picture. Indeed she defies all of us."

I contained my temper. What, I wondered, is a fetish? Maybe an obsession with a body part.

"It's also really quite comic," Delia, who had once dated Chucky, commented. "One wants to admire her, and laugh with her, and duck when she throws the brush, which presumably you did."

My middle daughter, who had taken her godson away from April Rosemary and was playing with him, remained silent.

"Moire Meg," the good April asked, "aren't you going to vote?"

"Oh, do I get to vote? . . . What do you think, Johnny boy? Do you think it's a totally bitchin' picture of your gram? . . . Well since you asked me, I don't think Chucky should hang it until Rosie agrees."

"Well, I don't agree," I snapped. "I might just as well be totally naked."

"Oh, no, dear," the good April remonstrated with me. "That would ruin it all. It's much more erotic because it is much more modest."

My foster mother was still a flapper, always would be.

"The picture says," Peg added, "that a beautiful woman can be erotic and chaste at the same time. And confident in her erotic powers too."

"That's bullshit, Peg."

My foster sister and dearest friend flushed angrily.

"You're the one that's filled with bullshit, Rosie," she fired back.

We've been arguing and fighting since I showed up outside their two flat in 1939.

"I wish my mother and my aunt," Moire Meg joined the battle, "would stop using vulgar language and acting like assholes."

"Now, darlings," the good April said, "we must control our tempers. . . . You know, Rosie dear, that all of us envy you because that picture is so wonderful. None of us would dare pose in a nightie like that for poor little Chucky."

"I would hope not," I said, simmering down. "Sorry, Peg."

"Be my guest."

"I have been for a long time." My eyes stung with tears.

"I don't think an artist could do a portrait like that of anyone who was not his wife or lover," Delia observed. "One would need to be in a confident and intimate relationship with a woman to dare to attempt it. Even then the photographer took a terrible risk."

Delia was from Lake Forest and talked like she had a Harvard degree. I ignored the drawl because she was so sweet. I was about to turn on her and then stopped myself.

"Maybe you're right, Deal," I said. "Himself didn't look very frightened."

"He wouldn't look that way, would he?"

She had dated Chuck when they were at Notre Dame and then rejected him so she could pursue a concert career, only to discover that she didn't quite have the talent. She did have some good insights into my husband.

"Too bad you didn't marry her," I would shout at him in some of our fights.

"Not enough passion," he'd reply, and our fight would end in laughter.

"No, I suppose not," I replied to her. "However, Chucky Ducky doesn't have enough sense to be scared when he's in danger. He didn't even think I'd throw the hairbrush at him."

Everyone laughed and we all relaxed. I felt like a real bitch.

"Well, dear," the good April summed up, "we could be wrong and probably are, but we all think it's a cute picture and it would look just fine in poor little Chucky's show. Still as darling Moire Meg says, it's your decision, not ours."

Darling little Moire Meg handed her godson back to April Rosemary and hugged her grandmother.

Why was it always "poor little Chucky"?

"I'll have to do a lot of thinking about it," I said, putting off a decision. "Thank you for being candid despite my rotten temper."

So the minifight ended early rather than late. I could easily have thrown the portrait at Peg and stormed out of the house.

"Did you expect anything different?" Moire Meg asked, as we went back to our house under a gray sky which hinted that Indian summer warmth could last only a day or two more. She would go on to class at Rosary and I to wrestle with my manuscript.

"I thought they'd understand. I guess they didn't."

"Maybe they understood all too well."

I resolved I wouldn't get in a fight with her. So I said nothing.

Why was I so afraid of a portrait that everyone else loved?

I made some progress on the manuscript, four or five paragraphs. At this pace I would be finished by Easter.

Chuck joined me at the end of the day, carrying a tray on which there was a teapot in a caddy and two mugs.

"Well, how did the Grand High Council of the Matriarchs rule?" he asked after he had poured my tea.

"You rigged the vote," I complained. "You stuffed the ballot box."

"Fat chance of that happening."

"They liked it of course. They keep saying it's my decision."

"Shame on them."

"It should be your decision. You're the photographer."

"All the other subjects have given their written consent. I won't hang your portrait without your written consent."

"It's a stupid, silly picture," I said, now without much conviction. "It isn't me at all."

"Your vote cancels all others."

The little bastard was enjoying the game, like he enjoyed most of the games he played with me.

"Why can't I just say that I won't scream and shout and claw in protest?"

"Wouldn't believe you."

"Can't I write you saying that I don't like the picture because it's silly and stupid and not me, but you can go ahead and hang it if you want to?"

"Hang myself too."

He had me where he wanted me and wouldn't let me sneak away.

"Well, first thing next week."

"After you've collected Maggie Ward's vote."

"I don't care what she says. I'll make up my own mind."

"Dare I ask how the manuscript is coming?"

"I'll be finished before summer. . . . Now we have to worry about what we feed Esther tomorrow."

✎ Chucky ✎
1978

Esther, nee Eileen, wore a pale gray shift and had put up her hair in a ponytail, thus heightening the impression that she was a solemn little waif. Our poor son hung around behind her in the parlor like a cashiered knight-errant who had no idea of what to do or say, poor bumpkin. Esther was frightened. She did not want to be with us for Sunday supper. She was afraid of us. She didn't exactly like us. Well, she had bonded with Moire Meg in a new generation of the monster regiment.

"Would you like something to drink, Esther?" Rosemarie asked politely.

Thank the good Lord that she did not adopt my mother's "dear."

"If I might have a small glass of dry white wine," she whispered.

"I'll have a large glass of the same, Rosie," the ineffable Moire Meg informed her mother.

We didn't serve liquor at or before family meals. Perhaps bottles of wine would be placed on the table when the extended family was around. Moire Meg had never before had an opportunity to order a preprandial drink at home.

"Not your usual dry martini with a twist?" I asked.

"Chucky!" she protested.

"Jews consider wine to be sacramental," Esther said softly.

"So do we," Moire Meg responded. "We believe that in some mysterious way Jesus is present in it."

"You eat and drink Jesus, don't you?"

"That's silly," Moire Meg dismissed the attack. "It doesn't understand what Catholics mean by 'sacrament.'"

Esther nodded solemnly as if she understood, which she certainly did not. The waiflike child did not stand a chance in the forthcoming Talmudic argument.

Poor Seano simply looked confused.

"You don't have to worry about the meal, Es," Moire Meg went on. "Everything fits with the dietary laws."

"The Lord gave us these laws," Esther said softly, "to remind us of His loving presence among His people."

"Yeah, well, I understand that similar food codes were widespread in the Near East. They were intended as primitive public health measures."

"Still, God gave them special meaning for us when He gave them to us through our rabbi Moses."

"Does your shul have a *mikveh*?"

Where had our daughter picked up all this stuff? Esther, however, seemed pleased with the questions. They gave her something to talk about.

"What's a *mikveh*?" Sean asked, in a tone of voice which said why are you talking about such stuff?

"It means a ritual bath in which women purify themselves after they've had their periods."

"Oh, no," Esther said, "only a few of the big Orthodox synagogues have them. I spend much of my time in the tub during those days."

"Why?" Sean demanded.

"To remove my impurity."

"Impurity!"

Moire Meg adopted the tone of an impatient full professor with her brother.

"The Torah requires that men not touch a woman who is ritually impure, during her monthly period and also after childbirth. Remember the Purification of Mary in the temple?"

"Why?"

"To protect the poor women from male lust!"

"Dinner is ready," Rosemarie intervened, her eyes wide with surprise at her daughter's "engaging" our guest in religious discussion.

We sat around the supper table. I said grace, which we

didn't do routinely every night. Esther bowed her head respectfully.

After Moire Meg helped her mother bring soup to the table, she continued her "dialogue."

"Same thing with circumcision, I gather," she said. "Public health measure in those days. Not clear anymore that it really works, but a lot of people thought so in those days."

"I'm sure you're right," Esther said. "Yet, those of us who follow the Torah also believe that the Lord demands these obediences of us because we are His people. That makes the observance of the law different for us than it is for others."

"Does your shul believe that women should have as many children as possible?"

Our guest's eyes brightened. "A good Jewish woman knows that it is her duty to bring children into the world so that the Lord's holy people may grow and prosper."

"Most Jews don't believe that, do they?" Rosemarie asked.

"Oh, no, Mrs. O'Malley. Only the very Orthodox. But the others, like my dear parents, are practically goyim—gentiles."

"Jewishness is passed on through the mother, isn't it?" Moire Meg said.

Setup question. My daughter undoubtedly knew the answer.

"Oh yes, Moire. It is the Lord's law that all of my children will be Jewish."

"I suppose the reason," Moire Meg said, "is that one can always be sure whether the mother is Jewish or not."

"Isn't it hard to be an observant Jew?" I asked because I figured I should say something. Rosemarie and Moire Meg slipped into the kitchen to bring the salad.

The clear soup which Moire Meg had bought at a kosher store up in Skokie was terrible. I finished as much of it as I could as a gesture of interreligious friendship.

"It is very difficult here in America, Mr. O'Malley. That is why I hope after graduation to emigrate to Israel, where I can raise my children to be good Jews."

"Does religion really mean keeping all those rules?" Sean asked in a tone which was a mixture of surprise and dismay.

"Keeping God's law is what makes us a holy people. You Christians believe in salvation, we Jews believe in sanctification. To become sanctified we keep the Lord's law."

"I don't get it," Sean said.

"You're not Jewish, Sean," Moire Meg dismissed him. "Esther is . . . Still, Esther, as I read the books, I am impressed by the fact that Christianity is really a Jewish sect. In the time of the Second Temple, most Christians thought that they were also Jews. It was only after the fall of Jerusalem that sectarianism infiltrated into Jewish religious culture and the two cousin religions emerged."

"I have not read that," Esther said, now on the defensive.

"I can give you a list of books," my daughter said. "The point is that the split between the synagogue and the Church was gradual and was not the intent of the best people on either side."

"Why did the Lord permit that?" Esther asked, her fork poised over her salad.

"I don't think it was a very good idea, to tell the truth," my daughter replied. "Yet any Christian who understands knows that Jews are still God's people."

I stopped eating, so struck was I by the knowledge of this child of ours, a woman with my hair and eyes and her mother's figure and grace and an intellectual brilliance which perhaps harkened back to the wisdom of some Druidic ancestor or perhaps a teacher in one of the hedge schools who was literate in Latin and Greek.

"And they will reunite someday?" Sean, still befuddled, asked.

"Who knows the ways of the Lord?" Moire Meg waved his question aside as irrelevant.

"Yet Christians persecuted Jews from the very beginning, didn't they?" Esther asked, as she picked at her salad.

"Not for the first ten centuries. And then the persecutions were limited to the Rhineland in Germany for a long time. Most of the popes and bishops tried to stop the persecutions. Remember when St. Bernard went from Clairveaux to Mainz to stop a massacre? Since then, of course, we've done a lot of bad things to you guys. If I were Jewish, I wouldn't trust Catholics very much, though to tell you the truth I'd trust Protestants even less."

Esther realized that she was outnumbered and gracefully ended the disputation.

"My parents didn't have many Irish Catholic friends, so I didn't know your people until I went to Loyola. I think the Irish are great. I admire their religious faith."

"Why did you choose Loyola?" I asked.

"I wanted to be near my poor parents who loved me so much and I couldn't stand the paganism at Northwestern."

The last thing those poor parents would have expected was that their daughter would become a strict Orthodox Jew at a Catholic university.

I felt very sorry for them.

We turned to discussion of classes at school, especially the advanced course in computer programming which Sean and Esther thought was wonderful. When she had discharged her obligation to outline her religious convictions to us, Esther became a delightfully witty young woman, full of laughter and fun and mimicry. She helped us clean off the table and fill the dishwasher and chatted merrily with us. Her family might be religiously secular but they must speak with the irony and inflections which are characteristic of American Judaism and which I have found delightful since my days in the darkroom in Bamberg with Max Berman, so many years ago.

No one can say, "So what can I tell you?" with as much expression and so many expressive gestures as an American Jew. I laugh every time I hear it.

Gram and Gramps delivered Siobhan Marie back home at the appointed time. I was surprised at how quickly the hours with Esther had passed. The child, always eager to exercise her charm, promptly embraced "Essher."

"You must be so proud of her, Mrs. O'Malley. What a lovely grandchild!"

"I'm the kid's mother." Rosemarie laughed.

"I'm so sorry . . ." Esther looked like she wanted to escape into the first available hole in the ground. "I knew . . ."

Rosemarie embraced her.

"No problem," my wife assured her. "Lots of people make that mistake. Sometimes I think of her as a grandchild too."

"You're certainly young enough to have a baby like this adorable little girl." She lifted the happy Siobhan Marie into her arms.

"Just barely."

When they were leaving to return to Loyola, she pecked at my cheek and embraced Rosemarie and Moire Meg.

"I was afraid to come for dinner, but I've had such a wonderful time."

Outside the temperature had fallen thirty degrees and a fierce wind was blowing.

We gathered in the family room to review the day, the child with her toys.

"Well," Moire Meg kicked off the discussion, "my sibling may well be an asshole, but he is certainly a gentle asshole . . . I suppose that no male raised in this family can help himself. All he knows is being gentle. No wonder she adores him."

"If someone is talking about me," I said, to cover my embarrassment, "I reject all the charges. I am not a gentle asshole."

"Not usually," Rosemarie agreed. "Always gentle and an asshole on very rare occasions."

Moire Meg ignored our banter.

"She's not ready to become engaged. If he were smart about women—like you are, Chucky—he'd forget about that until next year. Even then I don't think she'll be ready. She has too much of her own shit to straighten out."

"You will tell him these things?" I said.

"Sure"—she shrugged her lovely shoulders—"but he won't listen to me. He will have to learn painfully how the psyche of a woman works . . . She really likes us, you know. Wouldn't mind us as in-laws at all."

"Too bad by us it's not Jewish," Rosemarie sighed.

"No it isn't. Even if she doesn't stick with this Orthodox conversion, I don't think she'll ever go back to being a secular Jew. Sounds pretty hollow to me."

"You don't think she'll stick with it?"

"How would I know, Chucky? She sure is fervent, but she doesn't know much. You saw how I ran all over her, poor kid . . . She's searching for who she is. Who knows what she'll find out? She might make a nice sister-in-law. Ask me, I'll say nothing will come of it, even if my dear brother smartens up enough to listen to what she says, which he certainly wasn't doing today. Too bad, maybe."

"Do you know who you are, Moire Meg?" I asked.

"Who, me?" She seemed astonished. "Sure, I know. I knew the minute I was conceived that I was Rosie and Chucky's baby girl . . . Until this little brat came along and stole my identity . . . Didn't you, Shovie?"

She lifted the tyke off the floor, held her in the air, and then cradled her in her arms.

"More!"

"We'll scare dolly!"

"Can't scare dolly," the small one said, hugging the dolly the same way her big sister hugged her.

"Shovie loves Momeg."

"I'll put her to bed," Moire Meg told us. "She's dead tired."

"No!"

"Yes."

"Hokay."

"That young woman," I observed, "will make some girl child a wonderful mother someday."

"And drive some poor man crazy."

"I know the experience."

❧ *Rosemarie* ❧
1978

"What do you expect me to say about this portrait, Rose-marie?" Maggie Ward said sternly as she waved her little hand somewhat disdainfully at Chucky's picture. "It's beautiful and so are you, but is that appropriate material for our hour to-day?"

"I was hoping you'd tell me that it wasn't me."

"That's absurd. Besides, even if it wasn't you, it would hardly be appropriate for our conversation."

"Chucky and I are having a big argument over it," I admitted, feeling very guilty.

"You and your husband are arguing over this lovely picture? He doesn't want to hang it at his exhibition and you insist that he does?"

"You know that's not it."

"The reasons for your resistance are appropriate matter for our conversation?"

"It embarrasses me," I said, trying a new track.

"You are quite chastely covered."

"I might just as well not be."

"Come now, Rosemarie. You know very well that the appeal of this marvelous photograph is that the photographer has both covered you and revealed you. Very ingenious."

"People see my boobs and my belly and my thighs whether they're covered or not."

"And your nipples too."

"Right, so I should be embarrassed, shouldn't I?"

"The photographer has not objectified you or fetishized you.

Clearly he enjoys your beauty and wants the viewers to enjoy you too. There's surely nothing wrong with that, especially as he presents you as a person whose eyes and smile defy him and all his pretensions. You like being admired—what woman does not?—and you are still keeping him and us in our respective places."

"I threw the brush at him and then I tried to hit him and we wrestled and, well, you know what I mean."

"One would have thought it odd if you had not . . . Obviously you enjoyed the experience."

"I always enjoy it when Chucky takes my picture," I admitted.

"You don't want other people to see you the way he sees you, however. I wonder why."

"It's not me," I said stubbornly.

"I think, Rosemarie, that we can rely on a worshipful husband to know more about who you are than you do yourself."

"NO!"

"Yes, my dear. Definitely yes."

"I look like this to you? You know what a fouled-up, terrible person I am."

"I cannot appreciate your attractiveness quite the way a man might, especially a poor dear man, as we Irish say, who is in permanent thrall to you. Yet that's surely you in that picture, you at your best perhaps. That's what Chuck is supposed to capture in a portrait, is it not?"

"I don't know and I don't care."

I knew very well that it would do me no good to become angry at the little witch.

"Moreover, how many times do I have to tell you that I will not permit you to project your lack of self-regard onto me. I do not think you're a terrible person or even a troubled one, save on occasions like this."

"I don't like this portrait because I don't have enough self-regard?"

"Intermittently. This is one of those times."

What if she was right?

"I wonder how many of those who see this fine work of art will suspect that the woman is teasing the photographer and rather enjoying the tease and that in a few moments she will engage in rather aggressive sexual behavior with him."

"NO!"

"He is, after all, her lover. Why would that not happen after an encounter that is intimate, revealing, and patently titillating? Is that not the story? What is wrong with the story? Why are you ashamed of it?"

"I am NOT ashamed of it!"

"Are you telling me that you're proud of your abilities as a sexually attractive woman?"

"No . . . Well, yes. Why the hell not?"

"Indeed."

"I'm no Mona Lisa, Maggie Ward!"

"That's not exactly what I was suggesting."

"I still don't like it . . . You're trying to tell me that I can't admit to myself that this is me, some of the time anyway, because I don't have enough self-regard to accept myself?"

"Have we not made that point several times in these conversations?"

"Uhm . . ." I growled.

"And I'm afraid it's time."

I had walked over to her office at Marion and North Boulevard, despite the wind. It was worse walking home, especially because I was carrying a twenty-by-twenty-four print. Drizzle lingered in the air. We did not need snow flurries tonight.

I felt terrible. There was no escape from this damn portrait. My friends and family and now my shrink had told me that I was acting like a silly child. I *was* acting like a silly child. What would happen to me after the picture was hung? Others would admire me. I didn't want to be admired. My mother had been admired and she died a horrible death. I didn't want to be ordinary either. Couldn't I be kind of attractive in a nonspectacular sort of way?

I knew the answer. I didn't want people to know who I was, even at my best, which apparently is when I'm preparing to sexually attack my husband.

I was thankful that I had worn a warm jacket. Why had I not driven over to Maggie's office or called a cab?

Because exercise was good for me. It helped preserve my figure which I didn't want people to know about.

"Damnation!" I exploded as I collapsed into the easy chair

next to the fireplace. Missus somehow knew I'd come home cold, so she had lighted a fire for me. Then she brought me a pot of tea.

"Lady have nice time with doctor?"

"Brilliant time."

"Is good."

I unwrapped the picture and studied the face. Where had I seen that face before?

I sipped the tea eagerly. Lapsang Souchong. Strong enough to walk on. Missus understood.

In the hundreds of other pictures my husband had taken of me, I had become the Marthe of an Irish-American Bonnard. Shit!

No, I had seen her somewhere else. Where was it? All dressed up in nineteenth-century clothes. I never wore nineteenth-century clothes.

Then I remembered. I ran up the stairs to the second floor and then to the attic. Over in one dusty corner was an ancient armoire, the door hanging loosely on its hinges. It had been my mother's, poor dear woman. I stayed away from it because inside was all that was left of her, a few gowns, a wedding dress, some jewelry I could never bring myself to wear, a few pictures, a painting that Chuck's father had painted when they were all young together.

Even the sight of the armoire in the corner of the attic would make me weep. I avoid it as though it were infectious. How goofy can a woman be!

I looked at the painting. She had been so beautiful, a slender blonde with pale skin, not at all like me.

The tears poured down my cheeks. Why had I exiled her into the attic? It had been thirty-two years since she had died. I had told my kids very little about my parents. Was it not time to forgive? Should I not hang the painting somewhere in the house so the kids would at least know what she looked like?

I wept uncontrollably. Outside an insane chatter of rain against the roof joined the howling of an angry wind. Perfect background—insanity and anger.

Gradually my sobs subsided. The flow of tears ended. I had cried myself out. Then, with the painting in one hand, and the photo album from the bottom of the armoire in the other, I trudged down to the second floor. I left the painting in an empty bedroom and returned to my office.

I phoned the elder O'Malleys.

"April? Rosemarie. Is Vangie around?"

He was meeting downtown with an art dealer from Tucson who planned an exhibition of the watercolors that he had been doing since his retirement. Wonderful.

"I was up in the attic this morning," I said, trying to sound like I was in full control of my tears, "and I found a painting that he had done of my mom when you guys were flappers. Well, I know you still are! It's a beautiful work. I'd like to hang it, in the parlor I think. If we chase Moire Meg over this afternoon with it, could Vangie maybe clean it and touch it up if anything has happened to it?"

Both of us were crying. Such bittersweet memories, now perhaps more sweet than bitter.

Then I opened the photo album.

On the first page, flowery printing on a pink label said simply, "Rosemarie Finn McArdle 1857–1928."

Who had created the album? It must have been my mother. Despite the sentimental label, it was a very skillful job. The only memories I had of Mom were of a pale, vague woman, who was usually drunk. Now I was meeting her again, as a person who cared deeply for her grandmother and who had assembled an album of memories in her honor.

She had also named me after that grandmother.

On the first pages there were sacramental certificates, baptism, confirmation, first Communion, marriage—all from St. Patrick's Church.

She had married Colonel Michael Patrick McArdle also at St. Patrick's in 1875—eighteen years old. She didn't waste any time.

In the first photograph of her she was wearing an unattractive school uniform with a large bow. A neatly lettered caption said "Saint Xavier Academy 1870."

She was thirteen years old, five years before her marriage. So young. I was only a year older. I sighed loudly.

Then I looked at the face and cried out.

It was the one that I had seen in a mirror at that age. The

eyes were as dangerous as those in poor Chuck's portrait of
me, the smile the same as that smile. She was being pious for
the sake of the nuns. But there was just a hint of devilment.
How well I knew that look. That was the person who threw
snowballs at poor Chucky.

The next one was a wedding picture. Colonel Michael Patrick McArdle was a tall, ramrod-stiff Black Irishman with a
thick beard, low forehead, and pale skin. His genes were in
my three sons who, I had often thought, would look won-
drously fearsome in beards. How old was he when he married
my great-grandmother? He had ridden with Phil Sheridan in
the Shenandoah Valley between the Blue Ridge and the Al-
legheny Mountains in 1864 as an immigrant kid. Seventeen at
the most. So eleven years later he was twenty-seven, twenty-
eight, not too much older than his bride, an immigrant and a
soldier who had made a lot of money. He looked even younger
despite his beard and military bearing.

You hardly noticed him, however, in the wedding picture.
The young woman next to him, his Rosemarie, was unbearably
lovely. Her eyes were as dangerous as ever and the smile on
her lips said pretty clearly, "Mike McArdle, I have captured
you and I will never let you go."

I closed the album and struggled for breath. All right, she
wasn't wearing a sleep shirt, but she was me. Or I was her.
Mike's wife was Chucky O'Malley's wife.

More tears, a lot more tears.

Then I watched her life in news clippings and photos—
children, grandchildren, including my own mom. A son who
died from the flu, a lovely daughter who married. My mother's
wedding, her husband's death in the early nineteen twenties.
Summers at Geneva Lake in summer clothes which, while
again not sleep shirts, did not require absurd corsets.

Same eyes, same smile, same lovely figure, same radiance.

Same Rosemarie, always beautiful, also facing the world
with those dangerous eyes.

Maybe I would write a story about her, or a series of stories,
or even a novel.

"Grandma Rosie," I prayed to her, "I sense you're near me
today. I just know it. It's nice to meet you. Maybe you've
always been waiting around for me to introduce myself. There

was so much suffering between you and me. My poor grandmother married to an unfaithful tyrant. My poor mother married to a madman. Poor me until Peg and Chuck came along
to save me. I'm not a reincarnation of you, just because I have
your genes. Yet there is a communion between us, isn't there?
I don't know what that means. I don't know why we have the
same dangerous eyes and the same defiant smile and the same
sexual allure and the same passionate loves. All I know is that
we do. I won't let you be forgotten, that I promise, though I
don't think in heaven you and Colonel Mike—did you call
him that, I know you did—worry much about such things. I'll
show this book to Chuck, not right away because we have to
get through this exhibition business. He'll understand a lot
more. So will I. Will I let him hang that damn picture? Of
course I will. It's a picture of both of us, isn't it? Part of me
will resist the idea that the picture is me at my best. But you
and I know that it really is, don't we?

"And what about that gypsy woman at Twin Lakes fifty
years ago? She told Mom that she would have a daughter who
would be a great woman. Do I believe in gypsy predictions?
Certainly not! Still, if you see Mom—and I'm sure you do—
tell her that I love her and I'm sorry and I'm trying to live up
to that prediction as best I can."

I was silent for a moment and I filled up with peace and
love, quiet peace and gentle love. Was the original Rosie there
with me? I don't know. God was, I'm sure of that.

"See you later," I said, as the peace and love faded.

Outside, the rain was so heavy I could not even see Delia's
house across the street. Slowly I came back down to earth.

There was something I had to do. My manuscript! To hell
with it. Not today. They'd love it if I mailed the revision
tomorrow. However, there was still more I wanted to do. What
else was on my agenda?

Chucky! My own version of Colonel Mike. How does he
put up with me?

I pulled out one of my personal sheets of paper which pro-
claimed in large letters:

ROSEMARIE

> Chuck,
> I've been a real bitch. I'm sorry. You absolutely have to
> hang that portrait. I won't forgive you if you don't. It's
> beautiful. Again I'm sorry.
>
> Rosemarie.

I folded it and put it in a matching envelope. I wrote
"Chucky Ducky" on the envelope. Then I ran downstairs and
without permitting myself to think about it, slipped it under
the door. Then I returned to my office to await the expected
reaction.

It wasn't long in coming . . .

He rushed into my office and embraced me.

"I'll explain someday soon why," I said, as he smothered
my lips with kisses.

"No explanations required."

"I want to show you something," I said. I took him by the
hand and led him to the guest room where I had stored the
canvas of my mother.

"Wow!" he exclaimed. "Was she the ghost?"

"Oh, no! I'll explain about the ghost later. I've hidden that
picture too long. I want to hang it in the parlor."

"Great idea!" he said, though he had no idea what this
change in me was all about. "Dad's work, isn't it?"

He put his arm around my waist.

"Who else? I'm going to ask Moire Meg to drive it over to
their place this afternoon. The good April said he would clean
it off and touch it up if it needs anything."

"Shouldn't we bring it ourselves?"

"There's already been too many tears," I said. "It will be
easier for them and us if we ask herself to do it. I thought we
might put it in the parlor for Christmas Eve."

"Show it to Peg first. She won't object, but don't surprise
her."

I had forgotten completely in my rediscovery of my family
that it was Peg who pushed Mom away and sent her tumbling
down the basement stairs to her death. If she had not pushed
her, Mom would have bashed out my brains with the poker in
her hand.

I wondered then if maybe some of her anger at me when she was drunk was the result of her worship of her grandmother. I shouldn't try to figure everything out all at once. Most of it I would have to guess at. That's what stories are made of.

Both of us went back to work. It was hard for me to concentrate. Too many images of past and pleasant love.

"You want me to bring this over to Gramps?" Moire Meg asked me when I showed her the picture. "Sure, Grams makes the best cookies in all the world . . . This is your mother, isn't it? Why haven't we seen her before?"

"It's a long story, which I will tell you very soon when I have figured it out completely."

"She's beautiful, but you don't look like her at all."

"I look like her grandmother."

"Yeah? All I know about your family is that your mother had a hard life and died young. So did your father. Not that I need to know . . ."

"If I hadn't walked over to the O'Malleys' when I was nine or ten years old, I wouldn't have survived."

"To tell the truth, I think it might be the other way around."

"They say that sometimes."

"It's stopped raining and turning totally cold . . . They know this is coming?"

"Yes. There's likely to be a lot of tears."

"I'm immune . . ." She continued to study the picture, as she would a blank space in a crossword puzzle. "Anyway, I'm glad you did wander over to their house. Otherwise, I wouldn't be here and there'd be no one to threaten to confiscate all your clothes if you didn't lose more weight."

"I'm not planning another pregnancy."

"You never know."

She lifted the painting and walked toward the door of my office.

"Well, poor little useless Momeg is still good for running errands . . . Rosie, can I see a picture of your great-grandmother?"

I pondered her question.

"Certainly. Put down the painting for a minute and sit on the couch."

"Yes, ma'am."

I removed my mother's photo album from the bottom drawer of the cabinet in which I had locked it.

"I found this only today, though I must have seen it once before because I knew it existed. This is our secret, hon, till after we start the exhibition and I can show it to your father."

"Okay."

I gave her the album.

"Rosemarie." She glanced at the title page. "Same name . . . Omigosh! Omigosh! Rosie! Omigosh! You're a clone!"

"Just a great-grandchild that inherited a lot of her genes."

"It's like totally scary! Same eyes! Same smile. Same boobs!"

The color drained from her face as she turned the pages.

"It's the woman in Chucky's picture. The same one. No sleep shirt, but it almost doesn't matter . . ."

She hugged me.

"Rosie! How wonderful! How terrible and how wonderful! Do you feel close to her?"

"Right now I do."

"She looks like April Rosemary too, like she was before she went away."

"Her confidence is coming back, Moire Meg."

"Slowly . . . And this lug of a colonel is a clone of my brothers."

"They'd look good with beards."

"It would wear off."

"He was a good man."

"Rosie, he didn't have any choice in the matter . . . You going to write about them?"

"I think so. I have to get my head around it."

"Talk to Marina Keenan's mother too."

I had never told her about my relationship with Maggie Ward. Naturally, however, she knew.

She gave me back the album and stood up.

"Off to Grams and Gramps' . . . You're going to let Chuck hang the picture?"

"I think this one would haunt me if I didn't."

"Fer sure . . . Hey, which gown are you going to wear to the grand opening? The silver or the blue? I'll wear the other."

"You'll look great in the blue."

"I'd look better in the silver, but you have seniority."

At supper that night, Chuck asked her how his parents had reacted to the picture of Clarice Clancy.

"More water pouring inside than outside. Those guys must have been awful close back then. Gramps said that no one could dance the Charleston better than your mother, Rosie."

"She was a flapper, just like the good April."

"I bet they have lots of pictures of her."

"I'm sure they do."

"I'll have to check them out . . . How old was she when Gramps painted her?"

"Your age."

Our daughter shook her head. The mystery of time and generations and aging were too much for her.

"Well, like I go to Grams, at least she had all her clothes on when he painted her. That painting of Grams is really bitchin' isn't it? Both flappers. Sometimes I wish I were a flapper."

"What did the good April say?"

"She smiled kind of contentedly and said well at least we were married. Then she added 'almost.' "

"Standard answer. Your father dug it out of the basement of their house and made them hang it."

"Father and son both had a fixation on naked women, huh?"

"At the risk, hon, of sounding like my foster mother, most men do."

Chuck and I made love again that night, a lot more peacefully than we had in the afternoon. It was the last time, as I knew it would be, until the beginning of the show.

He grew more tense as the Tuesday after Thanksgiving approached, not irritable, not snappy, just quiet and distant. I figured it was best to leave him alone. One of the troubles of early success is that you have lots of time to wonder when your luck will run out.

I wasn't worried. The portraits were the best work he'd ever done. The men and women and children leaped out of the pictures and demanded your attention, even, God forgive me, the artist's wife, a West Side Irish Marthe to his Bonnard.

If the critics didn't like them, they were simply wrong.

Wait till they don't like my short story collection!

He did look simply adorable in the very expensive, tailor-made tux on which I had insisted.

"It fits pretty well," he admitted, as I struggled with his tie. "But I feel like the little guy on the top of a wedding cake."

"Cute little guy," I said.

"That's what they all say."

"Charles Cronin O'Malley, hold still!"

"Yes ma'am . . . I thought you were wearing the blue dress."

"Originally I was wearing the silver, then Moire Meg wanted to wear it, so I said all right, and then last night she said I should wear the silver because I did more for it than she did, which isn't true."

"Oh."

"She is a very sweet child, Chucky . . . Well, you look all right now, as all right as you'll ever be . . . Now help me on with my dress."

"Yes, ma'am."

He made no pretense at being fresh as he zipped me up.

He did admit, "As always, Rosemarie, you are magnificent."

"Thank you," I replied.

He would have been in deep, deep trouble if he had not said something like that. "It's disgraceful to be as nervous as I am," he said as he helped me on with my cloak. "I ought to know better."

"You do know better, Chucky. You've put a lot of work into those portraits. It doesn't matter whether some people don't like them, especially media people. They don't count. The subjects like them. You like them. The people will like them. You shouldn't give a few effete snobs control over your work."

"I always used to think that. Now for some reason I can't anymore."

"Everyone who is praised at one time will be attacked at a later time and then praised again. It's the system. Think of Mozart."

"When he was my age, he was already dead for sixteen years."

I gave up on him.

I insisted that a limo pick us up and take us to the Art Institute. No search for a parking place for Prince Charming and his Magic Princess. Besides, my silver outfit would look its best as I emerged from a long limo.

Prince Charming stumbled as he was getting out. This was going to be a long night.

The night was clear, the air was fresh and still, a mild winter evening on the shore of the Lake, as people in evening dress glided into the stately building. I loved these scenes. Chucky had a hard time climbing the stairs. I almost helped him.

"Is this the guy who speared me in Hansen Park?" Ed Murray asked, as we met them at the door.

"Defamation," Chuck insisted. "You attacked my head with your chest. Besides, I had not recovered full consciousness after you had committed unnecessary roughness on the previous play."

"It never stops, does it, Rose?" Deal Murray said. "You were there. What really did happen?"

"In those last seconds, Delia, Chucky was too frightened to know what he was doing . . . You look great tonight by the way."

"And silver is positively your color, you sparkle."

"No one has paid any attention to my new tux," Chuck protested.

"You have to take your coat off before they can see it, eejit."

Our whole gang was inside, an attractive and imposing extended family. Two surprises: Sean had brought Esther, who was wearing a pale gray gown which set off nicely her golden brown eyes. And Moire Meg had a date, an Ignatius/Marquette boy with whom she had gone to grammar school, one Joey Moran by name. He seemed dazed that he was among the Crazy O'Malleys. There was much hugging and kissing and shaking of hands. I wondered if the jazz group had smuggled in their weapons.

"Guard of honor?" I asked.

"Blocking backs against Carmel," Vince replied. "I think I see one of them among us. Don't worry, Chucky, we'll protect you."

My husband stood at the fringe of this circle of beauty and warmth, once more the bemused kid peering in the window.

"Vince, will you take the quarterback's coat and hang it up

somewhere? Treat it gently, he's owned it for thirty years. Now everyone, please admire him! It's his tailor-made tux, bought especially for tonight."

Applause from the crowd.

"Gingiss's didn't have my size. The old one fit fine."

"I think, dear, we should go into the dining room," I said, sounding again like the good April. "We don't want to keep the trustees waiting."

Esther brushed my cheek with her lips.

"You look lovely, Mrs. O'Malley."

"Thank you, Esther . . . Are your parents here?"

Her father was a trustee of the Art Institute.

"He thinks Mr. O'Malley is a conservative."

"Funny," I said without thinking, "I didn't see him at Selma."

Her feelings were not hurt.

"That's a good line, Mrs. O'Malley. I'll use it sometime."

"We brought the whole *meshpocha* here tonight."

"That's a Yiddish word, Mrs. O'Malley. It's not Jewish."

"What can I tell you, Esther! Yiddish *is* Jewish."

She smiled enigmatically.

Our wine and appetizers were being served in the rebuilt Chicago Stock Exchange room in the bowels of the Art Institute.

I had paid for the wine and catering. It would be the best wine and the best food for Chuck's coming-out party. Enough food so we wouldn't have to eat dinner afterward.

Chuck opposed the Stock Exchange for the party. It would remind him, he argued, of the Great Depression. He might forget where he was and shout out a sell order.

Neither the staff nor the trustees nor I took him seriously.

A crowd had assembled already, most of them in evening dress, though it was not strictly required—trustees, civic folk, journalists, gossip columnists, hangers-on, the usual suspects.

"You see that ugly woman over there in the brown suit and blond hair, the tall one?"

"She's not ugly, Chuck. She may not be Irish but she's pretty."

"She's from the *New York Times* and she's a monster."

"She doesn't look like a monster."

"That's all they send out these days."

The chairman of the Trustees would introduce my husband. He would say a few words and that was all. No speeches, I had decreed.

"Ladies and gentlemen, it is not often that the Art Institute devotes a major exhibit to a native Chicagoan. We are delighted tonight to present our Christmas treat for the city of Chicago. Ambassador O'Malley has won Pulitzer Prizes for his photojournalism. In recent years he has turned to portraiture and demonstrated, we believe, that his shrewd, probing eye is especially suited to that genre. Chuck, we are glad to have you with us."

Chucky sidled up to the mike.

"Thank you, Lawrence. I can't help but feel that this show is for someone else and that I wish my mommy would take me home. I'm never quite sure what a snot-nosed little brat from Menard Avenue is doing inside this august building. I had to come because my wife, about whom more inside, bought me a new tuxedo. She won't let me go home till everyone else has gone home. I hope you like my pictures. As I say in the catalogue, I have tried to capture my people not as they are at any given moment, but as they are at their best. I aim to challenge, not to flatter. Finally, there will be no collections, raffles, or door prizes, though to dispense with these traditions does deep violence to my Catholic soul."

Laughter and applause.

Not bad.

The doors opened and the first rush of viewers poured into the five rooms, each with twenty portraits. A gasp of awe and surprise trailed the first crowd and then was repeated frequently as though they were entering a fairyland of magic and wonder.

The design, which Chuck had planned with the curator, was dazzling. The lights, the stark black and white of the prints, the off-white walls, the glow which seemed to flow from the faces of the subjects created a slight and subtle impression that they were a group of live humans waiting for the viewers. I wanted to take the image of my Siobhan Marie grinning impishly at all of us into my arms and tell her not to be afraid of all the people.

"See why I didn't want you to view this stuff till opening night?"

"Hi, Mr. President," I whispered to Jack Kennedy, who seemed prepared to wink at me.

"That was a nice talk," I said to my husband.

"Yeah, well it was short."

He turned on all his very considerable charm for the folks who swarmed up to congratulate him, the creepy limp-hand holders as well as those who knew what they were talking about. I have never been able to make up my mind whether that charm is authentic or whether it covers up other and darker emotions. As best as I can figure out, the act becomes real after a while.

His opening remarks were a giveaway. My poor dear Chucky wasn't sure he belonged at this show. He suspected that he was a punk kid from the West Side who had perpetrated a fraud and would someday, like maybe today, be found out. His work was so instinctive, so easy, that it really could not be great photography, could it? Tonight was the night perhaps when someone would shout out the truth: he was nothing but a taker of snapshots!

I drifted around from room to room and tried to absorb the people, both those in the portraits and those staring at them. I avoided my own portrait, especially because there was always a large cluster of people ogling it.

"Voyeurs," I murmured to myself.

I encountered Joey Moran, his arm cautiously linked with that of his date.

"Who's the redhead, Joey Moran?"

"A brat who went to school when I did . . . You look beautiful, Mrs. O'Malley."

"In real life or in the picture?"

"Both," he replied with an unfazed grin.

"He's kind of cool, Moire Meg," I informed my daughter.

"He has possibilities," she replied.

"I may survive," Joey Moran said. "I'm not sure, but I think there's a good chance."

Had she found a guy who was something like her father?

I felt old for a moment. My teenage buddy would be leaving

home soon, if not with Joey then with some similar Irish blarney artist.

The crowd had thinned around the picture, which was labeled in the catalogue simply as *wife*. (And described in the following words: "She claims that this portrait doesn't look at all like her. She's wrong.")

There were only two people looking at it, the blond monster from the *New York Times* and a familiar woman in a gray gown and a cute figure.

"It's an incredible portrait," the *Times* person said. "Perhaps a turning point in the history of portraits of women in the twentieth century. She's not an object at all. She's a very attractive woman who engages the artist and us with a defiant self-confidence, somehow erotic and chaste and still erotic."

"The artist doesn't turn her into a fetish at all," Maggie Ward observed.

"I don't think he'd dare to," the *Times* said.

"I'd throw the brush at him," I said.

The *Times* person turned around in surprise.

"Ms. O'Malley! The portrait obviously does not lie!"

"That's the point we debate," I said, as my face turned very warm.

"I'm Christina Freeman. I'm with the *New York Times*. Do you know Dr. Margaret Keenan?"

"She tells me that she's from the neighborhood."

"The whole show is special," the critic went on, "though I shouldn't be saying it before I write the review. This portrait, however, is very special."

"Very special woman," the good witch of the East said with the ever-so-slight smirk which on rare occasions she permitted herself in her office.

"I won't tell my husband you like the show until he reads it tomorrow."

We all laughed and I drifted on, a huge burden of worry lifted from my shoulders. Chuck always said that nothing was ever officially true till it appeared in the *New York Times*. A good review in the *Times* would cancel all the bad reviews. It would not, however, deflect the fear of death which was eating at him.

Had Maggie spotted this woman and filled her head with our propaganda?

I wouldn't put it past her.

The crowd eventually thinned out.

"You doing all right, Mrs. O'Malley?" Chuck asked me.

"They accepted my revised manuscript this morning," I said. "So I'm doing fine."

"I didn't get a chance to read it!"

"You had enough on your mind."

"Can I read it tomorrow?"

"After the reviews."

"Fair enough . . . Do you think, Mrs. O'Malley, that we might quietly drift out of here now?"

"It's your show."

"I've had enough compliments for a couple of years. Besides, there is an important sexual ritual we seemed to have overlooked a couple of weeks ago."

"It's too late and we're both too tired," I said, as desire stirred within me.

"The warrior routs the forces of disorder and chaos"—he grinned—"then he revels in the prize."

"Prize," I said, "is a fetish term."

"No it's not," he said, taking my hand.

So we said good-bye to the few people that still remained and shook hands with the curator of the exhibit and her staff and went home.

In our bedroom, he made me undress and then began his finger's slow and delicate journey across the responsive geography of my body.

I woke up once later in the night and realized with brilliant clarity that Chuck's denial of his artistic insight and my denial of my womanly appeal were similar escapes from reality.

❧ Chuck ❧

1978

The day after our carnival at the Art Institute, Rosemarie read me excerpts from the reviews. As always the Chicago papers were able to control their enthusiasm. I was not part of the Chicago literary world's artistic establishment but irredeemably neighborhood Irish and that meant my success was depriving one of their own of the success to which they were entitled.

"Listen to this ditzy dame, Chucky:

" 'No one would ever accuse local photographer Charles C. O'Malley of being a member of the avant-garde. His venue has always been sentimental domesticity. Hence one did not expect and did not encounter anything particularly new or exciting in his current exhibition at the Art Institute. One would rather wonder why the Art Institute would turn over a substantial amount of its space for a show which is mostly an exercise in self-congratulation. The answer, one suspects, is money. Mr. O'Malley's photographs of the famous and the near famous, the pretty and the inspirational will attract large crowds of Chicago viewers who confuse his unquestioned technical skills with great photographic art. They will not even be repelled by sympathetic portraits of Richard Nixon and the late Senator Everett McKinley Dirksen. Mr. O'Malley, who was one of the many court photographers who traveled in the train of the Kennedy family, will not disappoint his Chicago fans, who are incapable of seeing through the flattery of court photography.' "

"They don't like me over there," I said complacently.

"How can anyone be so intellectually dishonest?" my loyal Rosemarie exclaimed.

"They know that their friends will praise them. What more do we need but the praise of our friends?"

"Listen to this headline: 'O'Malley suffers from limitations of Being Irish.' "

" 'It is not a secret that Charles C. O'Malley is Chicago Irish. It is perhaps a sufficient summary of his new show at the Art Institute to say that he still sees the world through the lens of Chicago Irish Catholicism. A lavishly, one might want to say tastelessly, mounted exhibition of his portrait work, it will surely please Christmas-season visitors with its 'too-good-to-be-true' depictions of popes and presidents, priests and pretty children. Only one portrait, displaying the now-familiar sexual attributes of Mr. O'Malley's aging wife, seriously ex-. ceeds the limits of good taste. One wonders what kind of woman, with no career of her own, would tolerate such exploitation. Yet there is no denying the quick eye and the skillful technique of Mr. O'Malley. It is a shame that he does not realize that there is a world beyond the neighborhoods of the West Side of Chicago.' "

"Son of a bitch," Rosemarie shouted, the light of battle in her lovely blue eyes.

"He must have missed my portrait of Conrad Adenauer," I said.

"They're so ignorant," my good wife insisted, "they don't know anything."

"They see what they want to see . . . I note you have the *Wall Street Journal* in your hands. Surely they have not covered the show."

"Yes, they have. Dig the headline: 'Kennedy Staffer Turns to the Right.' "

"I don't think I want them to praise me."

"Well they do, so you'll have to live with it.

" 'Charles C. O'Malley, Kennedy ambassador to West Germany and one of the architects of American defeat in Vietnam, has never heard a liberal cliché that he hasn't liked. However, when he turns to his well-publicized photographic art, he rejects the fashionable and politically approved style and subject matter of the left and celebrates the traditional values of the

American middle class. In his new exhibition of portraits at Chicago's Art Institute, he reveals himself as a man with a sharp eye and a sensitive heart. It is hard to believe that a left liberal like Mr. O'Malley could produce such a sympathetic portrait of President Nixon or such an intense celebration of family life. Perhaps that is what one would expect in Chicago, a city which has never been troubled by political consistency. His work would doubtless be greatly improved if he could match his left liberal political perspective with his deeply conservative artistic instincts.' "

She looked up from the paper to consider my reaction.

"I feel like an inkblot," I said.

"Or the blind men with their elephant . . . Here's the one from the monster woman."

"I'm not sure I want to hear it."

"Well, I'll give you the headline anyway: 'O'Malley Portraits Dazzle.' "

"I think I can suffer through it."

" 'Chicago.

" 'The last time we saw an exhibition of the photograph work of Charles Cronin O'Malley was in his brilliant photo-journalism essay *Year of Violence* about 1968. While Mr. O'Malley still practices that craft, as in his recent striking photographs of the conclaves in Rome, he has turned his major efforts in the last decade to portraits. A new show in Chicago, called *People*, shows that his quick, practiced eye has, if anything, improved. Indeed the exhibition, brilliantly mounted at this city's Art Institute, is dazzling. The various subjects, as different as John Kennedy, Martin Luther King, Richard Nixon, and Maureen O'Hara, seemed to leap out of their frames and join the crowds of viewers who came to the opening-night show. In the excellent catalogue Mr. O'Malley explains that he seeks to capture his subjects as they are at their very best, to challenge them rather than flatter them. He writes, "I am happiest when a subject says something like, I wish I were really like that, and his friends and family say, but you really are."

" 'A youthful-looking and self-effacing man, Mr. O'Malley said to a reporter, "I'm just a fast-talking punk from the West Side of Chicago who takes pictures." Well, yes, but that's precisely his secret. Solidly rooted in his own environment, Mr. O'Malley is able to empathize with those from other environments. He uses modern cameras, but claims he still sees the world through the fuzzy eye of a box camera. His work demonstrates, however, that it is not the eye of the camera which matters but the eye of the photographer.

" 'The most successful portrait in the exhibition is of a woman identified in the catalogue only as *wife*. It may well be a turning point in twentieth-century gender portraiture. Ms. O'Malley appears as a radiantly and yet chastely erotic woman in the middle years of life who is neither a fetish nor an object. Quite the contrary, her dangerous eyes and her intimidating smile suggest that she is challenging not only the photographer but all those who look at his work. She is a woman to admire, but also one you had better respect or you may be in serious trouble.' "

"It's just like the article they did about me in the magazine when we were in Germany," I said. "More about my family than about me!"

"Charles Cronin O'Malley! You are impossible!"

"Well, I can live with it," I said.

"You didn't tell me you spoke with her!"

"I didn't know what she was looking for in her questions . . . I don't suppose she talked to you . . ."

"As a matter of fact she did. I had to promise her I wouldn't tell you about her review till it appeared."

"You charmed her," I grumbled.

"Only as you saw me."

"Well, that was the idea wasn't it? . . . Any pictures in the article?"

"One of you."

"I'm surprised."

I had been hoping that they would reprint my shot of Rosemarie. The review was right, it could become a very important picture.

The review was an unexpected blessing. I could relax and begin to work on the conclave book. However, it did not, could not, heal whatever the ache was in the center of my soul.

"Maybe I put my finger on it to the woman at the *Times*,"

I said to Dr. Berman in our weekly lunch, this time at the Standard Club. "Maybe I'm afraid that I'm a kind of fraud, not the genius that even my poor wife insists that I am. I'm in way over my head. Someday they'll catch on to me. So this time I escaped."

"Fast-talking fraud, as you implied to the *Times* woman."

"Well, yeah."

"So."

He can say that word with more implications than anyone I know. Goes with being Jewish, I think. I'd have to see if I could repeat it with Esther.

"So what if you're wrong?"

"I've lived with that image for a long time."

"Where did it come from?"

"Not from my parents, Lord knows. Maybe from my experience in the early years in school, little troublemaker covering up with S'ter."

"Or poor kid from a family who pretended they were rich?"

"I hadn't thought about that. Actually I was the only one in the family that thought we were poor. So I guess I covered up . . ."

"So were you poor?"

"Not compared to many people I've seen around the world. Not compared to a lot of people in the parish in those days."

"So?"

"So I was the only one who knew we were living above our means. Or maybe the only one who cared."

"So."

"So?"

"So perhaps it was some small incident, like your mother crying when they had to sell your big home?"

"Something like that, which I don't remember, could haunt me after all these years?"

"So it has hardly incapacitated you. You are a success. You have won the woman you always wanted . . ."

"She always wanted me."

"Chucky, this is not a therapy session. It is a friendly lunch. I will not, however, put up with such nonsense."

"Okay. I wanted to take off her clothes when she was in

third grade. I finally did. I still do. I like it. So does she, I think."

"So."

I was silent for a moment. To win Rosemarie, then to save her from the wicked dragon, and finally to celebrate her—were not these enough achievements for one lifetime?

"So," I said, "Rosemarie might be enough justification for anyone's life."

"However, this sense of being a fraud, a game—which let's be honest about it, you always enjoyed—comes back to haunt you as you face the prospect of death, a death from which even Rosemarie cannot protect you."

"All right, that makes sense. How do I get over it?"

"You don't get over it. You shouldn't get over it. It is part of who you are. It is functional most of the time, especially when you know it really isn't true. You go beyond it more than you have already."

"So," I agreed.

He was right, I thought as I rode home on the Lake Street L. I had to accept the worth of my work just as Rosemarie had to accept her beauty. Maybe I should continue to take my pictures. Maybe of refugees around the world as I had planned. In the meantime I would continue the pleasurable activity of taking off Rosemarie's clothes.

Why not?

❧ Rosemarie ❧

1978

Maggie Ward leafed slowly through the photo album.

"This is an epiphany experience for you, isn't it, Rosie?"

"It is," I said meekly.

"Can you sort out for me why it is so?"

"Lots of different reasons . . . It brings me back into contact with my poor mother. I realize how I have ignored her. I have to correct that."

"Which you will do by hanging her painting in your house and discreetly explaining to them, especially that very dangerous adolescent. Moreover you will eventually share this album with them as a sign of her love for this very special woman."

"Maybe write a story about the original Rosemarie too."

"Ah, that could be a best-seller, couldn't it?"

"I don't need a best-seller."

"You wouldn't reject one, however?"

I felt a grin forming on my face.

"Certainly not . . . I want perhaps, I'm not sure yet, to imagine from the pictures what she was like and her life."

"You feel a special kinship with her?"

"I do, Maggie, I really do. Is that crazy, I wonder?"

"At worst, my dear, it is a harmless illusion. At best . . . Well, it might help you to clarify your identity."

"Can genes have that kind of power?"

"To reproduce over generations a person who looks a lot like an ancestor? Surely they can and do. Even to the temperament and personality."

She glanced again at the album.

"Perhaps."

"Yes," I said.

"Yet you are the present Rosemarie. Your husband is not a dashing Union Army officer, but a whimsical genius who probably could not ride a horse if his life depended on it. You are not the Rosemarie of a century ago. You are someone different."

Tears stung my eyes. I didn't want any dashing cavalry officer. I wanted my Chucky Ducky.

"I know that."

"Still, there's no harm in knowing that there was once another Rosemarie who looked like you and maybe acted like you and was beautiful all her life and was perhaps not nearly as conflicted as you are and never wrote a story like you."

"No harm?"

"At worst, as I said before, a harmless illusion."

"At best?"

"Maybe a positive reinforcement."

"Okay."

"You will show this to your children and your in-laws?"

"At Christmas?"

"Why not?"

"I showed the pictures to Moire Meg."

"Her reaction?"

"Admiration and many tears."

"Apples, it is said, do not fall very far from their trees . . . It is time, I'm afraid."

As I walked to the door, she said in an undertone, "Informed sources tell me that this Joey Moran is a nice boy, which in their terms means that he does not grope or grab."

"He wouldn't do it twice."

❦ Chuck ❧
1978

"Chuck," my good wife asked, "do you have a few minutes?"

She was dressed in a dark blue business suit with white trim, clothes for visiting the ineffable Maggie Ward. I wasn't sure that I needed another crisis.

"For you, Rosemarie Helen Clancy O'Malley, I always have a few minutes."

She was sitting on the leather couch in her office, the de facto family room despite her insistence that it was private. On her lap was an old photo album of the sort which were piled up in my parents' house.

"Would you look at this please?"

I sat down next to her, put an arm around her shoulder, opened the book, and turned to the first picture.

"Grandmother McArdle?" I whispered.

She nodded.

This album had become very important to her. I must strive for the proper reaction, to live up to the challenge every man must face, to listen to what his wife means, instead of what she says.

"The poor bastard," I said, pointing to Colonel McArdle. "I know how he felt."

She was laughing and crying, a good sign.

"He knows he'll be taking orders from her for the rest of his life. He's so happy he doesn't care. Later in the day, he'll take off her clothes and tell himself that he's conquered her. Even then, however, he'll realize that the prize taking goes in the other direction. Poor dear man . . . Looks like our kids, doesn't he? But then he should."

I went through the pages slowly. The pictures were astonishing. The elder Rosemarie not only looked like my wife; her gestures, frozen in the camera, look like hers, as did her facial expression. Her summer clothes at Geneva Lake were more modest than my Rosemarie's sleep shirt, but she was as defiant and amused as her granddaughter, no, great-granddaughter.

"Great-grandmother?" I asked.

"Right, my poor mother's grandmother."

The stories were racing through her body, her mind, her soul. Be careful, Chucky Ducky, don't blow it.

"What a wonderful, thrilling, scary experience for you, Rosemarie."

She hugged me fiercely.

"I knew you'd understand."

Ah, Chucky Ducky, so far so good. Now you let her spill it out.

"I feel guilty about my mother."

Now here the great big strong male says that she has nothing to worry about.

Neither big nor strong, Chucky Ducky falls back on wisdom.

"I can understand that."

"I've neglected her . . . I can't remember her as a beautiful, talented woman who cared enough for the original Rosemarie to save these pictures and to name me after her."

All I could remember was a lovely, vague drunk.

"I want to retrieve some of her memory if I can."

Time to make a suggestion.

"I don't know whether it would help. My parents have a stack of albums like this, not so neatly put together, because, alas, neither of them really knows what neatness means."

She giggled.

"Maybe you could go through them. I can borrow them for you, though I will have to search for them. Maybe you could even go through them with the good April. Will you show her this album?"

"Oh, yes, in a day or two . . . I think I'd like to look at those other albums . . . Do you think I'm silly, Chucky?"

"I've never thought you were silly, Rosemarie."

"It is all kind of silly. I can't bring my mother back to life. I can't protect her from the misery she suffered. I really can't do anything."

True but irrelevant.

"You can learn more about her, renew your love and respect for her, tell your children more about her."

"Yes," she said quietly, "that does make a lot of sense."

"Have any of the kids seen this album?"

"Only Moire Meg."

Naturally, daughter as confidante.

"And she was as moved as you were."

"Yes, oh yes!"

The next day, I searched all day the nooks and crannies, the corners and the cabinets, the attic and the basement of my parents' house. The good April followed me around for a while making many suggestions which were not helpful. Finally, she gave it up and pleaded that she had to address her Christmas cards.

I had learned to be patient with my parents' confusion, perhaps as a preparation for marriage. Few people, I discovered, understood as well as I did how important it was to keep neat records.

Finally, in a small subbasement under a stack of ancient blueprints—for which there had doubtless at one time been frantic searches—I found a stack of eight photo albums like the one over which my good wife was mooning these days.

I carried them up two flights of stairs to the good April's study (not to be confused in any respect with my wife's office). She was bent over a stack of cards and a disorderly pile of papers with addresses on them, some crossed out, others handwritten in corners and margins.

"I think I found them."

She took off her glasses.

"Pictures of flappers?"

"I didn't look."

We opened the album on top. It was nowhere as neat as the Rosemarie collection. Some pictures were mounted, others were piled between the pages, still others wrapped with rubber bands.

"Oh my," the good April said as she lifted the top picture from a pile. "Here we are. Clarice and I in 1924. Can you believe how young we look? And can you believe those swimsuits? Weren't they awful?"

"The young women in them are not awful," I insisted.

"You always were sweet, Chuck." She patted my arm.

"Tell you what, Mom. The woman I sleep with wants to rediscover her family past. She found an old album of pictures of an earlier Rosemarie . . ."

"McArdle of course. She was a legend. Grand woman."

"Clarice Powers went to a lot of work to create that album. That made Rosemarie think about her again."

"Poor dear woman," she said, dabbing her eyes with an ever-present tissue. "We tried to talk her out of marrying Jimmy Clancy. She wouldn't listen to us. Still, she gave us Rosie, didn't she?"

I did not intend to slip into this nostalgic swamp.

"I think it would be helpful to Rosemarie if I ask her to come over here and show you her album and then you and she can go through all of these."

"We will cry all day long," she said, with considerable anticipation I thought.

"Lay in an extra supply of tissue."

"Will she write about these times, Chuck?"

"I think that will be the best way for her to work it through."

"Have you ever shown her your father's account of our courtship, silly old thing that it is?"

"No, but that's a good idea. I'll give it to her tonight."

"Are you sure you can find it?"

Mother, you've forgotten that your son is an anal-retentive obsessive when it comes to documentation.

"I think so."

Rosemarie was in her office, briskly addressing Christmas cards. I had created a file system for her that made it easy. Soon we'd be able to put it on computer.

I reported my successful search and described my proposal for her visit to the elder O'Malleys' house.

"That sounds like fun," she said, glowing happily.

"The good April promises to lay in an extra supply of tissue. I would suggest, however, you bring your own."

"You think of everything, Chucky."

"I also thought of this. It's a journal my father kept of their, uh, love affair, if one could call it that. I don't know why I didn't show it to you before. Well, yes, I do. You will understand when you read it."

"My mom is in it?"

"Yes, Rosemarie, she is."

"I'll read it after supper."

I went downstairs to work on prints for the conclaves book. I made no progress. Something inside me simply collapsed. Perhaps I was suffering from a letdown after the excitement of the opening of the show. I was tired, so very, very tired. I had not slept well at night for the last couple of months. I'd fall asleep for a couple of hours, then toss and turn. For her part my wife slept soundly through the night and was unaware of my restlessness.

I assumed that Max Berman was right. I was afraid of being exposed as a fraud. My struggles to sustain the act were growing more frantic as death loomed ever more certainly around the corner. Possibly I wasn't a fraud. That alternative somehow didn't seem very likely.

Foolish, foolish, sad sack.

Supper was devoted to a discussion of the newly discovered love life of Moire Meg. She denied that there was anything to talk about, but patently wanted to talk about it.

"Joey Moran seems to be a nice young man," Rosemarie began.

"You sound like April," her daughter responded.

"Are we likely to see more of him?" I asked.

"Who knows?"

"Like on Christmas Eve?"

"Maybe. If he doesn't have anything else to do."

"What's he studying at Marquette?"

"Prelaw, of all the dumb things."

"Is he smart?" I asked.

"Smart enough."

"Smart enough to keep up with you?"

"No boy is smart enough to keep up with me."

"Is he that rare male who likes smart girls?" my wife asked.

"If he wasn't, would I have invited him to Chucky's show?"

"He certainly is cute."

Loud sigh of protest.

"Well, at least he's not tiresome like most boys?"

"Totally cool?"

She considered that.

"Well, cool anyway . . . Now I don't want to talk about him anymore."

"Can I ask one last question?"

"All right, Chucky, so long as it is the LAST!"

"Is he a Democrat?"

"Would I be seen in public with a Republican?!"

She swept out of the room, paused at the door, and turned around.

"He laughs at me a lot, which IS totally cool," she informed us, and departed under full sail.

Rosemarie waited till she was out of sight and sound and laughed.

I went down to the darkroom and tried again to pull some order out of myriad shots we'd taken at the conclaves. Recalling that experience made me angry once again at the leaders of the Church.

My fabled photographer's eye failed me again. I attempted several times to sort out the good shots from the bad. Then I shoved them all together in a pile and gave up. What if I had lost my eye? What if I could never tell a good shot a fraction of a second before it took shape? The fraud would be over and I would be finished and I could retire to scholarly ease of writing obscure articles for even more obscure economics journals, lose myself, so to speak, in the dismal swamp of the dismal science.

So I retreated to my workshop and began to plow through back issues of dismal journals. Perhaps I could become a fraud at dismal prognostications and win a Nobel prize. That would not only be cool, but in the jargon of my middle daughter, totally cool.

I gave it up as a bad business. Perhaps tonight I could get a good night's sleep. What I needed was a long rest, peace and quiet under an umbrella in the desert sun.

I peeked in the office. My good wife was poring over Vangie's memoir, probably for the third or fourth time.

Upstairs Moire Meg was at the screen of her new Radio Shack computer, her shoulders set in the businesslike manner of someone who would brook no serious interruptions. Miles Davis was playing softly in the background.

I peeked in the nursery. "Shovie" was sleeping the sleep of the just, her favorite dolly clutched in a chubby arm.

All that was left for Charles C. O'Malley was a ride with the steeds of night. I said my prayers, such as they were, and promptly fell asleep.

Sometime later there was the noise of a person entering my room and discarding clothes. She slipped into the bathroom and closed the door to perform her nightly rituals in silence so as not to awaken me. Then she emerged again, turned off the light, and crawled into bed with me.

"Are you asleep, Chucky?"

"Yes," I said.

She snuggled in beside me, smelling nice at the end of the day as she usually did.

"It's a beautiful story, and terrible, and beautiful. Will they know I read it?"

"I don't think they'd mind. Dad wrote it to be read."

"I understand so much more about my mother, poor dear woman. She was already doomed even then, wasn't she? I'm sure your parents tried to talk her out of the marriage."

"Uhm . . ."

As she is wont to do, my wife went into the land of Nod almost immediately.

It was one of those delicate moments in a marriage in which one partner is ready for love but not insisting. Normally, I am only too willing to take advantage of the situation. This time I did not. I was too tired, I told myself.

Charles Cronin O'Malley, you're a worse sad sack than I had hitherto realized. Not so long ago when you were young and healthy you would not have passed up the slightest opportunity to make love with that woman. Now she's endured a traumatic experience and needs loving pleasure. You turned her down. You're a jerk.

Why?

Because it would involve too much effort.

You're slipping not only into early senility but early

impotence. Who would have thought it! You've never failed to respond to the woman when she was fragile. You did it this time because you're a mess. You don't deserve her.

This sense of failure would lurk at the edges of my conscience for a long time.

❧ Rosemarie ❧
1978

Christmas was closing in on all sides. The O'Malleys have an elaborate Christmas schedule to facilitate the craziest time of their crazy year. Ted and Jane have the party on the Sunday before Christmas. Peg and Vince celebrate Christmas Eve for all the children and now grandchildren. We do the time after midnight Mass (including the adult gift exchange) and Vangie and the good April do the big festival on the afternoon of Christmas Day. We also do New Year's. Christmas morning and early afternoon are *ad libitum* for individual families.

The dramatis personae vary from venue to venue. However, the hard-core O'Malleys (of whom none are harder than Chucky and me) never miss a minute of the partying. The Lord has come among us again, so *certo* we must celebrate. Since the crowd is relatively abstemious (and I totally so), there is no heavy drinking. Good food, good music, good kissing, and good conversation are more than enough to make all of us light-headed.

There's always some people missing. This year the Nettletons would travel to Boston for Christmas Day and Kevin and Maria Elena would spend Christmas Eve with her family in the Pilsen neighborhood. Chuck and I swore we'd never be possessive about our kids at holiday time, but in our heart of hearts we both missed them.

Seano told us that Esther would not be with us for our celebrations.

"She really doesn't believe in Christmas," he said. "I don't quite understand why."

"Christmas is a Christian feast, hon," I tried to explain. "And she's not Christian."

"Jesus and Mary were Jewish."

"You told her that?"

"She said I didn't understand. Jesus was an apostate. I didn't want to argue."

"He talked to her about engagement," Moire Meg reported. "She turned him down flat and really hurt his feelings. I don't know what he expected. She's made it clear enough that she is not ready to marry. She expects to go off to an Orthodox kibbutz in Israel this summer and is not sure when or if she will come back . . . I don't think she'll like it that much. Those places are pretty patriarchal and she's an American woman who believes in her own rights."

"Poor child."

"I know."

"And will we see Joey Moran?"

"Can't tell," she said with indifference. "I gave him the schedule and told him he could show up if and when he wanted."

He'd show up all right.

This floating party with variable guest lists requires an enormous amount of work from the women members of the family, since the men don't have a clue about preparing food for parties, decorating trees, mailing invitations, and sending out Christmas cards. Chucky pretends to do his part by printing a schedule of events.

The cookie problem becomes worse every year. When we were married, I had not the slightest idea about cooking. The O'Malley daughters had learned the art from the good April. Somehow I seemed to have missed the lessons. Chucky never complained about my early efforts, nor did he complain when I began my lessons with Italian cuisine and he ate pasta every night. Through the years of cooking courses I became the best cook in the family—or so Chucky wisely says. However, my top specialty became pastry. That skill is not especially helpful for maintaining my figure, but if I have the willpower to beat the drink, I can certainly beat chocolate. Anyway, the extent and the variety of my cookie repertory imposes great demands every year at Christmas.

As in, "Rosie would you ever make some of those adorable . . ."

Naturally I do.

So as the joyous season approaches, I go into overdrive. I am convinced that I am the only one in the family capable of putting it all together. I have Missus to help me, which makes it easier, but still I become something of a raving maniac. My husband enjoys me when, as he says, the Christmas train rushes into the station.

Christmas 1978 was especially difficult. I fell behind schedule with all the work on my story and the exhibition, Chucky had gone into a deep purple funk, a letdown after the success of the show, and I was trying to cope with the discoveries about my family.

I left the first Rosemarie's album on a table in our parlor to be inspected by anyone whose attention it might catch. I had not brought the albums from East Avenue over to our house yet. Sorting through them and arranging them properly was a long-term task which I would probably have to delegate to my husband—if he ever struggles out of the purple morass. It would be the kind of archival work on which he dotes.

Sorting the pictures, however, was not the issue. I had seen enough of them and heard enough of the good April's stories to have a sense of the time and places described in Vangie's wonderful memoir. I knew my mother as I had never known her before—her goodness, her hopes, and her terrible destiny. I didn't want to know those things about her and yet I did. I had to put her at peace in my life and perhaps restore some sort of a relationship with her memory and indeed with her, other than a quick prayer before I went to bed every night.

It was not fair, I often thought, that God should have been so good to April Mae Cronin and so unconcerned about Clarice Powers. April had lucked out on parents, Clarice had not. Neither for that matter had I. Why do You do things like that, I demanded often in the days leading up to Christmas.

There were no answers. There never are.

Why did I make it, more or less anyway, and my mother didn't? Rosemarie Finn's genes? Surely that can't be all?

Ten days before Christmas I was working late in the kitchen with some Polish recipes which Missus had taught me and wondering about my mother and myself. My husband drifted in, wearing those terrible Army fatigue clothes he affects when he's playing photographer.

"Christmas train is coming into the station," he said.

"On time!"

"How many new varieties?"

"Only one or two, not counting the fruitcakes . . . Chucky, stop stealing my cookies!"

"Yes, ma'am," he said, grabbing for a third.

"If I let you near them, you'll destroy all my work."

"What better cause than to keep your husband supplied with energy?"

"You can have everything that's left over after Christmas."

"Always leftovers for the poor little guy . . . Who hasn't been much of a husband lately, I'm afraid."

The hormones were stirring in his bloodstream, at long last. I should pretend that I wasn't interested. Make him plead for it.

Dumb idea.

"You're the best husband I've ever had, Chucky. You're entitled to one of your deep purple moods every decade or so."

"I rather thought it was mood indigo."

Then and there in the kitchen, a spatula in my hand, we sang "Mood Indigo" together, danced as we hummed it, then sang again.

Nothing came of the interlude. My fault.

The next morning at breakfast, he murmured, "I got a good night's sleep last night."

"Haven't you been sleeping well? I didn't notice."

"Rosemarie, my love, I could reactivate our family rock group in the bedroom when you are asleep and you'd never notice it."

"That's true. You always seem to go right to sleep."

"And then wake up in a couple of hours and can't get back into my dream world."

"Why not?"

"Dr. Berman," he said, returning to the account of the previous day's fiasco of the Chicago Bears, "says it's a sure sign of depression."

"Do you take medication?"

"No, I'd never be able to hide that from you."

"True."

Our daughter joined us in the kitchen with a stack of toys. "Play with me, Rooshie?"

"Mom has cookies to make," Chuck answered. "She's promised us each two of them. I'll play with you."

"Hokay, Chookie."

❧ Chuck ❧
1978–1979

My spirits usually pick up as the Christmas train pulls into the station. The O'Malley clan loved Christmas as all good Christians should. While I disapproved in principle of all the money which was spent on cards, wrapping paper, gifts, and food, I had learned as a youth to keep my mouth shut on these matters. Thus I gradually became an unindicted coconspirator in the festivities. Indeed, as our house gradually filled up with small ones, I wisely opted to be on their side at Christmas because I felt that childlike wonder was the only sensible response to the day. The kids didn't exactly understand the reason for wonder, but they at least weren't swept away by the social demands of the season.

So I would take my position at the foot of the Christmas tree (which early on, Rosemarie realized I could not be trusted with) and play with them and their new presents. Unfailingly they let me into their world of make-believe, assuming perhaps that I was not really a grown-up. That's fair enough. I really wasn't.

I played with the kids and my wife was the Christmas train, bearing cookies, fruitcakes, pastries, chocolate cakes, and presents. After a while this division of labor worked out. Then suddenly our kids were grown-ups, but they soon produced kids of their own and we had ourselves a new kid who was quite content with me as a playmate because I understood her games.

As the Year of Our Lord 1978 wound down, however, the usual Christmas spirit pickup did not happen. I pretended that it did and fooled everyone but myself and maybe Rosemarie.

I continued to work with the conclave pictures, slowly seeing order and themes within them. Rosemarie, when not acting as engineer on the Christmas train, agonized, constructively, I thought, over her mother.

So we were drifting into Christmastime in a pleasant state of alternative sexual arousal and fulfillment. I even went so far as to descend on Marshall Field's and lay in an extensive supply of Christmas lingerie for her, not that she lacked for such accoutrements.

Then the November issue of the *Gramercy Blast* appeared in my mail. I opened it in my workshop in the basement. The paper was a second-generation attempt at imitating the *Village Voice*—its tone hip, worldy, knowing, cynical. Its problem was that, unlike the *Voice*, it appeared at a time in which people were tired of that tone. This issue contained a powerful blast against me.

O'MALLEY PHOTO FRAUD IN CHICAGO

Those of us who were together at the Democratic Convention in Chicago know that the city is about as culturally sophisticated as Addis Ababa. Thus we expect very little from it and are never surprised. Nonetheless, it comes as a shock that the city's once prestigious Art Institute would devote its space to the retrograde and degenerate work of Charles C. O'Malley.

Not to put too fine an edge on the matter, O'Malley, in addition to being an obscenely bad photographer, is a fraud as a human being. The detritus with which his propaganda machine befouls the environment is a tissue of falsehoods. He did not receive a medal for his service in Germany after World War II. Indeed, he was involved in the black market in that country. He never completed his doctoral dissertation at the University of Chicago. He was not beaten at Little Rock. He did not march at Selma. He was not assaulted by thugs during Martin Luther King's days of rage in Chicago. He did not go to Vietnam. He was not attacked by police during the 1968 convention.

He exploits his assistants who do all his work. He has

prevented his wife from pursuing a career of her own. He exploits the bodies of women. His prints celebrate patriarchal discrimination against women, the young, nonwhites, and gays and lesbians.

In the recent vomit show in Chicago he presents pictures of John Kennedy, Martin Luther King, Richard Nixon, Maureen O'Hara, and his naked wife in the same room, utterly unaware, it would seem, of the negatively transgressive context of such a statement.

The portrait of his wife is especially offensive. We must say that the aging woman should join a feminist group to have her consciousness lifted along with the other parts of her anatomy. In a quest for sexual titillation, he reduces the naked wife, a willing victim perhaps, to the status of a passive object, a fetishized whore, an aging *Playboy* bunny. As he himself admits, "I'm just a fast-talking punk from the West Side of Chicago who takes pictures. I still sees the world through the fuzzy eye of a box camera." Such a person may become rich pandering to the narcissistic needs of the aging white fat cats in his portraits. One cannot expect him to take a stand against such clients' racist, sexist, ageist, homophobic vision of the human species. Nonetheless, he is still open to the charge of profound immorality.

DIANA ROBBINS

My throat was dry, my stomach tight, my heart pounding. It was as though someone had pulled up to me as I stood on a street corner waiting for the light to change and drenched me with a bucket of vomit and diarrhea.

I didn't know what to do. Surely the woman couldn't get away with such an attack.

No, just as surely, given the fading but still virulent ideology of ten years ago and its influence in the media, she could. She would argue that she had written a "revolutionary discourse."

I stumbled upstairs looking for my wife. A tray of steaming oatmeal-raisin cookies had just been removed from the oven. I stole two of them.

I tried the office. She was poring over one of her many Christmas lists, manifests for the Christmas train.

"You stole one of my cookies," she said, looking up at me.

"Two actually."

I gave her the *Blast*.

"What's this, Chuck?" She began to read it.

Then she erupted from her chair, screaming, "Bitch!"

The dead out at Mount Carmel Cemetery might well have heard her.

"Cheap, lying bitch," she continued. "We'll kill her, bury her, wipe her from the face of the earth."

The fearsome pirate queen Granne O'Malley could not have been more terrible to behold.

"I'm not sure I want to get into a fight with her . . ."

"You shouldn't have to get in a fight with her. We have lawyers for that. I'll get copies of this to Vince and Ed and Charlotte and tell them we want to destroy this rag and everyone who works on it. They're dead!"

"I'm not a lawyer, I don't know what we can do."

"Plenty. We'll have to find out what their resources are and decide whether we want to sue them in federal or local court and in Chicago or New York."

"What good will a suit do?"

"It will catch them up in their lies, prevent the Photography Gallery in New York from backing out of their contract to do the show, and maybe enhance the sales of the catalogue. This article is reckless disregard for the truth. Not only are their statements untrue, they either know they are untrue or should know they're untrue. The punitive damages will be sky-high."

"We don't need the money!"

"We do need your reputation. I won't let this bitch harm your reputation."

"She's nasty to you too."

"An aging *Playboy* bunny? I think that's kind of funny."

"Do we have to do it before Christmas?"

"Good point." She bent over and kissed me slowly and lovingly. "No reason to ruin Christmas. I'll call a meeting of our legal team for St. Stephen's Day."

"Where did you learn all that stuff?"

"From listening to Ed and Vince and Charlotte. They speak

their own language . . . I'm a writer, Chucky, I study what people say."

"Just like the little redhead."

She grinned and settled back in her chair.

"Something like that. I know what he'll say before he says it."

"Do I have to go to this meeting?"

"Of course not. You should forget about it. We have lawyers to take care of this shit."

"Can we afford legal bills?"

"Chucky, don't be silly!"

"There's better things to do with our money."

"They'll pay plenty, don't you worry."

The die, I realized, had been cast. Granne O'Malley reveled in the possibility of battle in defense of the poor little redhead's honor. My heart continued to pound. My throat was still dry.

Merry Christmas from Diana Robbins and the *Gramercy Blast*.

On the way down to my workshop, I encountered Siobhan Marie, who informed me she wanted to play. I agreed. Actually she wanted to pump me about what Santa Claus might have in mind for her. She assured me that she had been nice, not naughty.

"You're always nice, Shovie!" I said, lifting her off the ground.

"Not ALWAYS," she giggled.

"Santa doesn't tell me his plans," I argued.

I wasn't quite sure what we were giving her. So I didn't have to lie when I denied all knowledge.

"Ah, tell me, da."

"No!"

"Chookie!"

Christmas was a huge success. Santa treated Siobhan Marie with accustomed generosity. The family rejoiced in two new engagements—Charlotte Antonelli had landed a River Forest lawyer named Cletus McGrath and Chris McCormack was engaged to a decorative but sweet blonde from Atlanta, whose name I didn't quite catch.

Charlotte and April Rosemary were laughing happily.

"I never thought it would happen!" Charlotte burbled.

"I knew it all along . . . And he's so cute."

"I love him," Charlotte said simply. "So do Mom and Dad."
Peg seemed content.

"He's one of our own, Chuck. I'm so happy that she didn't
join forces with some Rush Street hippy."

There was much music and singing and dancing and kissing
and, in various bedrooms, lovemaking.

My wife and I, the acknowledged leaders of song, led in
each of the venues our long repertory of Christmas carols—
including "White Christmas" in the quasi blues idiom with
which Irving Berlin had written. Sad stuff.

The stalwart Joey Moran escorted Moire Meg to midnight
Mass and showed up at our house with her afterward. He made
no attempt to corner her under the plenteous mistletoe. Later,
when he also appeared at the Big Party in my parents' home,
he did kiss her among universal cheering. Moire Meg did her
best to appear offended by his discreet brushing of her lips
but she was not successful.

Astonishingly, Esther came to the house on East Avenue,
where my parents greeted her warmly and pressed some
mulled wine upon her.

"We don't drink much in this family, dear," the good April
assured her. "A lot less than I did when I was a flapper."

"I think you're still a flapper, Mrs. O'Malley," she replied,
saying exactly the right words.

Seano was in attendance but did not seem happy.

"She didn't quite give him his walking papers," Moire Meg
informed me. "The poor kid is dazzled by him. She doesn't
want to end it, but she will."

In our own bedroom Rosemarie and I staged an extended
modeling of the new lingerie I had purchased for the Christmas train.

"This is excessive, Chucky Ducky. You bought too much."

"I'll take it back."

"You certainly will not . . . You don't expect me to put on
that thing, do you?"

She gestured disdainfully at a contraption that was part cor-
set, part bra, and part garter belt.

"Entirely up to you."

"Well," she said, "let's see how it works."

It worked just fine.

"The idea is that a woman puts it on sometime early in the evening and the man takes it off sometime later in the evening."

"Sometimes with fumbling fingers."

We were having so much fun that we forgot about the conference with our lawyers the next morning.

I enjoyed a good night's sleep.

The next day was a holiday, but we had scheduled our conference in Rosemarie's office for after lunch so that our legal minds would be clear after a good night's sleep. In fact no one but Charlotte seemed awake. Outside, large snowflakes were drifting lazily by the window.

"I have here copies of an article in a hip New York paper called the *Gramercy Blast*. Its ambitions are to be the *Village Voice* for the younger generation. Those ambitions seem to exceed their talent. The article is an attack on my poor husband. We seek relief, which I'm sure you can provide for us."

It all sounded so formal. My Rosemarie's ability to mimic the way lawyers talk was scary. She was a woman who was even more dangerous than her eyes suggested.

"I should add," she went on while they were reading the article, "that while Chucky is here today, I don't think he should become deeply involved in whatever action we might take. He has better things to do. I will act for him as befits an Irishwoman warrior witch. We will consult with him when necessary."

"That's alliterative," I offered. "Woman warrior witch. One could extend it to say 'wild woman warrior witch' and even 'wild wanton woman warrior witch.' "

The three lawyers glared at me. No laughter wanted here while we were doing serious business.

"This woman can't be for real!" Vince exclaimed. "There's a prima facie case for action here."

"I'd love to get her on the stand or even in a deposition." Charlotte smiled grimly, no longer a happily affianced bride-to-be, but a tough litigator closing in on a miscreant, a slick, sleek, polished shark.

"We have to find out what kind of resources they have to

litigate." Ed Murray smiled happily. "If their resources are
weak and if they don't have any insurance or their insurance
company won't pay, we can beat an abject apology out of
them."

"Would that be enough, Chuck?" Vince asked.

"Ask my wife. I favor the electric chair."

All four of them glared at me. They wanted no part of
Chucky the clown on this feast of Stephen. I looked out the
window to see if Good King Wenceslaus was wandering by
in the snow. He wasn't there yet.

"I'm inclined to think," my wife said, "that an admission
of defamation from the magazine would suffice to save my
husband's reputation and protect the contract we have with the
Photography Gallery for an exhibition in the spring. I wouldn't
mind keeping Diana Robbins swinging in the wind for a
while."

"Go for the jugular."

"There's a contract at stake?" Charlotte's brown eyes glit-
tered.

"It's been signed," Rosemarie said. "They could probably
get out of it."

"All the more grounds for seeking relief," Ed Murray chortled. "I can't believe that this paper has a lawyer read their
stuff."

"Rosemarie," Vince asked, "we can collect affidavits and
film clips and news stories refuting all her charges?"

"Sure," she said. "Most of what we need is in Chucky's
cute little archives, as his mother would say."

"I propose that we move on two fronts. Charlotte, you scope
out this rag and find out whether they lack resources to fight
litigation. If they don't have any lawyers, they might be difficult to scare because they could have mistaken ideas about
freedom of the press. Rosemarie, you and I, with my wife's
help—we won't be able to keep her out of it when she finds
out—prepare a dossier. Ed, maybe you could write a notice
of intent to sue to worry them a little, if they're smart enough
to worry."

It was time for me to fire my grenade launcher, something
I never did during my undistinguished career in the Army of
the United States.

"You have all doubtless perceived the curious matter of the scene she created at the show."

"Chucky," my wife said, kindly reciting Dr. Watson's line, "there wasn't any scene."

"That was what was curious," I said right on cue. "Do you think this crazy woman who wrote us this letter a couple of months ago"—I passed the letter to Vince—"would not have created a scene? Can you imagine that this veteran of direct political action would have passed up the opportunity to tear the picture of my naked wife from the wall and perhaps be arrested and thus become a martyr?"

"Aunt Rosie wasn't naked in that picture." Charlotte extended a protective arm to my wife.

"You noticed that? Odd that Ms. Robbins didn't notice it, isn't it?"

Silence around the room of the sort that good old Holmes loved.

"You also might have noticed that she writes that John Kennedy, Martin Luther King, Richard Nixon, Maureen O'Hara, and my naked wife are in the same room. You will have remembered, of course, that they are all in different rooms except my fully clad wife and Ms. O'Hara, also fully clad. Interesting, is it not?"

"You're saying, Chucky, that she wasn't there?" Rosemarie asked.

"I am suggesting that she cadged her facts from the review in the *New York Times*, which all of you have doubtless memorized. Consider her quote about my being a punk from the West Side who sees the world through a box camera. That's not actionable because I said it and it may even be true. However, the words are hardly changed from the quote in Christina Freeman's article, which also mentions John Kennedy, Martin Luther King, Richard Nixon, Maureen O'Hara. Ms. Freeman chose a subject from each room. Ms. Robbins, not having been there, thought they were all in one room."

"She's psycho," Charlotte murmured.

"Or just a hard-nosed ideologue who thinks that since she is virtuous she can do no wrong. Oh, yes, if you read her vicious description of my shot of my wife, you will note it is a reverse adaptation of Ms. Freeman's description."

"Astonishing," Vince exclaimed.

"Elementary, my dear Antonelli."

"When did you think this up, Chucky?"

"Last night when I was falling asleep," I said with a perfectly straight face.

"We can't absolutely prove she wasn't there," Ed Murray said. "But if we insist they print this in our letter, it will destroy her credibility."

"Not with her friends," I answered, "but with the New York art community. I suspect she has a rich father or mother or both lurking behind her. They probably have disowned her, but if she is sued, they might come riding to the rescue with tons of money for our respective charities."

"Uncle Chuck," my namesake said, her eyes open with astonishment, "you are a dangerous person."

"Sweetest old uncle you ever had."

My wife was watching me intently, as if she was recognizing me for the first time. She had known enough of my previous capers—and had cooperated in some of them—not to be surprised.

"Do you have any more bombs, Sergeant O'Malley?"

"Not for the moment . . . Well, one more thing. If this matter develops in the proper way, I think our good friend Christina Freeman of the *New York Times* newspaper might feel the need to engage in the controversy, since she is the one who has been plagiarized. That would help the show at the Photography Gallery and also the sale of the catalogue. You first-rate legal minds might factor that into your equations, you should excuse my odd metaphor."

Actually what I was hoping was that Ms. Freeman would print the controversial picture of my Rosemarie.

I shuffled out of the room, the incompetent little artist returning to his cave.

Rosemarie joined me later.

"That was quite a show, Charles Cronin O'Malley."

"I thought so too." I looked up from my piles of conclave pictures and kissed her.

"You shot down all those legal aces," she said with a disapproving frown.

"Not really," I said. "One of them would have caught the

secret in due course, Charlotte probably. It was fun playing Holmes again. You of all people shouldn't be surprised."

"You surprise me all the time, Chucky."

I touched her breast, firm and inviting under the red Christmas sweater that April Rosemary had given her.

"I have to go upstairs and clean up. I don't want to leave everything for Missus when she comes on Monday."

"And get ready for New Year's Eve. Do I hear that the jazz group is reviving itself? That should delight the neighbors."

"We'll have our next meeting on the day after New Year's. You're welcome to attend."

"I might just do that."

"Must you paw me, Chucky Ducky?"

"It's pretty hard not to . . . Any reaction to the Rosemarie album?"

"Maria Elena was the first one to see it. She cried, naturally."

"Those Latins are an emotional lot."

"Then she showed it to April Rosemary, who came running to me in tears to ask questions. I think it scared her.

"Finally, Peg picked it up, looked through it, then sat there in the easy chair with her eyes wide-open. I asked her what she thought. She said she didn't know yet, but she understood a lot more about me than she ever had before."

"A success then?"

"Maybe . . . Chucky, isn't one boob enough?"

"I don't think so."

I felt two nipples rise erect underneath the sweater and bra. I touched them gently.

"I have to do my work." She slipped away from me and ran upstairs.

Fine. I was in no hurry.

I had performed very well for the day after Christmas, reestablished some traces of the old Chucky image, exorcised however temporarily some of my demons, and dallied with my wife.

Then I realized what a narcissistic jerk I was to care about that old image. Still, they all had enjoyed it. Or I thought they had.

Then, as I was about to return to the conclave shots, my

youngest arrived and dragged me upstairs to the playroom to enjoy her Christmas toys.

It seemed like an excellent idea.

The next day I felt guilty about my performance at the legal conference. It was vintage Chucky O'Malley, but who needed that anymore? I was just showing off like I had done all my life, a fast mind and a faster mouth. I wanted to show the family lawyers that I was really smarter than any of them. As I had said to Rosemarie, Charlotte would have figured it out in a day or two anyway.

I then went into another tailspin. The "review" was so much nonsense. Yet what was the point of all the work I had done for thirty years if a bunch of punks could savage my reputation without any fear of punishment? There would always be some people who would believe them. If I had enough sense to stay out of the limelight, this attack on me and my wife would never have happened. Who needed it?

Besides, the woman might be right about my work.

I wanted it all to go away. I also wanted to get even with them. How could I achieve both goals?

I didn't know.

I just wanted to get into the warmth of the Arizona sunshine.

So I was a sad sack for the rest of the week.

I abandoned romance with my wife. She had switched from the Christmas train to the New Year's train and was out there roaring down the tracks at full speed. Doubtless she was worried about my gloom and about the attack on my work. She also was trying to cope with the rediscovery of her mother—the most important emotional crisis in her life so far. When April Rosemary disappeared into the miasma of the hippy underground and Kevin was reported killed in action, she had been severely traumatized, as any parent would. But her mother's story went to the core of her identity and dredged up the buried memories which she had avoided for so long.

So she needed my love no matter how sad I felt for myself. I was too tired, too disheartened to have any love to offer.

So we struggled to the New Year's Eve bash.

"This jazz is great stuff," young Joey Moran said to me, as the group, including my mom on the piano and my wife and Maria Elena on the vocals, attempted to blow the roof off our house to celebrate the advent of the Year of Our Lord 1979. I was able to contain my enthusiasm for the coming of the new year. Things, it seemed to me, always got worse.

"You listen to it much?" I asked, nursing my virtuous milk-nog—the younger O'Malleys refusing to spike their eggnog with rum.

"You won't tell my date?" he said with a broad grin.

"Anything I might tell her she already knows."

He laughed happily, "Yeah, she knows everything . . . Anyway, I've never paid any attention to jazz. Tonight is really the first time. It's sensational!"

Anything that happened on a date with Moire Meg would be sensational.

"You were really brilliant the other day, Uncle Chuck." My namesake niece smiled at me, her eyes glowing with admiration.

"I'm afraid that I was just showing off, Charley," I admitted. "You guys would have noticed it in a few days anyway."

"Maybe. But it's the kind of thing lawyers don't normally see for a long time. It strengthens our hand with them."

"I thought it was pretty strong."

"Now more so. Don't worry, Uncle Chucky. We'll get them."

"Let me know when the shooting starts, Charley, and I'll get my friend Doc Holliday and we'uns will meet you down at the corral."

She giggled.

"You like my guy?"

"Not bad for River Forest Irish."

"He's been around for a long time and I didn't even notice him. He's such a sweetie, Uncle Chuck."

"Which means he does what he's told, like all good Irishmen."

She laughed and bounded away. How had she ever come to believe that she'd never find the right guy?

Next her mother, the tall, elegant Margaret Mary, nee Peg, now the director of the West Suburban Symphony and a first violin at the Chicago Symphony.

She hugged me.

"Isn't that young woman wonderful?"

"Charley? Was there ever any doubt?"

"She scared a lot of boys off."

"So much the worse for them."

"Rosie let me read Dad's memoir."

"I should have given it to you long ago."

"No need . . . It's fascinating reading."

"I thought it might help her."

"I'm sure it did . . . Chucky, isn't it amazing that she's survived?"

"The genes of her great-grandmother and God's grace."

"And your love."

"Peg of my heart, are you becoming sentimental?"

She hugged me again.

"You're wonderful. Charlotte told me about what you said at the conference. Vintage Chucky!"

"That isn't necessarily good."

"Yes it is."

I'm not wonderful, Peg, not at all. But if I tell you that, you won't believe me.

Then, of all people, Esther.

"This is a wonderful party, Mr. O'Malley."

"The Celts, a savage people, created their tribe somewhere in Poland or the Ukraine and then swarmed across Europe first on foot then by horse. They always made a lot of noise. People let them run things because then they were a little less noisy. Then other people almost wiped them out, but the Celts were too stubborn to accept the judgments of their betters. We howl at the first full moon too."

She shook her head in mock dismay. "You are the craziest of all the Crazy O'Malleys, Mr. O'Malley."

She kissed my cheek and slipped away. A farewell?

"Holding court, Mr. Ambassador?"

"Just standing here minding my own business."

"You think we did all right with herself?"

"You mean Eileen?"

"Esther!"

"Oh, yeah, that's right . . . I think she likes us. But then I, at any rate, am a likable fellow."

"She has no intention of marrying Seano."

"Not now anyway. It would be against her religious faith."

"Do you think we've seen the last of her?"

"Maybe not."

"It's strange, I suppose, but I hope we see her again . . . Now, Chucky Ducky, our fans are demanding us. It is time for singing."

I started, "It's a Grand Night for Singing!"

And so it went.

Two days later we were back in her office with the legal team.

"Well, why don't we begin with Charlotte's report," Vince began, his broad shoulders tense, his face stern. Someone had insulted his daughter. Honor was now at stake.

"Well," said that lovely young lawyer, "the *Gramercy Blast* is the creation of a Harvard dropout named Creighton Carstairs. He is living off a trust fund doled out each year on a fixed rate by trustees. They disapprove strongly of his activities and would be delighted to see the *Blast* go under. Not enough money in his allowance to defray expenses of extended litigation."

"Are they liable for judgments against him?" Rosemarie asked.

The good Charley smiled. "You think like a lawyer, Aunt Rosie. Surprisingly enough the trust fund is liable. The trustees could force him to settle a suit under pain of their suspending all payments. Such a sanction would notably interfere with Crate's pot and coke habits."

"Ah," I said, suddenly enjoying myself again. Be careful, they don't need another chapter in the Chucky legend.

"I called Mr. Carstairs to discuss matters with him." Her fingers moved to the play button on an old-fashioned tape recorder. "Aunt Rosie, I apologize for the language."

"I'm the one with the tender ear," I pleaded. Nonetheless, I censor the conversation after the first couple of exchanges.

I was favored with a pair of womanly dirty looks.

"Mr. Carstairs, good morning, I am Charlotte Antonelli. I am a lawyer . . ."

"No shit?"

"I represent Dr. Charles Cronin O'Malley."

"Fuck that prick."

Charley was blushing even now.

"I would ask you, sir, to watch your language."

I censor his reply.

"We have reason to believe that in the last issue of the *Blast* you defamed Dr. O'Malley on twelve separate occasions. We have under active consideration a petition before the United States Court for the Northern District of Illinois to seek relief from this defamation."

"You don't scare me. I know our rights under the First Amendment. You can't sue me."

"Yes, sir, we can. We have prepared a dossier which documents the falsehood, and indeed falsehood with reckless disregard, of your allegations. I should like to contact your legal counsel in order to discuss our complaint."

"We don't need no legal counsel."

"Sir, I'm afraid you do. The First Amendment does not protect you against defamation actions."

I censor his reply again.

"Moreover we have substantial evidence to indicate that Ms. Robbins never viewed Mr. O'Malley's exhibition in Chicago, that she reviewed his photographs without seeing them."

There was a pause at the other end of the line.

"Bitch!" Crate exploded.

"I assume you mean Ms. Robbins, sir. You might ask her for the receipt for her plane ticket to Chicago."

"So what! You don't have to go inside a shithouse to know that it smells. She didn't have to go to your stinking city to know that O'Malley's work smells."

There was a click at the other end of the line.

"Nice metaphor," I said cheerfully.

"I'd like to break his neck," Vince murmured through gritted teeth.

"Settle down, Vinny," I suggested. "That conversation from a self-proclaimed feminist all by itself gets us a huge jury verdict."

I glanced at my knuckles. They were white as I clenched my fists.

"Chuck the pragmatist."

"I know good litigation technique when I hear it," I continued. "Charley tricked him into admitting that La Bella Diana had never seen the show."

Charley smiled, content with my acknowledgment of her skill.

Vince wet his lips, struggled with residue of old Sicily, and grinned.

"Give her a couple of years and she'll be a better lawyer than I am."

"What do you mean a couple of years?" Charley snapped back.

"You did most of my work for me," he admitted. "We know it's a fly-by-night operation and that we can bury them. Rosie and I have already created a dossier that refutes all of their allegations. We're still waiting for the videotapes."

"In light of these facts," Ed Murray, his silver hair in perfect place as it always was, joined the discussion, "I have prepared a plea to file in Federal Court here. We can follow up with a subpoena of all their records. That might be a bucket of cold water that Mr. Carstairs needs. It's up to you, Chuckie."

"Ducks in a shooting gallery, Chuckie?" Rosemarie said.

"Tell me reasons why we shouldn't."

"They're so unimportant that it might not be worth it to slap them down," Vince began.

"It will be a nuisance," Ed continued.

"They're vile people," Charley went on. "You can get contaminated by their vileness if you fight them."

"What do we get out of it, except revenge," my wife concluded. "Maybe it's not worth it, Chucky."

"What about the Photography Gallery?"

Rosemarie shifted uneasily in her chair.

"Well, someone down there read the review in the *Blast* over the holidays. They're nervous. For some reason they want to avoid controversy as though controversy does not make any art show a success."

"Well, that seems to be a good reason to go after these morons."

"There might be a backlash, Chuck. 'Rich Chicagoan Tries to Crush Paper of Young Activists.' "

"Who lied about him twelve times."

"I'm not sure it's worth the hassle."

She was probably right. Her bloodlust had dried up during the joyous season.

"That cokehead can't talk to my favorite first niece that way!"

"Uncle Chucky, I encounter that kind of guy every day in my business."

All of this was true, all of it was good legal advice. Even my fearsome wife had calmed down.

"Suppose they agree to publish a letter from us and admit that there were lies in her article. Then we could withdraw the suit."

"The problem is their providing a lawyer we can negotiate with."

"And if they don't withdraw the lies, we can still let the suit dic on the vine?"

"Sure."

"And if the suit gets any attention in New York, it will expose them as reckless liars without ever going to trial?"

"Yes."

"Go get 'em, Ed!"

"I agree."

"You bet, Uncle Chucky!"

So it was settled.

I had another Uncle Chucky scheme up my sleeve. It was a long shot. But there were no risks in trying. According to my scenario, at some point the *New York Times* newspaper might carry a big picture on the front page of their art section of my wife.

My scheme would probably require that someone proclaim a new doctrine of art criticism—you don't have to go into the shithouse to smell the stink. It was a solid Catholic philosophy, you don't have to see a film to know that it's dirty. There was not much I could do to arrange such a happy outcome, except to see that my legal team draft the kind of letter that might occasion such an outcry.

Why would I want to draw such attention to the portrait of my wife?

I had begun to believe the good Christina Freeman's claim

that it was one of the most important portraits of a woman in the twentieth century.

Chuck rides again.

That sustained me until we arrived in Tucson. Then I searched out my sad sack and climbed into it.

❧ *Rosemarie* ❧
1979

The elder O'Malleys—Vangie and the good April—had purchased a sprawling winter home in the Catalina foothills above Tucson.

"It's just too cold in Chicago during the winter for old folks like us," the good April pointed out.

In fairness to them, I chose the house, which was at least twice as big as anything they would have bought for themselves.

"You must have room for your children and grandchildren when they come to visit you."

"I suppose you're right, dear."

Vangie worked on his watercolors all year-round, but in Tucson he concentrated on them. A gallery owner saw a few of them at a private showing and offered to sell them. They quickly disappeared from the gallery walls, much to the delight of April and Vangie.

Chuck's father had always wanted to be an artist. Somehow his work never quite made it, though his best painting *Rom Women* did hang in the prestigious Worcester Gallery in Massachusetts. His fame rested on his architecture, especially church architecture, for which he had won several important prizes. However, the watercolors of his senior years were immensely popular.

"I'm glad you found all those old albums," he informed his son. "I'm going to do a whole series on flappers."

"Vangie, dear, that will be embarrassing, won't it?"

"If my son can celebrate his wife, why can't I celebrate mine!"

"Sauce for the gander is sauce for the gander, Pa," Chucky said.

Before we left for Tucson I called Max Berman.

"Max, I know you can't discuss your patient with me . . ."

"So who's a patient? Chucky? So we only chat at lunch once a week."

"All I want to know is whether you think we should get him some medication."

"So who are this 'we'?"

"Me, I suppose."

"So."

"So," I resolved to wait him out.

"Chuck doesn't need pills, Rosie."

"So."

"You know that of course, but like a good wife you want to be sure."

"So," I agreed.

However, by the time we arrived in Pima County, he did need pills—cold pills. Another cold had knocked my poor little husband over. He sneezed, he coughed, he slept, he stretched out under an umbrella and slept some more. When he wasn't sneezing, sleeping, or coughing he worked his way through Tony Hillerman's wonderful novels. When he felt up to it, he helped me arrange the most telling pictures of my mother from the flapper era.

"I can't tell the difference between the depression from my cold," he complained to me, "and the depression from my midlife crisis."

I bought him some model airplane kits. He actually made them and was very proud of his work.

The kids were with us, Moire Meg because Rosary had a long midyear vacation and Shovie because she wanted to come. The latter wore herself out every day in the pool and the former was content to read Graham Greene at poolside. Unlike most young people her age, she seemed to feel no compulsion to make phone calls back to her friends in Chicago. There was, however, a male voice on the phone every evening who identified himself to us as "Joey" and asked me dutifully about the weather and Mr. O'Malley's cold.

Naturally all of us, including the baby, went to the opening of Vangie's show. Crowds of people milled about the gallery, which was luminous with his bright, soft colors. It was like walking into a blossoming spring garden.

"You've got it this time, Dad," Chuck said in unfeigned admiration.

"It's taken a long time," his father replied. "Better late than never."

"Sold" signs appeared on many of the paintings while we watched. The elder O'Malleys didn't need the money, but they loved the popularity.

"Well, dear," the good April said repeatedly, "I've told you for years that you should do watercolors."

"Irish wife," Chuck whispered to me.

"Hush."

Then we saw off in one corner, three small frames with pictures of two flappers in swimsuits—undoubtedly April Mae and Clarice Marie long ago.

My eyes welled up with tears, as they often do.

"Oh, Chucky, it's the two of them! Aren't they beautiful!"

"Already sold."

"Don't worry, dear, your father is going to paint a lot of those two. They are kind of drippy, aren't they?"

"Springtime," he said.

"And that is the ultimate reality."

"Totally excellent," said Moire Meg, who had materialized behind us.

"Gram . . . ," Shovie observed, pointing at the flapper with the brown hair.

Later that day, as the sun was sinking behind the Tucson mountains and painting the saguaro cacti rose and gold, I approached my spouse, who was napping on a chaise, his face at peace.

"Dreaming of me?" I asked, sitting on the edge of the chaise.

"Actually I was dreaming of one of my mistresses."

"Fictional," I said. "Why do all these homes have walls around the patios?"

"Old Mediterrean custom. This is not a patio, this is an

atrium. The Latins like to protect their privacy. Even the older homes in the center of the city which don't have pools are into this atrium idea, though they probably don't know the word, much less the origins of the custom."

"Oh."

I touched his hand. He smiled contentedly. Mommy taking care of her baby because he was sick. He was wearing the chinos and beige sweater I had bought him, a nice ensemble for dinner at El Charro. On the table next to the chaise was a cheap and tattered windbreaker which said "Bonn"—almost eighteen years old.

"I suspect that we have them up here in the foothills," he went on, "so that folks can skinny-dip in their spas and swimming pools."

"People don't do that, Chucky!"

"Sure they do. This is the new 'let-it-all-hang-out' America."

"Only in California."

"This is vest-pocket Beverly Hills," he said, closing his eyes.

"Well . . . You can't do it when your children or in-laws are around."

He opened his eyes, then closed them again.

"Certainly not. No respectable Irish Catholics would think of such a thing."

"I've been thinking about what you said at the gallery."

"Hmmn?"

"About the flapper pictures of my mother and your mother representing springtime. Then you said that springtime was the ultimate reality."

"Did I say that?"

"You did."

"Must have been the medication."

"It was a very profound inspiration."

He began to sing, "It Might As Well Be Spring."

I joined in as the scenario required.

Then we did "Younger Than Springtime."

"That's what you think life means?" I asked, when we were finished.

His eyes remained closed.

"Eliminate some of the sentimentality, but only some of it, and you have what we believe. Life is stronger than death, right?"

"Some of us don't live to the next springtime."

"So they have to be content with the everlasting spring." He opened his eyes and examined my face very carefully.

He didn't close his eyes.

"You really believe that my mother is like that flapper in Vangie's watercolor?"

"Last time I looked at it we were still registered members of St. Ursula Roman Catholic parish. We gotta believe that."

"So I'm wrong to mourn for her?"

He sat up, with a touch of a sigh, and extended his arm around me.

"No. You mourn for the pain she suffered, for the loss you suffered, for the waste of life and talent, for terrible agonies of your youth. You still know that Clarice Marie Powers is younger than springtime."

"Then all of this agonizing is silly?"

"The only silly thing you've ever done, Rosemarie, is marry me."

He kissed my neck, a signal of reassurance, not desire.

"You're trying to rediscover her and part of your own life. I'm sure that in her springtime, where it doesn't get cold when the sun goes down like out here, she's happy that the two of you have rediscovered one another."

I started to weep. I'm sorry, I do that all the time.

He caressed the back of my neck.

"You'd better rush into the house and write this conversation down."

"Why?"

"For the next story!"

I pushed him back down on the chaise.

"Charles Cronin O'Malley, you're simply outrageous!"

He closed his eyes contentedly.

"I'd rather think of myself as outrageous in a complex and fascinating way."

"Anyway, I'll never forget what you said."

I leaned over and rested my lips on his.

"The fog is dissipating, Chucky. Thank you."

"I'm like one of those machines they used to have at the airports to break up fog. I like that metaphor."

"Now go in the house and find yourself a better wind-breaker, one that matches your sweater. And put on your shoes. The sidewalks get cold here at night."

"Such as they are."

The phone rang at eight the next morning. I grabbed it.

"O'Malleys'."

"Hi, Rosie, I hope I didn't wake you up. It's ten o'clock out there, isn't it?"

"No, Vince, it's eight o'clock here and nine o'clock in Chicago and ten o'clock in New York. The farther west you go the earlier it is."

"That's what Charlotte said, but I told her she was wrong. I guess I'll have to apologize."

"Indeed!"

"I hope I didn't wake anyone up."

"Besides me, only Chucky, who is pretending he is still asleep . . . Pick up the other phone, Chucky. It's Vince."

He buried his head in a pillow.

"I'm a sick man. I need my sleep."

"It's Vince."

"Vince who?"

He picked up the phone and put it inside the pillow.

"Vince who?" he repeated.

"Sorry to wake you so early, Chuck."

"When you and Peg are out here, I will call you every morning."

"I had a conversation with a nice lawyer in New York, a refined gentlemen. Very Talmudic. Turns out we know a lot of the same people in Democratic politics."

"I'm impressed."

"We chatted for a long time about a lot of things, especially the Mayor."

"That's the way Irish politicians do it, even when they're Jewish and Italian."

"His whole point was that we should try to settle this matter before it gets worse."

"I can hear the restrained agony in his voice."

"Exactly."

"On our terms!"

"He accepted that. Incidentally, I played the tape of his client's conversation with Charlotte. He was appalled."

"Doubtless . . . What's going to happen?"

"We draft a letter saying that Ms. Robbins has defamed you at least twelve times and that we have furnished evidence of this in our petition before the United States Court for the Northern District of Illinois. We ask that they acknowledge that her assertions are false and in reckless disregard of the truth. Then we say that we have no quarrel with the rights of Ms. Robbins and the *Blast* to their critical opinions but we are dismayed that she felt free to make them apparently without visiting the exhibition at the Art Institute. We ask them to acknowledge this also unless they are able to provide proof that she indeed visited Chicago at that time—"

"Do we have the right to demand that?" I interrupted.

"We have the right to demand it as an alternative to proceeding with depositions, which our friend does not want to happen, because he knows, though he doesn't say so, that his clients are cokeheads."

"Then what?" Chucky rolled over and looked at me like I was a complete stranger who had invaded his bed. Then he smiled and touched my face.

"They agree to publish the text of a letter which we have already approved, admitting the defamation and apologizing for it. Then, absent persuasive proof, they also admit that they cannot establish that she ever visited the exhibition."

Chucky looked at me. I nodded.

"When you get those drafts in final shape, you'll send them out here Federal Express."

"We sure will . . . You can trust us, Chuck. We won't let them get away with any tricks. If they do, we'll go after them in court. Our friend knows that."

"Good work," I admitted.

"Bad time, good work. Give our best to Peg and Charley."

"I'll listen to her the next time."

"Well?" I asked my husband.

"I'm a sick man. I need my sleep."

"You need your breakfast. Feed a cold, starve a fever."

"Old wives' tales, with all due respect."

❧ Chuck ❧

1979

My scheme to sneak my Rosemarie masterpiece onto the front of the Arts and Leisure section of the *New York Times* was proceeding apace.

In a dream the night before Vince's ill-timed call, someone—I'm not quite sure who—came to me and informed me that the woman was my masterpiece and that the shot merely captured that.

I don't believe in people that come in dreams, especially when I am perishing with a cold and my bloodstream is filled with strange chemicals. I dismissed the message as patently false. I hadn't done much besides be a good husband for her, especially when, however belatedly, I had lowered the boom on her drinking. Polished the jewel up a little bit maybe but nothing more than that.

On the other hand, a seditious inner voice whispered, if you had not married her—and you were strongly tempted not to—she'd be a terrible mess right now. Or maybe dead.

I married her only because I wanted to take her clothes off.

That silenced the inner voice.

Perhaps I had been a help at a crucial time and deserved some points from the Great Accountant in the Sky for that. Nothing more.

Besides, she had saved me many times, though she was unable to exorcise my current cold.

I was sitting outside, bundled up against the cold morning, in University of Arizona sweat clothes and fleecy blanket. I had reduced the possible shots for our conclaves book to about a hundred. They presented a fairly dismal view of the leadership of the Catholic Church. That was fine with me because my opinion was that they were a fairly dismal lot.

My wife appeared at poolside with a tray of food and a huge pot of tea. Naturally she did the cooking while we were at the elder O'Malleys' home. She was dressed in a vast, tightly belted white robe. Her hair was brushed out and, as always, she smelled lovely.

"Your parents are eating inside. Your daughters are still abed. You will note I have provided you with a wide variety of breakfast foods—raisin bran, English muffins, omelets, cinnamon rolls, and your choice of jellies and jams. Also orange juice, which is very good for colds."

"No bagels?"

"No."

"Well, I'm not paying at this hotel, so I'll have to make do . . . Would you please pour me a small cup of tea."

She did so with grace, but only after I had consumed my ration of orange juice, which everyone knows is good for a cold, right?

When I heard the door to the house slide open, I quickly hid the small clipping from the *New York Times* over which I had chortled.

PHOTOGRAPHER SUES VILLAGE PAPER

Charles Cronin O'Malley, a celebrated Chicago photographer, has filed suit against the *Gramercy Blast*, an underground newspaper, for a review of his current exhibition at the Art Institute in Chicago. In her review Diana Robbins asserted that Mr. O'Malley had not earned a military decoration during his service in Germany in the nineteen forties, was not beaten during the Little Rock school integration, had not marched at Selma, and had never been to Vietnam during the war. According to Charlotte Antonelli, a spokesperson for Mr. O'Malley, his lawyers have submitted affidavits, newspaper clippings, and television footage "which establish beyond any doubt that Ms. Robbins has written defamatory statements in reckless disregard of the truth." Asked why the *Blast* would publish such allegations, Ms. Antonelli said that perhaps the *Blast* staff felt that there were no limitations on the First Amendment. No one at the *Blast* office was available for comment. The woman who answered the phone informed a reporter that the *Blast* had no lawyer and did not need one.

Marvelous!

Now if only someone in New York would stir up more controversy! Our friend Christina Freeman would have to ride into the battle. What better opportunity for the newspaper of record to present to the world my picture *wife!*

I considered the scheme from every side. There was nothing I could do one way or another to move the scheme forward. It had never been within my power to do so. All I could do was to watch and wait. After the event, no one could blame me, though I doubted that the only one who would—Rosemarie—would complain in the slightest. If she did, I could say it wasn't my idea, a statement which in context was true enough.

I had engaged in only one minor ploy which might facilitate the scheme. I called the curator at the Art Institute before we had flown to Tucson and told him that if any important publication wanted permission to print a single picture from the collection, he might grant that permission.

How was I to know who would call for permission to reprint which picture?

I tried again to see what might go wrong. Nothing, as far as I could calculate.

This was all vintage Chucky stuff. I should be ashamed of myself. Somehow, despite my various depressions, I could not find shame lurking anywhere in my soul.

Maybe later.

While I had no appetite for breakfast, Rosemarie's insistence on feeding me was irresistible.

Later, when it grew warmer, she removed her vast robe and revealed a fetching two-piece suit which one might have called a bikini. Since I was ill and incapable of Eros, I experienced no reaction at all.

She dove into the pool and swam vigorous lengths for a

half hour. The very sight of such frantic activity exhausted me.

Soon after her daughter appeared and engaged in similar activity. Then her mother-in-law. Even her father-in-law eased his way into the pool.

Who was watching the child?

I looked around in some alarm. Then I discovered Shovie playing with her dolls right behind me. I gathered from her conversation that some of the dolls had misbehaved. She reasoned with them quite patiently.

"Good morning, Siobhan Marie," I said formally.

"Chookie no swim?"

"Chookie has a cold."

"Poor Chookie."

Indeed yes.

Despite all the vigorous activity around me, I somehow managed my midmorning nap.

Later the whole family gathered around me and wondered whether I had a fever.

If they awakened me rudely, I would certainly have a fever.

A wet hand touched my forehead.

"No fever," Rosemarie observed, "though he may not last the week."

I opened my eyes reluctantly and glared. My wife was standing over me, water dripping on the patio, a picture of athletic accomplishment and womanly beauty. I wanted her. Immediately. Then I realized that I was sick and could not possibly act on my desire.

What if I had a cold for the rest of my life?

"No fever and no peace," I sighed.

It was another perfect Arizona winter day, way above the normal temperature for mid-January. I was forced to eat lunch and then, while the rest of the family went off to see the Old Tucson film set (where half the Western films ever made were set), my wife constrained me to discuss our conclave book as we reclined on chaises underneath an umbrella, she with a towel wrapped around herself and I still clad in my sweat suit but without the fleecy blanket.

"How are you doing today?" I asked her.

"You're the one who is sick."

"You know what I mean."

"I do . . . I can't say that I'm completely at peace with my mother. I think that she could have protected me from her demented husband and that she could have stopped drinking and then I realize I have no right to make such demands on her and we're friends again."

"It will take time, Rosemarie."

"I know that, Chuck. I understand now that there's no rush. I have the time . . . Thank you for being so patient."

"I'm happy to be able to help."

I touched her hand. We were quiet for a moment.

"Now what about the conclave book?"

"No peace for the wicked"—I sighed—"even when he's sick."

Not much sympathy either.

"I've reduced the shots to approximately a hundred prints in these three folders. This first one is the best photos of the cardinals. These two we could label 'candidates.' "

I showed her Benelli and Siri.

Then I handed her the third picture, which I proposed we call "winner."

"These are two horrible men," she said. "The Pope looks much better."

"You think the first two are too cynical?"

"No," she said thoughtfully, "ugly maybe, but at least Benelli is smiling."

We went through the collection very carefully, approving most of them, rejecting a few.

"I have some backup shots in my briefcase," I said. "Why don't you check them out and pick the ones you like."

"Okay . . . I think our narration should be very low-key and objective, some essential history, some bland commentary on the issues, an explanation of how and why John Paul I."

"The so-called liberals thought he was one of them and he really wasn't, mostly because of his neighborhood."

"Not even that concise. We write a commentary full of respect for the Church and its traditions so that no one can find the slightest hint of anger or dissatisfaction. Let people judge the prints for themselves."

"That's fine with me. You're doing the writing."

"I know, but I'll want you to look at every couple of pages."

"I read everything you give me to read."

"This is different from one of my stories."

"You are not planning to reveal your anger that celibate males make all the decisions about sex for married women?"

"No, not in so many words. Let the readers judge that for themselves."

"I'm sure you'll provide them with many subtle hints."

She laughed happily.

Yes, wife, you can be happy and sing. Your poor aging, sad sack husband is a physical and emotional wreck.

I was advised that I needed a nap so I would not sleep during supper at the Arizona Inn. I took the nap.

The next morning a Federal Express pack came with documents from our legal team.

To the editors of the *Gramercy Blast*

Sirs:

We believe that there are several misstatements of fact in your review of the current exhibition of the photographs of Charles Cronin O'Malley at the Art Institute in Chicago. We have provided your attorney with evidence that these statements are false. This evidence consists of newspaper clippings, sworn affidavits, and television tapes.

1) He did receive the Legion of Merit medal for his service in Germany after World War II.

2) He was not involved in the black market in that country.

3) He completed his doctoral dissertation at the University of Chicago and graduated with distinction in the Spring 1956 Convocation.

4) He was badly beaten at Little Rock.

5) He did march at Selma with Martin Luther King.

6) He was assaulted by thugs during Martin Luther King's demonstrations in Chicago.

7) He did go to Vietnam in 1968.

8) He was attacked by police during the 1968 convention.

9) He does not pay his assistants poor wages because he does not have assistants.

10) His wife does have a very successful career as a writer and testifies in her affidavit that he has always been supportive of that career.

We believe that all these facts are on the public record and could easily have been verified. Hence we believe that they are published in reckless disregard for the truth.

We require that you acknowledge that they are false and apologize for the injury done to Dr. O'Malley's reputation.

We do not question the right of Ms. Robbins or the *Gramercy Blast* to be critical of Dr. O'Malley's work. However, we do question whether it is proper for her to do so without having viewed the exhibition at the Art Institute. Absent proof, such as a receipt for an airline ticket, we must express our suspicion that she never in fact viewed the photographs. Most notably she describes the portrait of Mrs. O'Malley as naked. In fact, as the catalogue of the exhibit would show, she was not. She describes the portraits of Mrs. O'Malley, Martin Luther King, Richard Nixon, Maureen O'Hara, and John Kennedy as appearing in the same room. In fact only the portraits of Mrs. O'Malley and Ms. O'Hara were in the same room. We think that it is no coincidence that the last four portraits are mentioned in the *New York Times* review by Christina Freeman. Also the quotes attributed to Dr. O'Malley appeared in that review and the comments about the portrait of Mrs. O'Malley also seemed to have been taken from the *Times* review and reversed.

Thus we require that you present evidence that the review
was based on an actual viewing of the portraits or
acknowledge that Ms. Robbins did not attend the exhibition.

We expect your prompt attention to these matters.

> Cordially yours,
> Vincent Antonelli
> Edward Patrick Murray
> Charlotte April Antonelli
> Attorneys-at-Law

The response demanded of the *Blast* was brief.

We acknowledge that the evidence shows that all of our
reviewer's allegations about the career of Dr. O'Malley are
false. We regret the allegations and apologize for them. We
have received no proof that Ms. Robbins visited Chicago
recently and conclude that she probably did not attend the
exhibition of Dr. O'Malley's portraits.

"What do you think?" I asked my wife.

"Looks good to me ... Let's call Vince and Ed and tell
them to go ahead."

Both lawyers were in court, a typical legal excuse. However, Ms. Antonelli was available.

"Hi, Uncle Chuck, Aunt Rosie. Senior counsel are in court."

"Probably out having a prelunch drink," I growled.

"No way!"

"Don't pay any attention to him, Charley. He's been kidding
your poor father since they were ten years old. We don't have
any problem with the letters. What if they fiddle with them?"

"Then we sue. All they have is our word that we'll withdraw
our petition. If they don't keep their word, we're free not to
keep ours—and they'll have admitted libel."

"Do they know that, Charley?" I asked.

"Their lawyer does. Hard to tell what they know and don't
know."

"Give your mother our love. Tell her to hurry out here."

"Well, I guess that's that!"

"Do you think so, Chucky? That kid with the foul mouth we heard on Charlotte's tape was stoned. Maybe they all are. They could still do something crazy."

I was hoping they would. I realized, however, that the improbable scenario I had cooked up in my head never really had much of a chance. Too bad.

My cold did not improve. Neither did my vague sense of sadness. Would there never be any more good news in my life?

I worked in desultory fashion on our conclave book in the Arizona warmth. Rosemarie scribbled notes—on her lined yellow pads—for the text as I tried to order my prints in a fashion most likely to convey the impression that there was something profoundly imperfect about the way our Church selected its leadership.

That made me feel even sadder. Perhaps I was becoming a typical elderly Irish male, the kind that would sit in front of his cottage while he smoked his pipe and gazed dreamily out over the bogs. I would murmur periodically, "Ah they were grand times and great people. 'Tis the end of them now. Sure, we won't see their like again."

That image somehow consoled me. I would spend my life being a character, a whimsical old man who lived mostly in the past.

"What are you smiling at?" herself demanded.

"Wasn't I dreaming that I had become a typical elderly Irish male, the kind that would sit in front of his cottage while he smoked his pipe and gazed dreamily out over the bogs. I would murmur periodically, 'Ah they were grand times and great people. 'Tis the end of them now. Sure, we won't see their like again.' "

She glanced at the desert and the towering Santa Catalinas. "I don't see any bogs. You wouldn't be murmuring occasional laments. You'd be telling stories all the time and driving your poor family to pray that you'd shut up occasionally so they'd have some peace and quiet."

Then she went back to her scribbling.

I'd be a poor old man with whose eccentricities no one sympathized.

My sadness was mixed with absurdity and laughter and self-ridicule. That made me even sadder.

It was the cold, I told myself. If I could only stop hacking, I'd feel fine again.

Moire Meg returned to Chicago for the beginning of the semester.

"Rosie," she said, "keep Chucky here till he gets over his cold. There's too much Celtic twilight around this place."

"He likes feeling sorry for himself."

That was true, but she shouldn't have said it.

The trouble was I didn't think I'd really like smoking a pipe.

"You could always try chewing bubble gum."

She actually brought me some bubble gum. I amused my daughter with my bubbles, especially when she learned that she could make them collapse all over my face (which was covered with sunblock to protect me from sunlight when I walked to the umbrella from the house).

"Chookie funny!"

The good April and Vangie were driving up to Carefree to visit friends who had a great-granddaughter visiting, just about Shovie's age. Would we mind if they brought Shovie along?

She endorsed the scheme.

"Shovie meet Patti," she informed us.

"She's punishing us for abandoning her when we went to Italy."

"Charles Cronin O'Malley! She would never do that. She just wants to show us that she can travel too."

Same difference, I thought.

Many hugs and kisses as she got into the car.

"I'll come back real soon, Chookie and Rooshie."

Just like you did, you bad parents.

I retreated to the patio with the prints for *Conclaves*, as we were now calling it in a burst of creative imagination.

A few moments later Rosemarie appeared in her huge white robe. She tossed it aside negligently—on me—and dove into the pool. An elegant dive as usual.

"Rosemarie! What are you doing!"

"Swimming!"

"You forgot your bathing costume!"

She splashed my perfectly neat sweat suit.

"Stop that!"

Then she pulled me into the water and somehow managed to despoil me of my sweat suit.

I don't know that our thirty-six-hour frolic cured my cold. It was probably departing anyway. I was not so deep into Irish melancholy that I could not enjoy it. Still I was badgered by the thought that this might be the last time.

When Shovie came back, she informed us, "I love Patti but I love Chookie and Rooshie more."

"First person singular," my wife said sadly. "The poor little thing is growing up."

The phone was ringing when we arrived home in Oak Park in the midst of a blizzard and with the promise of subzero temperatures the next day. Rosemarie beat me to it as she always does—a missed phone call could arguably be a matter of life or death.

"Yeah hi, Ed. Your partner picked a good time to get out of town. Chucky and Siobhan were homesick for Chicago . . . They did . . . Let me get Chucky on the phone."

"Our friends in New York played it cute," Ed told me. "They published the letters as we insisted. However, they also published a story about a 'Demand' made by a group called the Lower SoHo Women's Faction. I'll read it to you: 'We the Lower SoHo Women's Faction express our strong support for our member Ms. Diana Robbins, whose freedom of speech has been impugned by Charles C. O'Malley. We firmly believe that a woman art critic who is sensitive to the most advanced feminist theory need not physically view oppressive art to render a revolutionary opinion about such degenerate material. Because of this position we demand that the proposed exhibition of O'Malley's obscene art at the Photography Gallery be canceled. If it is not, we call upon our feminist sisters to rally against this male chauvinist oppression and storm the gallery to destroy its obscenity.' "

"Interesting," I said, more delighted by this idiocy than angered by it.

"Any idea about the size of this particular faction?" Rosemarie asked.

"Some of my friends in New York tell me that it's seven

or eight women who are angry at their rich parents. Not very big, but they could still make a lot of noise."

"Would that be bad?"

"We know that the Gallery is already feeling timid about the exhibition."

"They have to pay us if they cancel, don't they?" I asked, knowing full well that when my scheme began to work they would uncancel.

"Sure, though the litigation might cost something . . . They're scared shitless. They don't realize that it's the late nineteen seventies, not the late nineteen sixties."

"Ah," I said, "to quote someone who was never mentioned at Mount Carmel High School, *O Tempora, O Mores!*"

"M. T. Cicero, as I recall."

"I won't ask you what it means . . . Do you suggest that we take any action?"

"We could continue our suit against the *Blast* on the grounds that they violated our agreement. We could seek an injunction against the Gallery to prevent them from canceling the contract."

"That would look petty, Ed, wouldn't it?" Rosemarie asked.

"I think so too . . . Chucky?"

"I agree. No point in giving them any free publicity."

Especially since, unless I didn't understand how things work in the New York art world, they were about to give us priceless free publicity.

Then Shovie woke up and Moire Meg appeared to embrace her little sister. The child would grow up spoiled. Again I had more sense than to express my opinion.

❧ *Rosemarie* ❧
1979

When we returned from Tucson, I began to worry about Chuck. It was not the kind of worry that I ordinarily feel—the constant background fear that your husband will not act right and hence harm himself some way or other. Now I feared that Chuck might be edging toward a nervous breakdown or psychotic interlude as Maggie Ward would have called it. Max Berman had told me that Chuck didn't need tranquilizers. What if he was wrong? I could ask Maggie, but she would deflect the question as inappropriate.

So what if I told her flat out that I was worried about Chuck?

She would want to go into the reasons for my worry.

"Well, he was mercurial during our time in Tucson. His moods shifted back and forth. He spent more time than was appropriate on the prints for *Conclaves*. Normally he makes decisions about such matters and sticks with them. He seemed more thoughtful than usual some of the time."

She would demand to know how different all of this was from normal behavior. I would say that it was hard to tell. I was never quite sure about what normal is in him.

Sex?

A little erratic, but good enough. Sometimes he didn't seem altogether there when we were making love, but nothing I can put my finger on.

Interesting language, she would say.

I would flush and laugh.

Harsh to you?

Chucky? He wouldn't dare!

Another woman?

Not a chance!

Was I sure of that?

I would think for a moment and say, yes, I was sure. No mysterious phone calls, no going out in the car by himself, nothing at all.

In truth a woman can never be completely sure on that subject. Yet it was absurd to distrust him.

Maybe, Maggie would say, he's still coming to terms with mortality, something you did long ago.

Maybe.

Then she'd say that it was time and that would be that.

I might go through this dialogue with her sometime. I didn't have enough to go on now.

"No lunch with Dr. Berman today?" I asked him on Friday.

"He's gone to Florida to play golf."

"Psychiatrists play golf?"

"He's a doctor, isn't he? Anyway, I'm still not satisfied with the prints for *Conclaves*."

That would make me uneasy all over again.

❧ Chuck ❧

1979

The Photography Gallery canceled the show because of fear of violent protests. Ed Murray told them that he had a contract. The director of the Gallery said that the cancellation was our fault because of the controversy we had created in the *Blast*.

"No one in New York knows anything about the law," Ed complained.

"Not in the art world anyway."

"What do you want to do?"

"Hassle them."

I smiled with satisfaction when I hung up the phone. All the pieces of the plan were falling into place. The story had a marvelous inevitability. Greek tragedy, though I didn't think the director of the Gallery was a tragic figure.

To change mythologies a bit, I was Puck. Or maybe, given my recent sojourn in Arizona, Coyote. A Coyote who was always hungry but in this instance simply sat and watched.

I conveyed the news to my wife.

"You almost seem happy about it, Chuck."

"Who, me? I think it's great comedy. Who cares about New York anyway?"

She frowned uneasily. Still worrying about me, poor dear woman.

Was I worth worrying about?

I supposed so. I was the only husband she had. However, she would certainly do much better the next time around.

I was alone in the house the next day when Charlotte Antonelli called me on the phone.

"Uncle Chuck," she complained in her Sicilian voice, "why am I suddenly the press spokesperson for our clan?"

"Intelligence, charm, good looks, an instinct for the jugular? What can I tell you?"

"Yeah, well this woman from the *New York Times* called this morning to ask if you had any comment on the cancellation of your contract for a show at the Photography Gallery because of the controversy over the obscene picture of Aunt Rosie."

BINGO!

"Let me think about it, Charley . . . Well, first of all the picture is not obscene, secondly the Gallery may certainly decide not to show photography that it deems inappropriate, thirdly they are violating their contract."

"Yeah, I got that all down."

"What do you think?"

"It's you."

I had no idea what that meant.

"I'm glad you think so."

"She'll want to know whether we will go to court."

"This is Ms. Freeman?"

"That's her name. She seems real nice."

"First rule of being a spokesperson for the Crazy O'Malleys: never trust anyone who is a journalist."

This one we could trust, however. She had an agenda of her own, which doubtless included putting the woman who had cadged her work firmly in her place.

"Got it!"

"You can tell her that we are considering our options."

"This is all a direct quote from you?"

"Absolutely."

After Charley had hung up, I reflected on my comment. Any gaffes that might ruin my plan?

No way.

The next morning, I crept downstairs quietly so I wouldn't wake Rosemarie, opened the front door gingerly, winced at the blast of Canadian air which invaded our house, and rescued the *New York Times* newspaper from a snowdrift.

As I flipped through the pages to the Arts and Leisure section, I realized that if the virtuous Rosemarie knew I had opened the door and, indeed, gone outside in my pajamas and without anything on my feet, I would be severely reprimanded.

I didn't worry very long, however. The aforementioned wife, in her University of Chicago sleep shirt, leaped out of a full quarter page to wake up readers of both genders on this bitter winter morning.

The headline read,

WIFE'S PICTURE CREATES CONTROVERSY OVER O'MALLEY'S NEW YORK SHOW: DOES A FEMINIST CRITIC NEED TO SEE PORTRAIT TO JUDGE IT OBSCENE?

BY CHRISTINA FREEMAN

I rearranged the paper into its proper form—I hate to read a paper which has been pulled apart—and placed it on the table in our breakfast nook. Then, shivering from my imprudent charge into the elements, I slipped back upstairs, brushed the snowflakes out of my hair, and donned a robe and slippers. The article had to be savored over a cup of hot tea and toast with raspberry jam.

I opened the Arts and Leisure section again while the tea steeped.

> The Photography Gallery has canceled the long-awaited opening of an exhibition of portraits by the Chicago photographer Charles C. O'Malley because of opposition from a downtown feminist group. The SoHo Women's Faction denounced as obscene a photograph of O'Malley's wife, the author Helen Clancy. Diana Robbins, art critic of the *Gramercy Blast* and member of the Faction, denounced the portrait as obscene in a review in the *Blast*. The Faction also denied that a feminist critic needed to actually view a photograph to know that it was obscene and oppressive.
>
> Subsequently Dr. O'Malley's attorneys charged that Ms. Robbins had never visited the exhibition at Chicago's Art Institute. They pointed out that her review seemed to be based on an earlier *New York Times* review from which

she concluded that portraits of John Kennedy, Martin Luther King, Richard Nixon, Maureen O'Hara, and Ms. Clancy were in the same room. In fact only the pictures of Ms. O'Hara and Ms. Clancy were in the same room of the five-room exhibition. The *Blast* apologized to Dr. O'Malley for a number of false statements about his life made in Ms. Robbins's article and admitted that it had no evidence that Ms. Robbins had seen the exhibition.

Nothing daunted, the Faction issued a statement in the *Blast* asserting that a "woman art critic who is sensitive to the most advanced feminist theory need not physically view oppressive art to render a revolutionary opinion about such degenerate material." The Faction also threatened to storm the Gallery and tear the picture from the wall.

Lucien DePlante, director of the Gallery, said he decided to cancel the O'Malley show because the "Gallery does not wish to offend women." Asked if he personally considered the portrait to be obscene, Mr. DePlante refused to comment.

However, Mathilda Martin, a New York photographer, disagreed sharply with the Gallery's decision. "It's a wonderful shot," she said, "respectfully and chastely erotic. The woman in the picture defies the photographer and us. O'Malley has managed to present an erotically appealing woman who is not an object but a challenging person. The portrait is an amazing achievement."

Dr. O'Malley was not available for comment. However, a spokesperson, Charlotte Antonelli, pointed out that the Gallery was in violation of its contract with Dr. O'Malley. "In Chicago," Ms. Antonelli said, "we're old fashioned. We think you should see a work of art before you denounce it."

Ah, Charley, you've learned too much from listening to Uncle Chucky. It's a line I should have used but didn't.

The line under the copy of the portrait read, "Obscene or an amazing achievement?"

The shot dazzled me as it had since the instant I saw it falling into place as I squeezed the camera button. It was my

Rosemarie to perfection. I imagined the letters that would appear: a monsignor somewhere in the New York suburbs would denounce the *Times* for printing pornography; a woman with an Irish name would describe my wife as "shameless"; a couple of Jewish folk would accuse the Gallery of censorship; and several women and men would praise me for an artistic breakthrough.

I smiled happily. Who needs to pay for publicity when your enemies give it to you for nothing?

I glanced at Rosemarie again. Was the picture sexually arousing? No, I decided, but the woman in it was definitely arousing. A lot of men who would glance quickly at the picture as they opened the Arts and Leisure section would glance again and yet again and wish to themselves that this woman was theirs. However, she was not. She was mine. All mine.

That was, I warned myself, a sentiment which bordered on oppressive male chauvinism. So what? It didn't quite cross the border.

I was very satisfied with myself.

I folded the Arts and Leisure section so that the picture was on top of the newspaper, the first thing someone would see when she bounced into the breakfast nook.

Then the real-life Rosemarie bounced into the breakfast nook. She was wrapped in a peach silk robe.

"Why up so early, Chucky Ducky? . . . Oh, no! Not HER again! I figured this would happen! Whada they say! . . ."

She grabbed the paper and read the article with fierce concentration. I poured her some tea and prepared a piece of raspberry toast for her.

"Well!" She held the page up triumphantly. "I guess we showed that Feminist Faction bunch of bitches!"

"I guess we did!"

"That Charley is a clever little brat, isn't she?"

"It was her line. I wish it were mine."

"This Lucien fellow will change his mind?"

"Bet on it."

She sighed and folded the paper so her picture was still on top.

"She's me all right. I knew that from the time you pushed the shutter release. At first I tried to pretend it wasn't. But I knew it all along. I don't understand it exactly . . . She must be hell to live with . . ."

"Always challenging, like the woman says."

"Sexy?"

"Yes, but that is only the beginning."

"Passionate?"

"True enough."

"Wild?"

"On occasion."

"Seductive?"

"Generally."

"You're my husband." She frowned. "You should have a good one-word description."

I prepared another slice of raspberry toast and handed it to her.

"Exhausting and enchanting?"

"That's two words, but I'll settle for them. For the moment."

"Good. You've always been that. Since you were ten anyway."

"Not really!"

"Yes, really!"

Quick change of subject.

"I'll have to call the magazine. They'll want to use it. Maybe on the cover."

"You'll tell them not to?"

"Why? Better to be damned for a goat than for a sheep!"

This was not quite the reaction I had expected. I had thought I might be Pygmalion. Now I wondered if maybe the Baron von Frankenstein might be a better metaphor.

"What will people think about me?" She extended her teacup.

"Women will tend to envy you but many of them will be won over and will identify with you, like most of the women around here do."

She nodded.

"I hope so . . . And men? Will they lust after me?"

I took a deep breath.

"I assume that they will glance quickly at it and turn the page. They're not really interested in art controversies. Then they'll remember the image and turn back to look at it again and yet again and wish to themselves that this woman was theirs. However, she is not. She is mine. All mine."

"That's very arousing, Chuck," she said, lowering her eyes.

I had not meant it to be so.

"I am all yours," she continued, her eyes still averted. "Always have been."

"I think I know that."

Even in my depressed state, I couldn't take any more. I leaned across the table and pulled the robe off her shoulders. The sight of her exposed breasts, as always, hit the pit of my stomach with a jab of wonder, desire, pride.

"I think we'd better go back upstairs," she said hoarsely.

We did.

After I asserted my mastery again . . . or maybe only succumbed to her again . . . it occurred to me that this was not an outcome for which I had planned.

Indeed, I had only seen it coming. It wasn't my scheme at all. Rosemarie had seen it coming too. Instead of being upset and perhaps even angry as I had expected, she was delighted.

Big deal, Chucky Ducky!

In the midst of the phone calls and congratulations the next couple of days, I steadily grew more morose.

The women of the clan—the monster regiment—had swarmed over to our house by ten o'clock to celebrate, bringing their babies along as necessary. Poor little Shovie wandered around with a copy of the *NYT* to show to everyone.

"MY mommy!"

"Cool, Chuck!" Moire Meg observed.

"I didn't have anything to do with it."

"Sure!"

There were two offers of film contracts, which my wife modestly declined without consulting me.

If she had wanted to try film, I wouldn't have objected.

What right has the Baron von Frankenstein to complain?

"I don't know where my eldest got her tongue," Peg, beaming with joy over her foster sister's triumph, whispered in my ear.

"From grandmother April."

"Chucky!"

As for the good April, she merely said to everyone who

would listen, "Well, poor little Rosie has always been cute. She gets more cute every year."

"Chucky Ducky," poor little Rosie whispered in my ear, "I want a couple of life-size blowups. You can do that, can't you?"

"I suppose so . . . Where will you put them?"

"For starters one will go downstairs in your workroom."

She kissed my forehead.

"Okay," I said with little enthusiasm.

So.

So. I sat in the corner and listened to it all, up to my neck once again in the slough of despond. Why had I become so excited by a silly little scheme that I had not really cooked up?

Because I was desperate for excitement.

I rejoiced with Rosemarie. She was entitled to the celebration. I was only a fraud, playing a foolish game for quick laughs.

I'd better get back to work on the damn *Conclaves* thing.

❧ Rosemarie ❧
1979

In March I began to worry seriously about Chuck.

One cold day with the wind howling through the barren trees, the slush frozen on the streets and sidewalks, and snow flurries sifting a deceptive white sheen over the whole ugly mess, he appeared in my office with the same set of *Conclaves* prints. I was working on the galleys for my new story.

"My heart isn't in this anymore, Rosemarie," he said.

I'd never heard him say anything like that in all the years of our marriage. If Charles C. O'Malley, Ph.D., started something, he finished it.

He had gone into a tailspin after our triumph over the *Blast* and its allies. He should have been celebrating. I don't know how he pulled it off, but I knew that he would. It was a real Chuck O'Malley masterpiece. He had every reason to rejoice. Instead he stewed. He couldn't explain to me why he stewed.

"It all seems so silly."

"Why?"

He shrugged.

"I don't know."

When his show started at the end of the month, there would be some critical reviews from those New York narcissists who had to prove their worth by dissenting from the collective re-action and there would be those who believed that nothing good can come out of Chicago. However, the show would surely be a huge success. Everyone would talk about the portrait of Helen Clancy, the writer. I figured I could live with it, pretending to be flattered even at those times I might be a little bit embarrassed.

"Have you had cosmetic surgery, Ms. O'Malley?"

(No.)

"Do you dye your hair, Ms. O'Malley?"

(What do you think?)

"How do you keep your figure, Ms. O'Malley?"

(Genetic luck and hard work.)

"Is the character in your stories really based on your husband, Ms. O'Malley?"

(No way. My husband is a far richer, far more multifaceted character.)

"What do your children think about having celebrities as parents?"

(They don't believe it.)

ETC.

I had gone through this comic routine with him. His response was only mild chuckles.

He said he didn't think he'd go to the opening. He'd probably catch another cold on the plane.

Then he comes into my office and tells me that his heart isn't in the *Conclaves* book anymore.

This stuff was getting to be too much. I resisted the temptation to lose my temper.

"Why not, Chuck?" I said.

"I don't like attacking the Church. It's the only one we have. Sometimes it's not much. We could be doing a lot of harm."

"We're not attacking the Church, Chuck. We're honestly depicting its leaders and the cronyism which produces them. We're implying that the Church would be a lot better at its mission if this were changed. This is criticism, I admit. Didn't Paul criticize Peter? Didn't St. Catherine criticize popes? Is there not a public opinion in the Church like Father Ed says?"

"I know all these things, Rosemarie. All I'm saying is that I don't want to do it. Not now anyway. Maybe not ever. It's all right with me if you arrange the prints and write the commentary. My stomach ties up in knots when I think about it. The Church has enough troubles without my adding to it."

I thought of the birth control commission and our honest efforts to furnish good advice to Pope Paul. Now we were degenerates, outcasts. I didn't want to get even. I merely wanted change. I wanted women to have some input into decisions about the sexuality of women.

Someday maybe. Not today.

"All right, Chuck. I understand. At least I think I do. You don't mind if I work on it after I'm through with my galleys here?"

"No, not at all. I just can't do it anymore."

He trudged out of my office, like a sick little puppy.

I would have to talk to Dr. Berman again.

He agreed reluctantly to attend the opening in New York. On the plane he started to sneeze and cough.

"Three colds in a winter," he laughed. "Three strikes and you're out."

At the Photography Gallery he was his old charming self again. The leitmotif of his comments was that he was now the man who had made the portrait of Helen Clancy, the famous author.

"We better take him home first thing in the morning, Rosie," Moire Meg warned me.

I agreed.

He stumbled around at La Guardia like a man in a trance.

"I think I have a fever," he mumbled, as the plane took off.

"You're burning up, Chucky."

He went into chills twice on the trip.

It seemed to last forever. We circled Chicago several times because of a weather front that was coming through the city. Purgatory is waiting for a plane to land in Chicago during a winter snowstorm.

Finally, in the blowing and drifting snow we found our way to the emergency room at Oak Park Hospital. Fortunately, Dr. Kennedy was on the premises. He ordered X rays and blood tests. Then he put an oxygen mask on Chuck and sent him to intensive care. I knew that it was all a nightmare. I would wake up and he would be fine.

"It's very serious, Rosie," he said. "Chuck has a powerful, pneumonia-like respiratory infection and a fever of a hundred and four. We're doing all we can to bring the fever under control. I don't know exactly what it is . . . We're doing our best . . ."

"How serious?"

"Very serious."

"Potentially fatal?"

His face grim, he took a deep breath.

"I hope and pray not."

"Mom," Moire Meg whispered, "we better say the rosary."

❧ Chuck ❧
1979

One of the things that happened in 1979 was that I tried to die. I also met a very strange woman.

I was pretty sure I would die as soon as I heard Dr. Kennedy's voice at Oak Park Hospital. He was worried. Well, he should be worried. I was sick, burning up with fever, shivering with chills. I was, I told myself, not long for this world.

Really.

I didn't really mind. Everyone had to die sometime. Maybe I was a little young by current standards, but that was the way of it.

Some of the women in my family were murmuring prayers at the bedside. It was soothing, like the monotone of the living rosary in the St. Ursula schoolyard so long ago. May crowning. Rosemarie deliberately fell off the ladder into my lap. Terrible child.

I don't mind if You take me, I told God, but You have to take care of her.

The voice in my head wasn't God, but what was left of my own consciousness. "She can take care of herself. She always has."

Right.

I'd miss all the Crazy O'Malleys.

Then people were chasing me—rednecks, cops, blacks, Vietnamese, cardinals. Demons all of them. The Vietnamese kid whose head the Marines had blown off in the basement of the Saigon Embassy demanded his head back. I told him to bother the Marines, I didn't have it. Then a lot of black-clad nuns screamed at me. They were replaced by a swarm of feminists who tore the frames off the wall at one of my shows, then a horde of screaming critics who objected to my being Irish.

I kept ahead of them. I ran down alleys and side streets and main streets and expressways and swam across Twin Lakes and Lake Geneva and Lake Michigan and the Tiber and the Grand Canal.

A pope condemned me in Latin, then in Greek, then in broken English.

I shouted back at him. A swarm of Swiss Guards marched at me with their pikes at the ready. They were followed by cardinals with faggots and lighted tapers. They were burning me at the stake because I was a degenerate. The flames were burning all around me. I tried to think of something clever to say, but it was too hot. In self-defense I slipped down into the darkness of death. As I did I heard Edward administering Extreme Unction to me.

No, Sacrament of the Sick.

Later, much later, I opened my eyes. Rosemarie was smiling down at me.

"You had us worried, Chucky," she said.

"Sorry about that."

Then I caught fire again.

The next attacks were fragmentary, disorganized, terrifying. I could no longer run. I was lost in a frozen forest, buried deep in a cave, hiding among a pride of lionesses who didn't seem to notice me. I was immobile, doomed, almost dead.

Then I looked up and saw a woman standing next to the bed. She seemed to be wearing a red dress and a blue cape. Her wide brown eyes were kind and her smile gentle. I knew who she was.

Power, calm, love.

"Have you come to collect me?" I asked.

"Collect you, Chucky?"

"It is said that you or your friends collect people when they're dying."

Her smile broadened.

"We do that sometimes to help people who are frightened

to cross the line. Someone who is as reckless as you are won't need that kind of help."

"Curious." I sighed and closed my eyes.

Later, I don't know how much later, I opened them. She was still there, still smiling.

"Then why are you here?"

She seemed surprised.

"To take care of you."

"Why me?"

"That is the kind of question you should never ask of us."

"I see."

Again I closed my eyes.

"How do I know you're really out there? Maybe you're only a creation of my feverish brain."

"Fever and medication."

"Right."

"Couldn't it be a combination of both?"

"I guess so."

Then it didn't seem an unreasonable possibility.

How do I remember all this? Hey, if you have a visit from her, you remember it all, maybe because she wants you to remember it all.

"You're very sick," she said.

"Tell me about it."

"Rosie is terribly worried about you."

"Rosemarie," I corrected her.

"Sorry," she laughed.

Her laughter was like chimes echoing across a mountain meadow in spring.

"She can take care of herself."

"You will recover, Chucky. That's why I'm here. And don't ask why we're concerned about you. We're concerned about everyone."

I wondered who the "we" were. Better not to ask.

"I have a hunch I'm kind of special. Why?"

She lifted her shoulders in an unmistakably Jewish gesture.

"That should be evident."

"I don't get it."

"We are very fond of Rosemarie."

"You should be."

"You saved her."

"I didn't."

"Come on, Chucky, you know better than that. You were right the other day when you thought that she was your masterpiece and not that very clever portrait."

"You can read thoughts?"

"Only faces . . . I've had a lot of practice."

I sighed and closed my eyes again.

I was very sick. Delirious probably. Yet I was having a rational, more or less, conversation with someone from another level of reality.

I opened my eyes, much later I think.

"Are you Jewish or Catholic?"

She thought that was very funny.

"I mean you look Jewish, kind of, but you also remind me of Rosemarie."

"That ought not to surprise you."

"If you say so."

"We must get down to business, Chucky."

"Anytime you say. What's business?"

"Your identity crisis. It has to go."

"What does that mean?"

"It means that you must value your work for what it is, a major contribution in your field. It means you must value yourself as a great man who couldn't take himself seriously even if he tried. It means you must treasure the gift that we gave in your wife. It means that you must believe that there is much important work for you yet to do. It finally means that you must not question the depth and power of our love for you."

"Is that all?"

"It's not as much as it seems. It's really very simple."

"I can see that."

"People will come to you and tell you what you must do. Some will be completely wrong. You will have no trouble recognizing them. Others will be partially right. They will be very dangerous. Beware of them."

"Who should I listen to?"

She seemed surprised.

"Rosemarie, who else? She is your guiding star, your destiny, your illumination on the way home."

"I can see that."

"Remember, she is your reality check."

"Okay."

The Lady was preparing to leave. I wished she would stay.

"I would tell you to always love her, though you know that you have no choice in the matter."

"I can see that."

"Now I will get rid of this illness. As a bonus I'll see you contract no more colds."

"Can you really do that?"

She laughed and bent over to touch my forehead with the palm of her hand.

The sickness disappeared.

"Do you have to leave me?"

"I'll never leave you, Chucky."

The scent of flowers filled the air around me.

I opened my eyes.

All the women in my family were looking down at me, rosaries in their hands, tears rushing down their faces.

"The whole monster regiment," I said, and winked.

"Are you all right, Chucky?" my wife asked.

"I'm fine. I want to go home."

"His fever's gone," someone said.

I repeated my demand.

"I want to go home."

I looked around the room. Intensive care. No flowers. Yet the smell of flowers was everywhere.

Nice effect.

❧ *Chuck* ❧

1979

"So."

"So get me out of here."

"So you have been very sick, Chuck. Dr. Kennedy wants to be certain that you don't have a relapse."

"I won't have a relapse."

"You are also very weak. A severe trauma assaulted your organism. It will take time to recover."

"I have work to do. My wife and I are doing a book about the conclaves."

"Despite your rediscovered energy, how long do you nap every day?"

"A couple of hours," I admitted.

"So."

"So. I should cool it?"

"You will have no choice. You must be patient with yourself."

"That's what my wife says."

"So. You must listen carefully to me, Chuck. You will make no serious decisions for the next six months, do you understand?"

"If you say so . . ."

"Many physicians neglect to tell their patients that pneumonia leaves a terrible depression. It is not like your recent identity crisis. Your organism will protest against what was done to it. This protest on some occasions will be very powerful. You must be wary of it. Tell yourself that the depression is purely physical and that eventually it will go away."

"All right," I said. "Seems reasonable."

"With your permission I will also tell your wife."

They're ganging up on me. I feel fine. I just want to go home.

"That's a good idea. Thank you."

It would keep him happy.

"So."

After he left, Sister Mechtilde came to see me again. A tall, thin woman in her middle forties, she had returned to the hospital after years of work in South America. Her experiences with the very poor natives out in the jungle were fascinating. I was less enthused with her self-appointed role as my spiritual director.

"You have had a very easy life, Charles."

Nuns still did not like nicknames.

"Compared to your people, I have."

"Your lifestyle could sustain a whole village."

I had tried to argue economics with her. She dismissed my explanations with a wave of her hand.

"It is not right that Americans be so comfortable and these people so poor."

Her theme was that God had given me a new chance at life. I should dedicate this new chance to the service of the poor and the oppressed. I should live a radically simple life.

"God will judge you sternly if you return to your old ways."

I thought she was wrong. The Lady who had come to visit me had represented a different God. Yet perhaps this was a continuation of her message.

"You must humble yourself and serve the poor," she insisted.

Rosemarie was standing at the door. She was dressed in a severely tailored brown silk suit with a yellow scarf. Important writer in town. Her frown was a warning of a coming explosion.

"I wish, Sister, that you would leave my husband alone. He has been very sick. He does not need your preaching."

"Please yourself." Sister stalked out of the room.

"You never liked nuns," I reminded her.

"I cannot stand people, especially women, who think that their own generosity gives them the right to preach to others like they're a special agent of the Holy Spirit. It is time to get you out of this place."

"Now!"

"Tomorrow. I don't want that woman in here again."

"Yes, ma'am."

"I'll talk to the administration about it. They know they have a problem with her. She was too much for the people she was working with in South America."

Looking back on it, Rosemarie was probably right . . . as always. In my enfeebled condition I did not need a zealot whispering in my ear.

"You're looking better every day, Chucky Ducky," she said. "Time to get you out of here. We have already run up a huge hospital bill for you."

"We're insured, aren't we?"

"Sure . . . You shouldn't worry so much."

She brushed her lips against mine. I felt the first stirrings of desire. I'd been afraid it might not come back.

"How long have I been here?"

"Two weeks, half in intensive care."

"It must have been tough on all of you."

"It was a lot more difficult for you."

She kissed me again.

"You were delirious most of the time. You were babbling away most of the time . . ."

"Not untypical behavior."

She laughed and kissed me a third time.

"You were arguing a lot."

"Ghosts and demons."

"And you were talking very respectfully to someone, a woman I thought."

"Probably you . . . How's the show in New York working out?"

"A huge success. The Faction managed ten people for their demonstration. The critics are comparing you to the Chicago Symphony."

"Huh?"

"Unsuspected art treasures of Chicago."

I reached up and touched her breast. Despite the covering of silk and bra it felt awesome.

"Still fixated on my boobs." She laughed.

"Always."

My hand slipped away, too exhausted to try anything more.

"A lot of loving to catch up on, Chucky Ducky."

"I won't be doing anything else all spring and summer . . . except work on the *Conclaves* book."

"I'll count on that."

We were both quiet for a moment, perhaps being thankful for another opportunity in our lives.

"Rosemarie, there weren't any flowers in intensive care, were there?"

"No, they're afraid of the germs on them . . . Though the germs in you might have killed the flowers."

"When I came out of the fever and woke up, I thought I smelled some."

"Funny," she said, "I thought so too. Probably something out in the corridor."

"Probably."

Like I said, it was a nice effect.

I had not told Rosemarie about the Lady. My visitor had not warned me that it was secret. I thought, however, my story might spook Rosemarie. Better that I kept it a secret for a while. Maybe a long while. I wasn't certain myself what the story meant or even that the Lady had been anything more than a product of my fevered imagination.

It was indeed time to go home, time to get on with life and love.

❧ Chuck ❧
1979

I determined on the Memorial Day weekend that I would dedicate the rest of my life to taking pictures of immigrants. I would become a martyr for the cause of the poor and the oppressed.

"I think my next project will be refugees," I told Rosemarie on the deck on Saturday morning.

We were sitting outside in warm jackets and sweatpants pretending that the clear blue sky really meant summer despite the wind and the cold. We had put aside the final draft of *Conclaves*, which we would send off to the publisher on Tuesday. Both of us were reading mysteries.

"Great idea," Rosemarie replied. "Should be an important project."

"It's time I do something socially useful for the poor and the oppressed."

"Huh?" She put down the book she was reading and stared at me. "What are you talking about?"

"I haven't really showed much social concern in my work till now."

"Charles Cronin O'Malley, you're out of your mind! Little Rock! Selma! Marquette Park! Vietnam! The convention! Catholic schools in the inner city! No photographer in the country has shown more social concern!"

"Yeah, but it's time to move on to something else."

"I don't disagree. But don't do it as a rejection of all your previous work."

I thought about it. She was right.

"It'll be hard," I went on. "I'll be away from home for a year and a half, maybe two years. It'll be tough for Shovie, not having her father around. You'll be able to cover for me."

"It's that damn nun that was trying to brainwash you in the hospital! Max Berman warned us that you shouldn't make any decisions till the end of the summer. Poor little Shovie will not put up with an absent father, neither will poor little Shovie's mother, and that's final!"

"But I have to do this project—"

"No you don't. I won't permit it."

Clancy had lowered the boom.

"But—"

"See that up there, Chucky, that white streak against the sky?"

"Yes. It's contrails from a jet."

"Right. And where is the jet from?"

"O'Hare probably."

"So we go off for a shoot one week every month or every two months and come back here to work on the prints and put our notes in order. Sometimes I come with you. Sometimes, when it's safe, like filming Cubans in Miami, Siobhan Marie comes with us. Simple. None of this stuff about leaving your family for two years, understand?"

Clancy had lowered the boom for a second time. Oh, that Clancy!

"Besides, if I weren't along for the ride, you'd get lost the first week."

What had the Lady said?

Listen to Rosemarie, my guiding star.

"Damn fanatic nun," she said, still not ready to simmer down. "Should mind her own business."

I began to sing "Clancy Lowered the Boom!"

We sang it together and danced on the deck, much to the surprise of Kevin and Maria Elena, who were the first to join us.

I felt an enormous burden lift from my soul and drift off over the Lake.

❧ *Chuck* ❧

1979–1980

In the late summer as I relaxed in my newfound freedom, I received a call from Vince as I was sitting on the deck at Grand Beach.

"Chuck? Vince."

"I played football with you once, as I remember."

"I need a favor."

"I think the proper response is name it and you got it."

"It's about the people who work for Cardinal O'Neill."

"Yeah?"

"You ever hear of a guy named Hanraty?"

"Nope."

"Would you call your brother and see what the word is on him?"

"Sure."

Pause as Vince made up his mind.

"There's this first assistant United States Attorney that gives me a ring."

"Yeah."

"He says this Hanraty walks in off the street, says he works for O'Neill, and tells my friend over there that his conscience is bothering him about all the money that's misused."

"Hmm . . ."

"My guy says it looks like something really big."

"They'd go after him?"

"Sure . . . Anyway, he wonders if you can find out from Ed if they should trust this guy."

"I'll see what I can do."

I found Edward at his Youth Ministry office.

"Ed, a friend of mine wonders if you have a take on a guy named Hanraty who works for your good friend O'Neill."

Ed didn't hesitate.

"Good guy. Absolutely honest. Dedicated. Hardworking. I don't how he's survived so long over there."

"Thank you."

"Absolutely straight arrow," I told Vince.

"Yeah . . . I'm not sure my guy will like that . . . It'll be a big thing."

I thought about it for an hour or so. Vince had not bound me to secrecy. So I called my old friend the Apostolic Delegate.

"Ah, Mr. O'Malley! I heard you were very sick but are recovering nicely."

"I'm doing fine . . . I think I ought to tell you that the government may well be starting an investigation of our mutual friend."

"Mutual friend? . . . Oh, yes, of course."

"Money. Big. They have a good witness."

"Oh, that must be stopped."

"Too late now."

"That is most disturbing!"

"The Pope should have dealt with it when he was here earlier in the year."

"He did not think it appropriate."

"Well, he'll have a big mess on his hands now."

"I understand."

"I thought I would warn you."

"Yes, of course. *Merci*."

He phoned me the next day.

"The Pope will see our mutual friend tomorrow. You must pray that all will go well."

"Let me know what happens."

"But of course."

The next day he called.

"I have bad news," he said sadly. "The Cardinal shouted at the Pope. He refused to resign. He said he would fight publicly. The Pope thought it prudent to defer."

"He's going to have a big scandal on his hands. The press are on to the story."

"He prays that scandal can be avoided."

This was our tough Polish Pope who tolerated no nonsense, save from cardinals it would seem.

The scandal did break. The Cardinal sent one of his lawyers to Washington with a couple of hundred thousand dollars to bribe whoever he could bribe at the Justice Department. I don't know what happened to the money. The paper that had the story backed off because of pressure from conservative Catholics on its staff. The presiding judge refused to convene the grand jury which was considering the case, stalling till the Cardinal died. Everyone in Chicago knew about the story and the final attempts at cover-up. Packy says it will take twenty years for the Archdiocese to recover.

The Delegate was the only one who held the job never to be made a cardinal. He was blamed doubtless for the O'Neill mess. Strange bunch over there. I would not play their game again.

The Arabs turned off the gas spigot again and the cost of living index went sky-high. In November of 1979 a bunch of Iranian students seized the American Embassy in Tehran and held it and the Americans there hostage for 441 days. That fraud Walter Cronkite counted off the days each night, thus destroying completely the Jimmy Carter presidency and preparing the way for Ronald Reagan, whom I subsequently referred to on every possible occasion as "the Iranian candidate."

Poor Jimmy Carter would have gone down anyway without Cronkite. I was glad I wasn't working for him. I didn't know what advice I might have given. Probably I would have told him to continue the policy of trying to free the hostages by negotiation. The alternative—bomb the hell out of Iran—would probably lead to their deaths.

Better to sacrifice a badly scarred presidency than lose lives.

We baptized two new grandchildren. The first to make his appearance was Juan Carlos O'Malley, named for his maternal grandfather and his paternal great-grandfather and also, I guess, for his grandfather. He would be known, I was told, as Juan Carlos. The mix of the two heritages made him sound like an Admiral in the Argentine Navy. Unlike his red-haired sister, Maria Rosa, he was a sleek Latin type. The sister viewed him with considerable suspicion.

Next up was April Anne Nettleton, named after her mother and her grandmother (Polly Nettleton's real name being Mary Anne) and of course her great-grandmother O'Malley. She too missed the red-haired genes but looked so much like my Rosemarie that I was close to tears. We dug out the album of pictures of the original Rosemarie and realized that we had another clone.

There was considerable rejoicing at both baptisms that Grandpa Chuck looked so well again.

Sean graduated with his MBA at the end of the summer and went to work at the Board of Trade. He had not heard from Esther since she left for Israel. However, she continued to correspond with Moire Meg.

That latter turned twenty in August. Joe Moran continued to hang around. "He's always one step short of being a nuisance," Moire Meg explained to us.

Siobhan Marie became three in July. She thought she was in charge of everything.

Rosemarie and I flew over to Dublin to consult with some Irish missionaries about the places in Africa to find refugees. We brought along Shovie, who proved herself a durable traveler, though we tried to restrain her from walking around the Aer Lingus plane and introducing herself to all her fellow flyers.

I had pretty much forgotten about the woman at the end of the hospital bed. She was a product of fever and drugs though she was absolutely correct in her advice. I had always known in my subconscious the way out of my identity crisis—I was Rosemarie's husband and that was that.

I had escaped colds since my encounter with the Lady, but what did that mean? Maybe I'd absorbed all the virus that was "going around" as the doctors say.

We were ambling down Dawson Street. My wife stopped at the window of an art store.

"Isn't that a stunning picture, Chucky?" She pointed at a painting in the window.

For a brief moment, I felt dizzy. I had bungled into the world of the uncanny.

"Chucky?"

"It is wonderful . . . Let's go in and look at it."

It was the woman at the end of my hospital bed. How could she be here in Dublin? What kind of trick was this?

"Pretty lady," Shovie informed the owner of the store.

"It's Our Lady, dear," the woman said. "Mary."

"Jesus' mommy," Shovie agreed, proud of her religious knowledge.

Everyone has a mommy. Jesus is someone. So of course he has a mommy. Council of Ephesus said so.

"It's very striking," Rosemarie said.

"It's called *Madonna by the Hospital Bed*."

What else?

A chill ran through my body. Then it came back for a second time. I must not go catatonic. Chuck O'Malley never did that.

"Fascinating," Rosemarie said.

"The poor dear artist had a very difficult surgery. While she was in great pain and under severe medication, this woman came to visit her. I don't know whether she imagined her or . . ."

"It doesn't matter," I said softly.

So we bought the painting and it hangs in my workroom.

Right next to the portrait of Rosemarie.

Where it belongs.

AUTHOR'S NOTE

The art theories behind Chuck's portrait of Rosemarie are based on Wendy Steiner's book *Venus in Exile*.

The image of the Madonna by the hospital bed is based on a painting by Darina Roche.

The story of the year of the three Popes is based on my book *The Making of the Popes 1978*. However, the involvement of Chuck and Rosemarie is fictional. Their opinion of the process by which the Church selects its leaders is one I first expressed at that time.

There is no such place as the Photography Gallery in New York.

Siobhan is pronounced Shuvhan—hence "Shovie."

Look for

The
Priestly
Sins

by ANDREW M. GREELEY

Now available

❧

Turn the page for a preview

❧ Prologue ❧

(Printed in the *Plains City Plainsman and Gazette*)

(Partial transcript of hearing *in re Thomas Patrick Sweeney v Catholic Bishop*; Superior Court of Prairie County, Judge Arthur Sturm presiding. Mr. Vandenhuvel for the plaintiff, Mr. Kennedy for the defendant, Mr. Heller for the witness.)

Judge: Just what kind of priest are you Mr. Hoffman?

Hoffman: One that tries to be a good priest, Your Honor, not always successfully. I suppose I would say that I'm a sinful priest like all the others.

Judge: I will not play word games with you, Mr. Hoffman. Are you a Jesuit or a Dominican or a Franciscan or a Clementine or what?

Hoffman: I am a secular priest of the Archdiocese of Plains City, Your Honor. I do not belong to a religious order.

Judge: Not smart enough to be a Jesuit, huh?

Hoffman: I'm afraid not, Your Honor.

Mr. Vandenhuvel: Let the record show, Your Honor, that Father Hoffman has a doctorate from the University of Chicago in history and in addition to his pastoral work at St. Cunegunda parish teaches courses at State U.

Judge: A lot of education for a simple parish priest, isn't it Mr. Hoffman?

Hoffman: One might well think so, Your Honor.

Judge: Very well, Mr. Vandenhuvel. You may continue your questions.

Vandenhuvel: Where were we, Father? Oh yes, you heard Todd Sweeney screaming in Father Lyon's quarters. You ran into the room and pulled Father Lyon off of Todd, is that correct?

Hoffman: Yes, sir, though I didn't know it was Toddy at the time, only a child in great pain.

Vandenhuvel: Did you experience any difficulty in separating them?

Hoffman: Some difficulty. Father Lyon is not as strong as I am but they were stuck together pretty tightly.

Vandenhuvel: Did you notice any discharge of semen at the time?

Kennedy: Objection! Irrelevant and prejudicial.

Judge: Overruled. Continue, Counselor. I urge you to try to stay out of the gutter.

Vandenhuvel: Yes, Your Honor. I would observe that it is not my client or Father Hoffman who created this gutter.

Kennedy: Objection!

Judge: Sustained. No more program notes, Mr. Vandenhuvel.

Vandenhuvel: Yes, Your Honor . . . Father Hoffman, did Father Lyon say anything to you at that time?

Hoffman: Yes, sir. He said he would kill me if I told anyone about what I had seen and ordered me out of his room.

Vandenhuvel: Did you leave immediately?

Hoffman: No, sir. Toddy was still on the floor and still screaming.

Vandenhuvel: What was he screaming?

Hoffman: He was shouting, "Father Lyon hurt me. Father Lyon hurt me."

Vandenhuvel: Was he bleeding, Father?

Hoffman: Yes, sir.

Vandenhuvel: From his rectum?

Kennedy: Objection! Unnecessarily vivid question!

Judge: Shut up, Counselor. We are not talking about a Ping-Pong game in a rectory basement. Witness, stop sitting there like a bump on a log and answer the question.

Hoffman: Yes, sir. Yes, Counselor. He was bleeding from the rectum.

Vandenhuvel: Copiously?

Hoffman: Yes, sir.

Vandenhuvel: What did you do then, Father?

Hoffman: I lifted Toddy from the floor and helped him to pull his pants up.

Vandenhuvel: Was Father Lyon still in the room?

Hoffman: Yes, sir.

Vandenhuvel: Did Toddy say anything to Father Lyon?

Hoffman: Yes, he did.

Vandenhuvel: And that was?

Hoffman: "Father Lyon, you did a bad thing to me!"

Vandenhuvel: Did Father Leonard Lyon say anything in reply?

Hoffman: Yes, he said, "If you tell anyone, I'll come to your house at night and slit your throat with my big hunting knife while you're asleep and kill your father and mother too."

Kennedy: Objection, Your Honor! Witness would have us believe that a priest made that threat in the presence of another priest!

Judge: Shut up, Joe, and sit down! You'll have your chance on cross.

Vandenhuvel: What did you do then Father Hoffman?

Hoffman: I helped Toddy down the stairs to the door of the rectory.

Vandenhuvel: Did you take him to the hospital?

Hoffman: I'm afraid I didn't think of that.

Vandenhuvel: Why not?

Hoffman: I guess I was emotionally numb. I was a farm boy six weeks into his first assignment. I'd never been out of the state . . .

Judge: Mr. Hoffman, may I remind you that this is a hearing on plaintiff's motion *in re Sweeney v Catholic Bishop.* Court is not interested in your excuses.

Vandenhuvel: Did you say anything to him?

Hoffman: Nothing. I didn't know what to say.

Vandenhuvel: And Toddy?

Hoffman: He begged me to say nothing. "Father Lyon will really kill us all at night. He has secret powers."

Vandenhuvel: What did you do then, Father Hoffman?

Hoffman: I went to my room to think.

Vandenhuvel: Had you ever seen anything like that before, Father?

Hoffman: I had not. I knew there was such a thing as rectal intercourse, but I had never seen it.

Vandenhuvel: You were shocked that a priest would engage in it with a child in his rectory room.

Hoffman: Yes, sir, overwhelmed. It was all so ugly.

Kennedy: Objection! Witness is embroidering his testimony.

Judge: Sustained. Strike the words "all" and "so" from the record.

Vandenhuvel: Did Father Lyon speak to you at that time?

Hoffman: Yes, sir. While I was trying to sort it out he came to the door to my room.

Vandenhuvel: What did he say?

Hoffman: He waved a large knife at me, and said, "No one will believe you if you try to tell them. If you do, I'll slit your throat too."

Vandenhuvel: Did you reply?

Hoffman: No, sir. I was too confused. I just sat there, Your Honor should excuse the expression, like a bump on a log.

Judge: Order! Order in the courtroom! Witness will restrain his attempts at humor.

Hoffman: Yes, Your Honor.

Vandenhuvel: What did you do next, Father?

Hoffman: I finished my record keeping, ate supper, did a wedding rehearsal, and tried to sleep.

Vandenhuvel: Could you sleep?

Hoffman: No, sir.

Vandenhuvel: And the next morning?

Hoffman: I made up my mind to tell the pastor, Monsignor Flannery. The door to his suite was closed. So I had to wait.

Vandenhuvel: Anything happen while you were waiting?

Hoffman: Yes, sir. A young woman came to the rectory office, a seventh grader. She said that Father Lyon had told her he needed help in his room and she should go right on up.

Vandenhuvel: And what did you say?

Hoffman: I said that she looked uneasy about his request and she said she was. I told her that she should never go to his room and that she should tell all the other girls that I said they should never go to Father Lyon's room.

Vandenhuvel: And what did she do?

Hoffman: She said, "Yes, Father," and ran away. Happy to be excused.

Kennedy: Objection. Witness speculates.

Judge: Overruled. I think we can concede witness's ability to read the emotional reaction of a junior high school student.

Vandenhuvel: Do you recall the young woman's name?

Hoffman: No, sir, I do not.

Vandenhuvel: Do you think you saved her from sexual assault?

Hoffman: I hope I did.

Kennedy: Objection. Witness is speculating again.

Judge: I'll let it stand.

Vandenhuvel: Subsequently you talked to the Monsignor?

Hoffman: Yes, sir.

Vandenhuvel: And what did you say to him?

Hoffman: I told him what I had seen in Lenny's room.

Vandenhuvel: And he said?

Hoffman: Monsignor Flannery was very angry at me. He said that he was sick of hearing accusations against Lenny. He was a good priest who had been slandered in the past by false accusations. There would be none in this parish. Lenny had been cleared both by the police and the psychiatrist. He was a popular and effective priest. I was neither. I couldn't preach and I was—his exact words, Your Honor—nothing but a damned German bump on a log . . .

Judge: Order! Order! I'll tolerate no more outbursts!

Hoffman: He also said I was jealous of Lenny's success in the parish and that's why I made up such stories . . . I think he meant envious.

Judge: Witness, it is not necessary to correct the Monsignor's grammar . . . How do you know word for word what he said?

Hoffman: I wrote it in my diary, Your Honor.

Judge: Ah, how long have you kept that diary, Mr. Hoffman?

Hoffman: Since my senior year in high school.

Judge: Interesting—and in the present circumstances how convenient.

Hoffman: In my culture we're paper savers, Your Honor.

Vandenhuvel: Was this the first time you heard the implication about other charges against Father Leonard Lyon?

Hoffman: Yes, sir.

Vandenhuvel: Were you surprised?

Hoffman: At that time, sir, nothing would have surprised me.

Vandenhuvel: What did you do then?

Hoffman: That afternoon I went to visit Dr. Sweeney at his home down the street. I told him what I had seen.

Vandenhuvel: And his reaction?

Hoffman: He threw me out of the house. He said I was a lying Dutch dolt, that everyone in the parish loved Father Lyon and despised me. If anyone was a threat to his son, it was me.

Vandenhuvel: Were you surprised by this reaction?

Hoffman: I knew Dr. Sweeney had a temper, sir.

Voice: The Dutch bastard is lying, Arthur. He never came to my house, never!

Judge: Timmy, I'd suggest that you sit down and shut up. Witness is appearing in support of your family's suit. It is not wise to impeach his testimony as well as making a damn fool out of yourself. Not for the first time, either. Proceed, Counselor.

Vandenhuvel: Nonetheless, Father, you swear under oath that you did call on Dr. Sweeney?

Hoffman: Yes, sir.

Vandenhuvel: Did you try again to awaken someone else to the danger to the children of the parish?

Hoffman: Yes, sir. I walked over to the police station to report the incident to the chief of police.

Vandenhuvel: You were aware, Father, that even then there was a requirement to report the abuse of children to civil authorities?

Hoffman: I was not aware of it at that time. I thought a priest ought to report a rape that he had observed.

Vandenhuvel: What did the chief say?

Hoffman: He was very upset, sir.

Vandenhuvel: At what you described?

Hoffman: No, sir. He was upset that people would come to his office to complain about the misdeeds of priests. He said that it was the Church's problem, not his, and that the Church better straighten itself out now and not expect the police to do their work.

Vandenhuvel: Did you do anything more?

Hoffman: Yes, sir. I asked to see the Archbishop personally. He had said that the door was always open to his office for any priest who wanted to see him personally. His secretary gave me fifteen minutes for a week from Thursday.

Vandenhuvel: What happened during those ten days?

Hoffman: It was very awkward in the rectory. Neither Monsignor Flannery nor Father Lyon would talk to me.

Vandenhuvel: Did you see any more children go to Father Lyon's room?

Hoffman: I did not.

Vandenhuvel: Did you hear from any priests?

Hoffman: To my surprise, several of my classmates called me. They warned me about Lucifer Lenny as he was called in the seminary . . .

Kennedy: Objection! Your Honor, this is absolutely outrageous! It is hearsay, prejudicial, and completely irrelevant!

Judge: Counselor?

Vandenhuvel: Your Honor, our case argues that the diocese has systematically covered up sexual abuse and punished those who tried to report it: the victims, their families, eyewitnesses. We have here an example of a good priest who is trying to do what is right being systematically harassed by his fellow priests. It is entirely appropriate that he report the words of the conversations.

Judge: Which he happened conveniently to note in his journal, I suppose . . . Well, I'll overrule the objection for the present. Proceed, Counselor.

Vandenhuvel: "Lucifer Lenny"? Father?

Hoffman: Yes, sir. They called him that in the seminary because . . .

Kennedy: Objection!

Judge: I'll sustain that.

Vandenhuvel: All right, Father, can you tell me the substance of these conversations?

Hoffman: They warned me that Father Lyon had influence Downtown, that the past charges against him had been dropped, and that the police and the psychiatrists had cleared him, and that I was only making trouble for myself. They told me that I should stay out of it. Most of the guys thought Len was a good man. He denied anything had ever happened. You'll make enemies for yourself. There's no point in upsetting the Downtown.

Vandenhuvel: How did you respond?

Hoffman: I told them that I had personally witnessed the rape.

Vandenhuvel: Did that have any effect on the callers?

Hoffman: No.

Vandenhuvel: Did they seem to know that you had an appointment with the Archbishop?

Hoffman: Yes, they did.

Vandenhuvel: So someone must have told them both about your claim and that you wanted to see the Archbishop?

Hoffman: Yes, sir.

Vandenhuvel: Who might it have been?

Hoffman: Anyone to whom I had made charges, then someone at the Chancery.

Vandenhuvel: So you thought that the Archbishop might be prepared for you?

Hoffman: I didn't know, sir. I always felt that the staff tried to protect the Archbishop from bad news.

Vandenhuvel: And when you arrived at the Chancery?

Hoffman: I was not permitted to see the Archbishop. Monsignor Meaghan, Father Peters, Dr. Straus, and Mr. Kennedy were waiting for me.

Vandenhuvel: Now, help me to understand this. What are their roles in the Archdiocese?

Hoffman: Monsignor Meaghan was the vicar for the clergy, now he is the Auxiliary Bishop and the Vicar General. Father Peters was the victims' advocate, though that was not his title in the Archdiocesan Directory. Mr. Kennedy was and is the lawyer for the Archdiocese. Dr. Straus does psychological examinations for the Archdiocese.

Vandenhuvel: Father Peters is also a civil lawyer, is he not?

Hoffman: I believe so.

Vandenhuvel: Are they all in court today?

Hoffman: I believe that Mr. Kennedy, Dr. Straus, and Bishop Meaghan are present, sir. I don't see Father Peters.

Vandenhuvel: Are you aware that Father Peters has been suspended from the diocese because of credible charges of sexual abuse?

Hoffman: I have read that in the papers, sir.

Vandenhuvel: Thus the victims' advocate seems to have abused victims himself?

Kennedy: Objection! Your Honor, counsel is leading the witness.

Judge: Sustained.

Vandenhuvel: Did you know then that Dr. Straus is not a board-certified psychiatrist?

Hoffman: I did not, sir.

Vandenhuvel: You have read in the papers, I presume, that he is a family practitioner and not qualified to do psychological evaluations?

Hoffman: Yes, sir.

Vandenhuvel: All right, what happened when this foursome confronted you at the Chancery?

Hoffman: They did not give me much chance to speak, sir. They dismissed my story as a fabrication. Before I could say anything, they accused me of being a homosexual and reporting a homosexual fantasy as a fact.

Vandenhuvel: How long did the discussion last, Father?

Hoffman: A lot longer than the fifteen minutes. An hour and a half perhaps.

Vandenhuvel: Did you think they were sincere in their charges against you?

Kennedy: Objection!

Judge: I'll let it stand.

Hoffman: I can't be certain, sir. They seemed to be sincere. I don't have the gift of reading human hearts. I suppose they were trying to protect the Church from scandal.

Vandenhuvel: Are you a homosexual, Father Hoffman?

Hoffman: No, sir, not that I think homosexuality is sinful. I think the Church should leave them alone.

Vandenhuvel: Have you ever had homosexual intercourse?

Hoffman: No, sir.

Vandenhuvel: What happened then?

Hoffman: I drove back to Green Island, that's where St. Theodolinda parish is. I was troubled and confused. I couldn't understand what was happening. I was the only one in the rectory. The cook had not prepared supper for me. I scrounged some food from the fridge.

Vandenhuvel: You did not sleep well that night, I presume.

Hoffman: No, sir.

Vandenhuvel: Then?

Hoffman: The next morning, Monsignor Meaghan, Dr. Straus, and Father Peters arrived in a large Cadillac—the Monsignor's, I believed. They told me to pack a bag. They were taking me to St. Edward's Center for treatment. They said they believed that would help me to straighten myself out.

Vandenhuvel: You went along with their proposal?

Hoffman: I would never have thought in those days of challenging authority.

Vandenhuvel: Dr. Straus signed you in?

Hoffman: Yes, sir.

Vandenhuvel: A physician without any credentials as a psychiatrist signed you in to a mental institution?

Hoffman: A mental health center, sir.

Vandenhuvel: Very well. A mental health center.

Hoffman: I believe he's on their board of trustees, sir.

Judge: Sit down. I'm going to strike the question.

Vandenhuvel: How long were you incarcerated in that place?

Judge: Counselor, before our learned colleague has a heart attack, I'm going to ask you to reword the question.

Vandenhuvel: Very well. How long did you remain there, Father?

Hoffman: Six months, sir.

Vandenhuvel: Did Dr. Straus interview you during the course of, ah, treatment?

Hoffman: I believe twice.

Vandenhuvel: Of what did the treatment consist?

Hoffman: Medication to calm me down and tests.

Vandenhuvel: Did you take the medicine?

Hoffman: Not usually, sir, not after the first couple of months.

Vandenhuvel: And the tests?

Hoffman: They were designed to determine whether or not I was a homosexual.

Vandenhuvel: How was that done?

Hoffman: That's a little embarrassing, sir.

Judge: We're all adults here, Mr. Hoffman.

Hoffman: I wouldn't bet on that, sir.

Judge: Order! Order! Contain your sense of humor, Mr. Hoffman, and answer the question!

Hoffman: I don't believe you have the right to order me to, Your Honor, but I will anyway. For example, they would show me photos of women and of men in various stages of nakedness and engaged in various sexual situations. They would monitor my reaction.

Vandenhuvel: Would you not say that was a terrible way to treat a priest, Father?

Hoffman: What I said was not relevant, sir.

Vandenhuvel: And what was the nature of your reactions?

Hoffman: Embarrassingly heterosexual, sir.

Vandenhuvel: What did those who were testing you say?

Hoffman: Not much. They were very apologetic . . . One of them whispered to another, but loud enough so I could hear, "I don't care what Straus says. This poor guy is not gay."

Kennedy: Objection! Hearsay!

Judge: Sustained. Strike it from the record.

Vandenhuvel: How long did this treatment last?

Hoffman: About two weeks.

Vandenhuvel: And then?

Hoffman: Nothing at all.

Vandenhuvel: Nothing? You did nothing?

Hoffman: Oh, no! I presided over the Eucharist, anointed the sick, visited the troubled, preached every day on the closed-circuit TV, talked to my folks once a week to calm them down, read the history books one of my classmates brought to the door, and prayed. It was kind of like a long retreat.

Vandenhuvel: No visitors and only one phone call a week?

Hoffman: That's right.

Vandenhuvel: You like being a priest, don't you, Father?

Hoffman: Always have, always will.

Vandenhuvel: You were finally released after six months?

Hoffman: Three days short of six months. Monsignor Meaghan and Father Peters drove me back to Plains City and to the Chancery. They told me I had been cured, and they were very proud of my efforts.

Vandenhuvel: Cured of homosexuality in six months?

Hoffman: That's what they said.

Vandenhuvel: And you met with the Archbishop?

Hoffman: Yes, sir. For about a half hour. He was charming as he always is and vague as I have come to expect he will always be. He praised my patience and virtue, my strong will-power, and my excellent ministerial service to the people at St. Edward's.

Vandenhuvel: And then?

Hoffman: Then he said that he didn't think I'd really be happy in ordinary parish ministry so he was sending me to graduate school—any school of my choice, any subject of my choice. I said that I enjoyed parish work very much, but, if he wished, I would like to study immigrant history at the University of Chicago. He said that was fine. The Archdiocese would pay my tuition and living expenses. I thanked him and said I was sure I could get a fellowship eventually and would live in a parish in the Chicago area and be little if any drain on my home Archdiocese. He seemed quite relieved when I left.

Vandenhuvel: Glad to be rid of you?

Kennedy: Objection! Speculative! Irrelevant!

Judge: Oh, all right, Joe, I'll sustain that.

Vandenhuvel: Let me rephrase it: Did you feel that you were railroaded out of your parish and out of town by your Church?

Hoffman: At first I was just glad to escape all the mess, all the foolishness, all the dishonesty . . .

Kennedy: Objection . . . !

Judge: In a case like this, Joe, a witness's feelings are not irrelevant, the witness may continue.

Vandenhuvel: All the corruption?

Hoffman: I almost said that, but I didn't.

Vandenhuvel: And later?

Hoffman: Later, when I regained my confidence, I realized what they had done to me. I was furious; then I calmed down and worked on my research.

Vandenhuvel: Yet you returned.

Hoffman: Plains City is my home.

Vandenhuvel: That's all, Father.

Judge: I'm going to declare a recess, Father Hoffman. I'll turn you over to Mr. Kennedy on Monday morning. Before the recess I want to ask you just one question: After all you allege was done to you by your Church, your Archdiocese, and your Archbishop, why the hell did you stay in the priesthood? Surely with a degree from a great university you could have obtained a better job, perhaps married, and had a happier life?

Hoffman: I'm Volga Deutsche, Your Honor.

Judge: So?

Hoffman: You remember what they say about us Russian Germans? We combine the worst traits of both cultures?

Judge: Stubborn like the Germans and crazy like the Russians?

Hoffman: I like being a priest. I like being a Russian German. I like Plains City. No one is going to take any of those away from me.

Carnival Elation

7 Day Exotic Western Caribbean Itinerary

DAY	PORT	ARRIVE	DEPART
Sun	Galveston		4:00 P.M.
Mon	"Fun Day" at Sea		
Tue	Progreso/Merida	8:00 A.M.	4:00 P.M.
Wed	Cozumel	9:00 A.M.	5:00 P.M.
Thu	Belize	8:00 A.M.	6:00 P.M.
Fri	"Fun Day" at Sea		
Sat	"Fun Day" at Sea		
Sun	Galveston	8:00 A.M.	